Sheila O'Flanagan is the author of many bestselling novels, including *The Missing Wife*, *My Mother's Secret*, *If You Were Me*, *All For You* (winner of the Irish Independent Popular Fiction Book of the Year Award) and *Bad Behaviour*, as well as the bestselling short-story collections *The Moment We Meet*, *The Season of Change* and *Christmas With You*.

Sheila has always loved telling stories, and after working in banking and finance for a number of years, she decided it was time to fulfil a dream and give writing her own book a go. So she sat down, stuck 'Chapter One' at the top of a page, and got started. Sheila is now the author of over twenty best-selling titles. She lives in Dublin with her husband.

Readers love Sheila O'Flanagan's books:

'A fabulous tale with refreshingly inspiring heroines' *****
Heat

'Another first class bestseller. I read the book in one
sitting as it was so enjoyable, full of romance and kept
you riveted until the last page' *Woman's Way*

'Will keep you guessing right up until the end' *Bella*

'So beautifully described you can almost smell and taste the
oranges on the trees' *My Weekly*

'A heartfelt tale, told with the sincerity and humour
we've come to expect from Sheila O'Flanagan . . .
a real page turner' *Best*

'The perfect holiday companion . . . A thoroughly satisfying,
well-paced plot from a sure and experienced pen'
Irish Independent

'A feel-good story told by a funny and down-to-earth heroine'
Woman

'If you're seeking an escape of your own, this sunny, evocative
story is the perfect place to hide away' *S Magazine*

'A hugely enjoyable romance, written with pace and heart'
Sunday Mirror

'This *Gone Girl*-esque novel will have you gripped
until the very end' *Look*

'An exciting love story with a deliciously romantic denoue-
ment' *Sunday Express*

Sheila O'Flanagan

Her Husband's Mistake

REVIEW

First published in Great Britain in 2019
by HEADLINE REVIEW
an imprint of HEADLINE PUBLISHING GROUP

First published in paperback in Great Britain in 2020
by HEADLINE REVIEW
an imprint of HEADLINE PUBLISHING GROUP

3

Cataloguing in Publication Data is available from the British Library

ISBN 978 1 4722 5475 7

Typeset in ITC Galliard Std by Palimpsest Book Production Limited,
Falkirk, Stirlingshire

Printed and bound in Great Britain by Clays Ltd, Elcograf S.p.A.

Headline's policy is to use papers that are natural, renewable and recyclable
products and made from wood grown in well-managed forests and other
controlled sources. The logging and manufacturing processes are expected
to conform to the environmental regulations of the country of origin.

HEADLINE PUBLISHING GROUP
An Hachette UK Company
Carmelite House
50 Victoria Embankment
London EC4 0DZ

www.headline.co.uk
www.hachette.co.uk

Chapter 1

The morning after my father's funeral, I came home and found my husband in bed with the next-door neighbour.

The first thing I wanted to do, when I saw Julie Halpin bouncing up and down on top of Dave like a naked cowboy in a rodeo, was to unsee what I'd just seen. I wanted to tiptoe out of the house and pretend I hadn't been there at all. Which I know is a sadly weak response from someone who likes to believe that she's strong and resilient and good in a crisis. But at that moment I didn't feel one bit strong or resilient. Besides, my legs were far too wobbly to carry me out of the house without collapsing.

The thing is, I'd already been through a crisis. I'd managed to hold it together through the months of Dad's illness, when Mum was in denial and my brother too upset to be of any use. I'd coordinated hospital visits, talked to the nursing staff, made sure Dad was never alone for too long and even kept his business going. Strong and resilient stuff, no question. Both Mum and Aidan said so. Even Dad, weak as he was, had squeezed my arm and thanked me for everything I was doing.

But I hadn't given it a second thought because I'm the

one who always knows what to do when the chips are down. I pride myself on my ability to cope.

But I didn't know how to cope with seeing Dave and Julie together. I still don't.

If I'd ever imagined this scenario – not that I had, because I'd always believed that Dave was a keeper – I'd have pictured my total control as I hauled Julie's ample arse off my husband and dragged her down the stairs and out of my house. Possibly by her bouncy blonde curls. I'd have been in total control of throwing him out too. And though it would have been hard, I'd have got on with my life.

But it hasn't turned out that way. I'm frozen inside. I've no idea what to do. And no idea how to do it.

I trusted Dave absolutely, you see. We were a partnership. A team. We'd been a team for a long time. Dave and Roxy. Mica and Tom. He was the manager. I was the coach. Yet given the opportunity, he'd called in a sub and relegated me to the bench. I didn't want to believe it then and I wish I didn't have to believe it now. But it happened. I have to accept it, no matter how much it hurts.

The same feeling that engulfed me as I watched Julie's Clairol-enhanced curls bobbing around her shoulders, and heard the creak of the mattress springs, is still with me now. It's regret. Regret that I got up early and drove home wearing nothing more than a light coat over my silk pyjama top and matching shorts so that I could surprise Dave before he went to work. Regret that I didn't stay where I was, alone in the single bed at my mum's house, assuming that he was alone too, missing me as much as I was missing him. If I'd stayed at Mum's, in blissful ignorance, I wouldn't have had to re-assess everything about my life. I'd have coped with my sorrow about Dad, coped with making sure Mum was OK, and got on with my life.

But now I can't.

The only reason I went home at all that morning was because I craved some normality after the stress-filled weeks we'd all gone through. My head was still spinning from it. I don't regret for a moment having spent so much time with Dad and Mum. Of course I don't. I'd do anything for my family. But that morning, I just wanted to be in my own bed, with someone looking after me rather than the other way around.

I know I'm being silly. Not knowing that Dave had cheated on me would have been far worse in the long run. At least, I'm pretty sure it would. In the couple of months since it happened, I've read lots of articles about cheating partners. There's a view from some that you're better off in ignorance. But I can't help thinking that sooner or later you'll find out anyway. And then you'll feel an even worse fool.

If I hadn't gone home at six o'clock that morning, I might not have found out straight away, but I would've had a little longer to avoid dealing with stuff I don't want to deal with. I'd have carried on secure in the knowledge – now faulty – that my marriage was rock solid. I wouldn't have to make decisions that I'm still quite unable to make. Decisions that aren't only about me but are about Mica and Tom too. I'd still be the wife who'd been cheated on, but I wouldn't be feeling as poleaxed as I do right now.

And I wouldn't be blaming myself for allowing my coping energy to be depleted by what was going on in my mother's house and not keeping enough in reserve for what was happening in my own.

3

Moving into Mum's for a few days seemed like a good idea at the time. She needed someone with her, and the children were a welcome distraction. Dave agreed that it was the right thing to do too. But I didn't realise that while I was shoring things up on one front, I'd left another completely exposed.

As exposed as Julie's round and – it pains me to say it – rather bootylicious arse.

All these things went through my head at the sight of the two of them together, and I tried to stifle the choked gasp that had risen in my throat, but I couldn't. Which meant that when Dave's stricken eyes met mine over Julie's mop of shining curls, there was no escape for either of us. Things had changed forever. We could never be the people we were before. And we would both have to deal with the fallout.

Everyone has their own opinion on how I should deal with it. My mum. My best friends Debs, Alison and Michelle. Even the girls in my Slim to Win WhatsApp group. (I haven't been to a meeting since it happened, but they've sent supportive messages anyway.) Word gets round on the Beechgrove estate, especially as Becca Brophy from across the road, and the biggest gossip known to man, saw Julie running from our house with her knickers in her hand. I'm sure she was messaging everyone before Julie had even reached her own door. Since then, I've had more advice from other people than I could possibly need. Yet my views are the only ones that matter. If only I knew what they really were. If only I knew how to deal with what I'm feeling.

When I googled 'cheating husbands', there were over 32 million results, but regardless of all the advice, there are really only two options. Forgive and forget. Or break up.

The most recent article I looked at (I'm reading them obsessively at the moment) suggested that somebody else's cheating isn't about you; it's because they're unhappy with themselves. I don't think Dave is unhappy with himself. In fact, when I saw him with Julie, he looked far too self-satisfied for my liking. No – he saw an opportunity and took it. And he's broken my heart.

For the past few weeks, the flickering images of my husband and my neighbour are the last things I see every night and the first that come to me every morning. I don't want them to be. I've tried a million different ways to block them out. I've played meditative music to lull myself to sleep. I've focused on bringing myself to my happy place every night, although that's difficult, because the bedroom in Beechgrove Park no longer qualifies as my happy place at all. Sometimes, as I lie alone in my childhood bedroom, my mind wanders towards all the other stuff I have to get on with, and I spend five or ten glorious minutes not thinking about my total humiliation; but eventually the memories of Dave and Julie cavorting in my bed force their way in, taunting me and reminding me that even the people you love can make you cry.

I've loved Dave McMenamin since I was sixteen years old. We lived on the same housing estate in the Dublin suburb of Raheny and went to the same local school. Dave's younger brother, Phil, was friends with my older brother, Aidan. For a long time I was aware of him without taking any particular notice of him. I had short-lived flings with guys who burned bright in my life for a few weeks but then fizzled into nothingness. I had crushes on pop stars and celebrities, and, unaccountably, on Dean Marinaro, the rather nerdy guy in my class who was kind of cute. Maybe I should've held out for Dean Marinaro, who (as far as I know) had never gone out with a girl. But I didn't. The year I turned sixteen I went to the annual Halloween party in the community centre. I dressed as a rather sexy witch. Dave was a blood-spattered vampire. We kissed while standing around the bonfire and that was that. I forgot about the celebs and the pop stars and Dean Marinaro. I was Dave McMenamin's girl and I stayed Dave's girl all through school and after we left and started work. Dave and Roxy. Roxy and Dave. From that night we were always talked about as a couple, and that was fine by me. I wanted us to be forever. I believed we would.

When Dave was twenty and I was nineteen, he was offered a contract for a plumbing job in London's Docklands. Dave comes from a family of plumbers and it was the only thing he ever wanted to do. People may call plumbing a trade, but Dave is a craftsman and he's really brilliant at his work. The London job was a great opportunity and there was no way he was turning it down. Despite being in the middle of my accounting technician's course, I went to England with him. I couldn't bear the thought of us being long-distance lovers, even though London isn't really that far away. But it's overseas, so that makes it long-distance. Besides, being an accounting technician wasn't my dream. It was simply a qualification that would hopefully help me to get a job.

I didn't need my unfinished qualification, though. A few days after we arrived in the English capital, I landed a position as a receptionist in a Jaguar car dealership. Thanks to my dad, I know a lot about cars, although I'd never even seen a Jaguar up close before. But the job was perfect for me, I got on well with the staff and the customers, and despite missing home, I liked being part of London life.

We stayed for six great years. Then Dave was offered a contract on a massive commercial development back in Dublin. Returning was a no-brainer. Happy as I'd been in London, I was delighted to come home for good. We'd been talking about having a baby, but neither of us wanted to bring up a child in London. It was nothing against the city that had been good to us. It was simply that I wanted to start my family at home.

We bought a house in Baldoyle, a ten-minute drive from where we'd grown up, although we stayed with my mum and dad for a few months while Dave and his mates renovated it. I think I became pregnant on our first night there. A few months after Michaela was born, we were married in a ceremony that was way more lavish than we could afford given all the money we'd lashed out on turning the house into our dream home.

'Till death us do part, babes,' Dave said that night. 'So it's worth it.'

Or until Julie Halpin and her bootylicious bum moved in next door.

I'm awake ten minutes before the alarm is due to go off, and the image of the pair of them is in my head again. I always wake up ten minutes before the alarm, a somewhat useless talent that does, however, mean I have a few minutes to gather myself before getting out of bed. It used to be a time when I'd think about the day ahead, and I savoured those ten minutes as an oasis of calm before I had to throw myself into the fray. Now it always seems to be filled with images of Dave and Julie and the fact that she was on top.

Wiping away the hot tears that have filled my eyes, I pick up my phone and silence the alarm before it starts to ring. Then I tiptoe out of my bedroom and across the hallway to the bathroom, stepping carefully over the squeaky floorboard so as not to disturb anyone else. When I brought Mum up to speed on what had happened and asked if we could stay with her for a while, she wanted me to take the main bedroom with the en suite. She said it would be far more suitable. But there was no way I was turning her out of her own bedroom. I insisted that I'd be fine in the room I'd slept in as a girl, even though sleeping in a single bed after the comfort of the much bigger one I shared with Dave is really difficult. I thought I wouldn't miss him in the narrow bed. If anything, I miss him more.

I let myself into the bathroom and close the door behind me. In a further effort to keep things quiet, I don't switch on the ventilation fan but open the window instead, although the dawn light has only reached the very edge of the horizon and the early-morning air is more autumnal than height of summer. But Mum is a light sleeper too, and after the months of Dad's illness, she needs her rest.

She could have done without me turning into an unexpected lodger with two children in tow. But where else could I have gone? Who else would I have run to?

I pull my hair into a knot and cover it with a shower cap. Mum is as supportive as it's possible to be, but no matter how much it suits both of us for now, I can't camp out here indefinitely. The children are looking on this interlude with their grandmother as part of their holidays and have taken

8

it in their stride so far. But I can tell that Mica is starting to wonder if there's more to it than just keeping her granny company. Her questions are getting more and more pointed. Tom is blasé about things. I'm still a mess.

I turn on the shower and wait for the water to heat up. As it chunters into life, I tell myself that I might be missing the shower in my own home more than I'm missing my husband. It's a top-of-the-range power shower that's practically a workout for your skin. A fantastic bathroom is one of the advantages of being married to a plumber. The disadvantage, of course, is that he's a lying, cheating plumber.

I stop torturing myself with the train wreck of my life, lather up, rinse off and get out of the shower. As I pat myself dry, I pause, as I always do, to look at the faded scars of my two Caesareans. I remember being rushed into the hospital the second time, knowing that, once again, things weren't going to plan. While we were waiting for the ambulance to arrive, Dave used my lipstick to write 'cut along dotted line' across my enormous stomach. Even though I was sick with anxiety, it made me laugh. Dave has always made me laugh. I thought it was a sign that we were good for each other.

And now, as I sit in front of the dressing table and pull my hair into its work-day ponytail, I don't know what to think. I try not to think at all as I dab tinted moisturiser on my face and pearl-grey eyeshadow on my eyelids. It's the same look as always – I'm not one for experimenting. (Could that be why Dave was having it off with Julie Halpin? She's far more glamorous than me and has a range of make-up that accentuates her good cheekbones and bee-sting lips.) I use the same dark-brown mascara on my lashes as I've done since I was a teenager. There's no good reason to change.

Even Dave agrees my lashes are my best feature. They're long and thick and more than once I've been asked if they're real. So my Maybelline is fine. It and the Boots eyeshadow bring out the cool blue of my eyes. (Too cool, too blue? Julie's are a rich chocolate brown, eminently more seductive.) I finish my face by adding a peachy blusher and coral lipstick, before getting dressed in my working outfit of white cotton blouse and navy trouser suit. I slide a single pair of gold stud earrings into my ears; although I have a couple of extra piercings in them, I only wear more earrings if I'm going out socially, never when I'm working.

I assess myself in the long wardrobe mirror. Dave says I look like Claire Danes in *Homeland* when I'm in my suit. *Homeland* has always been one of our favourite shows, and of course I'm flattered whenever he compares me to her, but it's not true. I'm a watered-down version. I'm neither a Hollywood actress nor a super-spy. I'm a thirty-seven-year-old mother of two who can't tell the difference between the wrinkles and the worry lines that are etched across my face.

Julie Halpin doesn't have lines on her face. She doesn't have children. Nor does she have a husband any more. She moved in next door after her split with Doug and I did my best to be warm and welcoming, though clearly not as warm and welcoming as Dave. I stare at my reflection and wonder, fleetingly, if getting Botox or fillers would have stopped Dave from cheating on me. I don't know, and the Roxy staring back at me doesn't have the answers either.

I make another determined effort to push my unfaithful husband from my mind and pick up the satchel bag that contains my purse, credit cards and iPad. I let myself out of the bedroom and walk quietly along the landing, comfortable block-heeled shoes in my hand. I stop at the first door and open it gently.

Tom, who's seven, is lying on top of the bed, the sheets crumpled around his ankles. His red-gold hair falls over a face flushed with sleep. He doesn't move, even when I kiss him fleetingly on the forehead and whisper that I'll see him later. I close the door softly behind me and go up the steep stairs to the attic bedroom. Dad converted it years ago, when Aidan and I were still living at home. I desperately wanted to move into the conversion, but Aidan, being older, insisted that it was his by right. My complaints that it was stupid for him to have a room where he'd keep banging his head on the dormer roof fell on deaf ears. My brother got the attic room and I stayed where I was. To be honest, my own room is fine and gets the morning sun, but I was inconsolable for weeks. It made no difference. We were an equal-opportunity house. There were no concessions to weepy females. So eventually I stopped moaning and got on with it.

That's me. Getting-on-with-it Roxy. Accepting what's happened and moving on. Easier to do over an actual bedroom than what's gone on *in* a bedroom, though.

I thought there might have been a bit of an argument between Mica and Tom over the sleeping arrangements too, but Tom's such a happy-go-lucky person, and was so thrilled at the adventure of an extended stay at his granny's, that he didn't care where he slept. Mica (eleven, and veering between staying my little girl and starting to grow up) was delighted with her attic room, which is much nicer than her room in Beechgrove Park. But I doubt it will compensate for her dad if Dave and I make our temporary split permanent. Not that she'll have the attic room anyhow, because I simply can't inflict us all on Mum. If asked, she'll say we're welcome, but having us stay permanently is an entirely different prospect to putting up with us for a few weeks until I sort myself out. I've seen those TV programmes about children moving back with their parents. It's never a good idea in the long run. I love my mum to bits, but we have separate lives.

I'll have to make a decision soon. And I will. Honestly. But not yet.

Mica is also sound asleep, although in her case with the covers tightly wrapped around her. Tom takes after his dad, with his Viking heritage, but Mica is a mini-me. Her hair is buttermilk-blonde like mine and she has the same heart-shaped face and blue eyes. Additionally, like me, she wakes up in an instant, which is why I simply blow her a kiss rather than touching her.

'I hope nobody ever breaks your heart the way your dad did mine,' I whisper. 'Sleep well, pet. See you later.'

Then I close the door behind me and make my way quietly downstairs.

'What on earth are you doing up at this hour?' My tone is half accusing, half exasperated as I see my mother sitting at the table, a cup of coffee and a dry Ryvita in front of her. 'I couldn't have been quieter, for heaven's sake.'

'I knew you'd be up early,' she replies. 'So I woke up too. I'm sorry. It's a habit.'

'You don't have to be sorry.' I immediately regret my words as I notice Mum's still-too-pale face and the shadows under her eyes. 'I'm the one who should be sorry. I'm the one in the way.'

'You know you're not,' she says. 'You never will be.'

'On one level I'm aware of that,' I agree. 'On the other – I'm a grown woman with a family of my own and I shouldn't have had to come running back to my mammy like a child.'

'Aren't you still my child?' Mum gives me a smile, then picks up a knife and begins to smear Low Low on her Ryvita. 'I'd have been upset if you didn't stay with me.'

I don't know if Dave was supportive about me coming here while Dad was in the hospice because he knew it would give him the opportunity of some offside action with Julie. I like to think not, but he's spent a lot of time in her house over the last year. I always thought it was because Julie's brother, Robbie, had brought his seventy-five-inch OLED TV with him when he started to house-share after his landlord had jacked up his rent to unmanageable levels. I thought Robbie and Dave watched the footie on it together. That's what my husband told me. But maybe it was nothing more than an excuse and I'm utterly naïve.

'The coffee machine is still on,' Mum says, breaking into my thoughts. 'And there's hot water in the kettle. Are you going to have something before you go out?'

'I'll just have hot water and lemon.' I fill a cup with water, then slice one of the lemons on the worktop and drop it in. 'I'll get coffee at the airport while I'm waiting for Gina Hayes.'

'I didn't think that driving people around the place meant you had to follow their hare-brained ideas,' says Mum.

'If I had the willpower to follow everything she says, I'd be a sylph by now.' I run my finger around the waistband of my trousers. I'm comfort-eating and it's beginning to show. But I haven't the heart for Slim to Win. 'Lots of people have hot water and lemon juice in the morning,' I add. 'It helps with your digestion. It's not specific to Gina Hayes.'

13

'A decent breakfast would be better.'

'Says the woman with a Ryvita on her plate.'

Mum looks abashed and then smiles. Instantly, she looks years younger. 'You've got me there,' she admits. 'But it's only five thirty. I'll have something else when the kids are up.'

It's five thirty already! I have to go. I finish the hot water and lemon juice (secretly wishing I'd had coffee after all) and glance out of the window as I rinse the cup under the tap.

The sky has lightened but it's covered in a fine grey haze that's brought a soft summer drizzle.

'Take care,' says Mum. 'Let me know how things are going.'

'I'm sorry for leaving you with the kids,' I say. 'I know it's a long day today.'

'Don't apologise. I like it. You drive safely, OK?'

'OK.'

I pick up the car keys from the bowl on the kitchen table. I turn to leave and then turn back again. Mum looks at me questioningly and I walk around the table and put my arms around her.

'Love you.' I give her a hug that could crack her ribs.

'Love you too,' she says

And then I leave.

Chapter 2

The silver-grey Mercedes is parked in the driveway alongside my own car, a four-year-old red Toyota. Mum also drives a Toyota and it's on the road outside, in the cul-de-sac that forms the end of the street.

I unlock the Mercedes and slide into the driving seat.

The solid thunk of the door closing behind me is comforting. So is the rich smell of the cream leather interior. As I breathe in, I feel as though my dad is in the car beside me, looking after me as he always did. The luxurious E-class saloon is Dad's car. He bought it six years ago when he decided to give up a lifetime of being a taxi driver and become an independent chauffeur instead. He'd had enough, he told us, of driving in the middle of the night, of having random strangers sharing his space, of dealing with people who'd drunk too much or were high on drugs, people who – in Dad's opinion – shouldn't even be out on their own. 'I'm too old for it,' he said. 'But the economy is picking up again and I have good contacts with businesses around town that are looking for a more personal service. Lots of people want to hire an executive car rather than a taxi. My contacts with private hire companies are good too. I can make a go of it and then retire at sixty-five.'

He would have been sixty-five this year.

I exhale slowly and select reverse. The car rolls smoothly out of the driveway. When Dad was first diagnosed, I told him that I'd do the driving for him while he was getting his chemotherapy treatments. I hold a public service vehicle licence because I drove the taxi for a short time after Dave and I came back from England. We needed the money and I did the morning shifts when Dad was in bed after his night work. Mum looked after Mica and Tom while I helped out. I've always liked driving. It's one of the things that kept Dad and me close to each other. He trusted me behind the wheel of the Merc and I was happy to have his trust.

I looked after the company accounts for him too. I remembered enough of the accounting technician's course to be able to keep a set of books, and I'm quick with numbers. On and off, I helped Dad out whenever he needed, so it was logical that I'd drive for him while he was sick. I wanted him to believe that I was temporarily holding the fort; just keeping the driver's seat warm before he got back behind the wheel. We both knew it wouldn't turn out that way, but pretending helped both of us to cope.

He left me the car. When I went in to see him about ten days before he died, he told me that was his plan. I could keep running the business or not, he said, but the car would be worth a few bob anyway. I shushed him, telling him that it was the last thing on my mind at that moment. Which it was.

I didn't have plans to keep the business going after he died. But I didn't consider selling the car either. Truthfully,

I hadn't given any of it much thought. And then I walked in on Dave and Julie, and everything changed.

When my inadvertent gasp alerted him to my presence at the bedroom door, Dave's eyes widened with horror and he pushed Julie to one side so quickly she almost toppled off the bed.

'What are you doing here?' he demanded. 'You're supposed to be at your mother's.'

I couldn't speak as I watched Julie grab a light blue sundress that lay crumpled on the floor and slip it over her head. She'd been wearing a black dress at the funeral. A little short, maybe. But sombre. And appropriate. Of course the blue sundress was appropriate for a sneaky date with my husband. Even if it had ended up on the floor

'Obviously I wouldn't . . . we wouldn't . . .' Dave kept his eyes fixed on me. 'It's not what you think.'

'You're kidding me, right?' I found my voice, although it trembled. 'It's *exactly* what I think.'

Julie grabbed her leather bag (and her knickers), shoved her feet into a pair of jewelled flip-flops, then hurried out of the room without saying a word. I caught a waft of her perfume over Dave's familiar musky scent as I stood to one side to let her leave. Then I heard the bang of the front door and I was alone with my cheating, betraying husband.

'Sweetheart, I'm sorry,' he said. 'I didn't mean this to happen.'

'Which?' I asked. 'You didn't mean to shag someone else in our home, or you didn't mean me to find you at it in our bed?'

Now that I think about it, maybe I was resilient after all.

Or sounded it, at any rate, because I certainly didn't feel it. It was an effort not to burst into tears. But I didn't.

'Oh, come on, Roxy love. You don't have to make it out to be some big drama.' Dave's voice was cajoling. As if I was being unreasonable. As if it wasn't the biggest drama of my life to find him naked in bed with the next-door neighbour.

'What the hell are you on about?' I demanded. 'You were bonking Julie Halpin and I caught you. If that's not drama, I don't know what is. You cheated on me with the woman next door. For crying out loud, you . . . you . . .' I covered my face with my hands. But I still didn't cry. It was as though I'd used up all my tears for my dad.

'It just happened,' Dave said. 'I'm really sorry, you know I wouldn't have hurt you for the world. After I got back last night, Julie called around to see how you were. But of course you were still at your mum's and it's been nearly a week since you were home and—'

'Five days!' I choked. 'It's only been five days and you've moved someone else in already.'

'It's not like that at all,' he protested. 'I've been busy running backwards and forwards to the hospital and the funeral home and the church and all that sort of stuff, don't forget. It's been a difficult time for me too. When Julie knocked at the door, she could see I was upset and she insisted on making me a cup of tea. Then we got talking and—'

'There are loads of men I talk to but I don't end up bringing them home and sleeping with them!' I'd suddenly found my inner rage and it felt good.

'But it was an emotional day, wasn't it?' said Dave. 'And

I was thinking of life and death and stuff and I wanted to share it with you but you weren't here.'

'You're blaming *me*?' I stared at him. 'You slept with Julie Halpin and you're blaming *me*?'

'No. You needed to be with your mum. But I needed someone too. These last few weeks have been tough.'

'You *are* bloody well blaming me.' I felt the throb of a headache start at the back of my skull. 'You're saying that I wasn't here and you needed to sleep with someone so you took the first available woman. Not that Julie's without blame herself,' I added. 'She stood outside the church and told me she was sorry for my loss. Then a few hours later she's riding my husband.'

'I know it looks bad,' admitted Dave. 'I know I messed up. But don't get it out of proportion. It was a one-off thing because of the circumstances, that's all.'

'So everything's fine now, is it?' I rubbed my eyes. 'You've slept with Julie and we go back to being good neighbours and you pop next door on Saturdays to watch football with Robbie – where was he last night, by the way?'

'Out for a few pints, I suppose,' replied Dave.

I didn't remember seeing Julie's brother at the funeral but he must have been there. The church had been packed. Dad was a very popular man.

'How long?' I asked.

'How long what?'

'Have you had the hots for each other?'

'She's a good-looking woman,' he said. 'But I've never even noticed her before.'

'I'm going downstairs.' I ignored the contradiction in

19

his statement. 'I need a cup of tea. Don't even think about coming into the kitchen.'

'I have to get to work anyhow,' said Dave. 'I'll be late.'

I didn't say anything else. I walked down the stairs holding tightly to the handrail so I didn't fall. Then I opened the back door and went into the garden. I was still there when I heard Dave's van pull out of the drive.

As the Mercedes moves down the road, I switch on the radio, which is already tuned to my favourite easy-listening station. I prefer calming music when I'm driving around town; the early-morning shows with their relentlessly cheerful hosts are far too jolly. They remind me of Mica and Tom on a sugar rush.

I leave the housing estate and turn onto the main road. It's too early for a commuter build-up, so the drive will be relaxed even though the rain will mean more cars on the road later. I don't need the satnav to find my first client's house, because I've driven her before. She's Thea Ryan, the award-winning actress, and she and her husband are going to London this morning for a round of chat shows to promote her new TV series. Desmond Ryan is a playwright, and according to Ms Ryan (I can't call her Thea to her face, even though she's asked me to), the series is based around an incident that took place in a remote farmhouse during the Spanish Civil War. It sounds interesting and I'm looking forward to watching it.

Thea, who's in her seventies, was one of Dad's first clients. The production company that had made a short series narrated by her the previous year had always used Dad as a driver, and afterwards she began to book him rather than take taxis when she needed to be driven places. Although her business was irregular, Dad had liked her. He said she was 'a tough old bird', which I told him was surely a sexist way of referring to someone who was a national treasure. Dad rolled his eyes and told me to get off my feminist high horse. We both laughed then. I'm not a feminist. I'm not an 'ist' of any kind. I'm simply trying to do my best.

The Ryan house is on the south side of the river, which means having to cross the city, but that isn't a problem at this time of the morning. And hopefully I'll have Thea and Desmond at the airport long before it becomes an issue. I never drive through Dublin in rush hour if I can avoid it. Stop-start driving is far too stressy. But I enjoy driving through the centre when it's almost deserted. I'm a city girl and always have been. I like streets and houses and shops and buildings of every shape and size. I like knowing that there are people all around me. I like the buzz. The promise that anything can happen.

I arrive outside the old red-brick house in the chichi suburb of Rathgar twenty-five minutes after setting out. Usually I text clients to say I'm waiting outside, but almost as soon as I pull up at the kerb, the brightly painted front door opens and I see both Thea and her husband framed in the light of the hallway.

I get out of the car and take an umbrella from the boot. It has a vivid pattern of tropical palms and flamingos and is a vibrant splash of colour in the grey morning.

'What are you doing!' cries Thea as I make my way up the tiled pathway. 'We're on our way. There's no need for you to get wet.'

'Or you,' I say, holding the umbrella over her. 'By the

21

way, this is your umbrella. You left it behind the last time. I did ask you if you had everything,' I add. 'I didn't see it when I looked because it was under the seat.'

'Oh, I'm hopeless with brollies,' says Thea cheerfully. 'I leave them everywhere! Desmond has his today.'

Desmond, a tall, patrician man with an amazingly full head of almost white hair, holds up a black telescopic model in a faux-leather case.

'Honestly,' I say. 'Let me get you both to the car. You might need that umbrella for London and it would be better to keep it dry.'

They concede the point, although Desmond remarks that he should be escorting me, not the other way around.

'Roxy is a modern woman with a career of her own,' says Thea as they settle into their seats. 'She doesn't need men fussing over her.'

I can't help smiling when she says this, although the reality is, I don't have a career of my own. Driving the Mercedes is therapy, not a career choice. And I've no idea how long I'll keep doing it.

'ID, mobiles, credit cards?' It's a question I always ask on the way to the airport. You wouldn't believe the number of people who forget at least one of those items.

Desmond assures me that they've got everything and then Thea asks me about Mum. I reply that she's doing well, which, thinking about the shadows under her eyes this morning, I hope is true.

Some clients like to talk and some prefer to travel in silence. Thea is a talker, although from time to time she studies a script in the car. On those occasions she tells me not to feel insulted about being ignored. I would never feel insulted by

Thea Ryan, who was very kind when I first drove her after Dad's diagnosis. She asked lots of questions about his treatment and the prognosis. They could have been intrusive, but coming from Thea, they weren't. And because everyone else was sort of tiptoeing around his illness, it was refreshing, if a little daunting to have to talk about it. She sent the most enormous wreath to the funeral. Mum was very touched.

'I'm sure it's still raw for your mum,' she says now. 'It takes time to grieve and these days we don't allow enough space for it. We like to sweep it all under the carpet and pretend we're perfectly fine the next week. But we're not. The problem with today's world is that we don't allow ourselves time to recover from anything. It's crazy.'

I can't help agreeing with her. Sometimes it seems impossible to believe Dad has gone forever. I'll walk into the house and expect to hear his cheery 'hello, honey' and see his jacket hung over the kitchen chair as it always was. The realisation that I won't is like a knife cutting through my heart.

Thea then asks after me and I tell her I'm fine, which is obviously a lie because I'm not. She doesn't say any more, however, instead asking Desmond about their agenda for the day. It's all interviews and publicity for the new series. Desmond wrote it and Thea is starring in it, and I gather it's the first time they've worked together in years. It sounds glamorous and exciting and it's nice to have a bit of that in the car. Most of my clients are businessmen in suits, which isn't one bit glamorous or exciting.

'Excellent timing,' says Thea as I stop at the drop-off point. 'Thank you.'

'I'm collecting you next Monday evening, right?'

'Yes.' Desmond nods at me.

'Best of luck in London.' I retrieve the cases from the boot and hold the umbrella over my two clients. 'I'll be watching you on the chat shows.'

The national treasure gives me a quick peck on the cheek, which isn't usually part of my farewell to clients, but with Thea Ryan it seems entirely appropriate.

'You're a dear,' she says. 'We'll see you back here on Monday. Hang on to my umbrella till then.'

'I will,' I assure her. 'One last check that you have everything.'

Both of them assure me that they're good to go, and I wait beside the Merc until they've successfully negotiated their way into the terminal building. Then I get back into the driver's seat and start the engine again.

I've managed my bookings so that my next client is a pickup from the airport, but because Thea and Desmond are leaving from Terminal 2 and the nutritionist and celebrity cook Gina Hayes is arriving at Terminal 1, I have to circle around to park nearby. Gina's flight is due to touch down in about an hour, and although Mum's house is only ten kilometres away, the traffic will certainly be building up now, which makes it smarter to park and have a coffee at the airport rather than go home, even if it means I won't see Tom and Mica until later. I don't like not being there for them first thing, but it can't be helped.

I walk into the terminal and make straight for the coffee shop near the arrival gates. I'm desperately in need of caffeine and sugar – let's be honest, despite whatever health benefits it's supposed to have, hot water and lemon is an utterly useless way of starting the day. I'm pretty sure I once read that an enormous fry-up is good for you first thing in the morning, something that really appeals to me. I find it hard to believe, though, because the food I like is usually on the banned list. I'd love a sausage and rasher right now. Instead, I order a cappuccino and a muffin, which is probably worse. All the same, the aroma of the coffee is almost enough to revive me. Once I've taken a gulp of the cappuccino and a bite of the muffin, I open my iPad and begin to scroll through my Facebook timeline.

I stop at the picture of Dave and the kids that I posted a few months ago. They're all dressed in football gear, the strip of the local club the children play for. Both their teams had won a tournament in their age groups and they're posing with their trophies. Tom is standing in front of Dave, one foot on a football, his replica cup in his hand. Mica is beside him, holding hers aloft. Someone who's clearly not in the know about our marital situation has commented on it, which has driven it up my feed, and I feel a real pain in my heart when I recall how happy we were that day. I wonder if there's a chance we can ever be happy again. Having said that, Dave and I are still Facebook friends. Possibly that's more important than still being married to each other – which we still are on Facebook too. Neither of us has changed our status to 'it's complicated'. But it *is* complicated, even if Dave doesn't think so. In his view he made a mistake and he's sorry for it. He knows that being caught in the middle of his mistake was the killer blow. But he thinks I should forgive him. For his sake. For mine. And for the children.

Forgive and forget. Or walk away. The pendulum keeps swinging between the two. One of these days it'll have to stop. I still don't know where.

Dave called around to Mum's as soon as he finished work that day so that he could apologise properly to me, as he put it. I didn't want to see him, but Mum told me it would be wrong not to. She hustled Tom and Mica out of the living room, telling them that she wanted to get some McDonald's to take away. As Mickey D's is very much an occasional treat in our house, they were both thrilled by this. But I felt terrible that a day after burying her husband, my mother had to put my needs ahead of her own.

I said this to Dave.

'Mothers always do that,' he told me. 'Yours is no different.'

'Well, now that you've driven her out of her home, you'd better say whatever it is you want to say.'

'There's no need to be like this,' he said. 'I've told you I'm sorry and I am, Roxy. I really am. I know it was wrong. And I swear to you, I've never, ever been unfaithful to you before. Being with Julie was . . .' He paused. 'Meaningless.'

'It isn't meaningless to me.'

'I get that,' said Dave. 'I do. I was a dick. I'm sorry.'

He looked sorry. He sounded sorry. I believed him about that.

'I'm angry and disgusted,' I told him. 'That you could even think about it.'

'I was drunk.'

'And that excuses it?'

'No. But it explains it. I wouldn't have bothered with her otherwise.'

I felt a sudden pang for Julie, whose own marriage had broken down after a couple of years because her husband had cheated on her with a colleague. And then I clamped down

26

on any sympathy I might have had for her, because she should have known what it was like.

'Come home,' said Dave. 'I miss you and I miss the kids. I wouldn't have gone near Julie if I hadn't been missing you.'

I listened to his male logic without saying a word. On the one hand, I could feel myself wavering. Understanding, even. But on the other, five days on my own wouldn't have made me jump into bed with another man. And if Dave's explanations were to be believed, Julie had spent the whole night in our house. They'd undoubtedly been at it before I'd come home. So they'd done it more than once. I don't know if I would've forgiven once more quickly. But twice. Or maybe more. That wasn't a moment. That was premeditated.

The pendulum had swung towards walking away.

'I can't come home,' I said. 'I'm too angry.'

'I understand you might need a bit of time,' he said. 'But the children need their dad.'

'You should have thought of that before,' I said.

'What do you want from me, Roxy?' he asked. 'I'll do anything. I truly will.'

I believed that, too. Dave is a good man. He made a mistake. He has to pay for it, but according to another one of the cheating-husband articles, though a desire for punishment is understandable, it's not necessarily the solution.

The pendulum swung back towards forgive and forget.

'I need some time,' I told him. 'I'm sorry. But I do.'

'Please don't take too long,' he said.

And then he left.

I didn't hear from him for two days. Then he sent a long,

27

rambling text (from the local pub, I reckon) all about how much he still loved me and how he hadn't seen Julie Halpin since and if he did he'd turn his back on her and he was sorry, sorry, sorry.

He didn't say anything about me coming home, but he turned up at Mum's house on Saturday to take the kids for the day. He also had an enormous bunch of flowers in his arms.

'The flowers are for you. Football in the park for them,' he said as he handed them to me. 'The children can stay with me tonight. You could too, if you wanted.'

I buried my face in the flowers, which was a bit stupid as I immediately started to sneeze.

'For one night?' I put down the flowers and blew my nose.

'If it made a difference.'

I shook my head. He took the children and I stayed home alone with my mum. She divided the flowers between three different vases.

And that's how it's been since Rodeo Night. He texts me every day to say how sorry he is. All of his texts include a sad-face emoji and half a dozen hearts. Sometimes he adds a soppy romantic video. He asks me to come home. I delete the texts and videos and say that I need more time. He tells me I can take as much time as I like, but he needs me back. He needs the children to come home. He tells me that he'll never be alone in a room with another woman again. He says how much he loves me. And I always end up replying once again that I need more time. So far he hasn't asked how much more. But sooner or later he will. Sooner or later he'll stop being sorry and sending the videos and he'll get pissed off at me. I know he will, because that's how I'd feel too. And that means I can't swing with the pendulum forever. I have to make a decision about the rest of my life.

But no matter how good I'm supposed to be at decision-making, this is still one I don't want to make.

Debs, my closest friend, is trying to be even-handed about it. She says that all men are fools but that Dave is one of the better men even if he did do a very foolish thing. I know she's right. But I still can't cope with how let-down I feel. And although I truly want to forgive him, I'm not ready to do it.

I continue to stare at the photograph of my children and their father. They belong with him just as much as with me. Children need two parents. But even as my finger hovers indecisively over the message icon to type the words 'I'm coming home', I pull it away.

Why can't I accept that it was a moment of madness on his part? Why is it that every time I think I'm ready to let it go, another wave of pure rage washes over me and leaves me shaking? Why can't I simply forgive him? But why *should* I simply forgive him? He's broken my heart, after all.

My life used to be sorted. It might not have been glamorous or exciting, but it was perfect. Yet in the space of a few weeks, I no longer have the two men who meant the most to me in the world. I'm not living in the home that I love. All the certainties I've built up over the years have come tumbling down, leaving me bereft and bewildered. I'm not the person I used to be. Right now, I don't know who I am any more.

An announcement about a delayed flight jolts me back to my job. I glance at my watch, then check Gina's flight status.

The plane has landed, so I type the name 'Gina Hayes' in a large, bold font onto my iPad and go to stand in the already crowded arrivals hall.

'Roxy, sweetheart, how are things?'

I've wormed my way towards the barrier and it's another driver, Eric Fallon, who greets me. Meeting passengers at the airport is a bread-and-butter business and the drivers get to know each other. On one occasion a terrible thunderstorm delayed every flight coming into Dublin, and I spent nearly three hours in the coffee shop with Eric. It was one of my first jobs after Dad's diagnosis, and Eric, who's almost the same age as him, was kind and understanding.

'Good,' I reply. 'Which flight are you meeting?'

'The nine a.m. from Paris,' he says. 'A suit.' He tilts his iPad towards me. The name on it is Ivo Lehane. 'Heading to the convention centre. Something to do with ethical business models.' He snorts.

I smile at him. Like my dad, Eric doesn't believe that big business is ethical. He has a deep mistrust of anyone who wears a suit, and is wary of people who try to give him investment advice. Eric was burned in the financial crisis back in 2008. Ever since then, he's become an anti-establishment figure, having decided that nobody looks out for people like him.

I agree with him, at least in part. The system is rigged against the ordinary person. We don't get a say in anything. Laws are passed by rich people for rich people and there's nothing we can do about it. I'm not anything like as radical as Eric, who spent much of the recession involved in anti-austerity protest marches and was even, briefly, a member of a new political party. But I get really angry when politicians imply that if you're struggling, it's your own fault. I'm worried about what might happen to me and the children if I don't go back to Dave, because that would make me a single-parent family. I've no idea how I could possibly afford a home of my own. It's a mess and it's not my fault. But I'm pretty sure that some people would be happy to blame me anyhow.

The doors from the baggage area to the arrivals hall slide open and a stream of passengers walk through. Eric and I hold our iPads up so that our clients can spot us. Neither Gina Hayes nor Ivo Lehane is in the initial group and we lower them again. After a brief lull, more people appear, and eventually a tall man in a charcoal suit walks over to Eric and identifies himself as Ivo. I should be so lucky as to get a client who looks like Patrick Dempsey in his prime! Dr McDreamy is totally wasted on Eric. (I used to love Patrick in *Grey's Anatomy*. I was gutted when they killed him off.) Then I laugh at myself for caring whether my clients are as good-looking as TV stars. They don't notice me and I don't really notice them. Not after they get into the car, at any rate.

'This way, Mr Lehane,' says Eric. And then, to me, 'See you again soon, love. Take care.'

He leaves the terminal building with his suit. I keep my iPad held up and wait for my second client of the day.

Chapter 3

Dad did a good job of building up the business. Gina Hayes is actually a client of a PR firm that he did a lot of work for. He was very pleased to get Grady PR, because although it's a small firm, it has a great client list.

The issue of Dad's business is another pendulum swinging in my mind. Like I said, driving is therapy. I kept doing it after moving in with Mum, partly so that I wasn't continually obsessing about Dave (although I am, obviously); partly so that I wasn't under her feet all day; and also because it's bringing money into the house, even though she keeps refusing to accept it.

But now it's become more than that. For the first time in years, I'm doing something for myself, and despite the circumstances, I'm enjoying it. It wasn't until I took over from Dad that I realised how long it had been since I'd done anything of my own. I've never been what you'd call an ambitious sort of person. All I ever wanted was to get married and have a family. Work, no matter what the job, was a means to an end. My entire world revolves around my home and my family. Since Tom was born, I haven't worked outside the house – occasional driving and keeping Dad's books doesn't count because that's just helping out, and besides, it didn't take up too much time. I did some childminding for nearly five years, but the family moved to a new neighbourhood about eighteen months ago, and although there's always someone needing childcare on the Beechgrove estate (I'm part of a WhatsApp group of available mums), I wanted a bit of a break. Then Dad got sick and my priorities were elsewhere. I suppose Dave has seen himself in a very traditional head-of-the-household role, while I'm . . . well, I don't know what I am. But dependent on him is part of it. Now, I can't help thinking that perhaps Dave cheated because he'd lost some respect for me. Because he didn't think I contributed enough.

Julie Halpin is some kind of office manager. She might not have a husband of her own any more, but she heads off to work every day in her sporty blue car, goes on holidays whenever she feels like it and always wears the most fashionable of clothes. And I'm . . . well, I'm basically the same person I was twenty-odd years ago when Dave and I first started going out together, except with added stretch marks.

If we get back together – and it's still a massive if – something has to change. I need to find the part of me that I never knew mattered before. The rebellious Roxy. The Roxy who competed on the football pitch. The Roxy who thought of herself first and everyone else second (even if that's not a viable option now). Driving the Merc ticks some of those boxes. The problem is, even though it's a ready-made opportunity, continuing with Dad's business would be tricky. The hours are erratic and I'd have to be very organised about childcare. And yet . . . in the blur of the last few weeks, being a driver is the one thing that's kept me grounded. It's given me something practical to do. Feeling Dad's presence in the car with me, however tenuous, has been comforting too.

More people emerge into the arrivals hall, but it's another fifteen minutes before the nutritionist appears. I recognise her at once. Gina Hayes owns the space around her in a way I can only dream of. Even though she's not as glammed up as when she's on TV, she's tall and well groomed, with glossy nut-brown hair that curls gently past her shoulders. She's carrying a multicoloured tote bag and wearing a light fabric raincoat in pastel pink over skinny jeans, a white T-shirt and high-heeled boots. Somewhat weirdly, the raincoat is Gina's signature look. She started off presenting her show outdoors, where the raincoat seemed appropriate. Now, even though she's moved into a room made entirely of glass, she still wears it. It sounds silly, but it works.

I don't have a signature look. Unless you count today's navy suit, white blouse and tiny gold earrings, which is working Roxy, not real-life Roxy. Real-life Roxy prefers bright colours, lots of accessories and high heels; though after a day's driving, I usually pull on jeans, a T-shirt and trainers as soon as I get home. And 'pull on' are the operative words. I don't style my clothes the way Gina does. I just wear them.

I hold up my iPad. Gina sees it and strides across the arrivals hall towards me.

'I'm Gina Hayes.' She extends a hand. 'Are you my driver?'

'Roxy McMenamin. Pleased to meet you.'

I use Thea Ryan's umbrella again as I escort Gina to the car park – it's only a short distance, but I'm not entirely sure that the designer raincoat will be much use in the sort of Irish drizzle that can soak you to the skin before you even notice it's raining. Besides, I don't want her to get her artfully styled hair wet. Somewhat weirdly, the exotic umbrella gives me a certain confidence that I associate with Thea. It bestows me with a sprinkling of her personality and makes me feel less intimidated by the powerhouse that is Gina Hayes.

'I've never had a woman driver before,' Gina remarks as she gets into the back seat of the Merc. 'And it's never occurred to me that there might be women drivers out there. Which is annoyingly un-woke of me.'

'I'm not a driver to make a point,' I tell her. 'I'm a driver because it's my job.'

'But nice to see women doing jobs that were traditionally male,' says Gina.

Please tell me she doesn't want a conversation on gender equality at this hour of the morning. I know taxi drivers are supposed to have opinions on everything, but I'm a chauffeur and I don't. I glance in the rear-view mirror; fortunately for me, Gina has already moved on and is scrolling through her phone.

'We're going to the TV station for your interview first,' I tell her. 'Your PR agent will meet you there. Then to the bookshop for your signing session. And after that I'll be driving you to Belfast. I'll drop you off at the airport there after you've finished.'

'Fine.' She's totally concentrating on the phone and I wonder if she's a bit pissed off at me for not engaging in the feminist conversation. I'm all for equality and women's rights. But I can't bear people who bang on endlessly about it. Whenever I drove the car for Dad, I wasn't thinking about being a woman driver; just a driver. And yet, I acknowledge to myself as we leave the airport, all of the other drivers I know are men. There must be other women drivers out there, but I've never met one. So maybe, despite myself, I'm a feminist icon.

The very idea makes me laugh. Nobody I know, least of all my husband, would think of me as any kind of icon. Dave never made a thing of my driving in the past. He was matter-of-fact about it. Dad needed help and I stepped up to the plate. It's what you do for family. Simple as that.

I speed up as I turn onto the motorway. Gina is leafing through a folder of papers that she's taken from her tote bag. I wonder if she's nervous about her interview. But why should she be? She's used to being on TV. Her health show is very popular and I'm sure her cookbook will be a bestseller. I can't help envying her. It must be great to have it all sussed. To know exactly what you want from life and go out and get it. Gina Hayes is seven years younger than me. But she's still the grown-up in the car.

By the time we arrive at the studio, she's replaced the papers and has returned to scrolling through her phone. I get out and open the door for her, and tell her that I'll be waiting here when she's finished. She walks inside without a backward glance.

I get back into the car and drive to the small café that I always wait in when I bring people to the TV studio. Waiting around is an occupational hazard for a driver. So is drinking coffee. I'm ready for another caffeine hit and I'm feeling peckish again too. I'm not the sort of person who lets emotional turmoil affect her appetite. I've put on almost a kilo since I walked out on Dave. I don't need Gina Hayes to tell me that comfort eating isn't a good idea. But it helps.

When I'm settled with a coffee and a scone, I text Mum to ask if the children are up yet.

Tom in shower. Mica having breakfast. All good. How're you?

Also good. Everything on schedule.

What's Gina Thingy like?

A bit intimidating. But OK.

Nobody intimidates my daughter! Her text is accompanied by an angry-face emoji.

I send a laughing face and some hearts in return and add that I'll let her know how the schedule is progressing. Gina Hayes has to be in Belfast for a late-afternoon TV show, and although theoretically there's plenty of time, I like to make allowances for the unexpected.

I take a newspaper from the pile that the café provides and start to read. I've reached the letters page when my phone pings. My heart skips a beat, but when I look at it I see that, despite the signature, the message isn't from Dave.

Hope you're still OK for tomorrow night's fund-raiser. Dx

The fund-raiser is for the local soccer club, and Debs is on the committee. As both Mica and Tom are members of the club, I always go to the fund-raisers, and for this one I've donated a day's free use of my driving services as one of the raffle prizes. I wasn't going to go because I'm not in the mood to be in a room with people who I know will see me as gossip fodder. Not necessarily maliciously. But I'll be a topic of conversation all the same. It didn't matter what I said, though. Debs insisted. She said that I had to be strong, and despite my objections, she wore me down. Which goes to prove that my so-called strength and resilience is nothing more than an illusion.

I reply that I'll be at her house on time.

Looking forward to a good night out, responds Debs.

I send a thumbs-up while thinking it's a somewhat sad state of affairs for both of us to consider a fund-raising event in the community centre a good night out. In days gone by we would've scoffed at the very idea. Back then, it was all about clubbing in town and not coming home until four in the morning. These days, I sometimes get up at four in the morning!

I finish my coffee and return to the TV studio car park. I take out my iPad while I wait in the car. The TV subscription that Dave and I have covers our mobile devices, and although he's the one who manages the account, he hasn't blocked me from remote viewing. I'm not sure if this is deliberate or whether he's simply forgotten – Dave only watches sport, and on the biggest screen possible, so he probably hasn't even thought of me accessing the TV. Maybe now that he can't go next door to watch Robbie's supersized one, he'll remember.

The segment of the show with Gina Hayes has just begun. The nutritionist is poised and assured as she talks to the presenter and speaks about how healthy eating habits are good for both your body and your mind.

'It's not rocket science,' she says. 'It's simply good sense. If you want to be your best you, then eat the best food you can.'

Which is all very well, but when you have two children who go through phases of zoning in on one food group (with Tom, it's currently baked beans, with curry as a standby) and a husband whose tastes are very traditional, there is simply no point in trying to introduce stuff you know they won't like. I don't know if Gina has children, but I'm absolutely certain that if she has, and when they reach their point of food rebellion, it won't matter a damn what sort of pretty-looking treats she comes up with: they'll be ignored in favour of alphabetti spaghetti or chicken nuggets. And I also know she'll ultimately cave in, because nobody has the power to stand up to a determined child who refuses to eat what's on their plate. Or a determined husband who scoffs at the idea of a meal without meat.

Maybe it's just me, though. Maybe I'm as crap at being a mother as I am a wife.

Gina comes out of the building a few minutes later, accompanied by her PR manager, and they talk between themselves while I drive them to the bookstore where she's making her appearance. Already there's a line of people waiting to have their copies of *Eat Neat* signed. I don't have any cookbooks. Mum never bothered with them either. She's in the 'can't cook won't cook' category, and although I try to give the children reasonably healthy food, I can't be bothered with all the cookbook palaver. Debs, on the other hand, has an entire shelf-load, from Delia to Nigella, all full of sumptuous pictures and beautiful kitchens where women who look like Gina Hayes eat perfect food and live perfect lives with perfect husbands who would never dream of shagging the next-door neighbour.

I've arranged my day around Gina's schedule. She's going to be in the bookstore for an hour, and that gives me the opportunity to do some shopping. Not for me, sadly, even though I could do with some new clothes, especially as most of my summer wear is still in Beechgrove Park. Even though I know I could pick it up while Dave is at work,

I can't face going back to the house. Not yet, anyway. So my shopping is for Tom and Mica. Most of their stuff is now at Mum's, as they've brought it back after their visits to their dad, but they both get through clothes at an alarming rate.

The saturating drizzle has given way to a partly cloudy sky, but the temperature has risen and my walk down Henry Street is pleasantly warm. There are plenty of bargains in the shops and I pick up some nice tops for both of them. I add some red and yellow hairclips for Mica, and a Batman T-shirt for Tom as treats.

Gina would approve of Mica, whose deep loathing of pink sparkles is entirely of her own making and who is as sporty as, and infinitely more competitive than, her brother. She's also fiercely independent and doesn't hold back on her opinions. Tom is the gentler of my two children without a doubt. But perhaps that will change over time. Maybe he will suddenly embrace his masculinity and Mica will feel obliged to like pink. And then she'll become interested in boys and suddenly her independence and confidence will get cracked, because it always does when boys are involved.

I was a confident child too. It was only when I hit puberty, and the opposite sex became a thing, that I changed. Suddenly, what boys thought of me mattered more than what I thought of myself. Getting dirty on the football pitch became a stupid thing to do. I started thinking about the clothes I wore and how I did my hair and a hundred other silly details. And then, of course, I started going out with Dave McMenamin and the only thing that mattered in the whole world was that he loved me as much as I loved him.

My phone buzzes with a message from Gina's PR agent, Melisse, saying that they'll be ready in ten minutes, so I dump my shopping in the car and drive back to the store.

Gina and Melisse are delighted with how the event went and keep up a conversation for most of the drive to Belfast, which takes a little over two hours. Although I try to tune it out, I'm learning more than I ever wanted to about the inner workings of the digestive system. Rather than stop for something to eat, Gina insists we go straight to the TV studio, and when I park the car, she takes a couple of small containers from her tote bag. She offers one to Melisse while keeping the other for herself.

'They're an energy-giving mix – my own recipe,' she says. 'Much better for us than a mass-produced sandwich or wrap. I'm sorry.' She leans towards me. 'I didn't think to bring anything for you.'

'Not to worry,' I say. 'I'll get a sandwich on my way home.'

'No, no!' Gina is aghast. 'Have one of my bars. I'm working with a company to produce them commercially,' she adds as she hands me a wrapped square of pressed nuts. 'The key thing is not compromising.'

I thank her and look uncertainly at the bite-sized bar, which is an unappetising dark-brown colour.

'You should still get something a little more substantial to eat while you're waiting,' Melisse tells me as she gets out of the car. 'After we drop Gina at the airport, we'll head straight back to Dublin. I need to be in Sandymount as near to seven as possible.'

'I thought you were staying in Belfast,' I say. 'I didn't realise you wanted me to drive you back.'

'It makes no sense for me to stay,' says Melisse.

Of course it doesn't. But I took the booking myself on my mobile and I know that the person making it said nothing about driving Melisse back to Dublin. Not that it matters, as I'm going back there myself. But driving to Sandymount means driving past Mum's and will probably add another hour to my day. I wanted to be home as soon as possible to give her a break and spend some time with my children. I'll have to text her to tell her I'll be late.

Despite Gina's energy bar (which, being honest, was totally disgusting), I go for yet another coffee. I take Thea's umbrella from the boot of the car because the rain has started to come down again. Maybe it's the cheerful design, or maybe I'm still getting the vibe from the older woman, but using it definitely makes me walk a little taller.

I stop at the nearest café and don't bother with a wrap or sandwich but instead ask for a slice of chocolate cake. I'm a little tired now, which, I decide, means I'm probably low in sugar, so despite the chocolate cake, I also tip half a sachet into my cappuccino. I ignore the voice in my head reminding me that sugar is empty calories.

I text Mum to update her on the schedule. She watched the programme with Gina Hayes this morning and says that she seems a nice enough woman. I reply that she's pretty committed to all this healthy-eating lark and I feel like a leaden lump beside her. I try not to look at the chocolate cake as I send the text.

You're not a lump, replies Mum instantly.

I need to lose a few pounds.

Don't be ridiculous.

There's a baby belly there that never went away.

You should be proud of it, texts Mum. *It shows you've had two lovely children.*

Her message makes me smile. The scars from my Caesarean will always remind me, belly or not. I'm still smiling when the phone buzzes again, this time with a call.

It's Eric, the driver from this morning.

'How's things?' I ask.

'Grand. Grand. Listen, love, if you're not already booked tomorrow, I'm wondering if you could do me a favour. You remember that suit I picked up earlier?'

'Yes.'

'He's changed his plans a bit. He wants to be collected from the Gibson tomorrow and driven to Kildare. I can't do that, I've got a booking. How are you fixed?'

I tell him I've two early airport pickups.

'My man doesn't want to be collected until the afternoon. Would that work for you? If it doesn't, no worries, I can get someone else. I thought of you first.'

'Kildare and back?' I ask. 'Do I have to wait around for him?'

'No. Just there.'

I don't want to turn down work. The Kildare trip is reasonable – it will only take an hour or so to get there, and I'll still be home early enough in the afternoon to spend some time with the children.

'OK,' I say. 'Where did you say he was staying?'

'The Gibson.'

The Gibson is a modern hotel in the docklands area.

'No problem. Text me his number.'

'Will do. Thanks, sweetheart.'

I've tried a million times to stop Eric calling me love, or

pet, or sweetheart, but it doesn't make any difference. I don't think he even notices he's using the words. A moment later, his text with the client's number and the time of the pickup appears on my phone, and I add it to my contacts. Shortly after that, Melisse calls to say that Gina has finished her slot and is ready to be taken to the airport.

I wolf down the last of the chocolate cake and then high-tail it into the bathroom to make sure there are no telltale chocolate crumbs on my face. I freshen up, redo my hair and head back to the studio.

Dad used to do these types of trips all the time, but I'm still getting used to so much driving in one day. And I'm still getting used to tuning out the conversations from the back seat.

'Your car is like a confessional,' he told me the first time I drove for him. 'Always remember that. What's said in the car stays in the car. People discuss all sorts of stuff and they don't think you hear them. You don't, that's the thing. You close your ears and you let them talk and you don't ever remember.'

'What if they're talking about a crime?' I asked him.

'God almighty, girl, who do you think I have in my car?' he demanded. 'Nobody will be talking about crimes. Mostly it's sex.'

'Dad!' I rolled my eyes and made a face and we laughed together.

Gina and Melisse aren't talking about sex. They're congratu-lating each other again on a great day and I definitely want to tune them out, as all the talk about Gina's books and TV show and commercial deals is making me feel totally inadequate.

44

'What did you think of it?' Gina asks me suddenly.

'Excuse me?' I glance at her in the rear-view mirror.

'The Bite Boost,' said Gina. 'Did it fill you up?'

I check my own reflection to reassure myself that there are no cake crumbs on my lips.

'It was filling.' I'm trying to be diplomatic. 'I'm not sure it substitutes for a meal, though.'

'It's not meant to,' said Gina. 'It's instead of cake and biscuits.'

I feel as though the words 'chocolate cake' are tattooed across my forehead.

'It would certainly see you through,' I say.

'You see.' Gina sits back in the rear seat and gives a satisfied sigh. 'I *will* bring healthy eating to the masses.'

I'm not sure how I feel at being considered part of the masses. Although from Gina's point of view, that's exactly who I am.

I indicate and turn off for Belfast City Airport.

'That was quick,' says Gina.

'Small city.' I pull up outside the terminal building and get out of the car to open the door for her.

'Got everything?' I repeat the question I put to Thea and Desmond earlier as she steps out.

'Of course,' says Gina.

'Any promotional stuff you need to bring back?'

I ask my clients to check because most of them are in a hurry and it's easy to overlook personal items.

'Oh!' Gina reaches into the car and takes out a book. It's one of the copies she was signing at the bookstore and includes a free icing bag. 'Can't forget this,' she says. 'Not that I use traditional icing on anything, of course. I have a great vegan sugar frosting, though.'

Hopefully she doesn't see me shudder.

'Actually . . .' She hesitates and then thrusts the book at me. 'You keep it. You might find it useful.'

'That's very good of you, but—'

'You look tired,' Gina says. 'I didn't want to say before. I'm not sure what you were snacking on while we were busy, but I'm pretty certain none of it was optimal. Read the book. It will help.'

Have I been insulted by a famous person?

'There are recipes that kids will love too,' says Gina. 'I'm guessing you have them.'

'Do I look that exhausted?' I try a smile.

'Yes,' says Gina. 'Read up on my sections about sleep and healthy living. The book isn't only a recipe book. It's about how to live your best life.'

'Well . . .'

'You're welcome.' Gina reaches into her bag, takes out a Sharpie pen and signs the book with a flourish. 'Next time I see you, you'll look years younger.'

Definitely an insult, I think, even if she doesn't mean it that way. And how can I live my best life when I'm currently not living with my husband?

I wait while Melisse walks into the terminal building with Gina to point her in the right direction. I'm a bit edgy by the time she comes out again.

'All sorted,' says Melisse as I open the door for her. 'Now if you don't mind, I've some stuff to catch up on. So I won't be talking much on the way back.'

I'm stunned at how much time one person can spend on her phone. From the moment we leave Belfast until we reach the Port Tunnel at the end of the M1 in Dublin, Melisse keeps up a constant stream of texting, emailing and instant messaging. She briefly remarks that she's updating Gina's social media, tweeting about her appearances on TV and letting people know there are signed books in the bookshops.

'Got to squeeze every last bit of mileage out of her,' she says as we enter the tunnel.

I love driving through the tunnel, although some clients expressly ask me not to use it – nearly five kilometres underground makes them feel claustrophobic. Melisse says nothing. I'm guessing she's happy that it saves a lot of time in getting her home.

'Not just my home, my office too,' she says when we finally arrive at the single-storey-over-basement house. 'Office downstairs. I live upstairs.'

I guess my home (or at least my mum's home) is my office too. Or maybe Dad's car is.

'A lot of my clients are creative people,' Melisse tells me, even though I haven't asked. 'Musicians, writers, artists. I enjoy working with them. They don't try to interfere. Most of them, anyhow.'

'Do you have many people working for you?' Although all I want is to get home myself, I have to appear interested now that she's suddenly decided to become chatty.

'One intern, one admin person,' she says. 'You spoke to Jess. She made the booking.'

Jess, who didn't tell me I'd have to drive her boss home.

'We weren't sure about asking you after we heard about Christy . . . your dad,' remarks Melisse as she gathers a bundle of papers from the seat beside her. 'I got on well with him. He was a nice man.'

I nod.

'But you were very efficient today. So we'll use you again.'

'Thank you.' It's good to be appreciated.

'Have a nice evening.'

She gives me a quick wave and then hurries down the steps to the basement. I allow myself to release a relaxed breath and am about to drive away when I decide I'd better check to see if she's left anything behind. There's nothing on the seat itself, but a couple of brochures are sticking out from the passenger seat pocket. I lower the window and call after her.

'Sorry!' she says as she opens the rear door and takes them out.

'No problem.'

I give the rear section another quick glance, but Melisse seems to have taken all her stuff now, so I pull away from the kerb. I call Mum's landline when I'm stopped at the lights. Mica answers.

'I'll be home soon,' I tell her. 'I hope you had a lovely day.'

'Emma and Oladele came over and we played in the garden,' Mica says. 'Tom was out with Andrew.'

'Great,' I say. 'I can't wait to get home and cover you with kisses.'

'Mum!' Mica sounds horrified.

'Two kisses, then.'

'One.'

'Deal,' I concede. 'Is Gran there?'

Mica tells me to hold on, and a few seconds later Mum says hello.

'I'm on my way,' I say. 'Would you like me to pick up a takeaway?'

48

'Would you?' Mum is pleased. 'I did fish fingers and beans for the children a while back. I knew they couldn't wait.'

I don't know what Gina Hayes would have to say about fish fingers and beans. But it's fish and . . . and . . . pulses – though are baked beans actually pulses or are they some hybrid pretend-bean? I've no idea. So yes, I'm a crap mother who's allowing her own mum to raise her kids while she mainlines coffee, chocolate cake and Chinese takeaway.

Chapter 4

It's after seven when I finally walk in the door.

Mum takes the paper bag with its foil trays of food from me while I go upstairs. I open the door to Tom's room first, but there's no sign of him so I head to the attic. My son and daughter are both up there, reading. It's nice to see them with books rather than electronic devices in their hands, but to be fair to them, both of them have always enjoyed print books. Mica says she likes the feel of the pages and knowing how much of a story she has left. And Tom is a proper bookworm: he has an entire shelf-load at home. At home in Baldoyle, of course. Not here. He's brought some of his collection with him, but it only fills a fraction of the shelf in his room.

'Mum!' Mica looks up first and smiles at me. Tom drops his book and jumps up to hug me. The tensions of the day immediately slide from my shoulders. There is nothing in the world that can make you feel better than a totally unselfconscious, unconditional hug from your child. I hug Tom in return and then kiss Mica on her head.

'That's one,' she says.

'One more?'

She suddenly grins. 'Yeah.'

And then she hugs me too, and we're all in the middle of a group hug when Mum's voice floats up and says that the food is on the table.

'Chinese,' I tell my children.

'Did you bring home anything for us?' asks Tom.

'Curry chips.'

'I do so love you,' he says fervently, and is out of the room in an instant.

'I got you a spring roll,' I tell Mica, who doesn't like curry chips.

'With sauce?'

'Of course.'

'I love you just as much as him.' And she gives me another kiss.

'That's three!' I cry. 'You must be mad about me.'

She giggles and runs downstairs too.

I go to my old bedroom and change out of my Claire Danes outfit and into a pair of leggings and a bright yellow T-shirt. I put some extra earrings in my ears too and immediately feel more like myself again. Although to be fair, even if she isn't who I am inside, I like being the Roxy who wears the navy suits and white blouses. She might have a broken heart too, but she's in control of things, something the off-duty Roxy very clearly isn't.

We've all moved into the living room. Tom and Mica are on the sofa and Mum is in the armchair that used to be Dad's. I'm in hers. The TV is on and is showing a repeat of *Gogglebox*. I'm utterly convinced that all politicians should watch *Gogglebox*. They'd learn more about their constituents that way than they ever do talking to them on the doorstep.

51

We laugh at the families as we tuck into our food. Gina Hayes definitely wouldn't approve of eating like this, but I don't care. We're together. And that's all that counts.

Later, after Mica and Tom have gone to bed, Mum takes a large envelope from the sideboard and spills its contents onto the coffee table. It's Dad's memorial cards, and seeing them makes my heart constrict so much that it hurts. I pick one up. There's a picture of a sunset on the front, and inside is a photo of Dad with the words 'In loving memory of Christopher (Christy) Carpenter' beneath. Mum chose the photo – it's one of Dad on holiday, and he looks tanned and happy and healthy. There's also a poem about death and horizons, which is supposed to be comforting and which sort of is. But it doesn't bring Dad back.

'I miss him.' Her voice wobbles. 'I didn't think I would, especially in the evenings, but I do.'

'Why didn't you think you'd miss him?' I ask in shock. 'You were married to him for forty-odd years.'

'Yes, but he was out so much of the time,' she says. 'Driving at night. Leaving me on my own. I kind of got used to it.'

'It's not the same,' I protest.

'I know.' Her smile is rueful. 'I guess I thought I was a harder nut than I am. Thing is, Roxy, I thought I'd be ready for it. You get to our age and you know that the odds are shortening every day. Your grandfather, Dad's dad, was only fifty-five when he died. And his mother was fifty-nine. So I thought there might be a genetic thing in his family. Once he got past sixty himself, I sort of relaxed a bit. But I used to think about it all the same. To prepare myself. But you're never prepared for the finality of it.'

I don't know what to say. I never thought of Dad as an older person. I don't think of Mum as old either. I mean, she's in her sixties, so clearly not exactly a spring chicken, but she always looks great – better now than when we were younger because she has more time for herself. She gets her hair colour done every month and she's switched from using the own-brand ranges at Lidl and Boots to more expensive cosmetics. A month before Dad died, she went into Arnotts and had her make-up done at the Charlotte Tilbury counter. She came out looking absolutely amazing, and laden down with premium eyeshadows, blushers and lipsticks. She did her make-up every single day he was sick, although she hasn't bothered since the funeral.

'I know it seems mad,' she said to me then. 'But I need something to make me feel OK.'

I've used the Lidl stuff from time to time myself and it's fine. But sometimes it's not about the products themselves. It's about treating yourself. Despite being regularly told by advertising companies trying to flog the latest in shampoo or foundation or whatever that I'm worth it, I seriously doubt that I am. But Mum truly does deserve to treat herself. She's the glue that holds us all together. She remembers all our birthdays (and reminds us of each other's), she posts old family photos on her Facebook page that make us smile and . . . well, she's just there. Always. No matter what. Even if you turn up with a wheelie bag and say you need to stay a while because your husband is a cheating bastard.

I try to think of her as a person and not only my mother. But sometimes I forget.

'Anyway,' she says when I stay silent. 'I miss your dad, but I have to get on with it. That's what he'd want.'

I give her a hug and tell her there's no rush to do anything. But I know what she means. Life does move on. And we all have to move with it. I do too, even though I don't know the direction yet. I blink back the tears that have welled up in my eyes. I don't want to cry. Not when Mum is being so strong.

'Keep one in the car.' Mum nods at the cards.

I take one and stand up.

'I didn't mean to put it there straight away.'

But I do, going outside and sliding it into the pouch in the sun visor. I like the idea of having it with me all the time.

Mum has put the rest back into the envelope when I return to the living room. On the coffee table instead is a big box. I recognise it. It's one that we use to keep photos from the pre-smartphone era. Proper printed photos going back years. Some are so old they're black and white, but most are faded colour. She removes the lid and takes out a bundle. We smile as we look through them. There are lots of Aidan as a baby, fewer of me (second baby syndrome, according to Mum; she and Dad were less obsessed with charting my every move). All the same, I feature a lot in communion and confirmation shots, where I'm dressed up.

I catch my breath as Mum takes out a dog-eared snap of me when I was about ten. It's at the beach and I'm standing beside my brother, our arms around each other. I don't remember it being taken, but it was clearly a hot day – the sky is azure blue without a single cloud and I'm wearing a bright yellow swimsuit. It's a happy, cheery photo. I reach into my handbag for my phone, and show her an almost identical snap of Mica and Tom.

'Wow,' she says.

We're all bound together, I think. Me and Mum and Dad. My children. Their father. That link can never be broken.

'Can I ask about your plans?' She looks at me, perhaps thinking the same thing.

'You mean, mine and Dave's plans?'

'The plans you have for both of you,' she says.

'I don't have any yet.'

'You can stay here as long as you like,' she assures me, 'but you still have to make plans.'

I know I do. But what I'd really love is for someone else to make them for me. To be the coper. To show me that no matter what happens, everything is going to be OK. I want *her* to come up with a plan that will fix everything. She's my mother, after all. But she's not a magician.

'You have to decide if you're going to forgive him or not,' she says.

The swinging pendulum. Forgive and forget. Or leave.

'Do you think I should?' I ask.

'It's entirely up to you,' says Mum. 'But you need to weigh it up. One moment of . . . well . . . whatever, against all the years you've been together. All the years you've had a really strong marriage. Two children. Your future. Life is so short, sweetheart. You don't want to fill it with regrets.'

The pendulum moves slowly from side to side. Which would I regret more, though?

'We all make mistakes,' she adds.

'Not with the effing next-door neighbour,' I say. 'Not in my bed.'

'It was an emotional time.' Mum's voice is even.

55

'For me too!' I cry. 'Made twice as emotional by seeing that woman's fat arse bobbing up and down in front of me.'

'Roxy!'

'It's true. You weren't there. It was . . . humiliating.'

'Lots of people get over humiliation.'

'So I'm supposed to go back home and live next door to her like nothing happened?'

'Look, I'm not excusing Dave, I'm really not,' she says. 'But sometimes stuff goes wrong and you have to make up your mind how you want to play it.'

I look at the photo of me and Aidan. And the one of Mica and Tom. I think about the options.

'Dave is really sorry,' she adds.

'Has he told you that?'

'Yes,' she says, which surprises me.

'Have you been in touch with him?' I ask.

'He called me,' she says. 'He wanted to know how you were. He's devastated, Roxy.'

'Not half as devastated as me.' But I like hearing that. I like knowing he's unhappy. He deserves to be unhappy after what he did to me. And then I realise I'm wanting to punish him again. Is that what it's really about? Do I want to go home but make sure he suffers first? If that's really the case, I'm a horrible person.

'If you can get over something like this, it can make you stronger,' says Mum.

But the thing is, I thought we were strong already.

Until we weren't.

'I'll think about it seriously over the next few days,' I promise her. 'I really will.'

'You shouldn't have left the house,' she says abruptly.

'What?'

'You should have stayed there with the children and made him move out, if that's how you want to play it.'

'The house is part of the problem,' I tell her. 'I couldn't stay there knowing that Julie had been . . . Well, I couldn't stay.' I don't tell her that I walked around every room after Dave had gone to work and that I felt physically sick at the idea of that woman touching any of my stuff. And that it had been almost impossible to go into the bedroom to collect the few clothes I did, because I could still smell her there.

'I'm with you no matter what, Roxy,' Mum says. 'You know that.'

I can't talk about this now. I can't. I shuffle through the photos again, a lump in my throat, until I stop at an over-exposed picture of my dad and a young woman I don't recognise. She has long dark hair tumbling around her face and is barefoot, dressed in a white T-shirt and flared jeans. Her arms are raised over her head and she's laughing. Dad is also wearing flared jeans. His hair is almost to his shoulders and he has a kind of beardy growth on both sides of his face.

I hold it out to Mum and an entire kaleidoscope of emotions pass across her face.

'Christy was so proud of his sideburns,' she says as she studies it. 'They were all the rage back in the seventies.'

'Who's the woman?' I ask the more important question.

Mum is silent. She's turning the photo over and back in her hands and I can see tension in the corners of her eyes.

'Who's the woman?' I repeat.

She still doesn't answer, and I'm beginning to get a bad feeling about this.

'His first girlfriend.' She puts the photo back on the table just as I'm thinking she isn't going to say anything at all.

You always remember your first love. Though unlike me, you don't always marry them. I'm not surprised Mum is a bit upset at seeing the snap. I'd brain Dave if he kept a picture of another woman in the house. I'm surprised Dad did.

'Did you know her?' I ask. 'Was she one of your friends?'

'No,' she replies. 'It was only a short-term thing. Your dad's summer romance.' She's regained her equilibrium and shrugs. 'I didn't know he'd kept it. Sentimental old fool.'

I take the photo from her and study it more closely. It's difficult to see the woman's face behind her mass of hair, but her joy in the moment is very evident. I find it hard to imagine Dad before Mum. Before us.

'Did he tell you her name?'

Again I think she isn't going to answer, but eventually she says, 'Estelle.'

'How did they meet?' I ask the question before realising that there's no reason for my mum to know anything at all about the girl Dad was in love with before her.

But she's gazing into the distance, and it's as though she's travelling back in time.

'Your dad went on a camping holiday with some of his mates,' she tells me. 'She was staying in a mobile home on a nearby site with her parents. They met at some kind of disco and it was love at first sight. According to Christy, anyhow.'

'A summer of love.'

'Not exactly.'

'Oh?' Now I'm intrigued.

Mum hesitates as though she's going to dismiss it, but then releases a slow breath and starts to talk.

'It was definitely a love-at-first sight moment for your dad, and I don't blame him, do you? She was so pretty. Turns out, though, that she shouldn't have been at the disco in the first place. Her parents were very strict and she'd sneaked out of the mobile home they were staying in.'

'I suppose they found out and gave her grief about it. Did they split them up? Was it literally a one-night stand?'

'Not quite.' Mum picks up the photo and looks at it again. 'They met a few times in secret. But it was always going to end in tears.'

'What happened?'

'One night her mum and dad realised she wasn't in the mobile home and went looking for her. They found her and your dad together in one of the sheds on the campsite.'

I try not to imagine my dad (a man I've never seen with long hair and sideburns) in a shed with a pretty young girl.

'And?'

'Her father nearly beat yours to a pulp, by all accounts,' says Mum. 'Told him to stay away from his daughter and never to touch her again.' She picks up a different photo, one of Dad, and shows it to me. 'Remember the scar on his face?' I nod. It was a faint jagged scar that ran along his forehead. I always felt it gave him a slightly edgy look. 'Well,' says Mum, 'that was a result of the beating.'

'But that's dreadful!' I exclaim. 'Did he go to the guards?'

Mum shakes her head. 'He was afraid it would make things worse for Estelle. From what she'd said, he reckoned her father wasn't above giving her a beating too.'

'He should have said something. So should she!' I'm angry on behalf of them both.

'Times were different then,' says Mum. 'Especially for girls. She was from the country. A farmer's daughter.'

'Even so . . .' I try to imagine Dave beating Mica for anything, and thankfully I can't. And it's not because times have changed; it's because it's utterly wrong of a man to beat a woman. Especially his own daughter.

'They left the following day,' says Mum. 'Your dad was devastated. And he always regretted not going to the police.'

'That's so awful.' I feel sad for both of them. 'Did Dad ever see her afterwards?'

'Like I said, it was a different time. When he went to look for her, they'd already packed up and left, and he had no way of getting in touch.'

'Didn't he know where she lived? Couldn't he have phoned?'

'He only knew that it was Carlow or Kilkenny, somewhere around that area,' says Mum. 'They hadn't exchanged phone numbers.'

I find it difficult to imagine a world in which you can't find the person you're looking for. Between social media and smartphones, it's harder to stay off the radar than it is to be found.

'On the one hand, it's a tragedy,' I say as I return Estelle's photo to the pile. 'She looks so happy in that picture. But on the upside, Dad found you, so it worked out in the end.'

'Yes,' says Mum.

She picks up the photo and stares at it for a long time, a faraway expression on her face.

I'm trying both to visualise and forget my dad as a young

man chasing after a beautiful woman who isn't my mum. But even though I'm horrified for Estelle and what might have happened to her, I'm glad that my dad didn't get involved with her any further. Because if he had, I wouldn't be me. And even though my life is difficult right now, at least I can be sure of one thing. That no matter what, Dave would never be violent to me or the children.

And that makes me the lucky one.

Chapter 5

I'm up early again the next morning for my airport pickups, and then I drive to the Gibson for Eric's suit. I get there ten minutes ahead of schedule. I expect to have to wait – business executives nearly always make you wait – but Patrick's doppelgänger is already outside the glass doors, and when I pull up, he walks across to the car before I have a chance to text him.

He hesitates as I get out.

'Are you my driver?'

'Ivo Lehane? Kildare?' I ask the question anyway.

'Yes.'

'You're with me so.' I open the door to the back seat.

He gets in and I return to behind the wheel.

'Whereabouts in Kildare?' I ask.

'Banville Terrace,' he says. 'Number two.'

I'm surprised at this. I thought he'd be going to a hotel. But perhaps he has friends or family to stay with. His accent is Irish, after all, although it has a slight mid-Atlantic twang.

I put the address into my satnav and start to drive.

Ivo Lehane hasn't bothered to take out his phone or his

tablet or any papers. He's simply sitting in the back seat without saying a word.

It'll take about an hour to get to his destination. I don't mind driving in silence, but I want to give him the opportunity to talk if he feels like it.

'I'm using the Port Tunnel,' I say. 'Then the motorway. It's quicker that way.'

'Whatever you think is best,' he says.

'Would you like some music?' I ask.

'Quiet is good,' he replies.

I take it he means me as well as no music. So I shut up and keep my attention entirely on the road. Although obviously my mind wanders. I think about Mum last night telling me I needed to make plans. I know she's right. But I don't see why I have to do it yet. I need time to come to terms with things.

Since the first time I saw Dave after Rodeo Night, we haven't been alone together. Our communication – his apologies and my replies saying that I can't forgive him yet – have all been by text. The only times we've seen each other are when he's picked up the children, and Mum has always been there too. I've been super-cool but polite, trying to keep our conversations to the bare minimum and not talking about anything important. I haven't brought the kids to our home or collected them. I'm too mortified to be seen in the Beechgrove estate. I can imagine everyone peeking out from behind their curtains and the texts flying between them saying that I'm back. That's what happens. When Johnny Maguire left Brenna and her three children, it was like a bush telegraph every time he turned up on his doorstep afterwards. We all texted each other, and after he left, we texted Brenna to check if she was OK. We thought we were being supportive, but she probably cringed at every one of our well-meaning messages.

Maybe Mum was right and I should've told Dave to get out. But he might not have gone. You can't tell someone to leave the house simply because they've cheated on you with the next-door neighbour. Dave is perfectly entitled to stay. I know this because Brenna dumped all Johnny's stuff on the front lawn when they split up and he simply brought it back inside. And Brenna's solicitor told her there was nothing she could do about it because there was no threat of violence. They shared the house for nearly six months until Johnny finally decided to leave. It's fair enough. But it's no way to live. And I can't do it. I can't move back in with Dave if I'm going to divorce him. Besides, we only have three bedrooms. Where would I sleep? On the sofa? Like I was the one to blame? Because I couldn't possibly sleep in our bedroom, and I wouldn't dream of asking Mica and Tom to share.

My fingers tighten on the steering wheel.

I wish I hadn't gone home that morning. I wish I'd never seen them together. I wish everything was the way it was before.

The satnav directs me to a small street a short distance outside the town. There's a general air of neglect about the half-dozen small houses on each side, which I guess from their design were built sometime in the 1940s or 50s. I pull up outside the first house on the left-hand side. Like the others, it's narrow, with a tiny garden in the front. The green paint is flaking off the hall door and the net curtain at the front window is grey with age.

I'm surprised that a man like Ivo Lehane might be staying here.

He doesn't move and I glance in the rear-view mirror, wondering if he fell asleep on the drive and is still sleeping. But he's looking out of the window.

'Everything OK?' I ask.

'Yes.' He gathers himself and I actually hear him taking a deep breath.

I recognise it. It's the kind of breath you take when you're steeling yourself for something you don't want to do. I wonder if Banville Terrace is where Ivo Lehane grew up. If it is, he's moved a long way from it and clearly doesn't want to be back.

I get out of the car to open the door for him. Often my male passengers don't wait for me to do that. Like Desmond Ryan, they're uncomfortable with a woman opening the door – at least at first. But Ivo is still sitting in the back seat as I stand beside the open door. It takes him another few seconds to get out of the car.

'Thank you,' he says. 'That was a very pleasant journey.' He gives me the merest hint of a smile but it transforms his face and takes years off him. I'm actually hopeless at guessing people's ages, but Ivo must be around the same age as me. Early forties at most. There's a kind of grittiness about him that you don't often see in the polished, groomed businessmen that are my bread and butter as a driver. His stubbled chin is more a reflection of not shaving than a carefully studied designer style. His hair is tousled, but that's because during the journey he kept running his fingers through it. And there's a touch of hardness behind his blue eyes.

It sounds as though I'm studying him, but I'm not really. I notice people. It's a trait that's useful in a driver.

'If you ever need me in the future, you have my number,' I say.

'Yes. Thanks.' He takes a wallet out of the pocket of his suit and removes some notes, which he hands to me. I count them out and then return fifty euro to him, telling him he's overpaid.

'No, that's fine,' he says.

'I really can't accept it.'

'Honestly.' He looks from me to the house. 'It's a tip, that's all.'

'But—'

He puts up his hand in a gesture that means he won't take the money back, and almost immediately walks towards the house.

'Enjoy your stay in Kildare,' I call after him, still stunned by the amount I've earned for this trip.

But he won't enjoy it.

That much is obvious.

Chapter 6

I make everyone's favourite, spaghetti bolognese, when I get home, and we all sit around the table together: me, Mum, Mica and Tom. Nobody is using a device and the TV is switched off, so we have to talk. Even though Tom is the more reflective of the children, he's also the chattiest, and he's talking about the football club because of me going to the fund-raiser later.

'I hope we get new kit,' he says. 'That would be awesome.'

'Ooh, yes.' Mica looks enthusiastic. 'My top has a hole in it.'

'Already?'

'Where Shannon Wilson tackled me,' Mica says. 'Total foul, Mum, but she wasn't even carded.'

She sounds like her dad when she talks about football. I smile at her.

'Maybe she'll get it knocked out of her in summer camp,' says Mum.

'Nah.' Mica shakes her head. 'She fouls because she can't tackle.'

'But perhaps she'll learn.'

Mica looks a bit disconcerted by this. She's by far the best girl on the mixed under-12s team she plays for, and I'm thinking that she doesn't like the idea of Shannon getting better. I say that it would be a good thing for everyone to improve.

'Yes.' She nods and then shakes her head. 'I don't think Shannon can. She's not fast enough.'

'Mica's fast,' agrees Tom. 'I bet she'll be the best at the camp.'

His sister hugs him and I feel proud that my children support each other. I know I sometimes think I'm a crap mother, but actually I've done a reasonably good job. Then Mica takes the last piece of garlic bread and Tom goes mental and the two of them are shouting at each other and I stop the self-congratulation.

'If you're not quiet, neither of you will be going to summer camp!' I have to yell to make myself heard. The silence is instant. They've been looking forward to the camp, which starts in a couple of weeks or so, ever since the start of the holidays. 'Thank you,' I tell them.

'I'm finished.' Tom crams the half-slice of garlic bread that Mica gave him into his mouth and then stands up.

'Please may I leave the table?' says Mum, looking at him.

'Yes,' he replies, and he and Mica crack up laughing.

I laugh too.

So does Mum.

It's not that bad living with her again.

This is the first night I'll have gone out socially since I walked out on Dave. The community centre is actually in Mum's estate and not where Dave and I now live in Baldoyle, but everybody there will be completely up to speed with what's happened because we've known the people in Abbeywood all our lives. The women will be on my side, I'm pretty sure of that. Many of them are old friends, because a lot of people who left Abbeywood after school moved back once they got married. It was my dream to come back too. But not to my mother's house. Not without Dave.

I'm standing in my dressing gown looking into the wardrobe and wondering what the hell I'm going to wear. When I flung my clothes into the wheelie bag before turning up on Mum's doorstep, I just grabbed the nearest things I could find. So I'm missing the floaty floral dress that I bought at the beginning of the summer, as well as nearly all my sandals and light shoes. I'm raging about the dress because it did nice things to my boobs. I'm equally raging about leaving behind the new rose-coloured sandals that I hadn't even worn. I wonder if I could bear to flit back and get my stuff, but I haven't the courage. Instead I keep looking into the wardrobe as though new clothes will magically appear.

In the end I decide on a retro country look. It was one I rocked quite a bit in my teens when Shania Twain was one of my idols, and despite the fact that twenty-odd years have gone by, country chic is back in fashion. I nip into the shower and wash my hair, drying it with a diffuser to give it volume and a bit of a curl. Then I do my make-up again, only this time using a glittery silver-grey shadow instead of the matt colour I wear when I'm working. I add some blue eyeliner and blue mascara, something I used to do when I was in my twenties. Then I put on my red and black checked blouse over a short-ish denim skirt. I finish it all off with a selection of sparkly earrings, a chunky necklace and my open-toed boots. (I don't know what I was thinking when

I took my jewellery instead of my clothes. It's not like it's expensive stuff – I could have replaced all of it.)

I look younger, I think. I twirl in front of the mirror and then worry that if I remember this look from the first time round, I must be far too old to do it again. Am I trying too hard? Will I be making a fool of myself? But just as I'm wondering if I shouldn't haul my work trousers out of the wardrobe and team them with a plain T-shirt, my mobile pings and it's Debs to ask where the hell am I because she's ready.

With you soon, I send.

I still hesitate before leaving the bedroom. Maybe I should change the skirt for a pair of jeans? But then I think, feck it, who cares how I look? I'm dressing for me, not anyone else. As I close the door behind me, I realise that along with the earrings and necklace I'm still wearing my wedding and engagement rings. I've never even thought of taking them off.

'You look lovely, Mum!' says Tom when I walk into the living room.

Mica gives me an approving nod, but my mother raises her eyebrows.

'What?' I ask.

'Nothing.'

'I won't be late. Thank you for looking after them.'

'I'm not looking after them, they're looking after me,' she says.

'Of course we are,' says Mica. 'Granny is still bereaved.'

She learned the word at Dad's funeral. She uses it all the time now.

'Indeed I am,' says Mum with a grin.

70

It's the first time she's looked genuinely amused since Dad died. I smile at her.

'I truly won't be late.'

'No worries,' she says. 'Have fun.'

I leave them watching TV and walk down the road to Debs's house. It used to be her family home. Her parents now live next door, in a house they built on their large corner site. Like many Dubliners, they got planning permission during the boom to build another house in the garden. Then they sold the original house to Debs and her husband at cost. Debs always says how lucky she is, but I used to think I'd find it restrictive to live next door to my mother. I never thought I'd be living in the same house as her again.

'Roxy!' Debs opens the door before I have time to ring the bell. 'Come in. I've poured your drink already.'

I've hardly drunk any alcohol since moving in with Mum. Not because she'd disapprove – she likes a glass of wine in the evenings herself – but because I'm very aware that someone has to be on their toes in case anything should happen to either of the children. Weirdly, this didn't bother me too much when I was with Dave. I'd have a glass or two at the weekends even if he was also having a beer. But then there were two of us and it was different. Now, even though I know I can count on Mum, I feel as if there's only me. Besides, I've had so many early-morning pickups that alcohol the night before is definitely not a good idea.

'You've nothing tomorrow, though,' says Debs when I suggest that a single drink will leave me reeling. 'So tuck in.'

The vodka is smooth and I like the bite of the alcohol. All the same, I won't have any more when we get to the club. It's not worth it.

Debs was the first person to contact me after the incident with Julie Halpin. She texted to ask was it true that Dave had moved in next door. When we met up, I filled her in on the actual turn of events so that she could set the record straight.

'The bitch,' she said as she bit into a muffin. 'Shitting on her own doorstep.'

I nodded.

'What about Dave?' Debs asked. 'How do you feel about him?'

I knew she was being careful not to diss him right away in case I was forgiving him. Saying horrible things about him now might turn out to be awkward later.

I told her that I didn't know how I felt about Dave and I didn't know what I was going to do, but that Julie Halpin was indeed a bitch.

'Generally speaking, Dave's a good man.' Debs echoed what I think, what Mum thinks, what everyone thinks. 'You don't want to be too hasty even if he behaved like a total dick. You've got him where you want him now,' she added. 'Make him pay.'

I've been thinking that way too, of course. The only problem is, making him pay is making me and the kids pay too.

Debs's husband, Mick, walks into the kitchen and says hello. He warns us not to do anything he wouldn't when we go out, and Debs makes a face at him and jokes that he's leaving us with a long list of things we could do. Mick laughs and says he knows what 'you girls' are like when we get together, and then he leaves us to it.

Debs asks about Dave again and I say that I really haven't

got it in me to talk about him and can we forget about it for tonight? And Debs, because she's been my friend forever, doesn't get annoyed with me but simply gives me a hug and says, 'Of course.'

The club is already buzzing by the time we get there. The event is a fashion show followed by karaoke. Debs asked if I'd like to model in the fashion show because I'd done it once before. But in my current state, there isn't a chance I could stand up in front of people and sashay down a catwalk. Besides, back then I was younger and prettier and I hadn't got a wad of comfort-eating fat on my stomach.

There are about thirty tables arranged around the room. Debs leads me over to the one she has reserved for us. Michelle and Alison are already there, along with Rachel, another old school friend. It's a relief to be with people I've known most of my life. The girls have been sending me supportive messages ever since they found out about Dave's big mistake.

'Roxy! How's it going?' Michelle gets up and gives me a hug. Which is a signal for hugs all round.

When we sit down, I say that it's going well and ask about everyone else. I want them to be talking about themselves and not about me.

'I'm exhausted,' says Michelle. 'Darragh is like a cat on a hot tin roof over his Leaving Cert. Honestly, school exams were the pits when we were there and they're still the pits now.'

We all nod.

'He's hoping to get enough points for engineering,' she continues. 'He's actually really bright, but the competition is fierce and I'm worried that if he doesn't get what he wants, it'll totally knock his confidence.'

We make supportive comments. Michelle is the only one of us with a child old enough to be leaving school. She's a single mum – Darragh's dad didn't want to know back in the day, when he and Michelle were both nineteen. But Michelle never dissed Brendan in front of Darragh, and father and son have a reasonable relationship now. Brendan is married with two kids of his own. Michelle and Darragh live with Michelle's parents. Her mother is good friends with mine. Both of them strong women looking after daughters who picked the wrong men.

Rachel is also dealing with exam fever this year, as her daughter, Avery, is sitting her Junior Cert. She and Michelle share exam talk, while Debs, Alison and I chat about summer holidays. Alison, the only one of our group who doesn't have children (like me, Debs has a boy and a girl), has just come back from two weeks in Majorca.

'Puerto Pollensa,' she says. 'It was lovely. Brilliant weather, and the hotel was fabulous.'

Dave and I went to Majorca with Dave's brother and his wife a few years ago and had a great time. But money has been a bit tight recently, so we decided we'd be better off staying at home. Last year we rented a house in Cork. It rained the whole time. I'd love to go on a cheap sun package somewhere. Preferably by myself. But that's not going to happen.

'How's your mum?' asks Alison during a pause in the conversation.

'Doing OK,' I reply. 'It's hard, of course.'

'Selina is a strong woman.' Alison echoes my own thoughts.

'She was great when we were kids. Holding down two jobs and looking after all of you too.'

Back then, Mum worked in the local convenience store in the mornings and in a dental practice two afternoons a week. Later, she got a job as a part-time admin assistant in one of the local businesses. She gave it up when Dad became ill, but I wouldn't be surprised if she tried to get something else, even part-time. She doesn't like sitting around doing nothing.

'Your mum worked too,' I remind Alison.

'Being a hairdresser is different,' Alison says. 'She could set her own schedule because she worked for herself and because she went to people's houses rather than having a salon.'

'All mothers are wonderful,' says Debs as she gets up to go to the bar. 'Each one of us included. Except you, Alison, and I don't know if that makes you the luckiest one among us or a sad wretch.' She grins to show it's a joke. 'What can I get everyone?'

She's scathing when I ask for sparkling water but she doesn't try to force me. To be honest, I've got a bit of a headache already from the vodka. I wonder if I'm turning into someone who simply can't handle alcohol at all. I suppose it wouldn't be a bad thing. But I do like a glass of wine with a meal, or sometimes sitting in front of the TV at night. I don't think I could give it up completely.

As Debs arrives back with the drinks, Callum Phelan, the football club president, gets up and welcomes everyone. Then Tash, his wife, who's the chairperson of the committee, gets the fashion-show part of the proceedings under way. The clothes are all from local stores and the models are members

75

of the committee and their friends. It's nice to see normal-sized women modelling clothes. You get a much better idea of how they'd look on an average body. There are some lovely outfits and I tell myself that, as I'm not entirely opposed to treating myself, I'll have a day at the shops sometime soon. I haven't bought anything new in ages. The last thing was the floral summer dress I left behind.

We applaud wildly as the girls strut their stuff. I remember the thrill I got the year I did it. I was very nervous at the start, but when I stepped onto the catwalk, the energy in the room jolted me into action and I pranced and posed as though I was Kate Moss herself.

When we got home afterwards, Dave practically ripped the clothes off my body. He said he'd been totally turned on by seeing me up there looking so great, and knowing I was his. It was good sex. Sex with Dave has always been good.

The fashion show goes on for half an hour and then the karaoke starts.

'I'm putting our names in,' says Debs.

'No,' I protest. 'I can't.'

'We always sing,' Debs says. 'You can't not.'

'I'm usually half pissed when we do,' I point out.

'We can remedy that.'

'Honestly, no,' I say.

'I'm still putting our names in.' She grabs a pen and a slip of paper from the bundle left on our table earlier.

I say nothing. I'm not going to argue with her. Though I won't get up when we're called.

But when Tommy Clarke, the guy running the karaoke, announces our names and Debs grabs me by the hand, I can't help following her. There's a huge round of applause and the music starts. Our routine – like our friendship – dates back to our school days, when we were the leading lights in a production of *Grease*. I'm not the best singer in the world, but I was the best of a very mediocre bunch in our year. And with my blonde hair and peaches-and-cream complexion, I was always going to have a chance as Sandy. Frank Phelan, one of the male students, was Danny. Debs played the role of Rizzo.

For our duet tonight, though, she's Danny and we do 'You're the One That I Want'. I lose myself in the singing, becoming Sandy as I did back when I was sixteen. My curly hair and short skirt, if not exactly right for the musical, feel right for the song. The audience is clapping and whooping and I feel suddenly carefree and young again. Naturally they demand an encore, and many of them already know what it will be, because Debs and I only do two songs. The second is 'Islands in the Stream', which was a favourite of Dad's.

We're on the last verse and giving it total welly when I see someone move in the audience. And then my throat completely dries up, leaving Debs to sing on her own. She's looking at me in utter confusion, but I'm not able to say anything. Because it's Dave who's at the back of the hall, leaning against the wall, watching me.

And I'm back in my own skin again.

Chapter 7

Debs finishes the song and there's more applause as I drag her from the stage and back towards our table.

'Did you know he'd be here?' I hiss.

'Who?'

'Dave?' I nod my head in his direction and she glances across the room.

'God, no,' she says. 'But it's a fund-raiser for the football club, so . . .'

'He hasn't been to a fund-raiser since the year I did the modelling,' I remind her.

She looks a bit sheepish.

'What?' I demand.

'He asked about it,' she confesses. 'Not me,' she adds quickly. 'But he was talking to Belinda Danaher in St Anne's Park the other day and she mentioned it to him. I bumped into her in the supermarket and she told me. I didn't say anything to you because I was afraid you wouldn't come. I didn't actually think *he* would, to be honest.'

Belinda is yet another of my old schoolmates. She's also on the fund-raising committee, and a gossipy wagon. I bet she was delighted at the opportunity to find out what was going on between me and Dave.

'Did she tell him I'd be here?' I ask, slightly miffed that Debs didn't give me a heads-up.

'I've no idea,' replies Debs. 'But, well, you know Belinda.'

I do. We were never friends. She didn't like me when we were younger and I don't think things have changed over the past twenty years. There are times I wish Dave and I had stayed in London, away from everyone.

'Look, it doesn't matter,' says Debs. 'You're here for a good time tonight. Ignore him.'

Of course it matters. How can I have a good time when my cheating husband is in the same room as me? How can I ignore him? I bet nobody else is!

We reach our table and I sit down.

'Great singing,' says Alison. 'Even if you gave up there at the end, Roxy. Same again?' She nods at the drinks.

We all say yes and she asks if I'd like something other than sparkling water. But although I'm absolutely gumming for another vodka, I stick with the Ballygowan. I want to keep a clear head.

I've lost sight of Dave in the crowd of people. A man I don't know is singing Johnny Cash, and he's not bad. In other circumstances I'd be enjoying myself. But all I can think about is Dave. And all I can see in my head is him and Julie. Again and again and again.

Is there something wrong with me? I wonder. Lots of women go through problems in their marriage, but do they obsess like I am right now? Do they have palpitations (and not in a good way) every time they think about their husband? Do they endlessly replay events in their heads? Am I being ridiculous, making a mountain out of a molehill? Not that Julie's arse was a molehill, of course. But still . . .

The Johnny Cash singer finishes and Tommy Clarke announces the next.

'Eeeeelvis Presleeeeey!'

It's Dave who walks on stage. He takes the mike and the music starts.

Dave's a good singer, but we've never sung karaoke together. I always sing with Debs. And he likes to perform on his own. He has his favourite and I know what it is. He's singing it now and walking along the catwalk, which is still in place, until he's close to our table.

He hunkers down, as Elvis used to do, and leans towards me as he changes the words of the song.

'*I will always . . . be madly in love . . . with you.*'

He's looking straight into my eyes, and I want to look away but I can't. I'm staring at him and remembering all the good times.

'*Take my hand,*' he sings, and reaches out to me.

It would be a nice thing to do. Maybe it would be the right thing to do. But I can't.

'Ah, go on!' Michelle gives me a little push.

I shake my head wordlessly.

Dave touches the side of my face and then stands up.

'Shy lady,' he says, and then continues with the song.

I'm mortified. My heart is thumping and I can feel my cheeks burning. Why did he have to do that? He's embarrassed both of us in front of everybody. As if he hadn't embarrassed us enough already. I get up from the table and make my way to the ladies', where I lock myself in a cubicle until I feel my hammering heartbeat return to something near normal.

I wonder what people are thinking. Maybe that I'm an unfeeling, unforgiving bitch because Dave has put himself out there for me and I've let him down in front of everyone. But he let me down too, didn't he? So why should I feel like I have to forgive him just because he's trying to make up to me in public?

I open the cubicle door at the same time as Debs walks into the ladies'.

'You OK?' she asks.

I nod.

'I honestly didn't think he'd do that,' she says. 'He's an idiot.'

'Yeah.'

'Come on back inside, have a drink,' she says.

I shake my head. 'I'll head home. I've had enough.'

'I'll go with you.'

'No,' I tell her. 'Stay here with the girls. Have a good night. I'll give you a shout next week.'

'Ah, Roxy, no. I'll go if you're going.'

'That'd make me feel bad.'

'Are you sure?'

'Absolutely.'

She hesitates, then gives me a hug. 'Take care.'

'You too.'

I leave the ladies' and step outside. It's still not completely dark, but even though the air is warm, I pull my jacket more tightly around me. I've just walked through the gates of the community centre complex when I hear my name.

'Roxy! Wait up.'

I think about ignoring him and continuing on my way, but I stop and turn around.

'Where are you going?' asks Dave.

'Home.'

'Home where?'

'Home to my mother's.'

'That's not your home. Beechgrove Park is your home.'

'Is that why you brought another woman into it?' Even as I say the words, they sound melodramatic. My life has never been melodramatic before. There have been tough times, of course, but it's been normal. For the last few weeks, though, I've felt like I'm living on Coronation Street.

'Look, sweetheart, we have to sit down and talk.' Dave is using his most reasonable voice. 'I know I've done something awful and you can't imagine how sorry I am, even though I've told you at least a million times. But things can't go on like this. I tried to make it up to you tonight and you let me down.'

'I let you down!' My voice is a squeak. 'I'm not the one who . . . who . . .'

'I'm trying to show you how much I love you,' he says. 'I was prepared to make an arse of myself in front of everyone to prove it to you. I *did* make an arse of myself in front of everyone! Please come home.'

'Why?' I ask.

'Because I love you. I've always loved you and I always will.'

'Funny way you have of showing it.'

I obviously don't sound as bitter as I feel, because he gives me a small smile and takes my hand before I have a chance to react. And I don't pull away because I know he's sorry and wants to make things right again. Part of me wants to let him. Dave is my husband and he made a mistake, but being married is all about knowing that mistakes can be made

82

and forgiving them. And trusting that the other person won't do the same thing again. But I trusted him not to make that particular mistake in the first place. Can I trust him not to repeat it?

'I'm still angry,' I tell him. 'I'm not ready to come home yet.'

'But you will be?' He squeezes my hand.

'I . . . You really hurt me, Dave.'

'I wish I hadn't.' He sighs. 'She wasn't even that good.'

'She was on top,' I say. 'You never like it when I want to be on top.'

'That was just . . . Look, it doesn't matter, does it? What matters is it shouldn't have happened and I made an eejit of myself and risked everything and I'm really sorry.'

His remorse is genuine. I should forgive him here and now. I'd want him to forgive me, wouldn't I? But then I'd never have slept with someone else in our bed.

'I need a bit more time.' It's the best I can do right now.

'How long?'

'I don't know. A few weeks, maybe.'

'A few weeks!' He looks horrified. 'You've already had a few weeks.'

'Maybe it's a good thing,' I say. 'You know, a bit of time apart. So that we can get our heads together.'

'My head is perfectly fine,' he says.

'Mine isn't,' I tell him. 'What with Dad and everything.'

'Of course.' His voice softens and he releases my hand before putting his arm around me. Once again, I don't pull away, even though I tell myself I should. 'Christy's passing has made you much more vulnerable than you would have been.'

Has he been reading self-help books? I wonder. Or googling the same sites as me? I've never heard him use the words 'passing' or 'vulnerable' before. Unless he's talking about Arsenal's defence.

'I need to go,' I say. 'Mum will be expecting me.'

'Not for ages,' says Dave. 'Come home with me now. If you don't want to spend the night, you don't have to. But I miss you so much. I want to make it up to you, Roxy.'

I miss him too. And there's something warm and comforting about the familiar feel of his arm around me and the musky scent of his body. But nothing he can do right now will make it up to me.

'No,' I say.

'Roxy . . .'

'Honestly, I'll think about everything. I'll talk to you soon. But tonight – no.'

I can feel the tension surge through him and see a flash of anger in his eyes before he shrugs and then squeezes my shoulder.

'OK,' he says. 'I'll give you a bit more time. But you've got to understand that this thing with Julie Halpin meant nothing to me. It was stupid and wrong but it's irrelevant to our lives. We can get past it.'

'Right.'

'I love you,' he says. 'I always have and I always will. You know that, Roxy. You know you know it.'

I give him a small smile. But I don't tell him I love him back.

'I'll call tomorrow for the kids.'

He's being a responsible dad. He took them last Saturday too and kept them overnight at Beechgrove Park. He's doing everything he should do to make things right. And yet my heart still feels like a block of ice.

'I'll see you then,' I say.

'Do you want to share a taxi?' He takes out his phone and opens the app.

'It's OK,' I tell him. 'It's a short walk for me.'

'Suit yourself.'

'Dave . . .'

'What?'

'I'll see you tomorrow.'

'I wasn't expecting you home for ages.' Mum snaps her iPad closed when I walk into the living room.

It's eleven o'clock. Which isn't that early.

'I'd had enough,' I tell her.

'Everything OK?'

'Fine.'

'Sure?'

'Certain.'

She knows everything isn't OK. She wants me to confide in her. But I don't want to have the discussion again.

'I'm out of practice,' I say. 'I'm going to bed.'

'Would you like something first?' she asks. 'A nightcap? Or a hot chocolate?'

I smile at her. 'Thanks, but I'm fine. Honestly. Just tired.'

'You can sleep on in the morning,' she says.

'I know. I'm looking forward to a lie-in.'

'I'll do a fry-up for breakfast.'

Fry-ups for breakfast in the Carpenter/McMenamin family are generally restricted to big occasions. Like Christmas or Easter or St Patrick's Day.

'That would be lovely,' I say.

'You do look tired.' Mum gives me a once-over. 'I know you're under stress and—'

'Not talking about it,' I insist. 'It'll only keep me awake.'

'Right.'

'So . . . goodnight, Mum.'

'Night-night, sleep tight . . .'

'Don't let the bed bugs bite,' I finish.

We both laugh. Living with Mum is better than I expected. But I can't use her as a prop for my own life. I need to move on. Or back.

When my alarm goes off the next morning, I'm completely bewildered because I didn't set it. I blink a few times and see sunlight peeking through the chink in the curtains. The alarm keeps buzzing, and I realise it isn't the alarm at all, but an incoming call.

The caller ID says 'Lehane', and I have no idea who Lehane is and why he or she is ringing me at . . . six in the morning! Six o'clock on a Saturday? What the actual . . .

'Hello,' I say.

'Hi, is that Roxy McMenamin? The driver?'

'Yes.' I rub my sleep-encrusted eyes.

'This is Ivo Lehane.'

'I . . .'

'You drove me to Kildare yesterday.'

Ivo Lehane. The suit. I remember now.

'Mr Lehane.' I try to sound professional, but I truly think I'm entitled to be a bit ratty at six a.m. on a Saturday. 'What can I do for you?'

'You said to call if I needed your services again,' he said. 'And I do.'

'I . . . Right. When?'

'Now,' says Ivo Lehane.

I don't answer for a moment because I'm still in a post-sleep confusion.

'You mean, you want me to drive to Kildare and pick you up now?' I ask.

'Yes. If it's not too much trouble.'

'Well . . .'

'I realise it's short notice and that it's a Saturday. Of course I'll compensate you. I'll pay double the standard rate.'

I'm awake now. Double money for driving to Kildare early on a Saturday when there won't be any traffic sounds like a good deal to me.

'Where do you need to go?' I ask.

'The airport,' he says.

Of course it's the airport. He probably has some urgent suit-type business that needs his immediate attention even though it's the weekend.

'It'll be an hour or so before I get to you,' I say.

'I understand. I'll be ready and waiting.'

I suppose that's how all businessmen work. No messing around.

'OK,' I say.

'Thank you.'

I end the call and get up. After a quick shower, I dress in my work clothes and tiptoe downstairs. I'm leaving a note on the table for Mum when she comes into the kitchen in her PJs, carrying her iPad.

'What's going on?' she asks.

'A job.'

'At this hour? On a Saturday?'

I explain about Ivo Lehane and she shrugs and says it's good to have those kinds of clients even if they are a bit demanding, and I agree and make myself some coffee, which I then pour into my thermos mug.

'No hot water and lemon this morning?' she asks as I cram a breakfast bar into my mouth.

'No. Maybe you'd like to share your Ryvitas?'

She makes a face at me and I make one at her in return. Then she kisses me on the cheek and I leave the house.

I get into the car. Before I start the engine, I take a quick peek at Dad's memorial card.

He was a good man.

I wish I'd married someone like him.

Chapter 8

As I set cruise control to about five kilometres below the limit and revel in the comfort and power of the Mercedes, it comes as a bit of a shock to realise that I'm actually quite liking this part of my life. Obviously my heart is still broken and I'm in turmoil about my marriage, but driving people is something I enjoy. I liked it when I did it for Dad, and doing it for myself is . . . well, I don't know if empowering is the word, but it's making me happy. I don't always get to know the clients, but I like the variety of people I drive. Those I talk to – like Thea Ryan – are usually fun and interesting. But even those who sit in silence still allow me a glimpse into a different world. I can't help thinking that over the last ten years or so my own world has got smaller and smaller. It's all about Dave and the children and doing what's best for them. And it's not that I've entirely forgotten about me, but I've certainly forgotten what it's like to go to work and not think about home.

Determined to make the most of my solitude, I switch on the car radio and hit one of the preset buttons. If easy listening is my preferred music for the city, country music is my choice for the motorway. The station is playing Dolly Parton. I love

Dolly. She's smart and sassy and has never taken any crap from anyone. I wonder what she'd have done if she'd walked in on her husband with another woman. Whatever it was, it'd be final. She wouldn't keep second-guessing herself.

What would Dolly do? That should be my mantra. I laugh at myself, but it sticks with me as she sings that this dumb blonde ain't nobody's fool. Does Dave take me for a fool? Would I be a fool to forgive him? Or a fool not to?

I realise that despite my determination not to think about him, I am. Like the country singers who pore over their broken hearts, I can't stop myself.

The phone rings.

'Is that Roxy?'

'Yes.'

'This is Ivo Lehane. Can you pick me up at a different location?' he asks.

'No problem. Where would you like?' I make a face. I don't know Kildare very well, and I'd put Banville Terrace into the satnav.

'The Monasterevin Road,' he says. 'Opposite Tesco.'

It's always good to have a decent landmark. I tell him I'm about twenty minutes away and I'll see him soon.

Luckily, there's a sign for Tesco, which makes things easy. I turn onto the road and see him standing there, his leather case in his hand. I pull in, but before I have time to stop the engine and get out of the car to open the door for him, Ivo Lehane has already got into the back seat and dropped the case on the floor.

'Everything all right?' I ask.

'Of course. Why shouldn't it be?'

'I mean, are you belted in?'

90

'Oh. Yes. Thanks.'

I pull away and turn back towards the motorway.

I have to admit that I'm intrigued by the whole Ivo Lehane scenario. The trip to Banville Terrace. The crack-of-dawn phone call to be picked up again. The hint of anger in the way he dropped his case. I'm dying to know what the hell it's all about, but of course I can't ask. I wish he was a talker like Thea Ryan. She'd definitely tell me.

But he's not and he doesn't. He sits back in the seat and looks out of the side window as though the chequered green of the passing countryside is of great interest to him. Traffic is a little heavier now, but still nothing worth speaking of, and we get to the airport in just over an hour.

'Which terminal?' I ask as I turn off the roundabout.

'Two,' he says.

I pull up outside the building and this time manage to get out of the car before him, although I don't get to open his door.

'Thank you,' he says. 'Um, do you take credit cards?'

'Of course.'

Dad was totally up to speed on IT. He'd asked one of my brother Aidan's mates to sort it for him. Christy's Chauffeurs even has an app.

'I said I'd pay double,' says Ivo. 'Thank you for coming to get me at such an early hour.'

'No problem.' I smile at him. 'All part of the service.'

He pays the fee and then takes out his wallet and extracts another fifty euro.

'You tipped me yesterday, remember?'

'That was for yesterday. This is for today.'

Given that he's already paid so much, I can't possibly take another significant tip, and I tell him so.

'It's worth it,' he insists. 'You're great. No chatter.'

'I can chat,' I tell him. 'But only if the client wants it. Anyway, this is my job and you've already paid double, so I have to insist you keep the cash.'

He smiles, and suddenly he's a different person.

'Maybe one day I'll order your car and chat,' he says as he replaces the note in his wallet. 'But in the meantime, the silence was golden. I may be back again. Can I book you in advance if so?'

'Of course.'

I use the old-fashioned method of giving him a business card, which he tucks into his wallet along with the tip.

'Thanks again,' he says.

'Have a good day.' I get back into the car and drive away. When I look in my rear-view mirror, he's gone.

Tom and Mica are still in their pyjamas when I get back to Mum's. They're sitting on the floor of the conservatory playing a game that they're making up as they go along, but when I walk in, they jump up and hug me. I hug them back, secure in my unconditional love for them. And theirs for me.

Mum – who has always shown me unconditional love, even in my tearaway teenage years – asks if I'd like a coffee, and I say yes. I really must cut down on my caffeine intake. But as the aroma of the fresh brew drifts towards me, I know it won't be any time soon.

Mum brings the coffee to me, along with a Danish pastry wrapped in a paper napkin.

'I forgot I bought these yesterday,' she said. 'Have it while it's still sort of fresh.'

I was feeling quite alert after my drive, but the coffee and Danish revive me even more. I tell the children to hop under the shower and I allow Mica to use the travel-size bottle of Molton Brown shower gel that I got in a set as a Christmas present from Debs. It's been in my make-up bag since then, but I haven't travelled anywhere that would need a small bottle of shower gel. It's a treat for Mica, who loves the smell.

Tom prefers the Lynx gel that was Dad's. We don't have that, so he uses the Johnson's shower soap instead.

They both emerge from their showers looking bright-eyed.

I love them. More than anything. And I want to do what's best for them always.

Half an hour later, there's a ring at the doorbell and my heart flips because I know it's Dave here to pick them up. I hear them clatter down the stairs and their excited chatter when they open the door and he comes in. They miss him.

He's been a good husband.

Who made one mistake.

I should forgive him.

But it was a terrible mistake. And I can't.

The pendulum swings wildly from side to side as I prepare to go downstairs.

'Hi, Roxy,' he says when I walk into the hall. 'You're looking sharp this morning. Though you looked even better last night.'

I'm still in my suit and blouse, although I've exchanged my high heels for flip-flops.

'Have you got your overnight bags?' I don't respond to him but turn to the children instead. 'Toothbrushes, pyjamas, clean jocks and socks?'

'Mum!' Mica gives me a disgusted look. 'You can't say jocks and socks for a girl.'

'Knickers, then,' I amend.

'Mum!' She's even more disgusted. 'You can't say that out loud either.'

I grin, and she shakes her head. Maybe this is the beginning of the end of her unconditional love for me. Maybe we're getting to the point where I'm becoming an embarrassment to her.

'Why don't you come home with us now?' she asks. 'We can stay at Granny's again tomorrow.'

'Because Granny needs me today,' I lie.

'Because she's still bereaved?' Mica's blue eyes look thoughtfully at me.

'Yes.'

'When does she stop?'

'I don't know.'

She lowers her voice as she speaks to me. 'I understand she needs us, but so does Daddy.'

'You're right,' I agree. 'We'll sort something out soon.'

'I want you to come with us,' says Mica.

'Not this time.' I can't lie to her.

'Let's go.' Tom doesn't care whether I'm with them or not, and I'm grateful to him for butting into what was becoming an awkward conversation.

Dave hustles them out of the front door and they climb into the van. They love being in the van. It's more adventurous than a normal car, even Dad's Mercedes. He turns back to me and tells me he meant every word last night. Both the words of the song and what he said to me later. Then he takes a wrapped box out of his jacket pocket.

'For you.' He drops a kiss on my cheek and walks to the van.

I wave them away before unwrapping Dave's gift, which turns out to be a bottle of Happy, the perfume I've worn for the last ten years. He knows how to push my buttons.

I go upstairs and leave it in my room. I spend a few minutes sitting on the edge of my bed before coming down again. Mum's in the kitchen, peering inside one of the cupboards.

'Looking for anything in particular?' I ask.

'No,' she says. 'There's loads of stuff here, thanks to you.'

I've done the shopping for the past few weeks and have exchanged Mum's tendency to wait till the very last minute to get what she wants for my insatiable buy-one-get-one-free habit. The cupboards haven't been as full in years.

'Least I could do,' I say.

'Sooner or later I'll have to go to the shops myself. But I'm not . . . I don't want to yet.'

She hasn't been out on her own since Dad died.

'When you're ready,' I tell her. 'There's no rush.'

She puts her arms around me. 'You're a good girl, Roxy.'

I give her a kiss on the cheek. 'Tell you what,' I say. 'Why don't we go out for lunch today?'

She hesitates, and then nods.

'Avoca?' I suggest.

'In Malahide?'

'Of course.'

Avoca is a beautiful town in Wicklow, but there's a quirky shop and café of the same name that has a branch in the grounds of Malahide Castle, a local tourist attraction. It's only a fifteen-minute drive and I often visit with the children, although we don't always go into the café, where the cakes are decadent. Gina Hayes would approve of the high quality of the food, although she'd probably have a fit at the luscious slices of rocky road and caramel chocolate.

I change out of my suit and trousers into jeans and an almost new floral T-shirt that I'm thankful I remembered to pack when I left Beechgrove Park. The sun is splitting the sky now and I'm wearing a pair of Mum's sunglasses, because sunglasses were something I didn't think about when I left Dave. She says she'll do the driving as I've already clocked up a couple of hundred kilometres today. I agree, though I'm a terrible passenger and I keep braking involuntarily whenever she gets too close to the car in front.

The traffic is heavy on the way out to Malahide, which isn't surprising. The pretty coastal town is a magnet for tourists and Dubliners alike, especially on a day like today. But there's plenty of parking in the castle grounds, despite the hordes of people already walking around the extensive estate. You'd never guess we were just fifteen kilometres from the city centre, though, because as well as the beautiful gardens, the castle is surrounded by sports pitches. I love it here. It's an oasis of greenery.

'Walk or lunch?' I ask Mum.

'Better have a bit of a walk first,' she replies. 'So that we can have a cream cake without feeling guilty.'

I grin, and we link arms as we begin.

I'm expecting more talk from her about my situation with Dave, but instead she chats about the times she came here with Dad and how much he loved it, and how he was glad that local people had access to land that was once the preserve of the very rich.

'I can't imagine owning all this,' I say as I look across the rolling parkland. 'It must have been amazing.'

'But unjust,' says Mum. 'Your dad was right about that. Whatever you think about people who've made their fortunes today and are buying up land, at least it wasn't handed down to them for nothing like it was by those ancient landowners.'

My parents are big into the notion of inherited wealth being a bad thing. Even if Dad did leave me his car.

'Was her family wealthy?' I ask suddenly.

'Whose?'

'Estelle's. The farmer's daughter that Dad was in love with. Did they have a big farm? Is that why they were angry about her and Dad? Because he was a working man from Dublin?'

I've been thinking of Estelle and Dad on and off ever since seeing the photo. She looked so vibrant and full of life that it's hard to imagine she was basically assaulted by her own father. The knowledge has been niggling away at me. That it happened, that Dad was beaten up too, that he did nothing about it. I wish Mum had said that he'd gone to the police. I wish he'd looked after Estelle a bit better.

'I've no idea,' says Mum.

There's a finality in her words that nevertheless makes me think there's more to be said. And yet she's clearly not going to say it. So I don't push her and we chat about inconsequential things as we walk around the grounds before ending up at the visitor centre.

'We definitely deserve those cream cakes,' says Mum when we go into the café and stand in front of the (frankly sinful) cake display.

After a bit of soul-searching, though, we both go for individual vegetable quiches and decide to share a rocky road. Feeling virtuous, we carry our trays to one of the very few tables near a window and sit down.

It's ages since I was out anywhere socially with my mother. The last few months have been filled with hospital and then hospice visits, and neither of us was ever in the mood to go out after them. I realise that by coming here, we've turned a page.

And that feels good.

We're just cutting the piece of rocky road in half when we hear a sudden squeal and then a small tornado launches itself at Mum.

'Granny!' cries Tom. 'Have you saved a seat for us?'

There are two spare chairs at our table.

'Of course.'

Mum isn't in the slighted fazed by the sight of my son, but I look around anxiously and see Dave and Mica following him. Dave is carrying a tray laden with food.

'Mind if we join you?' he asks, putting it down on the table before we have a chance to object. Not that I would, with Tom already clambering onto the chair beside me. Mica takes the one opposite and Dave appropriates a spare one from another table.

'This is great,' he says. 'I didn't realise you guys would be here.'

'Did you know we were coming, Mum?' Mica's eyes are wide and I can tell from her voice that she wants me to say yes.

'Not for certain.' It's the closest I can get without lying to her.

98

'Have you already had something to eat?' asks Dave. 'Or is that it?' He nods at the shared rocky road and Mum explains that we had quiche earlier. Tom makes a face and Dave laughs.

'It's a lovely day, isn't it?' he says. 'We were in the play-ground earlier. Look.' He takes out his phone and shows us the pictures he took. Most are of the kids, but there's a selfie of the three of them too, which he says he's going to post on Facebook. I'm careful about posting pictures of the children on Facebook and only do it occasionally, but ever since I walked out, Dave posts one any time they're with him.

'You don't look very bereaved now, Granny,' says Mica. 'Are you better?'

'Nearly better, sweetheart,' Mum replies. 'A little bit longer with all of you living with me and I'm sure I'll be right as rain.'

It's not fair that she has to answer questions like this. I've brought it on her. I'm a selfish cow.

'I like living with Granny,' says Tom, who's digging into a huge slice of chocolate cake. As much of it is in his hair and on his face as has gone into his mouth.

'So do I,' agrees Mica. 'But it's only for the holidays. While she's bereaved.'

'Exactly,' I say.

Dave reaches across the table and takes my hand.

'I can't wait for you all to be back where you belong,' he says.

Mica is watching me, so I simply smile at him. I know it hasn't reached my eyes.

My stomach is churning too much to eat the rocky road,

so I wrap it in a napkin and tell Mum I'll save it for later. Much as I know the children would like it, I'm not letting them have any more chocolate today.

'We'd better go,' says Mum. 'I have things to do.'

'Can we help?' asks Tom.

'No, sweetie, you have a nice day with your dad. I'll see you tomorrow.'

'I'll be dropping them back a bit earlier than usual,' says Dave. 'I have to go out in the afternoon.'

I want to ask why, but I don't.

'See you soon.'

It's ridiculous to be kissing my own children goodbye like this. But if I leave Dave, that's how it's going to be in the future. And no amount of pretending to be a chauffeur with a business of my own will compensate for that.

I hurry out of the café.

I wait till I'm in the car before I cry for the first time since Dad died.

Chapter 9

Mum doesn't say anything about my tears even when we get home. Neither do I.

That night, we sit in and watch Thea and Desmond Ryan talk about their new show on TV, and I feel a surge of pride that I'm her driver and that the business is still doing well. It's my way of honouring Dad and keeping his memory alive.

'You don't have to, not for Christy's sake,' says Mum when I remark on it. 'He'd understand.'

I tell her that it's for me as much as for him, and she looks concerned.

'D'you think you taking on his driving has anything to do with what happened with Dave?' Mum asks.

'Huh?'

'Darling, you more or less gave up on your husband while you took over your dad's business,' she reminds me. 'And you spent the rest of your spare time running after me because I was so bloody hopeless. You don't know how much I appreciate it, but Christy certainly wouldn't have wanted you to end up with problems because he was sick. He knew you were driving to keep him motivated. It meant a lot to him. But if you want to save your marriage, you'll have to let it go.'

I've more or less come to this conclusion myself, but I don't want to admit it. Because this job has become very important to me. It doesn't matter that I only started doing it to keep Dad's spirits up. And it doesn't matter that I've kept doing it for a variety of reasons none of which are truly commercial. The bottom line now is that it makes me feel good about myself. And that's more than Dave has done lately.

'It's not possible to have it all,' Mum says while I stare at the TV without really watching it. 'I was brought up in a generation where we were told it was, but we knew it was a pipe dream. Something always has to give. Men like to be the most important thing in your life. And when they're not . . .'

I can feel my entire body clench as I pick up the remote and mute the sound.

'Dave tried to blame his decision to have sex with Julie Halpin on the fact that I wasn't there,' I tell her. 'And now you're more or less saying the same thing. As though a man can't be trusted to keep it in his pants just because his wife occasionally has other priorities. That's ridiculous.'

'I accept that it's not fair,' says Mum. 'But men are men. And Dave is very much a man's man.'

'I'm trying very hard not to think that you're actually taking his side.' I can hardly get the words out. 'He cheated on me with the woman next door, for God's sake. And I'm supposed to think it doesn't really matter.'

'Oh, I don't believe that for an instant,' says Mum. 'And I'm definitely not taking his side. Not at all. When you turned up with your case, the only thing I wanted to do was rip his balls off, to be honest.'

I can picture her doing it, actually. Mum can be very fierce when she wants.

'All the same, I think he's truly sorry about what he's done. He knows what a fool he's been. He adores you and the children. If you can't forgive him, that's your choice and I'm a hundred per cent behind you. Still, if you think you can, wouldn't it be better for Tom and Mica's sake to put it all behind you and get on with your lives?'

'He has a funny way of showing he adores me.' But even as I say the words, I recall Mica and her worried face this afternoon. I know that Mum is right about the children.

'It's not possible to have it all, Roxy,' says Mum. 'Really it's not. Everyone has to make compromises.'

What compromises am I prepared to make to save my marriage? I ask myself as I lie in bed that night. And if I make them, can I live with myself? And with him?

What would Dolly do?

Write a song and make a fortune, I guess. But that's not an option for me.

On Monday morning, I get up early to prep the car for my next job, which is collecting a young woman named Leona Lynch and bringing her to a photo shoot. Leona is what's known as an 'influencer', because she does weekly vlogs about her life and has a phenomenal following on YouTube and Instagram. I only know this because I did a search on her when I took the job. I'm not really part of the YouTube generation.

Mica, however, was very impressed when she learned that

I'd be driving Leona, and has made me promise to get a selfie with her. I didn't realise Mica knew who she was but apparently Leona is big with eleven-to-fourteen-year-old girls. My daughter has warned me not to pester her or be uncool. I promised to be as cool as a cucumber. (I also promise myself to check the parental control settings on Mica's phone to make sure she's not accessing stuff she shouldn't. I don't want to be an overprotective mother, but discovering that my daughter is more up to speed on my client than I am was a bit of a shock.)

I open the rear doors of the car and reach into the seat pockets to replace the magazines I leave there with ones I bought earlier. Although most people spend their time in the back of the car tapping away at their devices, I think it's a good idea for them to have something else to browse through. Every couple of weeks or so I put the latest copy of *Hello!* in one pocket and a business magazine in the other. I also leave bottled water in the cup holders.

I wipe the leather seats with a cloth and use the hand vac in the sills beneath the seats. I polish the fascia and the windows and I'm about to throw the used magazines in the recycling bin when a small card falls from one of them and lands at my feet. As I pick it up, I see that it's not actually a card but an old photograph of a young boy standing with his right foot on a football and his left hand on his hip. He's wearing an Ireland tracksuit, and from the appalling style of it, I reckon that it dates back to the 1980s. He's also wearing the oversized aviator glasses that were popular at the time. A dark floppy fringe hides half his face, and his expression, behind the glasses and the fringe, is a mixture of apprehension and defiance. It's the same look Tom has whenever I try to make him do something he doesn't want to.

Nowadays children are used to every second of their lives being digitally preserved, but I get the feeling this boy didn't want his photo taken. Back when I was as young as him (I reckon he's probably around my own age now, or a little older), none of us liked having to stand still for a picture. It was an unnecessary interruption in our lives.

I don't know the boy, but I feel a sudden connection to him, a shared time if not a shared past. And I feel sympathy for him too, because despite the tracksuit and the football, his expression hints at a deeper unhappiness than simply being made to pose for a photograph. Or maybe that's my overactive imagination getting the better of me, as it sometimes does.

I wonder which of my clients left it behind. There's no end to the amount of things that people forget to take with them. (Once, when Dad was driving, a man left his dentures in the car!) Usually I can reunite forgotten items with their owners because either I find them quickly enough to be able to figure out who was most likely to have left them, or the owners get in touch. But a photo is trickier, and heaven only knows how long it's been here. Just because it was between the pages of *Hello!* doesn't mean it wasn't already in the pouch behind the seat and simply got caught up in the magazine.

I turn it over, but there's nothing to say who it's of or who might have left it. I doubt it belongs to any of the many businessmen I've driven to or from their meetings. While they might have photos of their wives and children in their wallets, I can't imagine any of them bothering with an old photo of themselves! Nor is it likely that the young girls whose parents hired me to take them to a twenty-first birthday party and collect them again afterwards dropped it. But what about the couple I drove to Waterford? They were old enough for the boy in the picture to be their son. Or maybe it belongs to Melisse Grady? She was faffing around with a lot of paperwork in the back of the car and nearly left some of it behind. Perhaps the photo was from one of her clients – an author working on a biography or something similar who sent her some pictures to look at? Thea Ryan is another option. She's the scattiest by far of my clients and could easily have been looking at old photos in the back seat. I know she has a son, but I'm not sure if he's the right age for the boy in this photo.

I'll show it to Thea next time I see her, and in the meantime, I'll send a copy of it to Melisse, and to the couple I drove to Waterford. After that . . . well, I'll have to wait and see.

Once I've taken a snap of it and sent it in a text message, I put the photo itself in the small transparent folder I use for keeping receipts and other bits of paperwork and replace it in the glove compartment.

And then I forget about it.

Leona Lynch lives in a suburban housing estate, presumably with her parents. I imagined her in some ultra-modern apartment, surrounded by the latest in make-up and gadgets and whatever else she's sent to promote on her vlogs. Although, to be fair, we're talking about a girl who lives in Drogheda, which, though a nice town, isn't really cutting edge when it comes to cosmopolitan apartment living.

When I pull up outside the house with its neat front lawn and two cars in the driveway, I send her a text to say I'm here. A couple of seconds later the front door opens and a young girl wearing trainers, ripped jeans and an olive-green shirt with the sleeves rolled up hurries out. Her hair is an amazing cloud of red-gold curls around her oval face. As she approaches the car, I can see that her eyes match her shirt and that her skin is fair with a smattering of freckles. Leona Lynch is like a specially constructed Celtic maiden. She is, in fact, very pretty.

'Hello,' she says. 'Are you Roxy? Well, I hope you are, otherwise I'm getting into a complete stranger's car! Which my mother always tells me not to do. But then you're a lady driver, so hey, no worries.'

'I'm Roxy McMenamin,' I say. 'And yes, I'm your driver today.'

'Cool,' says Leona.

'We're going to Killawley House,' I confirm. 'After your shoot, I'll be bringing you home again.'

'That's it.' Leona settles into the seat.

Killawley House is about an hour's drive west. I'd never heard of it before, but it's an old country house that, according to its website, has been sympathetically restored. The pictures show a stone building with pink and red climbing roses growing up the walls and an extensive orchard at the back. Most of the interior photos were taken in the winter and are of blazing fires and cosy rooms. I'm not sure how it will look in the summer.

Gorgeous, is the answer. As we turn in through the gates of the house an hour later, we're shaded from the sun by an avenue of cherry trees – sadly no longer in blossom, but splashing colour with their vivid green leaves. The house itself stands in the centre of gardens filled with flowers, and is stately and magnificent.

What would my life have been like if my ancestors had been wealthy landowners instead of peasant farmers? I wonder. Actually, I've no idea if my ancestors were peasant farmers or not, but given that they certainly didn't own houses like this, it's a reasonable assumption. Thinking about Dad's surname, they were probably carpenters. Maybe they worked for the original owners of stately homes. Maybe they even worked on this one!

I give up my dream of an aristocratic life as I park the car. A short, balding man, who I learn is Leona's agent, scurries over and hugs her. There's a lot of talk between them about 'the product' and where she'll be photographed and what she'll be doing, and I gather from what they're saying that it's not a fashion shoot at all, as I'd imagined, but something for an ad.

They've asked me to hang around in case they need a driver for some unspecified reason, so I take a stroll through the beautifully maintained gardens. I can't help thinking that Leona Lynch is only twenty years old and already way more successful than I'll ever be. Even my own daughter admires her! It was Mica who told me that Leona is a brand ambassador for a range of hair products (not surprisingly, given her glorious Titian mane) and a children's charity. At twenty, all I was doing was working in a car showroom. Even if it was a Jaguar showroom.

I stop at a pretty summer house and take out my phone. Leona has already posted some photos to Instagram. In them she's standing on the steps of the house looking effortlessly gorgeous, even in her jeans and shirt. It's not just her looks, though. It's the enthusiasm and sheer joy of living she radiates that makes her so appealing.

I decide to take a few photographs myself. Perhaps I should set up an Instagram account of my own and post pictures of the places I drive to. There'd be a disproportionate number of airport pictures, of course. But I could take ones of different parts of Dublin, places the tourists don't normally see. It would be good for the business – well, if I managed to get a few followers. I don't really know how you do that. But I'll talk to Mica about it.

She's eleven. But she can be my marketing manager. Because she's obviously far more clued in than me on that sort of stuff.

The booking for Leona's shoot was for half a day, but they're running over time and I'm getting anxious because I have to collect Thea and Desmond Ryan at seven. It's only half an hour from Drogheda to the airport, but I'd like to be there in plenty of time because I don't want the Ryans to have to wait around for me. It's not professional, and the most important thing for me is to be professional when I'm driving.

But eventually Leona walks over.

'See you soon, Danny,' she says to her agent as she waits for me to open the car door for her. 'Thanks for everything.'

She's very businesslike with him and she reminds me of both Gina Hayes and Thea Ryan. These women all believe that they're due their success. That it's a direct result of their own hard work because they know what they want and they're not afraid to go for it. They're strong and sassy and not afraid to speak their mind. I need to be more like them. I need to be . . . well . . . feminist-y.

'Good day?' I ask.

'It was fun,' Leona says. 'I don't know if it's what I'd like to do all the time – too many people giving instructions and telling me how I should look and what I should say. But the money was great and my mum wouldn't let me turn it down.'

I laugh. It doesn't matter how strong and determined and feminist-y you are. When your mother tells you something, you listen.

'Anyhow, I like the covers, so it's not entirely selling out,' Leona says. 'But in future I think I'll stick with reviews.'

'Covers?' I ask.

'Oh, I thought you knew. It's a campaign for a set of phone covers and cases. Here.' She digs into her bag and takes out a few, which she hands over to me. I put them on the passenger seat beside me. They're pretty much standard issue, but the colours are vibrant and all the cases are embossed with little crystals along the edges.

'Nice,' I say.

'They have my initials on them.' Leona can't keep a hint of pride out of her voice. 'That's what I do instead of a signature.'

'Your mum must be delighted.'

Leona laughs. 'She thinks it's mad. That's why she wants me to make as much money as I can as quickly as I can so that I can buy my own house before it all goes horribly wrong and I regret dropping out of college without my degree. She's probably right.'

I probably would've hated college. I'm not academic enough. But it was never a consideration for me, not once Dave moved to London.

When we arrive outside Leona's house, I gather the phone covers from the passenger seat and hold them out to her.

'Oh, keep them,' she says. 'I already have tons.'

'Are you sure?'

'Absolutely.'

'My daughter will be thrilled.' I smile. 'Actually, I know this is really naff and totally unprofessional of me, but she asked if I could get a selfie with you. I'm awful in photos and it's deeply embarrassing, but . . .'

'It's no bother at all.' Leona takes my phone, shakes her hair a bit so that she looks rumpled and messy, and then leans in towards me. I'm hopeless at taking selfies and usually end up including my finger in the shot, but Leona is a pro and the picture she shows me afterwards looks amazing.

'What's your daughter's name?' she asks.

When I tell her, she taps away at the screen and then shows me the picture again, which now says: *To Mica – me and your lovely mum! Hugs and kisses. Leona Lynch.*

'That's so good of you,' I tell her. 'Mica will be thrilled. And I'll have to learn how to do stuff like this.' I tell her about my own Instagram plans.

'Brilliant idea,' she says. 'I'll follow you.'

'Oh God, not yet. I have to work out how to take decent photos first.'

Leona asks to look at the ones I took today, then fiddles around with my phone for what seems like about ten seconds before handing it back to me. 'I used some filters on them,' she says. 'Look . . .' And she gives me a quick lesson on editing photos. I'm not entirely stupid, I know everyone does it. I've just never bothered before. But the difference is astounding.

111

'Thank you so much,' I say.

'No bother.' She grins. 'Don't forget, I'll be following you. So make them good.'

'I'll do my best,' I say. 'It was a pleasure to drive you today.'

'I liked being driven by you,' she says. 'You're nice. Mica is lucky to have you as a mum.'

'Thank you.'

'And I love that you're a lady driver.' She makes a fist. 'Girl power.'

'Girl power.' I bump my fist off hers.

Maybe I am a bit of a feminist after all, I think, as I drive away.

Chapter 10

I make it to the airport in time for Thea and Desmond, who swamp me with stories of their exploits in London. I hope I'm as fit and interested in life as them when I reach their age, and I say this to Thea when they get out of the car again. She laughs and says she's sure I will be, and then tells me to keep her colourful umbrella in case it's raining the next time I pick her up. I'm delighted to think that there'll be a next time. She's definitely my favourite client.

Then I remember the photo of the young boy and ask them if it's likely either of them left it behind. I take it out of the folder and hand it to her.

Thea shakes her head as she studies it. Desmond, looking over her shoulder, shakes his head too.

'It's probably a memento,' I tell them. 'So I'd like to reunite it with the owner if I can. I'm surprised whoever lost it hasn't missed it.'

'Boys and their football,' says Thea, turning it over to see if there's anything written on the back, which there isn't. 'It's hard to make out his face properly, though it looks a little bit like Butler when he was a child. But our son was more interested in sonnets than soccer, which was tricky back then.' She smiles. 'Gosh, to think we thought that was style! The tracksuit. Those glasses. The hair.'

I laugh. 'My dad had a pair of specs like those too.'

'I'm sure if it's important to someone they'll get in touch with you.' Thea hands the photo back to me. 'Especially if it's a keepsake.'

We're all silent for a moment as we think about the boy, who he might be and what might have happened to him.

'And if nobody contacts you, don't worry,' says Desmond. 'You're not responsible for reuniting everyone with their forgotten items.'

I usually do, though.

'I'll call you next time I need a car,' says Thea.

I thank her and Desmond for their continued business. Then I put the folder back into the glove compartment and wait until they've made it inside their house before I drive away.

It's rush hour now, so it takes me ages to cross the river to the north side of the city. Once again I phone Mum and suggest a takeaway, and once again she tells me that Tom and Mica have eaten but she'd kill for a king prawn curry from the Chinese. I tell her I'll pick one up and hope that she didn't give the kids anything too awful from the freezer. I swear to God I'll do some proper home cooking soon. I know I've inherited Mum's lack of prowess in the kitchen, but I can do fairly decent one-pot dinners. I just haven't had the time.

Two messages flash up on the dashboard screen. The first is from Melisse Grady to say that the photo isn't hers but that she's forwarded it to Gina.

The second message is from Dave. He says he's going to work on a new job, a fit-out of a hotel in Wexford. It'll take two or three weeks and he's probably going to stay there, because otherwise it's a massive commute and what's the point when there's nobody at home. He adds he won't be able to pick up Tom and Mica at the weekend.

I'm not sure what to think about this. Dave has done jobs before where he's had to travel some distance and perhaps stay over for a short time. Never more than a few days, though. Does this mean that he's the one making decisions about our future, not me? Has he changed his mind about me coming home?

I use the voice recognition to text my answer to him, saying that I'm driving. He knows not to call me in the car, because even though I use an earpiece, I don't like taking personal calls if I have passengers. It's distracting. And I don't need distractions. But in my message I say that it sounds like a good opportunity and not to worry about the children. I add that perhaps we'll talk later.

When I arrive home, I'm astonished to see Mum sitting at the table surrounded by balls of purple, white and black wool.

'What on earth are you doing?' I ask as she swiftly closes the open iPad that's also on the table and moves the wool out of the way so I can load the curry onto plates.

'She's making octopussies,' cries Tom, who comes clattering down the stairs.

'For early babies,' adds Mica, who's right behind him. 'Did you get a selfie with Leona Lynch?'

I show her the selfie on my phone, which sends her into paroxysms of excitement. She insists that I forward it to her immediately. When I also take out the phone covers, she nearly faints with joy.

'You have to use one too,' she insists after she's attached the electric-blue cover to hers. I choose the shocking pink, which, to be fair, looks quite good on the phone.

'Did you bring home stuff for us to eat?' Tom isn't interested in phone covers.

I hand over spring rolls to my children and remind myself that I'll be moving our family to healthy eating from next week. Then I ask Mum about the wool.

'June called around today,' she tells me. 'She's involved with a project at the maternity hospital and she asked me if I'd do it too. I was quite good at crochet when I was younger. Remember the jacket I made you?'

Actually, I do. It was pale blue and the pattern was of sculpted seashells. I felt quite glamorous in it. I think I was about five.

'Anyway, this is for preemie babies,' says Mum. 'The nurses put a small crocheted octopus in the crib with them. Apparently the tentacles remind them of the umbilical cord. You have to be exact in the way you do them. Look.' She hands me an information leaflet and I read it with interest. It seems that the little knitted creatures soothe the babies. Who'd have thought?

'What a brilliant idea,' I say.

'I thought it would be nice to do something useful,' says Mum. 'I want to get . . . well, back in life's saddle, I suppose.'

'What saddle?' asks Mica. 'Octopussies don't need saddles.'

'Not a real saddle.' I don't bother to correct her about the plural of octopus, because I'm not entirely sure what it should be. 'It's an expression,' I add. 'It means getting on with things.'

'Have you stopped being bereaved, Granny?' she asks. 'Is that it?'

'I'm getting better,' says Mum.

'Oh good,' Mica says as she stuffs the last of the spring roll into her mouth. 'That means we can go home.'

But can we? If it hadn't been for Dave's text, Mica would have made the decision for me. She's swung the pendulum back towards forgive and forget and I want to stop it there, because I know deep down that it's what I need to do for the sake of my family. But I'm suddenly afraid I've left it too late.

I go into the living room and call my husband. He doesn't answer. I wonder if he's the one punishing me now. Have our lives become a series of mini battles? I left him. He's leaving me. Does he want me to beg him not to?

While I wait for him to call or message me, I sign up for Instagram. Then I upload the photos I took today to my new account. I'm quite proud of how they look. I switch to Leona's page and there I am in her selfie, in one of the best pictures ever taken of me, with a comment below saying that I was a brilliant driver and an inspiration, along with *#girlpower #ladydriver #inspiring*. Obviously that's poetic licence, because I'm not an inspiration to anyone, but it's nice to see all the same. I like the photo and follow her straight away. Almost immediately she becomes my own first follower, and then she tags me in her photo and next thing I know another ten people have followed me too. It's actually quite exciting, though I worry that I won't have enough great pictures to keep followers of Leona Lynch interested. Still, it's a new part of my business empire!

I glance at my phone again. No missed calls from Dave. No messages.

If he's changed his mind about us, if he doesn't want me back, what am I going to do? Not just about my domestic life, but about the business too. How will I cope? Living with Mum has been easy – we never argue, she's always there as a backup and a support for me, as I try to be for her. I never have to ask her to do anything. She does it automatically. But the big difference to living at Beechgrove Park is the way she simply assumes that whatever I do is necessary and important. She's worked her timetable around me. Not that there was much timetable for her to have to worry about in the early days after Dad died, but she still continually put me ahead of herself. I know mothers do stuff like that – I do too – but it's lovely all the same. Managing on my own would be very different. Despite having spent the last few weeks thinking about it, now that it could be a possibility, the thought terrifies me.

I can't be a working mum. It's too much hassle. And yet, as I look at the likes accumulating on my Instagram post, I feel a sense of pride in what I'm doing. I've found a part of me that I don't want to let go. Not yet, anyhow. Besides, I have a busy week ahead because a multinational corporation has retained me exclusively to ferry some visiting businessmen to various meetings and conferences around town. I was pretty chuffed to get the booking. It was good that the company considered me a suitable ambassador for our country, which, as one of the first people they'll meet, I am. Dad used to say that a lot. That when he picked up people from abroad, he might be the first Irish person they ever met. He always wanted to give them a good impression, and I want to do that too.

'What are you doing?' asks Mum as she walks into the room with her crochet hook and a ball of purple wool.

'Oh, work stuff. Look.' I open Instagram.

'They're great,' she says as she studies the photos. 'Very professional-looking. Will you keep doing it when – if – you go back to Dave?

I don't tell her about Dave's job in Wexford. It's an added complication. But despite my doubts about being a working mum, I feel as though I'm making progress in my life, moving forward. A sense of resolve hardens within me. I can do this, no matter what. So I tell her that it's all up for discussion.

She says nothing to that, but goes into the kitchen and makes us both a cup of tea.

It's late when Dave calls me back. I ask him about the Wexford job and how long he expects it to take.

'Not sure,' he says. 'It's a big hotel and we're lucky to get the business. Jimmy Corcoran's family have a holiday house nearby, so that's where we'll stay. I reckon it'll be three weeks at least. It'll be nice to be out of Dublin, near the sea, in the height of summer. Good for relaxing after work.'

'Are you planning to come back at all?' I ask.

'Is there anything for me to come back to?'

'Oh, Dave . . .' I'm suddenly choked up. 'Of course there is.'

He's silent.

'I'm sorry,' I say. 'I'm sorry it's taken me so long to realise where I should be.'

'Does that mean you want to come home?' he asks.

'Yes.'

Even as I say the word, I wonder how it is that I suddenly feel as though I'm the one in the wrong, as though I've been the person who needs to be forgiven.

There's silence at the other end of the phone again.

'Dave?'

'You hurt me, Roxy,' he says. 'I understand I hurt you too, but walking out like that without giving me a chance . . . and at the fund-raiser, humiliating me when all I wanted was to show you how sorry I was . . .'

'I know,' I say.

'I have to do this job,' he tells me. 'We're contracted now and it's worth a lot of money. But,' and suddenly his voice is cheerful, 'I'll come home at the weekends.'

'Great.'

'So . . . are you planning on being back tonight?' He sounds a little anxious.

'I need to sort a few things out with Mum first,' I tell him. 'I can't just up and leave. When are you heading off?'

'Sunday afternoon. But I'm doing a lot of late nights this week to finish off the job we're currently on. So maybe leave it till then, huh?'

Suddenly he doesn't want me back? Or is this part of the game? I'm so confused. I don't know what either of us wants any more.

'I'm glad you're coming home.' His voice softens. 'It's where you belong.'

'I know,' I say. 'I love you.'

'I love you too,' he says in return.

* * *

120

Mum hugs me when I tell her, and Debs, who I arranged to meet that evening, says she's happy if I'm happy. All the same, she asks if I'm a hundred per cent sure that going back is what I want to do.

'Yes,' I reply. 'What Dave did was horrible, but he's not a horrible person and he's the father of my children. I'm giving him a pass because it was a one-off and a tricky situation, and . . . well . . .'

'Would you?' she asks suddenly.

'Would I what?'

'Jump into bed with someone in a one-off tricky situation?'

'I've never wanted to jump into bed with anyone but Dave,' I say. 'Neither would you. Jump into bed with anyone other than Mick, I mean. I'm assuming you don't want to sleep with Dave.'

She makes a so-so face at me, and for one chilling moment I think that she's going to confess that she has. And I feel the bottom drop out of my world.

'Of course I haven't slept with anyone other than Mick,' she says. 'But I came very close once.'

I listen in astonishment as she explains that it was on their holiday to France a couple of years ago. She and Mick had rented a place in Provence and went there with Mick's sister, his sister-in-law and their respective families. I was totally envious at the time because it was a wet and woeful summer in Ireland and Debs messaged me pictures of the gorgeous farmhouse surrounded by lush vineyards and vast meadows of purple lavender. However, from Debs's point of view, all of the gorgeousness was tempered by the fact that halfway through the stay she tripped and crocked her ankle. She was full of praise for the local doctor who strapped it up, but she had to spend a few days sitting under a sunshade in the farmhouse garden with her leg propped up on a wicker chair. She sent me lots of photos of that too.

'The owner lived in a small cottage at the opposite end of the vineyard,' she says now. 'Whenever Mick and the rest went off and left me for a while – which was fine as I didn't want them faffing around anyway – he was the one who brought me glasses of home-made lemonade. And wine from the vineyard, too. He was a fine thing, Roxy, typically tall, dark and smouldering.'

She's never said a *word* about him before.

'Anyhow, on the third day, when they'd all headed to the beach or something, he came to make sure I was OK and brought a lovely little bowl of fruit along with the wine and two glasses. I felt like I was in some sort of arty-farty movie when he opened the bottle and sat down opposite me. His English was OK, but not great. And you know me, terrible at languages. Five years of it at school and I still can't speak a word of French. Naturally there was a lot of gesturing going on because there wasn't any funky music to do the talking.'

I smile. 'Can't Speak French.' The Girls Aloud song was one that we all loved back in the day, when Dave and I and Debs and Mick used to go out as couples. We did some very dirty dancing to it. I look at Debs, who's lapsed into silence.

'And?' I demand.

'And then he got up and stood behind me and started massaging my shoulders. It was fantastic, he really knew what he was doing. Then before I knew what was happening, his hand was down the front of my blouse, and I swear to God, Roxy, I nearly came there and then.'

122

'Debs!'

'He kissed me and he was going to carry me into the farmhouse, but I came to my senses and told him that I was a married woman and that I couldn't. Which made him laugh. He said I was a married woman but my husband was off enjoying himself and I should enjoy myself too. It was very French.'

'But you didn't?'

'No,' says Debs. 'I wasn't going to cheat on Mick. But I guess what I'm saying is that sometimes it's all about a sensation, and I know it *would* have been sensational and sometimes I regret not doing it with him.'

I'm shocked. And I'm wondering if Dave thought it was sensational with Julie.

'Why didn't you tell me about this when you got back?' I ask Debs.

'I tried to put it out of my mind,' she admits. 'I felt awful, both for letting what happened happen and for even thinking that it would've been great to take it further. Sometimes,' she adds, 'sometimes when I'm with Mick, I think about that guy and it's always bloody amazing.'

I don't know what to say. I've never even looked at another man since Dave. If a complete stranger shoved his hand down my blouse, I certainly wouldn't fantasise about him; I'd deck him.

'It was the situation,' Debs says. 'The sun and the warmth and the wine and his accent. So damn sexy. Anyway, I kind of felt that what happened in Provence stayed in Provence even though nothing actually happened.'

Dave doesn't have the excuse of the warmth and the wine and the sultry French accent. He was at home. And Julie's from Donaghmede, which is a ten-minute walk away. I feel myself suddenly tense up and second-guess my decision again. But I remind myself that I'm doing the right thing for me and my family.

'All I'm saying is that you can get carried away,' says Debs when I don't say anything. 'It doesn't make you a serial cheater. I wasn't proud of myself,' she adds. 'But for all of ten minutes it was magic.'

My phone rings, which is a bit of a relief because I don't know what to say. I understand getting carried away, I really do. But maybe I'm totally out of touch with reality to think that my marriage vows meant not ever being in a situation where I *could* get carried away. Even for ten minutes.

I look at the caller ID and this time I know exactly who it is when I see the name Ivo Lehane.

'Mr Lehane.' I raise my voice slightly over the hubbub of conversation in the bar. 'What can I do for you?'

'Are you available to drive me to Kildare tomorrow?' he asks. 'And pick me up on Saturday? And if so, would you be able to make it a standing arrangement for the next few weeks?'

Now I have to make another decision. If I go home and Dave isn't there, how can I carry on with my so-called business empire? And yet it's been the thing that's kept me going this last while. So how can I not? Especially now that I've set up the Instagram account and I have all these followers. I laugh at myself then. People I don't know and who don't know or care about me shouldn't be influencing decisions about my future. I need to get a grip on reality.

And yet the reality is that no matter how difficult I've told myself it might be, I can keep driving if I really want to. After all, if Dave comes home for the weekends, he'll be around on Friday nights and Saturday mornings, which means he can keep an eye on the children. Besides, I like the idea that Ivo Lehane might be a regular client. He was very easy-going.

I take a deep breath and tell Ivo that I'd be delighted to drive him, and ask if he wants to be collected from the Gibson again.

'No,' he says. 'Directly from the airport.' He gives me flight details and I ask if he wouldn't mind texting them to me as well.

'I'll see you tomorrow,' I say when he agrees. 'Thank you for choosing Christy's Chauffeurs.'

My business empire definitely needs a better name, though.

'Are you going to keep on driving after you go back?' Debs looks surprised.

I talk her through my thought process. 'I'll be more selective with the clients,' I add. 'And with the times, too. But I need to work, Debs. I need to be me again.'

'That's how I felt in France,' she says. 'For those ten minutes I wasn't Debs Moriarty, mother of two, chief bottle-washer and solver of problems. I was Debs McDonald and anything was possible.'

I nod slowly. I understand what she's saying. Because when I'm in the car (not that driving the Merc is anything like having sex with a French farm owner), I feel like I'm Roxy Carpenter again. And I too feel like anything is possible.

We don't say any more about her moment of passion in the sun. We talk about my plans and she doesn't point out something that I've suddenly realised – that being selective about clients might not be profitable, even if one of them is paying way over the odds. But I don't get into the financial side of things with her; I just repeat that I enjoy it.

'Well, I'm not surprised given that it's been all glam stuff for you lately,' she remarks after she orders another round. 'The Ryans, Gina Hayes, Leona Lynch. You're living the high life.'

'If only.' I take some crisps from the open bag on the table. 'I'm looking in at the high life; I'm not experiencing it myself. But that's fine. They do their thing and I do mine.'

'You really do like it, don't you?'

'Yes, I do,' I admit. 'Maybe Dave's dalliance was a blessing in disguise. It's meant I've had to do some thinking. And the net result is that although my family means everything to me, I'm going to be far more proactive about myself and what I want too.'

'Way to go.' Debs grins.

'Don't laugh at me.'

'I'm not,' she says. 'I'm deadly serious. You've taken a bad moment in your life and turned it around.'

'I kind of have,' I agree. 'And it would be nice to be successful as me. As Roxy Carpenter.'

Debs looks at me speculatively. 'Is one of your conditions of going back reverting to your maiden name?'

'No.' I look at her in horror. I like being Roxy McMenamin. 'It's that . . . well . . . you're right about reclaiming yourself. When I was Roxy Carpenter, I only had to worry about me. Now I'm a whole heap of different Roxys with a whole heap of different worries and I've kind of lost sight of myself in all of them.'

'No need to worry about the future, though.' She raises her glass and clinks it against mine. 'Everything's right in your world again.'

'Thankfully,' I say as my phone pings with Ivo Lehane's message and I save the flight details to my calendar.

Chapter 11

The children are pleased to hear that we'll be going home. Mica looks relieved.

'I was afraid we were staying here because you didn't love Daddy as much as Granny,' she confesses.

'Oh, sweetheart.' I pull her towards me and she allows me to hug her. 'Of course I do.'

'Because it's been a bit weird,' she says. 'I know Granny is bereaved, but Dad is lonely without you.'

'I know,' I say. 'Everything's fine now.' Then I explain that Dave has to go away to work for a few weeks and she looks concerned.

'But that's cheating!' she cries. 'You have to both be home at the same time.'

'We will be,' I promise.

There's a scepticism in her look that makes my heart ache.

'Honestly,' I say. 'You know Dad has worked away from home before.'

'I don't like it,' she says. 'I don't like how things are different.'

'They'll be back to the way they were before you know it,' I assure her.

'Cross your heart?'

I do.

That seems to satisfy her.

As my only job for the day is bringing Ivo Lehane to Kildare, and because he's not arriving at the airport until that afternoon, I take the children to St Anne's Park, where they exhaust themselves playing football with some of their friends. It's boys against girls, which sounds unfair, but the girls have the advantage of being older and faster. They also have Shannon, the teammate Mica reckons is a dirty player. My daughter has a point, I think, as Shannon floors Tom with a late tackle, but he gets up and keeps going, only to have his shot blocked by Mica's friend Emma, who whoops in delight. Mica then scores at the other end, much to the disgust of the boys.

'She's so like you it's unreal,' remarks Emma's mum, Audrey, as the girls clap Mica on the back. 'You were a demon on the pitch too.'

I was. I was also a demon in other ways. I stayed out late, wore too much make-up, smoked cigarettes and occasionally sampled alcohol in the field surrounding the community centre. I did all these things because I didn't want to be one of the nerdy, boring girls that nobody wanted to know. And yet, I think, as I watch Oladele send another ball into the goal while the boys look on in despair, I became friends with Alison King, who was studious and determined and who was seventeen years old before she even kissed a boy. So perhaps I could have been quiet and studious too if I'd really wanted to.

'How are things with you?' Audrey asks as the boys regroup for an attack. 'Not that I want to pry or anything.'

I tell her I'm fine and that I'll be moving back to Beechgrove Park shortly. I see a flicker of surprise on her face.

'I hope Selina will get on OK without you,' she says.

I wonder if that's the line the other women in the estate will take. That I was with my mum because of Dad's death, not because I caught Dave with Julie Halpin. I'm kind of happy to allow that to be the story. So I tell her that Mum is doing well and that it's time I came home, even as I know that I'll be sorry to leave. We've been a good team, Mum and me.

Girl power.

There's a roar of joy from the pitch, where the boys have pulled a goal back. Tom, who set it up, and Andrew, who scored, are celebrating wildly and then have to cut their celebration short to defend a fast break from Emma.

In the end, the girls win by five goals to three and everyone piles happily into the cars. Fortunately we're in the Toyota, because their muddy gear makes it filthy within seconds. I toot goodbye to Audrey and then head home.

Mica and Tom run inside, where Mum doles out ice creams she bought earlier, and I go and transform myself from a dishevelled mother of two to a sleek, professional chauffeur.

'You always look very smart like that,' Mum says when I come into the kitchen to collect the car keys.

'Thanks.'

'Your dad would be proud of you. He *was* proud of you,' she adds. 'Like I am.'

'Thanks,' I say again, touched by the sincerity in her voice.

'You're a strong woman,' she says. 'Going back to Dave is a strength too, not a weakness.'

'I wasn't thinking of it as anything else,' I say.

I give her a kiss, grab the keys, yell goodbye to the children and get into the Mercedes.

It's such a pleasure to drive after the Toyota. Not that Cherry (as Tom named my car when I got it) isn't a good one. But it's a family car, and after today, it reeks of sweaty children and earthy mud. The Mercedes smells fresh and clean. I turn on my country hits mix and hit the road.

I get to the airport just as Ivo Lehane's flight from Brussels lands, and see him before he spots me, tall and rangy as he strides across the hall, his dark hair neater than the last time I drove him. He's looking altogether more groomed despite his still stubbly chin and the fact that this time he's wearing a casual jacket over jeans. Still a touch of the Dr McDreamys, though!

'Hi,' he says. 'You didn't need the iPad. I remember you.'

I smile.

'The only female,' he adds.

People seem obsessed with the fact that I'm a woman chauffeur. But plenty of women drive taxis. I know. I've been driven by them myself.

'There are others,' I tell him.

'I'd still recognise you.'

He's chattier today, in a better mood and significantly warmer.

'Next time you shouldn't bother to come in,' he remarks as we cross the road to the car park. 'You can pick me up outside.'

Dublin airport is awful for pickups. There's no decent area to wait and you have to time it with almost military precision. I say this to him.

131

'Let's play it by ear,' he says.

We reach the car and I open the rear door for him. He seems quite unfazed by me doing this, which is nice. It means he regards me as a professional. Alison (who never did get a boyfriend while we were at school) works in a finance company and she occasionally has to take clients to dinner. Sometimes the waiter will place the bill in front of her male guest, even though Alison has asked for it and is paying. The client nearly always makes a joke about it, but she finds it very annoying. It's odd, isn't it, that women are supposed to be equal in so many ways and yet it's those tiny moments that prove we're not really. I once said this to Dave, and he asked, in a slightly offended tone, if I'd prefer that he didn't hold doors open for me or let me go ahead of him when we're getting on a bus, or if I'd like him to not bother being courteous at all. And I see his point. But it's about the situation, isn't it? Not the act itself.

Ivo Lehane has done what nearly everyone in the back seat does by now and has taken out his phone. We're exiting onto the M50 when it buzzes with an incoming call and immediately he starts talking in French. It's probably a boring business call, but it still sounds very sexy.

Then he switches to English.

'Of course I'm sorry I can't be there tonight,' he says. 'I wish it was different. But I made a promise.'

There's a pause while he listens to the person at the other end.

'It's not choosing one over the other,' he says. 'I have obligations.' His tone is conciliatory and not very businesslike. So perhaps it's a personal call.

He switches back to French again and it's softer and

132

definitely more personal than before. But even if he was reading a shopping list, it would sound seductive. No wonder Debs was tempted by her French farmer.

I glance in the rear-view mirror.

Ivo's not a hunky farmer, but he's certainly one of my more attractive male clients.

I exhale slowly.

Maybe it's fortunate there's no funky music in the car.

It begins to rain as we arrive at Banville Terrace, and Ivo doesn't wait for me to open the door for him. He hops out and tells me he'll see me in the morning.

'Here or near Tesco?' I ask.

He hesitates for a moment and then says, 'Tesco.'

'You can send me a message if you change your mind,' I say.

I drive away. In my rear-view mirror I can see him standing outside the house in the rain.

OK, he's one of the most attractive clients I've ever had, and one of the most laid-back, but he's also one of the weirdest – and there've been a few. All the same, like Dad said, what happens in the car stays in the car, so I put his eccentricities out of my mind and switch on the radio. I sing along to Dolly, Shania and Taylor all the way home.

Mum has sent out for pizza and it arrives at almost the same time as me. She brings the boxes into the kitchen (which now looks like a scene from *Invasion of the Octopussies*, as they seem to be on every available surface), then pours us both a glass of wine before we dig in. Tom and Mica squabble, as they always do, about who has the biggest slice, and who

133

has the most chips, and whose turn it is to refill their mugs with water.

I suddenly feel bad for Dave, who is home alone while we're behaving like one of those happy TV families where it's nothing but laughter around the dinner table. I lick my fingers, take out my phone and call him.

It takes a while for him to answer, and when he does, I can hear clattery noises in the background and a sudden spurt of laughter.

'Where are you?' I ask.

'In the pub,' he tells me. 'With Jimmy. For one. It was a busy day.'

'Oh. Right.'

I can't begrudge him going to the pub. I can't expect him to stay at home when there's nothing there for him.

'Is everything OK?' he asks.

'Yes, sure. I wondered . . . well . . . we're all here having pizza and I thought that maybe you'd like to come over.'

'Better not.' His tone is regretful. 'I've had a pint now.'

Dave wouldn't even dream of driving once alcohol has passed his lips. My husband is a good man. A good father. I've been an idiot. I get up from the table and walk into the living room.

'That's a pity,' I say. 'I miss you.'

There's silence at the other end.

'Dave?'

'I miss you too,' he says. 'I'm sorry now that I came out for the pint. Listen, why don't you come here tonight? Just you and me, no kids.'

I think about it for a minute. I want to, and I've only drunk half a glass of wine. But I'm a professional driver and even a mouthful is too much. So I tell him I've been drinking too, and it's out of the question. I can't get a taxi because I need the car to pick up Ivo Lehane early in the morning, although I don't say that to Dave. I don't want him to think I'm putting work before him. So I tell him that I'll see him soon and I'm glad I'm coming home.

'Me too,' says Dave.

'I'm sorry you're going away.'

'Can't be helped.' His voice is cheerier now. 'But at least you'll be there when I get back.'

'Love you,' I tell him.

'Love you too,' he says.

It's good to be loved. It's even better to love the person who loves you back.

It continues raining all night and is still raining when I wake up the next morning to collect Ivo Lehane. The house is quiet, and when I go downstairs, I see that, for once, Mum isn't in the kitchen before me. I'm glad. She needs her sleep.

I pour coffee into my thermos cup and slip out as quietly as I can. The day is grey, the clouds low and the streets slick with water. The fields are no longer a bright emerald green but a darker, duller shade, and the leaves of the trees are weighed down by the deluge falling from the heavy grey skies.

I don't get any messages from Ivo asking to change the meeting point, so I head to Tesco, which hasn't opened yet. He's there already, standing in the shelter of the building and holding his jacket to his face.

I pull up beside him, and yet again, he doesn't wait for me to open the door but just gets in.

'I hope you weren't hanging around too long,' I say.

'Five minutes, that's all.'

Why did he walk ten minutes in the rain to be picked up here instead of waiting at the house for me? What the hell is going on in his life?

'I'm sorry to drag you all the way down here on a day like today,' he says.

'No problem.'

'All the same, it's very early and I'm sure you'd rather have stayed in bed.'

I glance in the rear-view mirror. He's looking at me.

'I'm one of those people who don't mind getting up in the morning.'

It's nearly true. Once I'm awake, I'm awake. So getting up isn't a hardship.

'Good,' says Ivo.

There's no seductive French conversation this morning as he takes out his phone and begins to tap. He only speaks as we approach the airport, and that's to tell me he's leaving from Terminal 1.

'The first available flight to Paris was with Ryanair,' he adds, as though that's a burden.

Whenever I get a flight anywhere – which isn't that often, obviously – I go Ryanair. I don't think I've ever flown with anyone else.

'ID, mobile, credit cards?' I didn't ask him my standard question before because I didn't feel the need, but today I put it without thinking.

'Yes,' he replies. And then he swears.

'Problem?' I turn to look at him.

'I've just realised I've done something very stupid,' he says.

136

'Oh?'

'I bought Annabel perfume on the way over. At Charles de Gaulle. It's one she's been wanting for a while, a limited edition.'

Annabel must be the woman he was speaking to in French yesterday evening. I don't see why buying her perfume is such a mistake. And then, suddenly, I do. The ban on carrying liquids in cabin baggage still hasn't been completely lifted. People forget all the time.

'Over a hundred millilitres?' I ask.

'Easily. The bottle is huge. It won't fit in the stupid resealable bag.'

'You could check your cabin bag in,' I suggest. 'Or they can take it from you at the door to the plane and put it in the hold.'

'I don't want to let it out of my sight.'

If it's business papers or something, surely he could take them out.

'My laptop is in it,' he clarifies.

'Can't you carry the laptop separately?' I ask, but he shakes his head.

'I don't have a bag for it.'

I'd carry it under my arm – or buy something else in the duty-free so that I get a plastic bag. But maybe Ivo Lehane is the sort of man who thinks carrying things in plastic bags is naff.

'In that case, buy her another bottle in the duty-free and bring this one home next week in a checked bag,' I suggest. 'I can hold onto it till then. You can give it to her for a different occasion.'

He considers this for a moment, then nods slowly.

'I doubt I can get the same perfume in Dublin,' he says. 'It was a limited edition. But if you don't mind keeping this bottle for me until I can give it to her, that would be great.'

'I'll look after it,' I assure him. 'You could always buy her an atomiser on the plane, too. They're about a hundred mils each, so she can decant some perfume into one and bring it onto a plane herself any time.'

He smiles suddenly. 'I should've thought of that. Thanks.'

I wonder how he has such a high-powered job (because clearly he must do, given that he jets around the place the same way I take buses) and yet is so unaware of ways to make travel simple.

He takes the perfume out of his cabin bag and hands it to me. The box is enormous, as is the bottle itself, which is jade-green glass, shaped a little like an urn and gilded with gold. There's a big green lid with a gold rim. It looks unbelievably decadent and beautiful.

'I'll keep it in the car,' I say. 'So that I won't forget it.'

'Thanks,' he says again. 'It's very good of you.'

'Hey, you're a great client.' I grin. 'Why wouldn't I look after you?'

'Speaking of which.' He takes out his credit card and gives it to me to scan. 'See you next week,' he says. 'I'll text you when I know whether I'm coming from Brussels or Paris.'

'OK. Safe flight.'

And then he's out of the car and striding towards the terminal.

I look at the bottle of perfume again and wonder how much it cost, before putting it carefully in the glove compartment, where it barely fits. I know I told Debs that I was only looking in on the high life. But for a nanosecond, I feel part of it.

Mum has arranged a celebratory lunch for all of us on Sunday (fortunately the weather has returned to being glorious, so we're having a cold chicken salad, which doesn't require much effort on her part).

To keep Mica and Tom amused until their dad arrives, I suggest baking a cake. I saw the recipe in the Gina Hayes book when I was leafing through it, and it was probably the simplest thing in there. Anyhow, this is a 'healthy citrus cake' and Mum has most of the ingredients in the cupboard already – though the flour is actually a month past its best-before date, which means she bought it years ago. I'm hoping that semi-skimmed milk is a good enough substitute for the soya milk Gina has specified, and that a squirt of Jif lemon will do instead of the zest of the actual fruit. I've lined up all the ingredients when the doorbell rings and Mica and Tom abandon the kitchen to greet their dad.

'We're coming home!' Tom cries in excitement. 'Is the trampoline OK?'

The trampoline was his Christmas present last year. He loves it.

'It's waiting for you,' Dave assures him, as though Tom wasn't on it only last week.

'Will we jump together?' asks Tom.

Dave shudders as he nods. I can't help noticing that his eyes are bloodshot. I bet he had more than one in the pub last night. Not that I can complain. Mum and I polished off the red – although in our defence it was only a half-bottle that someone had brought to the house on the day of Dad's funeral.

I make the cake on my own while Dave and the children have a kickabout in the back garden. Mum comes into the kitchen when the aroma of baking begins to waft through the house.

'I'll miss you,' she says.

'I thought you'd be glad to see the back of me.'

'Don't be silly. It was a joy to have you and the children. But you need to get back to your husband and I need to get back into my groove.'

She tells me that the hospice where Dad spent his last days is looking for volunteers to read to the patients, and that she's thinking of signing up.

'That sounds lovely,' I tell her. 'Won't it be hard to go back there so soon, though? It would be for me.'

She shakes her head. 'I don't think so. The staff were so wonderful that although it was a horrible time, I felt comforted by them. So I'd like to do something in return.'

'And you've got your octopussies too.' I grin.

'I know. They're fun to do. To tell you the truth,' she adds, 'it'd be nice to have a part-time job, but employers won't look past my age.'

Even though she has fine lines around her eyes and lips, and even though there are a few more wrinkles than I know she'd like on her face, she's still an attractive woman who could be anywhere between forty-five and sixty-five. Before Dad became ill, I'd have put her at the younger end. Now, though, she's showing the strain a bit more.

'Anyone would be lucky to have you,' I tell her.

'I'll stick with the crochet and the volunteering for a while.'

140

She leans back against the counter as I tidy away the debris from my cake-making. 'And you're right,' she adds suddenly, which makes me look at her in confusion. 'To want to keep driving,' she clarifies. 'I only realised how important it is to you when I said I'd like a job myself. Everyone needs to have something of their own. And if you need me to look after Tom and Mica any time, just say.'

My heart almost explodes with love for her, and I'm about to say something sentimental when the oven pings and I take the cake out. It hasn't risen as much as the Gina Hayes one, and has a decidedly lopsided appearance.

'I'm sure it'll taste great anyhow.' Mum eyes it critically.

I decide not to bother with the vegan frosting and put the free icing bag back in the cupboard.

'We're hopeless, the pair of us,' I say. 'Maybe we should do a proper cookery course together. I could learn more than spaghetti bolognese and chicken curry from a jar, and you could start whipping up fabulous meals for one.'

'I probably should've done a course when you and Aidan were younger,' admits Mum. 'Now I have to be honest and say I quite like the variety of my M&S meals. If I had to buy all the ingredients to make them from scratch, I'd go mad. Besides, there's always the Butler's Pantry and Avoca if I want to push the boat out. All the same, I suppose I could try to be a little more adventurous on my own.'

'Gina Hayes has made me think how I should cook better stuff for Dave and the children,' I say. 'But they like baked beans and spaghetti bolognese and curries and pretty much anything that can be served with pasta or rice. I don't think any of that is really bad for them. And you know Dave – he'd go ballistic if I put tofu on his plate.'

I flick through the cookbook again.

'Shiitake and snow peas with quinoa,' Mum reads over my shoulder. 'Is that how you say it? Key-noah?'

'I think it's actually keen-wah,' I say. 'But I'm not sure.'

She takes the cookbook away from me and turns a few more pages. 'Smoked salmon and red onion omelette,' she says, stopping at a full-page picture that looks nothing like any of the omelettes I've ever made. 'You fire ahead if you think Dave will be happy with an omelette after a day on site.'

I laugh. Then I put my arms around her and we hug until Mica comes running in and asks for something to eat.

Chapter 12

We go back to Beechgrove Park after an enjoyable lunch where I felt like I was me again, laughing at Dave's jokes and doing our usual good-cop bad-cop routine when the children started acting up. I'm always the bad cop, but I don't mind really. Someone has to be.

I've left the Mercedes at Mum's and driven the Toyota home, behind Dave, who's in the van. When he unlocks the front door, Tom and Mica burst into the house and race up the stairs to their rooms. I cross the threshold a little more slowly. I don't know if anyone has seen us arrive, but I'm pretty sure the bush telegraph will be in full swing soon enough. Which is fine, really. I've stopped the pendulum and I'm putting it all behind me. People can say what they like. It doesn't bother me.

The house smells overwhelmingly of Airwick Ocean Breeze, and I'm guessing Dave has done extra spritzing over the last twenty-four hours. The living room is tidy and so is the kitchen, which sort of surprises me because my husband often uses the kitchen as an extension of his van and I'm forever moving washers, taps and bits of piping out of the way. But the table is free of both plumbing implements and leftover food, and I turn to him and smile.

'Everything looks good,' I say.

'I did a whizz around with a duster and brush. I even wore my pinny.' He grins at me.

'Must get you to do it more often,' I tease. 'Especially in the pinny.'

He glances at the kitchen clock. It's almost two thirty.

'I said I'd pick Jimmy up before three,' he tells me apologetically. 'But I don't want to leave you.'

'It's OK,' I say. 'I'll be here when you get back.'

He kisses me then in a way I haven't let him since Rodeo Night. He pulls me close and I can feel the strength of his body and the hardness of him against me. I hold him tight and wish that the children weren't in the house right now. He whispers exactly the same thing into my ear and we break apart, both a little breathless from the unexpected lustfulness of our encounter.

'Keep the bed warm for me,' he says.

I nod.

His bag is in the hall along with his tools. He yells up the stairs and the children hustle down to say goodbye. He hugs them and me and then he gets into the van. He toots the horn as he reverses past the Toyota and out of the driveway.

Tom and Mica run upstairs again. I take my time about going back inside. Let the neighbours see me. Let them know I'm home again.

I put the kettle on, but when I go to get my favourite mug out of the cupboard, I realise that most of the crockery is missing. I open the dishwasher and grimace. It's full to overflowing but it hasn't gone through a wash cycle yet. Dave and I argue about the dishwasher all the time. He never stacks it properly but shoves crockery in any old way. And he's a reluctant emptier of it too. If he needs something, he'll take whatever it is from the basket and leave everything else. Once he'd plumbed it in, his interest in it sank to zero.

I put a tab in the container and turn it on. Then I take a different mug from the cupboard and make myself a coffee. I look around the kitchen in a slightly more appraising way than when I first walked in, but I have to be fair to Dave and say that there are no other unwelcome surprises.

While I drink my coffee, I open the kitchen door to let air in, and then open the living room windows for the same reason. After that, I go upstairs, bringing my case with me.

The duvet is pulled up over my favourite plain white sheet – not the one with sprigged flowers that was on the bed when I found him with Julie Halpin. There's no scent of her left in the room. All I can smell is the muskiness of Dave and the faint traces of the aftershave he likes to use.

Mica comes running into the room and asks if she can call around to Emma.

'You've only just come home,' I say. 'Are you sure you want to go out?'

'Yes.'

'OK then. But be back by six.'

She consults the yellow and blue Flik Flak watch on her wrist and nods.

'What about your brother?' I ask.

'He's reading.'

I go into Tom's room. He's curled up on his bed, engrossed in one of his many books about dragons.

'You OK?' I ask, and he nods, only barely aware of my presence.

I'm happy to leave him there, so I go back to the bedroom.

I strip the bed and replace the sheet. Dave has washed the sprigged flower one and left it untidily folded in the airing cupboard. I take it out and bring it downstairs. Then I go outside and shove it into the bin.

As I close the lid, the front door of the house to the right opens and Daina Gadrim steps out. Daina has been my neighbour for the past six years, ever since she came to Ireland from Lithuania. She's married, in her twenties, and works at a call centre in Blanchardstown. Her English is crisp, clear and almost perfect.

'Hello, Roxy.' She beams at me. 'It's good to see you again. How is your mother?'

'She's fine,' I reply. 'Still getting over it.'

'But of course,' says Daina. 'It will take time.'

'Yes.'

'Everything is OK for you?' she asks.

'More or less,' I say.

'If there's anything you need, you ask me, yes?'

'Of course. Thanks.'

Daina isn't a gossip. Nor is she someone who asks lots of questions. I'm grateful to have a neighbour like her. And then, as I'm standing there, I see Julie Halpin walking up the road. I feel a wave of nausea wash over me. I've thought and thought about what I'll say to her on the day I inevitably meet her, but I wasn't expecting it to be so soon, and I can't remember any of my witty, cutting lines in the wave of panic that overwhelms me. I want to turn and go inside before she reaches our house, but I can't move. So I stay where I am and open the lid of the bin. As Julie walks by, I'm staring into it as though mesmerised by the contents.

When I'm sure she's inside her home, I drop the lid and

go back into mine. My heart is pounding and my head is throbbing. I'm angry with myself for not confronting her, but I still can't remember a single one-liner other than, 'Stay away from my husband, bitch.' But I discarded that one on the basis it would've made me seem pathetic. Perhaps I should have called her over and asked if she'd noticed Dave's bizarre habit of clearing his throat the second before he comes. Though that would be sharing, wouldn't it, and I don't want to share with Julie. Even though I already have.

I spend the rest of the day cleaning because it helps me to work off the tension that built up inside me from the moment I saw her, and because Dave's efforts, though welcome, are superficial. More importantly, I think that cleaning the house will make me feel as though it's mine again. Ever since I walked in the door, I've had the feeling that something has changed, and it's not only the fact that Dave has put some things back in the wrong places. It's more like a feeling that *I'm* in the wrong place, even though my home has always been my refuge. I know I'm being silly, so I keep cleaning and polishing until I'm utterly exhausted. All the same, when I go to bed that night, I don't fall asleep for a long, long time. And when I do, I dream about Julie Halpin on top again.

The following morning we FaceTime Dave, who brings us on a virtual tour of Jimmy Corcoran's holiday house. It's much bigger than I expected, and I tease him that he's living in the lap of luxury. He then brings the phone outside to show us the sea view, and I wonder if Jimmy would rent us the house later in the summer for a family holiday. I don't say this to Dave yet, though, but file it away for future reference.

Afterwards, I sit down and consult my grid so that I can coordinate the jobs I have with childcare for Mica and Tom. I can't help a slight feeling of guilt as I do this. I've never been the sort of mother who farms her offspring out to other people before. I've only ever used the Beechgrove Park mums' WhatsApp group in an emergency. In fact, I was the one who was usually able to help the other mums out because I was at home. Anyhow, I'm not using the WhatsApp group this time either. Mum has offered to look after Mica and Tom this week, coming to my house instead of me dropping them at hers, because I don't want them to feel that me and Dave getting back together is some kind of a con job.

I drop over to her later in the day, getting the bus because I have to collect the Merc. She brings me into the conservatory, which is now overrun with crocheted octopussies.

'Have you been up all night making them?' I demand. 'There weren't this many yesterday. It's like Marine World in here.'

She laughs. 'They're not all mine,' she tells me. 'June dropped off ones she's collected from other crocheters earlier. I'm bringing them to the hospital later this afternoon.'

'I'm sort of relieved to hear that,' I say. 'I was beginning to picture you as some mad old dear who can't stop knitting. Or crocheting,' I amend.

'It's very therapeutic,' she says. 'I'm listening to audiobooks while I work. It's a great way to catch up on the latest releases while doing something useful.'

'You look well on it,' I remark. 'In fact I'm thinking me and the kids were holding you back. You're looking amazing today.'

She's wearing a pretty pink top over flattering jeans, and

I'm sure she's had her hair coloured again. She's also returned to wearing her Charlotte Tilbury make-up.

She looks a little embarrassed and then thanks me for the compliment.

'How are you getting on otherwise?' I ask.

'I'm fine.'

'Not too lonely or anything?' I pick up the iPad that's on the seat beside her and she makes a sudden grab for it. I look at her in astonishment.

'Sorry,' she says. 'I was listening to my book on it. I've never lived on my own before,' she adds, answering my original question. 'So that's a bit weird. I suppose I'll get used to it.'

'Maybe we should have stayed this week—' I begin, but she shuts me up.

'You need to look after your own life, Roxy,' she says. 'Let me worry about mine.'

'We're sorted,' I assure her. 'I just want to be sure you are too.'

'I'm sad, of course I am. And I know it will take time for me not to look up and expect to see your father in the room. But I'll be OK.'

She's a strong woman. Stronger than me, that's for sure.

She clears her throat. 'Speaking of your dad . . . there's something I wanted to mention to you. I probably should have done at the time.'

I look at her quizzically.

'It's actually about that photo you saw.'

For a moment I think she's talking about the one of the young boy in my car, and I wonder how she knows about it because I never said anything, but as she continues, I

149

realise she actually means the one of Dad's first girlfriend. Estelle.

'There was a little more to her and your dad than I first told you,' says Mum. 'And not that it's important now or anything, but I . . . I didn't mention it because I was a bit thrown when I saw the photo. But I felt I should share it with you.' She hesitates and I stay silent, waiting for her to continue. 'Estelle got in touch with Christy again,' she says. 'She'd had a baby.'

I can guess what's coming even though I don't want to accept it.

'She said the baby was your dad's. But . . .'

There's a but? Dad had a relationship with this woman and she had a baby afterwards. I don't think there can be a but.

'Christy always insisted it was impossible,' Mum says. 'He told me the dates didn't add up. Estelle said the baby was premature.'

'When did she confront him with this news?' I ask. 'Did you know about it when you were going out with him?'

Mum shakes her head. 'She didn't turn up until after we were married. After Aidan was born, in fact.'

'Oh, Mum!'

The wave of sympathy I feel sweeps away the realisation that Aidan and I could have a half-brother or -sister out there who we've never met.

'I was still in the hospital. So I didn't know anything about it.'

Poor Mum. She'd just had her first baby, and now this Estelle person was saying that Dad had another child. She must have been devastated.

'Why did she wait till the baby was born before telling him? Was it a boy or a girl? What did she want him to do?' My questions come tumbling out.

'The baby was a boy,' replies Mum. 'She'd run away from home with him and she needed some help.'

'I suppose her parents weren't too happy with her ending up pregnant,' I say. 'Given what you already told me about them, I'm surprised her father didn't come after Dad with a shotgun to march him up the aisle.'

'He would've come after your dad with a shotgun all right if he'd known Estelle had run away to him,' says Mum. 'But not for the reasons you think. By the time she had her baby, she was married to somebody else.'

And now I'm back to feeling like I'm a resident on Coronation Street.

'Apparently she'd been going out with someone in her home town for a while before she and your dad met at the campsite,' explains Mum. 'They weren't engaged, but there was a general understanding . . .'

'For crying out loud!' I exclaim. 'I know it was over forty years ago, but it wasn't the Middle Ages. Surely if she'd changed her mind, that was her choice. I can't believe there were "understandings" even back then.'

'Oh, but there were,' says Mum. 'Maybe not so much in the city, but in small towns, yes. Being a farmer's daughter sort of explains it too.'

'Estelle was to be married off to someone because he had a few acres?' I'm struggling to believe this.

'More or less,' says Mum.

'And it doesn't matter that she was pregnant by someone else?'

151

'That's the thing,' Mum says. 'Everyone assumed it was her fiancé's.'

'In that case why did she run away and come after Dad?' I ask. 'Surely if she was pregnant and married, that was the end of it. Not ideal, but satisfactory. Why didn't she keep quiet?'

'Because, like her father, the man she married was violent. And he suspected the baby wasn't his. Estelle was afraid he might hurt the child and so she left. Back then, your dad was working in a builders' suppliers. Estelle knew that he had a trade. She eventually tracked him down.'

I always thought that my parents had lived uneventful lives. To be honest, I never much thought about what had happened before I was born. To me, they were always just Mum and Dad. Always there. Always in love with each other. I forgot they were also Christy and Selina. Now I'm trying to imagine Dad's reaction when a woman from his past turned up with a baby she claimed was his. I'm also thinking that this woman was pretty resourceful to find him in an era before mobile phones and social media.

'Was she expecting Dad to . . . to leave you and move in with her or something?' I ask. 'Did she think he still loved her? Did she say she still loved him?'

'Well, as she was insisting he was the father of her baby, she was definitely looking for something from him,' says Mum. 'Obviously when she discovered he was married with a newborn himself, that changed things.'

'Obviously,' I murmur.

Dad and Estelle are no longer a romantic story. If anything, they're a tragic one. She was in a terrible situation and Dad couldn't do anything to help.

'Actually, he did,' says Mum when I say this.

'How?'

'He gave her money. Money he didn't really have to give. It was the deposit for our house.'

'No!' I'm shocked. 'Did you agree to this?'

'I didn't know,' says Mum. 'Not for a long time. When we were looking at houses, your dad kept putting things off and I thought that he regretted marrying me and having Aidan. I was really upset about it. It wasn't until I eventually went back to my own mum that he confessed.'

I stare at her. This is nothing like the narrative we were given as children, in which Mum met Dad and they fell in love and lived happily ever after. The only part of the story that was different from a fairy tale was that they'd met in very unromantic circumstances. He'd come to fix the loos in the place where she worked. They always joked that their eyes had met over a ballcock. There was never anything about old girlfriends and babies and handing over money that shouldn't have been handed over at all.

Mum must have been devastated.

'On the one hand, I was fuming,' she says. 'He was utterly adamant the baby wasn't his. They'd used protection, and despite what she was claiming about it being premature, he insisted she'd got it wrong. In which case, he didn't have an obligation to her and he'd given her money that was as much mine as his. But if the baby *was* his, despite what he was saying . . . if that was what he thought . . . well, he did have some responsibility. But not at the cost of our home.'

'What did he say to you?'

'He wanted none of it to have happened,' says Mum. 'He kept saying it wasn't his life, it wasn't his plan.'

153

That's so male, I think. Shit happens and men blame other people. It's a bit of a blow to realise that my dad, who has always been my hero, was like every other man.

'But Dad didn't want to be with her instead of you, did he? Despite her being his first love and all.'

'Well, it would've been very difficult in any case,' Mum says. 'After all, she was married and she couldn't get a divorce – it wasn't made legal in Ireland for at least another fifteen or sixteen years. I think if it hadn't been a bit Romeo and Juliet when they first met, he wouldn't have given her a second thought. It was a summer romance with a sad ending. When this all blew up, your dad insisted he loved me and only me. Despite what he did with the money, I believed him.'

'So you went back to him,' I say. 'What did she do?'

'Moved to England, as far as I know. At any rate, he never heard from her again.'

'And you never found out if the baby was his or not?'

She shakes her head.

I sit in silence as I process the information. Much as I want to believe my dad's story, I'm not sure that I do. Maybe I'm doing him an injustice. But there could still be a boy – a man – I haven't met who's related to me. Who doesn't know anything about our family or about his father. It's hard to get my head around the idea. And equally hard to dismiss it.

Out of the blue, I think about the photo in the car and my heart misses a beat. What if the boy in it is the baby? What if Estelle sent it to Dad so that he could see a picture of his son? I'd been reminded vaguely of Tom when I first looked at it, but I thought that had more to do with the boy's expression than anything else. I'd felt a vague connection too. But what if the connection was real, and the photo reminded me of my son because I was looking at his uncle?

'What's wrong?' Mum's expression is puzzled as she looks at me.

Should I tell her? Does she need to know? I don't want to hurt her, but I can't hide it from her. I can't hide it from myself, either. The unknown boy could actually be my half-brother. And that means that my dad, who I always thought of as the most straightforward, honest person in the world, kept secrets from us.

'Back in a second,' I say as I get up and walk out of the room. I go to the car and take the photograph from the glove compartment. I walk inside again and put it on the table between us.

'What's this?'

I explain about finding it in the car and my so-far-unsuccessful attempts to trace the person who left it behind.

'Is it possible that this is Estelle's son?' I ask. 'That she sent a photo to Dad and he kept it because he thought the boy might be his too? I know it's weird and sort of spooky, but I got a feeling that I was connected to this boy when I first saw it. If he *is* Dad's son . . .'

'Oh my God.' She stares at it. 'But Roxy, this boy is at least six years old. If your dad had this photo, it would have meant he'd stayed in touch with Estelle after he'd given her the money. Or that she'd got in touch with him again later.' Her voice wobbles.

'I know.' I put my arm around her shoulders. 'I . . . I can't really believe he would have done this, and yet it sort of makes sense.'

'He never said.' Mum is turning the photo over and over in her hand. 'Not a word. But . . .' She looks up at me in puzzlement again. 'You said it was in the back seat pouch and fell out of a magazine. So Christy couldn't possibly have left it there. He hadn't been inside the car for months.'

She's right about that. It's niggled at me too. 'Maybe he dropped it and a passenger picked it up and shoved it into the seat pouch,' I suggest. 'And I didn't notice. And it ended up in the magazine.'

'But that means he would have been carrying it around for nearly forty years without telling me.' Mum looks distraught.

I shouldn't have told her. I should have kept quiet no matter how bad I might have felt at keeping it from her. Especially as I could be completely wrong and this boy has nothing at all to do with Dad. I'm angry at him for possibly keeping secrets from us, but I suddenly realise why he might have done it.

Mum gets the big box that we looked through before. She finds the photograph of Estelle, but the rest of them are family snaps. At the beach. At school. In the garden. Communions. Confirmations. Weddings. Normal stuff. No unfamiliar faces. Nobody who shouldn't be there.

'We're probably adding two and two together and getting five,' I say when we've gone through them all. 'My first thought was the right one. This is a keepsake that a random client dropped, and maybe eventually they'll notice and get back to me.'

'I'd like to think it's all a coincidence.' Mum is holding on to the photo of the boy with a certain grim determination. 'After Christy told me about the deposit money, he swore he'd never keep anything from me again. And I always thought he never did.'

'Dad wasn't a liar.' I'm not sure who I'm trying to convince – her or me.

'He wasn't a damn saint either,' mutters Mum as she returns the photos to the box and closes the lid. 'Though I know you'd like him to have been.'

'That's not true,' I say. But she has a point. I always believed my dad could do no wrong. I still want to believe that. So I don't want this boy to be anything to do with our family.

'Does Aidan know?' I ask.

She shakes her head.

I tell her that I've already saved a snap of the photo on my phone and that I'll send it to him.

'Why?' asks Mum

'Maybe Dad talked to him, you know, man to man.'

She looks horrified. 'I hope not,' she says. 'I don't want to think that Aidan was keeping stuff from me too! Anyway, don't send it to him, Roxy. Send it to me. I'll do it. It's not right that you should have to.'

'I'm sure it's a random stranger,' I say as I forward the picture to her. 'I'm making a mountain out of a molehill.'

'I hope so,' she says.

But I don't know if she truly believes it.

Or if I do either.

I deliberately haven't taken jobs for the first week Dave is away (except Ivo Lehane on Friday), because I want to keep lots of time free for Tom and Mica. As it turns out, they spend most of their days out on the green in front of the house, in their rooms with their friends, or in other people's homes. So I spend some time being a domestic goddess (at least as far as cleaning is concerned) and then turn my attention to the other aspects of being a driver and work on my accounts spreadsheets. I also upload some photos that I took at Malahide Castle to the Instagram account, which, despite my benign neglect, has accumulated more followers.

I follow a few more people myself, including a woman who posts old photographs of people and places. I wonder if I uploaded the photo of the boy onto Instagram, would the power of social media mean that someone might recognise him? But even as I think about it, I know I'm not going to do it, because even though he must be a middle-aged man now, it's still a photo of an unknown child, and I'd feel uncomfortable putting it out for everyone to see. But unless the owner contacts me, I don't see how I'm going to reunite them with it.

The old photos on the account I'm looking at are very clear. I wonder if there's a way to enhance the one I have, so I do a search for relevant apps, which brings up a number of different possibilities. I download a couple, but none of my efforts make much difference. After a while I abandon it and go into the kitchen to resume my domestic goddess status. I'm making jacket potatoes for our dinner. It's a Gina Hayes recipe, super-simple, and when Tom and Mica sit down to it later, they give me an impressed thumbs-up, which makes me feel good about myself.

Debs, Michelle and Alison drop by later that evening bearing bottles of wine and bags of crisps for an impromptu welcome-home party. Obviously I'm the chief topic of conversation, but I manage to steer it away from Rodeo Night to my plan to continue with Dad's business.

'What does Dave think?' asks Michelle.

Why does everyone ask what Dave thinks when I talk about my plans for myself?

'It's not up to him,' says Alison. 'Roxy can make her own decisions.'

'Not entirely.' I take a handful of crisps. 'He'll have to be supportive, and I have to make sure I'm there for Tom and Mica. Of course it does make it more awkward that he's going to be away for a few weeks.'

They exchange glances.

'There's nothing sinister in him being away!' I cry. 'He's done it before.'

'Actually, it's not a bad thing,' Alison says. 'You get to ease yourself back into the house, make it your own again. Gives you time to set yourself up, too, in how you want to run Christy's Chauffeurs.'

'I'm changing the name,' I say.

'Oh – to what?'

'I haven't decided yet,' I admit.

'Well, whatever, you have to make sure you're not trying to be Superwoman,' says Debs. 'Dave has to be flexible in the future too. I'm sure Lauren would be delighted to look after the children for you if you need help. She's keen to make some babysitting money.'

Lauren is Debs's daughter. She's three years older than Mica, who hero-worships her.

'If you want advice on the business side of things, I'll set you up with a guy at my company who specialises in SMEs,' says Alison.

159

'SMEs?'

'Small and medium enterprises,' she clarifies.

'I'm not an enterprise,' I tell her. 'I'm just a driver.'

'Still a business.' She refills our glasses. Despite being the responsible adult at home tonight, I don't object. For once, I want to kick back a little.

'A driver to the stars!' Debs laughs as she turns to the other girls. 'Roxy's had some very famous people in her car. Thea Ryan and Gina Hayes.'

Michelle looks impressed. She's a big fan of *Clarendon Park*, the soap that Thea appears in from time to time.

'And Leona Lynch,' I add. 'To show I'm down with the kids.'

'Who the hell is Leona Lynch?' asks Alison.

Debs fills her in, and I tell them how getting mentioned on Leona's Instagram account meant more followers to mine, which makes everyone check both accounts on their phones.

'She's gorgeous, isn't she?' Michelle tries to keep the envy out of her voice. 'What I wouldn't give for skin like hers. Is it like that in real life? Or is she airbrushed out of existence?'

I say that Leona is lovely and really sweet and that she's pulling in a six-figure sum from her vlog and other media stuff.

'Jeez, maybe we should do that too.' Michelle giggles. 'We could call ourselves Women of a Certain Age. With Wine. I bet we'd go viral in seconds.'

We all laugh, and then Alison says that it's great to see women doing well for themselves, and that I should definitely keep up with the driving and the Instagramming and maybe I could do a blog as well.

'If there were forty-eight hours in a day,' I say. 'Because

I also have to do parenting and housekeeping and a million other different things.'

'It's important to have your own stuff, though,' she says. 'Driving wouldn't be my thing, but it's definitely yours. I'm glad you're going to make it work, Roxy. You've been putting yourself in second place to Dave forever.'

Am I going to call out my friend for saying that I put myself in second place to my husband? Hardly, when she's right. But I'm not having her talk to me in that tone either.

'I don't mean to get at you,' she insists when I say this. 'All I mean is that . . . well, you make allowances for him that you don't make for yourself. You need to be stronger and more out there, Roxy. This is a good opportunity to take no more shit from him.'

'You think he treats me like shit?' My voice is dangerously calm.

'No!' She shakes her head. 'But you let him treat you like a doormat. You've come running back to him when he doesn't deserve you, and I bet you'll put his job ahead of yours when you shouldn't.'

She may be saying things I've thought to myself, but it's not up to her. It's Debs that says this out loud. I'm too annoyed.

'I think you're letting him off easy, that's all,' says Alison.

'You think I shouldn't have come back?'

'I'm not saying that.'

'But you're thinking it?'

She sighs. 'Everyone is different. I've had more breakups than hot dinners, Roxy. I've never gone back. But you're a nicer person than me.'

I probably am. Alison has a cold streak to her. Maybe it

161

came from being the nerdy one who was outside the pack. All the same, I'm not going to argue with her. She's only trying to be helpful, even though telling me I should have dumped my husband when we're supposed to be celebrating my return home isn't a great way to help.

The bottle of wine is empty. I get up and fetch another one from the kitchen. The girls are sitting in silence when I return.

'It's fine,' I tell Alison when I open the wine. 'I know you're just giving an opinion.'

'I shouldn't,' she says. 'You've got your own life to live and I haven't walked in your shoes.'

'You wouldn't want to.' I glance down at my feet. 'They're a size eight. And you only take a four.'

There's an almost palpable lessening of the tension in the room, and we start talking about fashion. Which is a much safer subject than errant husbands and keeps us going until it's time for the girls to leave.

Chapter 13

On Friday, because I leave to collect Ivo Lehane before Dave gets home, Mum comes to keep an eye on the children. Tom and Mica fling themselves at her.

'I've missed you,' she says.

'I miss you too, Granny,' says Tom.

'How are you feeling?' asks Mica. 'Are you still bereaved?'

'It takes time, but I'm getting better, sweetheart,' replies Mum.

'Baby steps,' Mica says. 'That's what our teacher says when stuff takes time. You have to do baby steps.'

'Exactly.' Mum kisses her on the top of her head. Now that they're downstairs, the kids go into the living room and turn on the TV. I don't mind them watching it; they've been out for most of the day.

'Has anyone come back to you about the photo?' Mum asks me when I put the kettle on for a quick cup of tea before I leave.

I shake my head and say I haven't had time to follow it up further myself either. 'I've already asked the clients I thought were possibles and they've said no,' I add, 'but I don't want to send a random picture to people I've only picked up once or twice.'

'What if one of them *is* this boy and is trying to contact us?' asks Mum. 'What if he left it there deliberately?'

'Hiding a photo in the car is hardly an efficient way of making contact,' I point out as I put a cup of tea in front of her and shake some biscuits onto a plate. 'All he had to do was ask. Or even put a contact number on the back. I wish I hadn't shown it to you now. I thought you might have already known . . .'

'I forwarded it to Aidan,' she says. 'Your dad never said anything to him about having a son, and Aidan says that even if it were true, Christy wouldn't have kept a photograph hidden from me for years. He also said that if I was worried that he was still carrying on with this woman while we were married, I was being very stupid, because everyone knows that your dad could be trusted a hundred per cent.'

My brother is probably right. Nevertheless, Dad did use their joint money to help Estelle out. He broke Mum's trust on that. So he isn't entitled to a free pass on random photos now.

I gulp back the tea I didn't really want, then pick up my bag and tell Mum I've done a bowl of chopped salad for the evening meal.

'There's enough for everyone,' I add, 'but you can throw in some oven chips if you like.'

'Chopped salad? Is this more Gina Hayes in action?' she asks.

'Chopped salad is a thing right now,' I inform her. 'It's not exclusive to Gina. Though I got the recipe from her book.'

Even as I say the word, I think that 'recipe' sounds odd for what's simply a whole heap of veg and lettuce chopped up and put on a plate. It's arranging, not cooking.

164

'You're taking this healthy-living thing to heart,' says Mum.

I think of the wine and crisps I had with Debs, Michelle and Alison and I laugh. 'I make lots of salads,' I tell her. 'I've never chopped it before, but it looks quite good.'

'It's all the same when it's in your belly.' Mum echoes a favourite saying of my Granny Carpenter as she takes her crochet from her bag. She might think I'm taking the healthy living a bit far, but there can't be enough preemie babies in Ireland for all the crocheting she's doing.

'Thanks for coming over,' I say.

'No problem.' She looks around her. 'Have you been cleaning or did Dave keep the house looking like this?'

I stick out my tongue at her. I admit that I can be a bit OCD when it comes to housework. Within the confines of the chaos the children inevitably bring, my home is always neat and tidy. I can't bear disorder. When everything around me is messy, I feel messy inside too.

'He was an idiot,' she says. 'But good men can also be idiots.'

She's absolutely right, I say to myself as I get into the car. But although the familiar sense of calm descends on me, I can't help wondering if Dad did something really idiotic when he was younger too.

As I drive to the airport, I have to admit that I'm regretting having said that I'd pick up Ivo Lehane, because it means I won't be there to welcome Dave when he gets back from Wexford. All the same, Ivo could end up being my most profitable client ever, and it would be stupid to turn him down. In fact between Dave's Wexford job and Ivo as a client, the pair of us are bringing in some serious money this month. Maybe we'll be able to afford a family holiday abroad before the end of the summer. Or if the house in Wexford isn't available, we could even stay in a hotel.

I'm exiting the airport roundabout when a message pops up on the screen in front of me.

Leaving terminal building now, it says. *See you outside.*

I drive past the car park and slow down as I reach the drop-off point – which is where, perversely, I have to pick Ivo up. I scan the crowds for him and then spot him at the furthest possible distance. I pull in, and before I have time to get out of the car, he's already in the passenger seat beside me.

'Don't want you to fall foul of the parking police,' he says as he fastens his seat belt. 'They've been shooing people away like nobody's business.'

'It's daft,' I remark. 'There should be a proper short-term parking solution for pickups.'

'Doubt it'll happen. This is Ireland, after all.'

I give him a slight smile and pull into the evening traffic.

Although I'm not a fan of clients sitting in the passenger seat, I don't feel crowded by Ivo Lehane, who has leaned slightly towards the door and is leaving plenty of space between us. Nevertheless, there's an intimacy in having someone beside you that's at odds with my professional desire to transport clients in 'quiet luxury' (which is what it says on Dad's business cards). I don't want to feel intimate with my clients. In fact I keep a small Mace spray in the pocket of the driver's door in case any of them try to take the intimacy a bit too far. I've never had to use it, but it's always best to be prepared.

'Don't you ever get tired of it?' Ivo puts the phone he's

166

been tapping into his suit pocket and stares at the traffic ahead.

I glance at him and raise an eyebrow enquiringly.

'This bumper-to-bumper stuff.'

'Of course,' I reply. 'But it's not always like this. I love it when there's an empty road ahead of me and I can put my foot down properly.'

'You like driving fast?'

'Who doesn't?'

'Um. Me. Possibly.'

'You don't like driving?'

'It's never been a thing for me,' he says. 'I don't really need a car in Brussels.'

'Have you been there long?'

'Ten years,' he replies.

'Do you like it?'

'It's OK. It's nice to be on mainland Europe. I get the train a lot, which I much prefer to flying.'

'Less stressful,' I remark.

'Yes. And you get to see places you wouldn't otherwise.'

'Where do you go?' If he wants to chat, I'll chat.

'Well, not very far in Belgium,' he says. 'But I go back and forward to Paris a lot. I lived there for a while too.'

It sounds so romantic. Back and forward to Paris.
I can't speak French . . .

'Amsterdam,' he adds. 'Frankfurt. Vienna. Berlin . . .'

'I've never been to any of those places,' I say. 'Well, Paris, yes, for Disneyland.'

'Disneyland hasn't been on my list so far.'

'No, I wouldn't imagine so.'

I feel him glance at me.

'Why wouldn't you imagine I'd go to Disneyland?'

'It's for kids,' I say. 'And I didn't think you were a family man. I'm sorry if I'm wrong.'

'No,' he says. 'You're not wrong. I'm not married. I don't have children.'

But he has a girlfriend. Annabel, I remember. I picture her as a tall, willowy blonde. Dewy skin. Long legs. Sexy. High-maintenance.

'My children loved Disneyland,' I tell him. 'They were positively sick with excitement when we went.'

'How many do you have?'

'Two.' I chuckle. 'Though I always say three. One big kid – my husband, Dave. And then Mica and Tom. They're eleven and seven.'

'Do you go often?'

'Are you mad?' I ask. 'Once. It was our holiday.'

'Right. Sorry.'

'Which would you recommend?' I ask.

'Which what?'

'City. For a city break. Paris, Vienna or Frankfurt?'

'Did you see much of Paris when you were at Disneyland?'

'Not a bit,' I reply.

'It's beautiful,' he says. 'Really beautiful. So that's where you should go first.'

There's a romantic vibe about Paris, I think. It's the city of love and passion. Not that you get either in Disneyland.

'Do you go there a lot?'

'Yes. It's only an hour and a half from Brussels by train. Brussels is work. Paris is fun.'

I didn't know it was such a short journey. I suppose I think that everywhere on the Continent is a huge distance from everywhere else. I wish it was possible to drive to a different country. I love the idea of starting out from Dublin and ending up in Paris, or Rome, or Madrid, then getting out of the car and hearing different languages being spoken all around me, even if I don't understand a single word.

Quel dommage. Out of nowhere, the phrase comes to me: Mrs Behan, our French teacher in school, saying it after I'd got a terrible mark in my French exam. *Quel dommage.* What a pity. It's certainly a pity I didn't listen more in her classes.

'What do you work at?' I don't usually ask that question. I don't generally care.

'I used to work for the EU,' he says. 'Then I got a job in the private sector.'

I recall that when he'd been picked up by Eric, he was going to a conference on ethical business models.

'A pharma company,' he adds.

'I thought you were some kind of banker.'

'No. But I do ask them for money.' His tone is matter-of-fact.

Although our conversation is a little formal and stilted, it's quite nice to talk to him. He's very different to the usual type of suit I drive. There's something very studied about him, as though he thinks before he speaks. But there's an underlying warmth there too, and even though our lives are light years apart, I feel strangely at ease in his company.

'Did you go straight into the EU after college?' I ask.

'More or less,' he replies. 'I liked it. It was interesting. Then this other opportunity came up and I took it.'

'I worked in London,' I said. 'But I was homesick.'

'Right.'

'Do you ever get homesick?' I ask.

'No,' he says, and there's a finality in his answer that means I stop talking and concentrate on the road ahead.

We turn into Banville Terrace an hour and a half after leaving the airport. Apart from the bottleneck getting onto the N7, there's a delay exiting the motorway too. And the traffic in Kildare is also heavy.

'That's great,' he says as I bring the car to a stop.

'What time would you like me to pick you up tomorrow?' I ask.

'Seven?'

'Here? Or near Tesco?'

'Near Tesco,' he says.

'Sure?'

'Absolutely.'

'OK,' I say.

'See you then.'

He almost visibly straightens his shoulders. Then he takes a deep breath, picks up his bag and gets out of the car.

By the time I get home, Dave is there too. He's in the living room watching TV, with Mica and Tom stretched out on the floor at his feet. Mica is engrossed in her mobile phone, Tom is reading. My heart warms to see them.

'Hi, honey, I'm home!' I smile at him and he looks at his watch.

'I thought you'd be back ages ago.'

'Friday traffic,' I say.

'And you're picking him up again in the morning?'

'Yes, but early. I'll be home all day.' I flop onto the sofa beside him.

'I was going to send out for food but decided to wait till you got back.'

'I left you some chopped salad,' I say.

'I had that when I came in. But it's hardly food, is it?'

I glance at Mica and Tom. I don't want them thinking that salad isn't food. But they're not listening to us.

'Takeaway?' I ask.

'Chicken curry,' he says, straight away. 'Boiled rice. Side portion of chips.'

I pick up my phone and put in the order.

Dave suggests an early night. I haven't slept well since I came home. I still don't feel as though I belong in my own bed. I can't help thinking that Julie Halpin has been where I am. That she put her head on my pillow. That she wrapped my duvet around her shoulders. That she slept with my husband. I tell myself that to make this work, I have to put these thoughts out of my head.

And as Dave pulls me close to him, I do.

I wake, as expected, exactly ten minutes before the alarm is due to go off and mute it so that it doesn't disturb Dave. I shower and get dressed as quietly as I can and leave the house.

It's raining.

There's a film of water on the roads but they're almost deserted, so the drive is relatively stress-free. I think about calling Ivo and suggesting that I pick him up at Banville Terrace after all, because he's going to get soaked on the ten-minute walk to our meeting point. But in the end I don't. He's the client. If he wants to change anything, he'll call me.

171

I arrive exactly on time, but there's no sign of him. I wait in the car, watching the rain sluice down the windscreen, blurring everything outside. I sit in silence and wonder about my client and his weekly visits to Kildare and his other life that involves commuting between Brussels and Paris and travelling around Europe. Is he happy? Will he marry his French-speaking girlfriend? Will they live a life of luxury, flitting between Brussels and Paris and goodness knows where else? Will money insulate them from the kind of day-to-day problems that can chip away at relationships? Does being in a different country help?

I wish I'd spent some time in France or Spain or Germany before heading to London with Dave. It would have been a great experience, although I know I'd have been hopeless at living on my own in another country. I wouldn't have been able to learn the language, I wouldn't have been able to make friends, and I would have missed my family too much. As I face up to these facts, I can't help feeling that I haven't done much with my life. It's mundane in comparison to people like Ivo Lehane. And all my other clients, who are unfailingly proactive and decisive and dynamic. I've simply allowed myself to be carried along by events, reacting to them, doing things because they've become the default option.

I'm so engrossed in my thoughts that I almost don't see Ivo hurrying down the road towards the car. I start the engine and drive towards him. He jumps in immediately I pull up at the kerb, once again leaving me no time to get out and open the passenger door.

'Sorry I kept you waiting,' he says as he runs his hands through his damp hair. 'Filthy day.'

'I would've collected you at the house,' I tell him. 'Save you getting drenched like this.'

'I prefer here.'

Why? Obviously I don't ask the question out loud, but why on earth would he prefer to walk ten minutes in the teeming rain instead of waiting in relative comfort for a car he's paying a fortune to hire?

'People are funny.' I hear Dad's voice in my head. 'They do crazy things. At least, they do things that seem crazy. But we don't know what's going on in the background.'

What's going on in Ivo Lehane's background? What brings him to Kildare every Friday evening? And what makes him so eager to leave every Saturday morning? I remember he mentioned an obligation when he was talking on his mobile. So it can only be family. But clearly it's an obligation he doesn't really want to fulfil. I can't imagine that. The obligation, yes, of course – we all have family obligations. But wanting to rush away again so quickly? That's almost inconceivable to me. My family is tight-knit. We look after each other. We put ourselves out for each other. That's why I stayed with Mum while Dad was dying. That's why I'm forgiving Dave. So what if it means my life is boring in comparison to other people's? It's still hard work. Being part of a family doesn't come easy.

'Terminal 2 today.' In contrast to his chattiness of last night, Ivo has been quiet on the journey to the airport. I didn't even ask him if he wanted music. We've done the entire drive in complete silence.

I take the appropriate slip road to the terminal, and Ivo is just about to get out of the car when I remember.

'The perfume!' I exclaim. 'I meant to give it to you yesterday.'

And then I realise he hasn't brought an extra bag for his computer.

'I wasn't at home, so I forgot,' he admits. 'And I didn't get an atomiser either. They weren't for sale on the plane.'

I make no comment about the bag but suggest that he might be able to buy an atomiser in Boots.

'I'll have a look,' he says. 'In the meantime, do you mind hanging on to the bottle for another week?'

'Not at all.' It doesn't matter to me, but I can't help thinking that it's a waste to have it sitting in my glove compartment when he has someone who wants it back home.

'I bought her a necklace instead,' he says. 'It was probably more meaningful from her point of view.'

'Was it a special occasion?' I ask.

'A birthday.'

'Oh. And you'd bought her the perfume she wanted. So annoying!'

'Wanted, not needed,' says Ivo. 'Besides, her gift was something else. The perfume was more of a . . . a stocking filler.'

'Well, I hope she had a fantastic day anyway,' I say.

He says nothing and I start to think that maybe his girlfriend is even more high-maintenance than I first imagined and was annoyed when she didn't get the perfume and took a strop for the night.

'I didn't make her actual birthday,' he confesses. 'That was Friday. So I missed the party.'

'Was it a significant birthday?' I ask.

174

'Her thirtieth.'

We hired the GAA hall for my thirtieth. There was a huge gang – all of my friends, Dave's friends, joint friends, his family, my family . . . Aidan, my brother, paid for the band and Dave hired a karaoke machine. I was hung-over for two days. I blame the fact that it was shortly after Tom was born and my tolerance for alcohol was very low.

'Where was the party?' I ask.

'She had a private room in a restaurant in Paris,' replies Ivo. 'She booked it last year. I was supposed to be free, of course.'

'I'm sure it couldn't be helped. Did you bring her somewhere nice to make up?'

'The Plaza Athénée,' he says.

That means nothing to me, so all I say is that I'm sure it was fabulous and she enjoyed it immensely. I love being taken out to dinner. It's great to have someone else do all the work.

'I don't think it made up for missing the day itself,' confesses Ivo.

Clearly his girlfriend – Annabel – *is* ultra high-maintenance. But why wouldn't he have a high-maintenance girlfriend? A man who uses a chauffeur service is pretty high-maintenance too. I smile as I think this.

'What?' he asks.

'Sorry?'

'What are you smiling at?'

'Nothing much.' This time my smile is professional. I don't want him to think that I'm laughing at him or anything. Which I'm not. Obviously.

'What would be your ideal birthday treat?' he asks.

'It's always going out to dinner,' I reply. 'I don't know that restaurant in Paris you're talking about, but last year Dave brought me to Roly's in Ballsbridge. It was brilliant.'

'And that's it?' he asks. 'Any other presents?'

I grin. 'My hair colour. He gets me a voucher for my favourite hairdresser.'

'He knows what you want, I guess.'

'Absolutely. I tell him in advance. Dinner. Then my hair or my nails or a facial. Some kind of treat. That's all I want.'

'Easy to please,' says Ivo.

I suppose that's the gulf between someone like him and someone like me. He moves in the kind of circles where you keep having to outdo yourself to please someone. And I move in those where not having to worry about cooking and washing up is the greatest treat life can give you. In all honesty, I might have the better deal.

'Are you OK to pick me up next Friday?' he asks. 'Same flight?'

'Of course.'

'I'll see you then.'

He gets out of the car and closes the door. Then he opens it again.

'Is there a Boots in Dublin airport?' he asks.

'Yes,' I reply.

'Thanks.' He closes the door and I drive away into the rain.

Chapter 14

Dave and the children are having breakfast when I get back. There are three different boxes of cereal open on the kitchen table, and a mound of toast piled high on a plate between them all.

I drop a kiss on Dave's head, then go up and change out of my suit and blouse into a sweatshirt, a pair of capri pants and my navy Skechers.

'Anything you want to do today?' I ask.

'Just chill,' he says. 'It was a busy week in Wexford.'

'I know we had to be with Granny because of her bereavement.' Mica stops shovelling Rice Krispies into her mouth to speak. 'But I've missed you, Daddy.'

'And I've missed you!' He picks her up and whirls her over his head. Tom jumps up and demands to be whirled too. Next thing they're all out in the back garden, bouncing on the trampoline, even though it's still drizzling and the children aren't even dressed yet. I watch from the kitchen window, my heart bursting with love.

I text Mum to ask how she is and invite her to lunch tomorrow because I don't want her to be on her own. She replies almost immediately saying that she's great but refusing the lunch invitation because, she says, I need to have time with my own family. She's right, of course, so I don't insist. But I text Aidan and suggest he might have her over instead. Aidan lives with his wife, Kerry, and their two children in Dunboyne, which is about half an hour away. He was great at the time of Dad's funeral, but he hasn't been around much since, which isn't entirely surprising given that I was with Mum myself. But now that I've moved home again, he'll need to do a little more.

He replies about ten minutes later saying that Mum will be with them for lunch tomorrow. He also mentions the photo that Mum forwarded to him, saying that I was an idiot to show it to her and there wasn't a chance in hell it was anything to do with Dad. I make a face at his message, but text back an agreement that maybe I was overreacting to the photo and thanking him for taking Mum for lunch. After I've sent it, I relax, knowing I can be with Dave and the children without worrying about Mum. She'd say I was stupid to worry, but I can't help it. She might have had her hair cut and be wearing make-up again, but that's just appearances. It's what's underneath that counts. I suddenly think of the way she keeps her iPad close to her and it hits me that she's probably looking at photos of Dad all the time. I feel a lump in my throat.

'Penny for them,' says Dave, and I realise that I haven't even noticed him coming back into the kitchen.

'Thinking about Mum,' I say. 'Hoping she's all right.'

'Of course she's all right. She's a tough old bird, your mother.'

'She wouldn't thank you for calling her old,' I tell him. 'She's only sixty-two.'

'It's a term of affection,' he says, and I laugh.

Then Tom, jumping from the trampoline, lands awkwardly and cries out in pain, and the two of us are beside him in an instant, Team Parent, making sure he's OK.

'I hurt my ankle!' he yells.

Mica sits on the edge of the trampoline and watches while I run my fingers experimentally over my son's ankle and Dave pats him on the head.

'Nothing broken,' I assure him. 'You'll be fine.'

'You got a fright, buddy,' Dave says. 'I'm not surprised you cried. But if Mum says you're OK, you're OK.'

'It hurts!' Tom sniffs.

'I bet,' I say. 'Come inside and I'll put some ice on it for you.'

We troop inside and I put some ice in a freezer bag, wrap it in a tea towel and place it under Tom's ankle. I give both him and Mica an ice cream from the stash in the freezer and calm is suddenly restored. Being a parent is all about lurching from crisis to crisis. Trying to keep things on an even keel. Dealing with disasters. Hoping things turn out right in the end.

Which they do. The ice cream works its magic far more quickly than the ice cubes. After ten minutes, Tom is back running around the garden again.

'They're good kids,' says Dave as we watch them play. 'They get on well together too. You've done a great job with them, Roxy.'

'We've both done a good job,' I tell him. 'So far. The crunch will come when they're teenagers and want to stay out all night and I won't be able to fix things with ice cream and cuddles.'

'You'll always fix things,' he says. 'That's what you do. Roxy the fixer.'

Yes, that's me. The fixer. The coper. The one who's always there for them. For him. Even if, for a while, I wasn't.

'Seriously.' His tone is indeed quite serious. 'You're a good mum and a good wife and this is the last time I'm going to say it but I'm really sorry about what happened.'

I nod but don't trust myself to speak. Because I might have forgiven him but the hurt is still close to the surface. And so is the niggling feeling that having done it once, he might do it again. All the same, it's good to hear him say the words.

He puts his arms around me and holds me tight. Then his hand slides down the front of my blouse and cups my breast. I close my eyes. I've missed him. I've missed this.

I was right to let the pendulum stop at forgive and forget. This is where I belong.

I don't think of Julie Halpin later that night when Dave and I are making love in our king-sized bed. I don't think of anything except that my husband and I are good together, we've always been good together and we always will be. He knows what I like and I know what he likes and we don't have to ask if we're doing the right thing because instinctively we are. And when I feel myself reaching the tipping point, I hold tightly onto him and cry out that I love him.

He falls asleep immediately afterwards. I read somewhere that some kind of protein is released into men's bodies after sex and that's what causes them to drop off. Dave must have loads of whatever it is, because he conks out every time.

Sometimes it irritates me, but tonight I simply spoon into his back and put my arm around him.

It's just as well tomorrow is Sunday. Because even though for once I'm not thinking about Julie Halpin, I don't fall asleep for hours.

The rest of the weekend goes by in a blur. I thought Dave might want to go back to Wexford on Sunday night, but he stays home and leaves at about six the following morning. The children are still asleep so they don't get to say goodbye, but I stand at the front door in my heart-stamped pyjamas and watch the van until it disappears around the corner.

Melisse Grady calls me later in the day to ask if I can drive a retired US general and his friend, a PGA golf professional, to Mount Juliet the following Thursday. Mount Juliet is an exclusive hotel and golf resort in Kilkenny, about a two-hour drive from Dublin.

'He's involved in a tourism push back in the States,' Melisse tells me. 'We've organised a number of events for him, but he's particularly keen on a golf trip. You'd drive him down on Thursday afternoon and then pick him up on Friday lunchtime.'

Dave and I didn't really talk much about my driving plans over the weekend. I told him that I was continuing to take on some jobs, and he frowned and said that wasn't really feasible now that I was home again, was it, and I dissembled a bit and said it was partly to make Mum feel helpful looking after the children. He nodded at that and we dropped the subject, but it's something we'll have to discuss properly in the future.

My vague business plan centres on a select group of

clients, and the retired US general doesn't fit the profile. But I've never been to Mount Juliet before and I'd like to see it. Besides, I'm keen to stay on the right side of people like Melisse who have the power to give me work in the future. So I tell her I'd be delighted to take the job and she sends me the general's phone number and asks that I pick him and his companion up at the Westbury Hotel at ten o'clock on Thursday morning. I text back a confirmation and save the number.

Despite what I told Dave, I've actually decided not to ask Mum if she can look after the children this week when I'm working. I know she said she'd do it any time, but I've never depended on her as a one-stop childminder before and I won't start now. Instead, I'm paying Natalie Hughes, who lives across the road. Natalie used to work in a bank until her third boy in five years was born. Now she makes scented candles at home and sells them online as premium products. They don't make a lot of money, she admits, but it keeps her sane. And the added advantage is that her house always smells like a fresh meadow.

Mica and Tom like being at Natalie's, and as she's really good with kids, I'm happy they'll be well looked after. And outside of the general and his friend, the schedule is pretty much driving around town, which leaves me lots of flexibility to drop home if I need to.

I'm pleased at how I'm managing to keep it all under control.

I tell Dave about the job when he calls me later that night, thinking that he'll be chuffed at the idea of me driving a retired general around the country. But he isn't. Instead he says again that it's not possible for me to keep driving on any long-term basis.

'I understand that it was important while your dad was alive,' he concedes. 'But it's far too inconvenient now. Besides, your dad always intended you to sell the car.'

'No he didn't.'

'Of course he did. You don't for one minute think he wanted you to be haring around the country with strangers in the back seat, do you? He expected you to sell the Merc, pocket a nice bit of money and enjoy yourself.'

It's not up to Dave to tell me what Dad thought.

'I want to keep the business going,' I tell him. 'I like driving.'

'But it's impossible,' he says. 'Especially when I'm away.'

'But you won't be away for long,' I point out. 'I can manage. I *am* managing.'

'Listen to me, Roxy.' Dave puts on his firm voice. 'Selling it will give us a lovely lump sum. We can go on a fabulous holiday and raise a glass to Christy in thanks. The Caribbean,' he adds. 'How brilliant would that be?'

It sounds wonderful actually. But I still don't want to sell Dad's car.

The images of lying on the beach in Barbados or Antigua or Jamaica fade. Maybe the real reason I want to keep driving has nothing at all to do with wanting to channel my inner ambition and says everything about not being able to cut the link to Dad.

'I definitely want to keep driving for the client who goes to Kildare,' I tell Dave. 'He's paying a lot of money and it would be crazy to pass him on to someone else. As for the rest, I'll work on the timings so that nobody is inconvenienced too much. Like I said, it's only going to be select customers. Him. Melisse Grady's clients. And people like Thea Ryan. Dad was very fond of her.'

'There's no point in maintaining an expensive car for one or two clients, no matter how much they're paying or how selective you think they are,' Dave points out. 'Or for the sentimental reason that Christy was very fond of a doddery old lady.'

Thea Ryan is the least doddery person I know. But I can't argue with him about the rest of it. However, he can clearly hear how I feel, because eventually he sighs. 'OK, OK. How about you keep doing it till I get back and then we'll have a proper talk? I can't see you being too keen in the winter,' he adds. 'It's all very well getting up when it's bright in the mornings, and being away from home when it's still light, but you'll think differently when the days are shorter.'

I don't say that in the winter I get up in the dark anyway.

No matter what Dave says, it's not us who's going to decide. It's me. The Mercedes is mine. And I'll choose the when and the how of what happens to it in the future.

The general and his friend are good company on the way to Mount Juliet, and I can't help thinking that Dave would have actually enjoyed chatting to them himself. After I've dropped them at the hotel, I take some stunning photos of the surrounding countryside for my Instagram account. There is nowhere like Ireland when the sun is shining: the fields truly are forty shades of green, and yellow gorse blazes on the hillsides. I don't need a filter on the photos to make them any more beautiful than they are already, and when I upload them, Leona Lynch likes them almost at once. I see that my followers have doubled over the last few days and feel a jolt of pride. I don't have anything like Leona's number, of course. But it's a kind of validation all the same, and it makes me feel like I'm doing the right thing.

I get back into the car and take a final look at the ivy-clad stately house before heading back to Dublin. As I reach the N7, I think of Ivo Lehane. Maybe I should recommend Mount Juliet to him as a place to bring his high-maintenance girlfriend for a romantic weekend. I googled the restaurant they'd gone to for her birthday dinner. The main courses were all at least a hundred euro each. I literally rubbed my eyes when I saw the prices because I thought that maybe it was for the whole meal. But no. That was for one dish. I don't care how good the chef is – a piece of fish isn't worth a hundred euro.

At that moment my phone rings and I see from the display that it's Ivo himself calling.

'Hi,' he says. 'Just to let you know I'll be an hour later tomorrow night. I'm flying in from London. I'll text you the flight number. I hope that doesn't disrupt you too much.'

'Not at all.' In fact I'm happy he's a bit later. It gives me more flexibility in picking up the retired general.

'But still the same time on Saturday morning,' he adds.

'No problem.'

'Thank you,' he says.

'See you,' I reply.

I've disconnected the call before I think I should have reminded him to bring an extra bag for his computer. Or asked if he'd bought the atomiser. Not that it's up to me really, but I like to add value for my clients, and besides, I can't keep his high-maintenance girlfriend's perfume in the glove compartment forever.

Chapter 15

When I arrive home, I find a cranky Mica, who's had a row with Emma and Oladele, neither of whom wanted to come to Natalie's house to play with her. I'm not going to intervene in the argument between the girls, who've been friends since they first started school, but I assure Mica that everything will turn out OK. She has a little cry on my shoulder and then she heads upstairs to watch the latest Leona Lynch vlog. Hopefully I'm right and the girls will sort it out among themselves, though I know my daughter can be stubborn if she thinks she's in the right.

Tom runs out to the trampoline and I make myself a cup of coffee. I drink the coffee and am nearly halfway through a packet of chocolate biscuits before I realise that I'm eating them. So much for my healthy-living regime! I take a deep breath and pull Gina Hayes's signed book from the shelf. Another round of chopped salad, I think. According to Mum, the children liked it. But of course, she did add chips . . .

I put the book on the countertop and gaze out of the window. Tom is leaping higher and higher on the trampoline and the words 'it'll all end in tears' are rattling around in my head, especially after his awkward landing a few days ago.

But he's happy bouncing away and there's no reason to worry about him. All the same, I can't shake the sense of unease that seems to have settled on me since I've come back to Beechgrove Park. A feeling that I'm outside my own life looking in. As though it's all a con and nothing is real. I don't know why I should feel like this. But I do.

I shake my head and go out into the garden, where I kick off my shoes and jump on the trampoline with my son. I don't hear my phone ring and it's nearly an hour later before I realise I missed a call from Dave.

'Hi,' I say when I call him back. 'Sorry I missed you. I was on the trampoline.'

'I was getting worried,' he says. 'I thought maybe you'd had an accident.'

Dave never worries that I've had an accident.

'You said you were driving to Mount Juliet today,' he adds.

'Oh, it was lovely!' I tell him all about it, and about the charm and courtesy of the US general, and Dave snorts.

'He's probably sent men to their deaths,' he says. 'Courtesy, my arse.'

'Well, he was courteous to me,' I tell him. 'And I'm looking forward to picking them up tomorrow.'

'I had a nightmare of a day.' Dave proceeds to tell me about a problem the team encountered with the old pipework in the hotel. It's incompatible with the new annexe he's working on. Or something. I'm not really listening. I'm deciding what time I need to set out to Mount Juliet and hoping that the weather will be as lovely as today, and wondering if Mica will have made up with Emma and Oladele, and thinking that maybe I should call Mum later.

'What d'you think?' he says, and I hesitate, unsure of what the question was.

'I'm good with whatever you think,' I say eventually.

'Great,' says Dave. 'Listen, I've got to go, the lads and I are heading to Dicey's for something to eat.'

Dicey's, I've learned, is the nearest pub to the holiday house. It's become their unofficial canteen.

'OK,' I say. 'Have a good night. I'll see you tomorrow. Don't forget I have to pick up my client from Dublin airport and take him to Kildare. Mum won't be here tomorrow, so the kids will be at Natalie's.'

'Doesn't Natalie have enough of her own to be worried about without you leaving ours with her too?'

I haven't told him I'm paying her. It's none of his business really. I say she's fine with it and then I tell him he'd better have a quick word with Tom and Mica before he goes.

The drive to collect the general and his friend the next day is wonderful. The sun is high enough in the sky not to bother me as I cruise through the lush countryside of Carlow and Kilkenny, and the traffic has thinned out sufficiently to make it stress-free. I put on my country music station and sing my heart out to Dolly and Shania, who are both giving me the same message. Which is pretty much that men are useless but women can't live without them. The ladies may have a point.

I arrive at the golf resort ahead of schedule, but the general and his friend are ready and waiting. They won't let me load their clubs into the boot of the car, insisting on doing it themselves.

'Where I come from, ma'am,' the general says, 'a gentleman always does the heavy lifting.'

He's sort of sweet. For a man who has ordered armies around and sent people to their deaths.

After I drop them back to their Dublin hotel, I text Mum to say that I'll call in to her on the way home. It'll be nice to see her without the children and have a little bit of mother–daughter time. It's not until I've pulled up outside her house that her reply appears on my screen, saying that she's going out to lunch but hopes to be home before I show up.

I have keys to the house, of course, but I ring the doorbell anyway. I hear her footsteps in the hall and then the door opens. She looks a bit flustered.

'I'm only home this minute,' she says.

'I'm sorry if I made you rush. I thought it'd be nice to drop by when you're not having to look after my children,' I tell her as I kiss her on the cheek. 'Did you have a nice lunch?'

'Very.'

Her face is flushed, which means she's had a glass of wine. Her face always goes a bit red after a glass of wine. But I'm glad she had a good time.

I make myself a coffee while she takes out her crochet needle and begins on a new octopus.

'You're like a machine,' I tell her.

'I'm really enjoying it,' she confesses. 'I'd forgotten how much I like crochet and knitting. I'm thinking that maybe I should do some other things too. Jackie could sell them.'

Jackie is another of Mum's friends. She's very much into art and design and brings her stuff to craft fairs all around the country. I don't know if she makes a living out of it, but she always seems to be busy.

'Great idea,' I say as I pick up one of the octopussies. It's so cute, with its curling tentacles for the babies to grasp. I think that maybe I should get involved with this too, but I've never been much for knitting or crochet.

'You'd pick it up,' Mum assures me when I say this to her. 'And it would be good for you to have something restful to do. I'm worried you're burning the candle at both ends.'

'How can I be?' I wrap one of the tentacles around my own finger. It's actually quite comforting, even for an adult. 'The last time I went out, it was to the football fund-raiser! And that was ages ago.'

'Mount Juliet and back and then Kildare and back all in the one day,' she says. 'That's a lot of driving.'

'Not really,' I object. 'It's an easy run and it's less than five hundred kilometres altogether.'

'How many hours behind the wheel?'

'Probably six,' I admit. 'But think about it, Mum. People spend eight hours at a stretch in an office. And Dave's days can be twelve hours long depending on his jobs. So I'm not doing that much by comparison.'

'But you won't be home when he gets home.'

'I'm not a little housewife in a pinny waiting for him all day,' I say. Although in some ways that's what I have been until recently. Without the pinny, of course.

'Well, no,' she admits. 'But it's a bit of a turnaround all the same.'

'He'll get used to it.'

'For how long?' asks Mum.

'For as long as it takes.'

She concentrates on her crochet for a minute and then swears under her breath.

'I'm making a mess of this.' She shakes her head and confirms my suspicions of a glass of wine at lunch.

'Where did you go?' I ask.

'Bay.'

It's one of her favourite restaurants when she goes out with the girls, because it's buzzy and fun and overlooks the coast. She used to go there a lot before Dad became ill, but this is the first time she's been since he died. I'm pleased that she went, and pleased that she had wine, too.

'Who were you with? June and Jackie?'

'Not this time.'

My phone beeps and I take it out of my bag. It's an alert about Ivo Lehane's flight, which now looks like it's going to be delayed by half an hour.

'You'll get stuck in traffic,' says Mum when I tell her.

'The scourge of all drivers.' I drain my coffee and stand up. 'I'll go home, say hello to the kids, then head out again to meet him.'

'Take care.' She's pulling the wool from her hook. I'm betting there won't be any more crocheting today.

Fifteen minutes before Ivo's flight is due to land, I'm in the airport café. I've substituted a smoothie for my usual coffee and take a picture that I filter and upload to Instagram with the caption 'Driver in Waiting'. It gets a couple of likes straight away.

Another alert tells me the flight has landed, so I forget social media, text him that I'm in the arrivals hall, and wait. Twenty minutes later, he emerges, tall and confident as he strides through the crowds.

'Hi,' he says. 'I'm so sorry about the delay. It's meant you having to hang around here again.'

'Not a problem.'

We walk together to the car park and he gets into the front seat. Clearly he's decided that he's not going to be a back-seat passenger any more. I ease the car out of its space and head yet again for the M50. Ivo sits silently beside me. He's not bothering with his phone, just gazing into the distance. It could be uncomfortable, this silence, yet it's not. And despite his presence in the front seat, I honestly don't feel that he's invading my space.

I realise that I'm more relaxed in Ivo's company than with anyone else I've ever driven, even my other regular clients. I think it's because, although he sometimes talks to me, he doesn't bother with idle conversation.

The traffic has built up over the past hour or so and it's moving more slowly than usual. It's more like a wet weekend in winter than a summer's evening. But at least we're moving.

'It's like the M25,' Ivo says suddenly.

He has a point. I've driven on London's orbital route too and there are definite similarities. Mainly that the speed limits can be aspirational rather than achievable at certain times of the day.

'Have you lived in London?' I ask.

'For a year,' he says. 'My company had a research facility there. After that, I went to Paris and then Brussels.'

'You get around,' I say.

'So do you.' He grins. 'Maybe not as much as me, but you obviously do a lot of travelling in your car.'

'Definitely not as much as you.' I move lanes to overtake a tanker.

'Is this a good job for a working mother?' he asks. 'Can you be flexible?'

'You should really be asking if it's a job for parents who need to be flexible.' I astonish myself with my reply. 'It shouldn't matter whether you're talking to a working mother or a working father.'

'I'm sorry,' he says. 'You're right.'

Clearly I've been influenced by driving Thea Ryan, Gina Hayes and Leona Lynch, and have become a card-carrying feminist after all.

'It can be flexible,' I say into the silence that has descended between us. 'But you need to have good support mechanisms.'

'And you have, obviously.'

'Well . . .' I shrug. 'My mum helps out. And – oh crap!' The slow-moving traffic finally stops after Junction 6, Blanchardstown. In the far distance I can see the flashing blue lights of a police car. And I know there's been an accident. I groan.

Ivo sees the lights too and glances at his watch.

'Hopefully it'll clear soon.' My voice betrays the fact that I don't actually believe what I'm saying.

'Can we exit?' asks Ivo.

I shake my head. 'The next junction is after the accident,' I tell him. 'It's three or four kilometres away. There's nothing we can do but hope that they clear the road quickly. And pray that nobody is badly injured, of course.'

I hate seeing accidents on the motorway. To be honest, I'm always surprised there aren't more of them. An astonishing number of people haven't a clue about motorway driving. They switch between lanes, undertaking and overtaking in a ridiculous attempt to shave a couple of seconds off their journey, and . . . I smile to myself. I sound like my dad. He was forever complaining about fools on the road.

'Music?' I glance at Ivo.

'It might help,' he replies.

'You can pair your phone with the system if you like,' I tell him.

'Oh, I'll go with whatever you've got,' he says. 'Unless you're into heavy metal.'

I switch on the sound system but I can't imagine my country music station is Ivo Lehane's thing. Instead I select a popular classics playlist. I'm not what you'd call a classical-music buff or anything, but I recognised a lot of these when I first heard them. They've been used in ads. So what I see in my head as the music fills the car is people buying bread, or using computers or spending money on credit cards or driving fast cars. Still, it's soothing, and we need to be soothed as we've been sitting here for twenty minutes without moving. I can feel Ivo's agitation coming off him in waves. I'm agitated too, but it's not like I have anything else to do. Ivo has paid for the car and I'm here for as long as it takes. I don't bother trying to cross the lanes of traffic to gain a couple of inches as some other cars are doing. It's futile.

'This is ridiculous!' Ivo takes his phone out and makes a call, which I obviously try not to listen to but which is basically him saying that we've been on the motorway for ages and his lateness isn't deliberate and he'll do his best to get there as soon as possible and that he'll ring back when we're moving again.

But ten minutes later we're still sitting here and his phone buzzes.

'We haven't budged,' he says. 'I'm sorry.'

There's silence while he listens to a tirade from the other end. Even though I can't hear the words, I can make out the tone of the woman's voice and she's not one bit happy.

'Perhaps you'd like to talk to my driver?' he suggests. 'Would that help?'

Thankfully the irate woman doesn't want to talk to me, and Ivo puts his phone back in his pocket.

Finally, after almost forty minutes of inaction, the police open the road again. I put the Mercedes into drive and we inch forward, slowly building up speed. Ivo takes his phone from his pocket, but it rings before he has a chance to dial out. He listens to what's being said and then interjects to say that the road has been cleared.

'I can be there in . . .' He glances at me and I suggest a little over half an hour. That's probably being optimistic, but I think we need a little optimism right now. He relays this information to the woman he's talking to. 'Oh for crying out loud!' he says in exasperation. 'After all this! I'm on the way . . .' Another pause, and then he says, 'Fine,' in a way that's definitely putting an end to the conversation.

'Take the next exit,' he tells me.

'Are you sure?'

'Yes. And head back to the city.'

I don't argue. Unsurprisingly, there's a bit of a tailback at Junction 7, but I say nothing. Ivo is making another call. He's reserving a room for the night somewhere.

'The Crowne Plaza,' he tells me.

I know it well. It runs a shuttle service to the airport and I've often picked up clients from there.

'I'm sorry your plans have been messed up,' I say as we finally reach the top of the exit ramp.

'Oh, something was bound to go wrong sooner or later,' he says. 'Giving in to my sister's demands was a mistake from the start.'

So it's a family matter like I always thought. I never get into conversation with people about their families if I can help it. I have enough to worry about with my own without hearing their problems too.

I rejoin the motorway travelling in the opposite direction and it's not long before I'm pulling into the car park of the hotel. Truthfully, Ivo could've got to Banville Terrace quickly enough once we'd started moving. But there's a part of me that thinks he's just as happy not to have had to bother.

'Would you like a coffee?' he asks when I stop outside the main entrance. 'You must be as tired and fed up as me.'

'Oh, don't worry, it's all in a day's work.'

'Please.' He turns to me. 'I feel bad about . . . Well, you had to listen to me and Lizzy and it'd make me feel better if you'd . . . I'm sure you could do with something.'

Actually, I'm dying for a cup of coffee. And maybe accepting it would make him feel less uncomfortable about our non-journey. But it's not very professional. At the same time, I'd quite like to use the loo. So I say yes and tell him I'll join him after I park the car.

He goes into the hotel and I find a parking space. He's already checked in by the time I walk into the reception area. I indicate that I'm going to the ladies' and he nods.

After I've washed my hands, I look at myself in the mirror. I take my hairbrush out of my bag, and even though it's perfectly fine, I redo my ponytail. I also reapply my lipstick and spritz myself with Happy. I'm suddenly afraid that Ivo Lehane will think I've done this for his benefit, but then decide he won't even notice. Because the thing is, no matter how nice the client is, they know they're the client. And they don't really see you as an individual. You're the driver. You're part of the furniture.

He's still standing in reception when I return.

'There's a bar over there,' he says.

The bar is like hotel bars everywhere and is mainly occupied by men and women in suits.

'Coffee?' asks Ivo when we've found somewhere to sit. 'Or would you prefer something else?'

'Coffee's fine, thanks,' I reply.

He goes to the bar and returns empty-handed. 'They'll bring it to us,' he says.

'OK.'

'I'm sorry about today,' he says.

'Not your fault.' I shrug. 'These things happen.'

'But such a waste of time for you.'

'Not at all.' I smile at him as a waiter arrives with the coffees. 'You hired the car. Whether it's moving or not is irrelevant.'

He laughs, which is nice to see. Because ever since we got stuck in traffic, his face has been like thunder.

'I guess I wasn't thinking like that,' he says. 'I was working on the assumption that you prefer to actually be driving.'

'Of course I do,' I tell him. 'But when you drive for a living, you have to accept that there will be days like this. What I'm sorry about is that you didn't get to Kildare and that your entire trip has been a waste.'

'It doesn't matter.' The thundercloud crosses his face again for a moment as he rubs his stubbled chin. 'It was a mistake to come in the first place. But I was strong-armed into it and . . .' He suddenly gives me an apologetic look. 'And I'm just as bad – I sort of forced you into this coffee too, which I shouldn't have done. You said no and I insisted. I'm sorry. You probably want to get home.'

I glance at my watch. 'I wouldn't be home from Kildare yet anyway,' I assure him. 'And I'm always happy to knock back a coffee or three. It's a sad addiction. Don't worry about it.'

'Are you sure?' he asks.

'Absolutely.' The coffee is great – strong and aromatic – and even though I wasn't feeling at all tired, it revives me.

'What made you choose driving for a living?' asks Ivo, after we've sat in silence for a moment.

As he's asked, I give him a quick résumé – leaving out the more intimate aspects such as Dave's night with Julie Halpin, which, after all, has been a major catalyst in my continuing role as a chauffeur.

'I'm sorry to hear about your dad,' says Ivo. 'He sounds like a great man.'

'We were close,' I admit. 'I miss him terribly.' I feel a sudden lump in my throat, and for the first time in ages, my eyes well up with tears. I blink them away, hoping he hasn't noticed, even though he's looking straight at me.

He doesn't say anything. It's peaceful. I can't think of the last time I sat in a bar in peace. I could sit here forever.

I'm completely lost in the moment when he asks me about Mica and Tom. After I drag myself back, I tell him a little about them and realise that, in a complete turnaround from what usually happens with my clients, I'm doing all the talking and he's listening to rubbish mum conversation, so I stop.

'You're lucky to have such a lovely family,' he says.

'Yes, I am.' And then I add that I'm sure he'll resolve his differences with his sister.

An entire kaleidoscope of emotions pass across his face.

'I never should have listened to Lizzy in the first place,' he says. 'I allowed myself to be manipulated, and as I'm usually the one doing the manipulating, it's a new experience for me.'

I'm not sure what to say to this. Eventually I murmur that I didn't mean to upset him.

He gives me a brief smile. 'I'm not upset,' he assures me. 'I've learned how to deal with being upset. I was just thinking how different our two family experiences were.'

And still are, I suppose. Him with his high-powered job and high-maintenance girlfriend. Me with the driving and Dave and the kids.

'Ah, look, everyone has family trouble at some point,' I say as brightly as I can. 'I'm sure it'll pass.'

Ivo is unaware that he's tapping his spoon against his saucer when he remarks that his family issues have kept his therapist in business for years. I know it's common enough, but I've never known anyone who's had therapy for family issues. Debs and Mick went for counselling after she had a miscarriage a number of years ago, and it helped both of them. But that was a kind of specific thing. Most of the people I know opt for the 'just get on with it' approach, same as me. And yet I wonder now if I should have had therapy after seeing Dave and Julie Halpin together. Although I'm not sure if it would have made any difference.

I wonder, too, if the therapy has helped Ivo Lehane. After all, he clearly still has problems with his family. He accused his sister of manipulating him even though he said he can be manipulative himself. And all this cloak-and-dagger stuff about not being picked up outside the house in Banville Terrace is definitely weird.

I say to him that I hope he's getting over whatever it was that necessitated the therapy.

'My father and I are – were – estranged,' he says, and I can't help thinking that 'estranged' is a very old-fashioned word for 'had a big row and don't speak any more'. Which happens all the time in families. 'I left home when I went to college and until now I never went back.'

That's a long time not to be speaking. Maybe he's carrying guilt for the row.

'I won't go into the boring details,' he continues. (Which is a bit of a disappointment, because the boring details of other people's problems are often the juiciest bits.) 'But he had a stroke earlier this year and was in hospital for a couple of months. Eventually he came home and my sister took special leave to look after him. Obviously it's very demanding and she needs a break from time to time. I offered to pay for him to go into a nursing home for a week or two while she went on holiday. But that's not the sort of break she wanted. She wanted a night off every week.'

'So that's why you come to Kildare?' I say. 'To give her a night out?'

'More or less,' replies Ivo. 'I would have paid for someone but she said Dad didn't want a stranger staying in the house.'

'I can understand that,' I say. 'Elderly people don't like their routines disrupted. Anyway, I'm sure your dad was pleased to see you, no matter what you fought about.'

Ivo says nothing.

'Blood is thicker than water,' I add. Just because it's a cliché doesn't make it untrue.

'Lizzy has always wanted us to reconcile. I think she hoped that if I came often enough, one day we'd turn into the type of warm and loving family you have. In her dreams!' He shrugs dismissively and I wish he'd tell me the details of the row. But he doesn't and so I ask about his mum, who didn't feature in his narrative.

'She died when I was small.' There's a finality in that statement that means I don't say anything more, although I'm wondering if she was part of what went wrong between Ivo and his father.

'Well, I accept it must be difficult for you to come back and look after your dad, especially when it means having to take a flight from wherever you are. But it is only one night a week, and Lizzy is doing all the heavy lifting.'

'You're on her side.'

'I'm not taking sides,' I say as mildly as I can. 'All I'm doing is pointing out that she's there all the time, which must be hard.'

'She doesn't have to be,' says Ivo. 'Like I said, I was prepared to pay—'

'Sometimes it's about more than money,' I interrupt.

'Are you sure you're not her secret sister?' he asks. 'That's what she said too. She made me feel . . .' He breaks off; clearly he can't find the right word to express his emotions.

'He's your dad,' I say. 'No matter what kind of difficulties you've had in the past, he's still your family.'

He exhales sharply. 'There are some things I can't forgive.'

'You don't have to forgive him if it was that awful,' I point out. 'Being there is enough.'

'Perhaps.' He picks up his coffee cup but puts it down without drinking anything. 'I can't believe I caved in. I bet Dad would've come around to an overnight nurse or something in the end.'

'Maybe deep down you *do* want to reconcile with him,' I suggest.

'No, I don't.' There's a certainty about his words that's quite shocking.

'If you're going to keep coming over, you should do it with a good grace,' I tell him. 'There's no point in being angry about it every single time. You are,' I add, before he says anything else. 'I can feel it as soon as you get into the car.'

Ivo gives me a sceptical glance.

'Honestly,' I say. 'I knew there was something.'

'I thought I was cool,' he says.

'You were,' I assure him. 'But possibly not the way you mean.'

He laughs suddenly, and the atmosphere, which had been getting tense, lightens considerably.

'Lizzy tells me I can be a right pain in the arse,' he says.

'I would never say that about a client.'

'Do you think I'm a pain in the arse?'

'No,' I say. 'I don't. I think you're a great client and you seem like a decent person. So did the therapy help with the row?' The words are out of my mouth before I can stop them.

He shakes his head. 'That was more for the childhood stuff.' His voice is calmer now and I know he's not going to tell me what that was. 'It worked. After all, I managed to go home for the first time in nearly twenty years, no matter how little I wanted to. Maybe it's easier because I didn't grow up in Banville Terrace. There aren't any memories for me there.'

'You might be right,' I agree. 'Listen to me, Ivo – you've done great. You have a fantastic job and a wonderful girlfriend . . .'

'How do you know that?' He looks amused.

'Because you couldn't afford to do all this if your job wasn't fantastic. And you clearly love . . . Annabel . . . if you're bringing her out for flashy dinners and buying her expensive gifts.' I suddenly feel awkward again. I'm not the one to be lecturing him about his family or telling him who he loves. So I drain my cup and stand up, saying I should go. For a moment I think he's going to ask me to stay, but he stands up too, his coffee still untasted.

'Thank you for today,' he says. 'I'm sorry to have dragged you halfway to Kildare and back again. And sorry to have bent your ear about my problems, which aren't really problems at all in the grand scheme of things.'

'Everyone's problems matter in their own lives,' I say.

'I guess so.' He smiles. 'I'm not sure if I'll be coming back again. I'm fed up with it all.'

I want to say that today was a storm in a teacup, but I don't.

'I'll let you know, of course. I'm sorry if it inconveniences you.'

'Not in the slightest,' I say. 'I have plenty of other clients to take your slot.' Then I give him an apologetic look. 'That sounds terrible. As if I'm happy to bump you for someone else. I didn't mean it like that. Simply that you don't need to worry about my business.'

'No,' he says. 'I can see that.'

'But I'll be sorry if you don't come back,' I add. 'I enjoy the drive to Kildare.'

'I've been very demanding in getting you to pick me up so early on Saturday mornings.' He frowns. 'It's because I didn't want to stay a moment longer than I had to, but I'm sure you're busy on Saturdays with your children. The last thing you need is a crack-of-dawn start.'

'I'm quite happy to be up at the crack of dawn,' I say. 'I like driving best when there's no traffic on the roads. So it's never been an issue.'

'Nevertheless, I've been thoughtless.'

'You're the client!' I remind him. 'You're paying for my time. You don't have to be thoughtful. Besides, you've been paying me over the odds, which has been great. So I'll actually be quite sorry if I don't see you again.'

'That's nice to know.' He takes his phone from his pocket, checks it, and then leaves it on the table.

'Will you need me in the morning, or would you prefer to get the shuttle to the airport?' I ask.

'The shuttle will be fine,' he says.

'OK.' I suddenly think of something else. 'Um . . . if you're not coming back, you'd better take the perfume.'

'The perfume?'

'That you bought for your girlfriend's birthday? That I've been keeping in my glove compartment for the past couple of weeks?'

'Oh, yes, the perfume.' He thinks about it for a moment, then shrugs. 'Keep it,' he says.

'I can't possibly do that.'

'Please,' he says. 'I'm not going to bother to check my bag in just for the perfume, and besides, as you said yourself,

I brought Annabel out for a very flash dinner. *And* bought her a necklace. *And* got her a voucher for some ridiculously expensive spa as well as a vintage Hermès bag she'd been wanting for ages. So I've more or less clawed my way back into her good books and she's forgiven me for missing her birthday dinner. The perfume would be too much.'

'It really wouldn't,' I say.

'I'm not a big believer in massive birthday celebrations,' says Ivo. 'We've done hers. I truly don't want to revisit it.'

'You can give it to her as a "just because" present,' I say.

'Just because?'

'Just because you love her.' I grin. 'People should do things for other people not only on birthdays and Christmas, but "just because".'

'Hmm. You're clearly far more generous than me.'

I'm not. Because I've never brought anyone for a dinner where the main course costs a hundred euro!

Ivo's eyes light up.

'You can accept the perfume as a "just because" from me,' he says with a note of triumph in his voice. 'Because you've been so patient today and because you listened to me talking complete bollocks about my family and were nice about it. Think of it as a thank you.'

I'm not at all certain I should accept a gift from a client. I don't remember Dad ever doing it. Though I took Gina Hayes's book, didn't I? And the phone covers from Leona Lynch. And I have a sort of long-term loan of Thea Ryan's beautiful umbrella. So it wouldn't be something out of the ordinary for me to take the perfume too. And yet it feels like it would.

'I'd really like you to have it,' he says.

It would be a shame not to accept it in the spirit in which it's being offered. Besides, he's right, he's already given Annabel loads. And I might never see him again.

'In that case, thanks very much,' I say.

'You're welcome.'

He moves closer to me and for a nanosecond I think he's going to kiss me. My heart somersaults. But then he extends his hand and I shake it.

'Goodbye, Mr Lehane,' I say.

'*Au revoir*, Mrs McMenamin,' says Ivo.

I can't speak French. But I understand that.

So perhaps he's saying he'll be back after all.

Which is a surprisingly cheery thought.

Chapter 16

I'll be home pretty much at the time I expected, thanks to stopping off for the coffee. I've never, ever had coffee with a client before and I'm feeling a little guilty. At the time it seemed the right thing to do, but now I'm thinking that if Dave went for coffee with a female customer I'd be peeved with him. I wonder why I should feel that way – is it because I wouldn't have trusted him even then? Or because plumbers usually don't have coffee with their customers? At least, not in fancy hotels. Their right to have coffee at any time on the job is, of course, unshakeable.

I think again about Ivo's relationship with his dad and wonder how it all went wrong. Nobody I know has had long-term estrangements from their families, although there are plenty of short-term arguments and fallings-out. Sometimes even defriending on Facebook! But no matter what, we all manage to resolve our differences. Nevertheless, it must have been something massive between Ivo and his father to lead to such a long silence. And then Lizzy got him home. It's always the women who fix it in the end.

I stop thinking of him as I get into a brief pissing contest with a truck driver who seems to want to force me off the road. I break the speed limit to get ahead of him and then berate myself for feeling the need. I hate being behind huge lorries, that's my excuse.

I'm five minutes from the Beechgrove estate when the phone rings. For a moment I think it's Ivo Lehane again, changing his mind and wanting to be brought to Kildare after all. And I'm actually planning on how I'll turn the car around, and what I'll say to Dave, when I see from the caller ID that it's Thea Ryan. She apologises for the relatively short notice but she's to be a guest speaker at a charity lunch the following Friday and she'd like me to drive her. Just there, she adds; her daughter – who's involved with the osteoporosis charity – will drop her home.

Even if Ivo changes his mind and comes back to stay with his father next week, I'll have time to drive Thea to her lunch. So I confirm her booking. I turn down the next offer, less than five minutes later, to collect some businessmen from Heuston station on Tuesday evening, though. I need to be home for the children.

I'm pulling up in front of the house when the phone rings for a third time. I can't believe I've become so in demand all of a sudden. But this call is from Alison, who tells me that her tax friend can see me on Monday morning. I didn't realise that she was going to make an actual appointment for me. Even though I'm nervous about the idea of meeting a proper business person as their client instead of their driver, I can at least ask him about the merits of selling the car versus keeping the business going. And that will mean I can have a sensible conversation with Dave about it, with all the relevant information at my fingertips. I'm not going to say anything tonight, though. No need for him to know.

When I walk into the kitchen, he's tucking into pizza and chips at the kitchen table with Mica and Tom, even though I left more chopped salad in the fridge. Emma and Andrew, their friends, are there too and they chant a 'hello, Mrs McMenamin' at me before they all head into the living room to watch TV. Emma and Mica have obviously resolved whatever differences they had, which I'm happy about. If only adults could do it as easily.

'Want some?' Dave asks as he opens the pizza box to reveal the last slice.

It smells great and I'm starving. But I take the salad out of the fridge and put the kettle on for a cup of tea, even though the coffee I had with Ivo is still swilling around my stomach.

'Good day?' asks Dave as he puts the last piece of pizza on his own plate.

'Not bad.'

'There was something on the news about an accident on the M50,' he says.

I nod. 'Caused a delay.'

'But you made reasonable time.' He glances at the clock on the wall.

'Yes.'

I don't say anything about coffee with Ivo Lehane. It's not important.

'We have to talk properly about this taxi stuff.' Dave goes to the cupboard and takes out a box of Mr Kipling pies. He opens it and puts a cherry Bakewell on the plate in front of him.

I'm absolutely not going to have this conversation until after I meet Alison's mate. But I can't stop myself from telling

Dave that I'm a chauffeur, not a taxi driver, and that he's already said he's fine with me driving until he comes back from Wexford. So there's nothing to talk about.

'I know what I said,' he tells me. 'But I honestly think it's going to be impossible for you to keep a schedule going during the rest of the school holidays.'

'I've managed so far.'

'But is managing enough?' he asks. 'Surely the kids deserve more than that. I'm not trying to be obstructive,' he adds. 'All I want is what's best for everyone.'

Which I'm sure he does. But do I count as everyone? Because if continuing driving is something I want to do, isn't he obstructing me? Does what I want not count? Or am I being monumentally selfish?

'I want life to be easy for you,' Dave says when I stay silent. 'Back and forward to the airport all the time, getting up at the crack of dawn to drive to Kildare – those things are making it hard.'

'Actually, I won't be going to Kildare in the morning after all,' I say. 'Mr Lehane doesn't need me.'

'Well, that's a bit of good news.' A wide grin breaks out on Dave's face. 'I can think of quite a few ways to pass the time instead. And all of them are good ones!' He leans across the kitchen table and kisses me.

As I kiss him back, I realise that there are two things I haven't told him about today: the proposed meeting with the tax adviser, and the coffee with a client. I don't usually keep things from Dave. But now, it seems, I do.

Even though I don't have to wake up early, my eyes snap open exactly at the time they would have done if I'd been

211

picking up Ivo. Through the shade of the curtains I can see that the sun is already up. Dave is out for the count, but I'm totally alert. I slide out of bed and go downstairs, first peeping into the children's bedrooms to check on them. Like their dad, Tom and Mica are sound asleep.

I decide on tea instead of coffee for a change, and sip it as I look out into the garden, where a red fox is balancing precariously on the dividing wall between our house and Julie Halpin's. Our eyes meet for a moment, his as tawny as his fur. Then he seems to shrug as though I'm not interesting enough for him, and shimmies down the other side of the wall. I hope the lids are secure on the bins in the front so that he can't scavenge from them, and I go into the living room to look out and check. They're fine, but seeing the Merc reminds me that I left the perfume Ivo Lehane gave me in the glove compartment. I won't get it now because the sound of the front door opening and the beep of the alarm disarming would probably wake either Dave or the children. But I make a mental note to take it out later.

I return to my tea, open my iPad and check my Instagram account. Leona Lynch has liked the photos of Mount Juliet and added a comment that if she ever stays there, I can drive her. I like her comment in return. As I scroll through Leona's most recent photos, I think of Gina Hayes and check to see if she's on Instagram too. Of course she is – naturally her photos are mostly of fabulous food, including the chopped salad that has become a staple in my healthy-living regime. I like the chopped salad post and comment that it's delicious. I'm still looking at food pics when Dave, tousle-haired and sleepy-eyed, walks into the kitchen.

'What on earth are you doing up?' he asks as I close my iPad.

'Internal alarm,' I reply. 'I'm used to waking up to go to Kildare on a Saturday morning.'

'You only did it a few times,' he objects.

'Yes, but you know how I am. It sort of imprints itself on me.'

'Come back to bed.'

'Tom and Mica will be awake soon.'

'Soon, but not yet. Come back to bed. I told you I had things I wanted to do with you.' He puts his arms around me and his hand slides down the front of my pyjamas.

I leave the iPad on the table and go back to bed with him. But even as he's doing things to my body that are very pleasurable indeed, I'm thinking of Instagram filters and how to make my posts more interesting.

The children are surprised to see me when they get up later.

'Why aren't you off with Ivo?' asks Mica.

'Ivo?' Dave looks at me questioningly.

'That's the Kildare client's name,' I tell him.

'Mum told Granny he was a bit weird.'

'Weird? In what way?' Dave looks at me in concern.

'Not weird weird,' I say. 'Just . . . odd.'

'For God's sake, Roxy, what on earth does that mean?'

'Oh, it's nothing.' I'm not going to share Ivo's life story with Dave. What happens in the car stays in the car, even if it was actually in a hotel. 'Family trouble mainly. And Mica . . .' I turn to my daughter, who looks up from her phone. 'We don't discuss clients ever. Their lives are private.'

'You were discussing him with Granny,' she points out.

'That was different.'

'I don't see how.'

'It just is.'

'What sort of family trouble?' demands Dave.

'Nothing sinister,' I reply. 'I thought it was a bit strange at first that he wanted to be driven to a pretty run-down part of town, given that he's so well-off, but it's where his dad lives.'

'How run-down?' Dave won't let it go.

'I'd say it's more neglected than run-down,' I amend.

'Have you met the father?'

'Of course not!' I exclaim. 'I drive people where they want to go. I don't meet their friends and family.'

'What did you say this guy did?'

'He works for a pharmaceutical company.'

Dave pours himself some tea from the pot.

'What kind of pharmaceuticals?'

'How should I know?' I ask.

'Because . . .' He lowers his voice, but Mica and Tom have taken their cereal bowls into the living room. 'What are pharmaceuticals, Roxy?'

'Huh?'

'Drugs,' he says dramatically. 'Have you considered that he might be a drug dealer?'

Ivo Lehane? Dealing drugs? It's laughable. Ivo is a successful man who had a row with his dad but is coming back to see him even though he doesn't want to. That's all. Then I think about his apparent wealth and his reluctance to check his bag in at the airport, and a niggle of doubt creeps in. Nevertheless, I tell Dave not to be ridiculous.

'Back and forward every week,' Dave says. 'It could be some kind of network. He could be a mule.'

'I really don't think so.' I shake my head. 'He's a businessman.'

'There's something not quite right about it,' says Dave. 'And I'm not sure you should be mixed up in whatever it is.'

'For heaven's sake!' I'm getting annoyed now. 'He's a client, he's paying over the odds . . .' and then my voice trails off as I consider that he might be paying over the odds *because* he's in the drugs business, and that everything he's told me might be a whopping lie.

Dave is watching me carefully.

'He's a businessman,' I repeat. 'Honestly, Dave, it's fine. He's a decent person. And the fact that he's obviously pulled himself up from his roots and got on in the world doesn't make him some sort of criminal.'

'Hmm. Well, I'm not happy about it,' says Dave. 'I know I said you could keep driving until I was back for good, but I'm having second thoughts now.'

I don't need Dave's actual permission to drive. He doesn't own me.

'And you should be finished by five o'clock anyway,' he says. 'It's not right you being out so late.'

I clamp down on my annoyance with my husband. He's concerned for me, that's all.

But he doesn't need to be. I can look after myself.

Chapter 17

The office where I'm meeting James Mallon, Alison's tax-adviser colleague, is in the docklands area. I know it quite well because there are a lot of businesses here and I've collected many of their executives from their various glass buildings. It's also quite close to the Gibson Hotel, where I first picked up Ivo Lehane. But I've never gone into any of the offices before and I'm a little overawed by the reception area of Hunter Crowe, where James and Alison work. It has a huge marble atrium that allows natural and internal lighting to combine, and it's furnished with potted plants, leather seats and rugs with piles so deep that my H&M high heels leave indentations in them. In the centre is a futuristic fountain with LED lights changing the colour of the water, while the glass walls of the offices mean that visitors can see the hive of activity on each floor.

A perfectly groomed receptionist tells me that James will see me shortly, so I perch on one of the leather chairs, glad that I'm wearing my newest navy suit and that my white blouse is the one with the snazzy silver buttons. The H&Ms are also my highest-heeled shoes. It's good to be wearing them again, even if I'm a bit out of practice. Those extra inches give me more confidence.

The lift pings and I look up. A sandy-haired man wearing a dark grey suit, white shirt and red tie steps out and walks towards me.

'Roxy McMenamin?' he asks. 'I'm James Mallon.'

I shake his hand and he leads me to the lift, which whisks us up to the fourth floor. I follow him to a large meeting room with views over the River Liffey.

'Coffee?' he asks, and I say yes, even though, possibly for the first time in my life, I don't really want any.

There's a machine on a sideboard and he makes two cups, handing one to me.

'So,' he says. 'Alison King told me to look after you.'

I'm too intimidated to do anything but nod.

'And what Alison wants, she gets.' His smile is relaxed and friendly and I release the breath I didn't know I'd been holding.

I emailed Alison information about Christy's Chauffeurs as well as some spreadsheets of the accounts a few days earlier, and James Mallon now takes them out of a transparent folder and fans them out on the desk in front of him.

'So you and your dad ran the business?' he says.

I explain exactly how things worked, and he nods and makes occasional notes. The more I talk, the more at ease I become and the more I feel like James is actually listening to me. He asks a few more questions and I'm able to answer them, and then he shuffles through the papers again.

'My husband thinks we might be better off selling the car and using the money for other stuff,' I say. 'I'm trying to decide if he's right.'

'It's two completely different things,' says James. 'On the one hand you're talking about continuing a going concern. On the other you're winding it up and selling its major asset.'

He talks to me as though I'm a knowledgeable business person myself, and even though I have to ask him to explain some of the more complicated issues in greater detail, I'm able to follow his line of thought. And he's right, of course. Running the business would be a long-term venture. Selling the car is a one-off transaction.

'In the end, it's entirely up to you,' he says after we've gone through the numbers. 'I can't advise you on what's best for you and your family. Only on whether the business can continue to be run profitably.'

I nod.

'You have some good clients and good contacts,' he tells me as he skims through the list again. 'Grady PR is a great outfit, and so is Hegarty Construction.' Grady is Melisse's firm. Hegarty Construction is owned by a man who grew up near Dad and made a fortune in the Celtic Tiger years.

'And you've got excellent business connections,' he adds. 'Which gives you almost daily access to a wide range of clients.'

He's right about that. I turned down four jobs so that I could be at today's meeting.

'Can it be run profitably?' I ask.

'It's bringing in a good annual income,' says James. 'You have to decide if you can continue to work the necessary hours to sustain it, and accept that the car will depreciate over time, but there's no reason it can't continue to make money. Of course, selling the car would be a nice short-term bonus for you.'

I don't want to get rid of it, that's for sure. But I truly do understand why Dave thinks it's a bonkers idea for me to keep working. Because looking at the figures and calculating the amount of work I'd have to do, it is.

'Obviously if you decide to stick with it, there's some paperwork that will need to be dealt with,' James tells me. 'I can look after that for you at a reduced fee.'

'How much would that be?' I ask. I also ask about changing the company's name, although I don't have a new one yet.

He does a quick calculation and mentions an amount that makes me wonder what on earth the non-reduced fee would be. They've got it made, I think, these people who sit in their glass offices and don't do anything other than move paper from one side of a desk to the other.

'Obviously I'm not charging you for today,' says James. 'Our discussion was a favour to Alison. But if you want to continue with it, getting the paperwork straight will include some legal charges; that's what pushes it up.'

Did he see it in my face?

'That's OK,' I tell him.

'You don't have to decide here and now,' he says. 'You should think about it. Talk it over with your husband.'

Is he saying that because he thinks Dave is the one calling the shots? Or that he'd have a better idea about it than me? Or . . . I pull myself up. It's probably because I mentioned that Dave was concerned about how we'd manage.

'It was good to talk to you,' he says. 'If you decide to stick with it, I'm very confident you'll be successful.'

I'm surprisingly overcome by his support and have to blink away the tears that are prickling my eyes. I hope he doesn't notice. I'm pretty sure successful business people don't routinely cry in their flashy offices.

'Alison asked me to tell her when we were finished,' he says. 'I'll call her now.'

He picks up his phone and dials a number. I hear Alison's voice asking him to bring me to her. We leave the meeting room and go up another floor. This time he leads me to an office at the end of the corridor. Alison's name is on the door. Before he has time to knock, she opens it and beams at me. She thanks James for looking after me, and he leaves us to it.

'How did it go?' she asks as she ushers me to a leather chair.

'Eye-opening.' I sit down. 'Jeez, Alison, I never imagined you worked in a place like this. That you had an office with your name on it. That you were so . . . so important.'

'I'm not that important,' she says dismissively.

'But you are!' I cry. 'When James talked about you, he talked with respect. Do you work with him a lot?'

'I'm his boss,' she admits.

I look at my friend in astonishment. I knew that Alison liked her job and had done well, but I never quite realised before exactly how well. She spoke about getting promoted and moving departments, but I didn't imagine her as someone who could be senior to the kind of man I'd drive in my car. Which makes her someone who could hire me and my car. Why didn't I ever think she could be . . . well . . . so successful?

'It's all relative,' she says.

'Alison King! You have a big office in an amazing building. You're senior to a man giving me professional advice. And . . .' I look her up and down, 'you're wearing a very expensive suit that I've never seen before.'

'Yeah, well, I wouldn't wear this on a girls' night out.' She grins. 'Far too corporate. But you have to dress well for the office.'

'I can see that. What I didn't get until now is how brilliant you are.'

'Don't be daft,' she says.

'I'm stating a fact. And I might be too thick to have realised before now that you're mega-successful, but everyone else must know.'

'Success depends on your point of view, Roxy.'

Debs said that to me too. But Debs works in B&Q, not an impressive place like this.

'From any point of view you're doing great,' I tell her. 'Who wouldn't think so, for heaven's sake?'

'My mother, for one.' She makes a face. 'All Mum wants is for me to be married and settled down and to give her a grandchild.'

'She has about eight grandchildren already,' I remind her.

Alison has four brothers, all married with families of their own.

'It's not the same as far as Mum is concerned,' says Alison. 'She thinks it's more important for me than for the boys.'

'That's mental.'

'That's Mum.'

We both laugh. I like Alison's mum, who used to allow all the kids in the neighbourhood to play in her garden and would treat us to lemonade and ice creams during the summer. But her thinking is very old-fashioned.

'She believes I'm not fulfilling my role as a woman,' adds Alison.

'Seriously?'

'Seriously. Until the day I'm married and pregnant, she'll never think of me as a success.'

'I'm sure you're—'

'I'm not.' Alison's tone is grim. 'When I told her last year that I had some great news, she wanted to know if I was pregnant at last. She couldn't have cared less about my promotion.'

'Just as well you weren't pregnant!'

Alison was living with her boyfriend of two years, Peter Brandon, back then. They've since split up.

'She probably wouldn't have minded. I might have been without a father for my child, but at least I'd have had one.'

'I'm sure you're wrong, Ally.'

'I'm not.' Alison sighs. 'Sometimes it seems as though women haven't made any progress at all over the last fifty years. We talk the good talk, but as long as our mothers still want us to be mothers too, we're not seen as people who are allowed to make choices.'

'Your mum must be very proud of you,' I say.

'She is. But she'd like to be proud of me for different reasons. However . . .' Alison smiles. 'I'm a director of a company with two hundred employees, and I'm pretty proud of myself, which is the most important thing.'

'Two hundred!' I gasp. 'You have two hundred people working for you?'

'Not all for me,' she replies. 'My department has fifty.'

I'm awestruck all over again.

'I wish you'd said before,' I tell her.

'What would I have said? Hey, girls, look at me, I have fifty people working for me?'

'Um . . . yes,' I say. 'I drive men around in my car all the time and they never shut up about how great they are. Or the deals they've done. Or how much they'd like to put the knife into someone else.'

'Oh really? Tell me more.'

I suddenly remember Dad's words.

'What happens in the car stays in the car,' I say. 'But believe me, it's a war zone sometimes.'

She laughs again and then asks what I'm going to do about Christy's Chauffeurs.

'I thought of myself as a bit of a businesswoman before I came in here,' I say. 'Now . . .'

'You *are* a businesswoman.' Suddenly her tone is serious and she's morphed into the kind of person who could definitely have fifty people working for her. 'I looked at those spreadsheets too, Roxy. You're good at what you do.'

'It was mostly Dad,' I say. 'I can't be sure that I'll have the same level of business as him.'

'Why wouldn't you?'

Because of Dave, I think, but don't say. Because of Dave and Mica and Tom.

'How are things at home?' she asks when she realises I've stayed silent. 'How's Dave?'

'OK,' I reply. 'We're getting on pretty well. But as far as this goes, he'd rather sell the Merc and take the money.'

'But you'd like to drive?'

I think about it again for a moment. Just to be one hundred per cent sure.

'Yes,' I reply.

'Then you should do it,' says my successful businesswoman friend.

'It's not that easy.'

'Nothing is easy.'

I look around her fabulous office with its huge windows and panoramic views of the city. I guess I always thought that me and the girls – the Abbeywood Girls, as we used to call ourselves – all had more or less the same kind of lives. I know Alison is the unmarried one, but I didn't think things were all that different for her. And yet they are.

'Was this hard for you?' I ask.

'Yes.'

'Why?'

'Oh, for all the reasons you've already mentioned.' She shrugs. 'The egos. The deals. The back-stabbing.'

'Have you been stabbed in the back?'

'Countless times.'

'Really?'

'Yes. But I get up and carry on,' she says. 'And I don't let it upset me.'

'You're as hard as nails.' When we were small, though, she wasn't. She used to cry when we teased her about the freckles dotted across her nose, or the fact that she was hopeless at sports, or that she was the only one of us never to get a Valentine card. Even though she insisted that Valentine's Day was a stupid con.

'You toughened me up,' she says when I remind her.

'We were bitches.'

'Ah, no.' She reaches out and gives me a hug. 'We were friends. And we still are.' She pauses for a moment, then gives me a considering look. 'We run workshops for business start-ups,' she says. 'There's one very soon. Next week, I think. You should come. I'll check the exact date.'

'Oh, I couldn't,' I protest. 'Driving Dad's car isn't a proper business.'

'Of course it is,' says Alison. 'And it's not your dad's car any more. It's yours. You owe it to yourself to be the best you can be.'

I stare at her, in her corporate suit, in her corporate office. A successful businesswoman. The best she can be.

And I agree to go on the course.

I'm feeling strong and proud and successful business-woman-y myself as I drive to Mum's. She's looking after Mica and Tom again, but when I arrive, she tells me they're in the Slevin house, a few doors down, watching movies with some friends.

'How did you get on?' she asks as she makes space for me at the kitchen table, which is still swamped with little purple octopussies.

'Are you ever going to bring those into the hospital?' I ask instead of answering.

'I was going to go in today, but I'll go tomorrow instead,' she replies.

'Sorry I've messed up your plans.'

'It doesn't matter what day I go,' she tells me. 'I'm not on an octopus deadline or anything.'

225

'All the same . . .'

'Chill, Roxy,' she says. 'And answer my question.' She picks up her crochet and starts working while I tell her how successful Alison is and how astonished I was to find out she has her own enormous office and staff.

'She was always the ambitious one,' Mum remarks.

'I didn't realise how well she'd done,' I say. 'It's amazing.'

'As long as she's happy,' says Mum.

'Of course she's happy. Why wouldn't she be?'

'She's never settled.' Mum stretches the tentacles of the octopus she's working on and looks at it critically. 'Flits from man to man like a demented butterfly.'

'No she doesn't.' I'm irritated on my friend's behalf. 'OK, she might go out on dates with a number of them, but she was engaged to Michael McGuirk for over a year and she lived with Pete Brandon for two.'

'I'm not sure she ever got over Michael breaking off their engagement.'

'Actually it was Alison who broke off the engagement,' I remind her. 'She had the chance to work in Portugal for a few months and Michael didn't want her to go without him.'

'That's understandable,' says Mum. 'Michael had a good job and he'd have been mad to leave it. And if you remember, you didn't let Dave go to London without you.'

But maybe I should have, I think now as I pick up one of the little octopuses and roll it around the palm of my hand. Maybe it would have been better for him and for me to have some time apart, to live separate lives for a while. And yet I loved him so much, I couldn't bear the idea of not being with him. Until I moved in with Mum while Dad was in the hospice, the only nights we'd spent apart were when I was in hospital having the children.

I don't say any of this to her. Instead, I continue to play with the octopus.

'I'm not saying Alison can't be happy on her own.' Mum breaks the silence. 'All I'm saying is that when you've found the right person for you, your happiness is increased.'

My happiness was increased a thousandfold when I met Dave. His love for me and mine for him gave me an inner strength. I still have that strength. But there's a part of me that hasn't got over it being tested. And – I don't want to think this, but I do – there's also a part of me that doesn't trust him the way I did before.

'Would you like a cuppa?' Mum abandons her crochet.

'I'll make it,' I tell her, but she insists on doing it and tells me to sit in the conservatory. I leave her in the kitchen and walk into the sun-filled room, picking up her iPad from the cane sofa so that I can sit in the warmest spot. Unlike mine, she hasn't got it on auto-lock, so I can't help seeing the page it's opened at.

It's a picture of a silver-haired man dressed in a bright orange cagoule and matching skin-tight leggings, standing beside a mountain bike. Beneath the picture is a description:

My name is Dean. I'm 65 years old, divorced, still fit and athletic. I'm looking for someone fun and outdoorsy, with a zest for life. Could it be you? Preferred age range 45–55.

I read the description at least half a dozen times before it sinks in that Mum has obviously joined Tinder.

When she comes in with the tea (and some mini Jaffa Cake rolls), I ask her about it. I try not to sound as shocked as

I feel. It's not that I don't want her to get on with her life, but it's not that long since Dad died and I can't believe she's already looking for someone new.

'It's not Tinder!' she exclaims as she takes the iPad from me. I realise this is why she's been so edgy when I've picked it up before. She wasn't looking nostalgically at old photos; she simply didn't want me to know what she was up to. 'It's a site for older people to connect with each other. June told me about it so I thought I'd check it out.'

'Are you seriously considering dating someone?'

'It's not necessarily dating,' she says. 'It can be for companionship too.'

Yeah. Right.

'Have you been out with anyone?' I demand.

She blushes.

'Oh my God, Mum!' I cry. 'You have! You . . . Was it lunch?' I ask. 'When you went to Bay? You'd had wine!'

'I'm a grown woman, Roxy,' she says. 'I'm perfectly entitled to go out to lunch with another person.'

I'm speechless.

'But to put your mind at rest about that particular day, although I did go to lunch, it was with Donie Haughton.'

Donie is an old friend of Dad's. He was married for thirty years before leaving Marion because he's gay. He now lives in an apartment in Drumcondra. I feel slightly better knowing that he was Mum's lunch date.

'I'm a little surprised that you've joined a site,' I say. 'And it does seem very soon to be checking men out. A bit . . . a bit disrespectful to Dad,' I add awkwardly.

'Checking them out is all I'm doing,' says Mum. 'You

know, just scoping to see what sort of man is out there. A bit of market research before I ever think about dipping my toe in the water.'

I look at her in astonishment.

'I'm sixty-two,' she reminds me. 'I can't afford to waste my time.'

'Do you want to get married again?' I can't get my head around this. I really can't. My parents were rock solid. And it's not that I expected Mum to be in mourning forever, but I can't believe she'd want to marry another man.

'Ah, here.' She makes a face at me. 'You're getting a bit ahead of yourself there, Roxy. I'm not sure I'd be bothered with marrying anyone. But a bit of male company would be nice.'

Is 'male company' simply another way of saying 'sex'? I don't dare ask. I don't dare to think of my sixty-two-year-old mother in bed with a sixty-five-year-old man in orange cycling shorts!

'The trouble with this,' she adds as she swipes away from Dean's picture, 'is that all of the men are looking for women who are about twenty years younger than them. This site is supposed to be for over-fifties, but no matter how old they are, they all seem to want women in their forties.'

She's right, I realise, as I watch the names and photos go by. Tom (66) is looking for a woman in the 40–50 age bracket. So is Des (68). And Maurice (72). None of these potential boyfriends are oil paintings. Do they seriously believe that a woman of forty-five would be interested in them? I suppose they do. After all, they see it all the time in the movies. Some grizzled old actor is paired with a gorgeous young woman. I guess they think life is like that. I say this to Mum.

'I don't know what they're thinking.' Mum grins. 'You're nearly forty, for heaven's sake, and would you be on a site looking for men as old as your dad?'

I make a face. And then remind her that I'm only thirty-seven.

'They'd probably prefer a thirty-seven-year-old.' There's a hint of acid in her tone.

'Probably.' I'm continuing to skim through them, and not one – even Reg (78) – has specified a woman over the age of sixty.

'I keep telling myself it's ageist to think of them as too old for a forty-year-old,' says Mum. 'But they're being ageist about me! I didn't realise before that, as a woman, I've clearly been placed on the discards shelf.'

'Oh, Mum!' I put my arm around her and hug her. 'Of course you haven't. These guys – well . . .' I stop at Henry (69). His photo – clearly a selfie, from the weird angle and bad focus – has been taken in his kitchen. There's unwashed crockery on the worktop behind him, along with an open box of Rice Krispies and a badly wrapped loaf of bread. He describes himself as 'laid-back and positive but needing a woman in his life'. I'm wondering if he's actually looking for a cleaner. Or perhaps a carer.

'I think some of them are,' agrees Mum when I say this out loud. 'They're getting old and rickety and they need a fit young wan who might be able to push their wheelchair in the future.'

I burst out laughing. I can't help it.

'Though how they expect that to happen when their photos are so awful, I don't know,' she says. 'I got my hair and make-up done before I uploaded mine.'

'I thought you were only stalking them?' I say.

'Yes, but you have to put up your photo and details to join,' she explains. 'I haven't tried to connect with anyone yet.'

'Have they tried to connect with you?'

'I've had a few likes,' she admits.

'Have you liked them back?'

'No,' she says. 'I'm not that desperate.'

'At least it proves that their age requirement is aspirational,' I point out. 'If they only wanted the forty-five-year-olds, they wouldn't give you a like.'

'I think they do it when they get to the desperate stage,' confesses Mum. 'After they've been rejected by the forty-five-year-olds.'

I'm overcome with the giggles and it takes me a while before I can ask another question.

'Haven't you come across anyone at all?'

She sighs. 'Not really. Truth is, sweetheart, if I'm looking for anyone, I'm looking for someone like your dad. And I don't honestly think he's out there.'

'I'm sure there are other good men.' I realise that I've suddenly switched tack and am encouraging her in her quest.

'But they all come with a trainload of baggage,' she points out.

'It's not baggage,' I protest. 'It's life experience.'

She puts the iPad on the glass table, out of my reach. 'All I want is someone to go to dinner with from time to time. I'm not disrespecting your dad or anything. We talked about it before he died. He wanted me to be out there.'

He probably did. Dad wouldn't like to think of Mum being on her own in the house and not going out.

'Actually,' she says, 'women do much better than men

231

on their own. We have more friends. We're more open to going places and trying new things. I think that's why the men on the sites are so desperate. They need women to stop them skulking around at home. I read about it before. Women mourn, men replace.'

I think of Henry in his kitchen with the unwashed crockery and the packet of Rice Krispies. And then I think of Dave living at home while I was at Mum's. It only took five days for him to replace me with Julie Halpin, even if it was only a temporary measure.

I hope he hasn't replaced me in Wexford too.

That night, after Tom and Mica have gone to bed, I phone him. At first I don't say anything about my meeting with James Mallon, but it was the biggest thing of my day and in the end I tell him. He's shocked that I went to talk to someone without him, and I can hear the annoyance in his voice.

'You're in Wexford,' I point out. 'There's no way you could've come.'

'I'm not sure I would have wanted you to go,' he counters. 'We agreed you could drive till I got home, even though it's hugely inconvenient. We never said anything about having meetings with so-called experts about the future.'

'Driving till you got home was a suggestion, not an agreement,' I remind him.

'You're being totally unrealistic about this, Roxy.' I can feel his exasperation with me flowing down the line.

'James Mallon thinks it's a good business. And Alison has offered me a place on a course for start-ups.'

'Oh for crying out loud!' he says. 'You didn't need some

kind of consultant to tell you the business was sound. Your dad worked all the hours God sends to make it that way. And you don't need a course to tell you how to pick up passengers and charge them for it. But you do need me to remind you that it's not a good long-term proposition.'

'It'll be easier when the children go back to school,' I point out. 'Besides, I like working and—'

'Then look for part-time stuff in the mornings. There are loads of places hiring now. You could get something in one of the retail parks, maybe? Or at a checkout? Why don't you ask Debs if there's anything at B&Q?'

I don't want to work on a checkout. Or as a temp in a retail park. I've done that in the past, during my school holidays when I was employed by the café at the Clare Hall centre. I made sandwiches and coffee and cleared tables and it was fine but it wasn't a career. I want to do something more than that. Something that makes me feel valuable. And valued. I tell Dave that I don't want just any sort of work; I want to drive – I nearly say 'Dad's car' but I remind myself I'm a businesswoman and change it to 'the Merc' instead. Dave picks up on it all the same.

'Isn't it more that you don't want to let Christy go?' he asks.

'I'm tired of people thinking that,' I say. 'It's true I felt it a bit at first, and it's nice to continue his business, but I'm doing it for me, not him.'

'Only if everyone else helps out,' says Dave. 'Like they've been doing recently. But you can't expect your mum to step up to the plate forever. And Natalie has her own stuff to do. Your children have to be properly cared for.'

'Our children,' I correct him.

'You know what I mean, Roxy. Don't turn this into some male against female argument.'

But in some ways it is. Dad's business is a proper business. It provided for my mum, my brother and me. It's not a game. And yet because I'm doing it, it's become dispensable. Less important than Dave's plumbing. Which is also a good business, of course it is, and Dave works hard to provide for all of us. But in the early years he couldn't have done it without me, and without the money that my other work brought in. I don't see why I should feel bad for wanting my own thing.

'We'll work something out,' says Dave when I say nothing.

I hope he's right.

Chapter 18

I ring James Mallon the next day and ask him to do whatever paperwork needs to be done. We agree that the new name for the business will be StyleDrive, though until that's registered I continue to accept bookings for Christy's Chauffeurs. Meantime Alison sends me a link to the business start-up course. She says it's subsidised, though it still costs three hundred euro. I reckon it's money well spent, so I sign up.

This week, my driving is mainly in the city, which isn't as much fun as longer trips. The summer camps have started in, so I don't have to worry about Mica and Tom. I bring them to St Anne's Park each morning, and Oladele's mum, Grace, collects them in the evening, which is ideal; although Mum is picking them up on Friday because Oladele has a dental appointment. I think she was quite pleased when I asked her, as she hasn't seen them all week.

'You're quite determined then?' she said when I dropped in to see her in a break from airport pickups.

'Quite determined about what?'

'To keep the business going?'

'Yes,' I said.

'Don't let Dave feel like you're neglecting him.' She gave

235

me a warning look and I had to bite back the retort that Dave never worries about neglecting me when he's working. I reminded her that he was living the life in Wexford at that very moment, but I wondered if Mum used to worry that Dad might find someone else if she wasn't at home whenever he walked in the door. Does she think that if I'm not around, Dave will fall into the arms of Julie Halpin again?

'Dave has learned his lesson,' she said when I asked her. 'And as for your dad, I never had the slightest concern about him. It was that he worked mad hours and I liked to be there when he was home. That's why I preferred to work mornings. He was mostly in bed then.'

Dad used to do a lot of evening shifts as a taxi driver. We had to be quiet getting ready for school in case we woke him up.

'Which are you worried about more?' I asked. 'That I'm doing too much or that I'm pissing Dave off?'

'Neither!' Suddenly her tone was softer, more understanding. 'I simply don't want you chasing your tail to prove a point.'

'I'm not trying to prove a point.'

'When you were driving before, it was the odd time,' she said. 'You've only started talking about turning it into a proper job since Dave . . . well, you know. You've never felt the need to have a practically full-time job until now.'

'Mum, this has absolutely nothing to do with Dave cheating on me,' I insisted. 'It's about me wanting to step out for myself. It's about time I did. And that's it. I promise you.'

'So long as you know what you're doing,' she said.

I do. And I told her that very firmly indeed.

* * *

236

Julie Halpin walks out of her front door at the exact same moment as I'm getting into the car to go and pick up Thea Ryan for her charity lunch on Friday. I'm already looking in her direction and I don't want to glance away as though I can't meet her eye. She doesn't look away either and so the two of us are locked in some kind of death stare for what feels like an eternity.

I've forgotten all the cool and cutting things I planned to say to her and I'm afraid that if I open my mouth I'll call her a skanky bitch. Which might be cathartic but is neither cool nor cutting. In the end, it's Julie who speaks.

'Look, Roxy,' she says. 'Dave and I were a one-night thing. You don't need to worry. I'm seeing someone else.'

'How nice for you.' I suddenly find my voice, and the words come without me even thinking. 'Will I let his wife know?'

Then I get into the car and close the door behind me. I realise my hands are trembling as I start the engine and move out of the driveway. In the rear-view mirror I can see Julie still standing in her garden, looking after me.

I release the breath I didn't know I was holding. And then I smile a little. I didn't realise it before, but the need to say something, anything, to Julie Halpin had been hanging over me. And now it's done, and it's the start of getting over her as much as I've had to get over Dave.

By the time I reach Thea Ryan's house, I'm actually feeling quite pleased with myself. Thea notices, and tells me that I'm looking cheerful today. I don't say it's because I finally looked the woman my husband had slept with in the eye. Instead I tell her that I'm having a better day than I expected.

'I hope mine is as good.' She gets into the car and begins practising her speech to the osteoporosis people. It's funny and serious at the same time and I'm sure it will go down well. I also make a mental note to get Mum to have a bone density scan, to be on the safe side.

'Are you sure you don't need me to drive you later?' I ask when we arrive at the hotel and I open the door to let her out.

She shakes her head. 'I'm staying for a meeting with the organisers and then going home with my daughter,' she says.

I know, because she told me before, that her daughter is on the board of the charity. Thea's other children are equally successful.

It must be amazing to be part of such a talented family.

'Not always,' says Thea when I remark on this. 'We've had our problems like everyone else. Sometimes different people don't feel as valued as others. But I do my best to encourage all of my children, and now my grandchildren, to be the person they want to be. Otherwise what's the point? Does anyone want to live a life of regrets? I very much think not. I love how you're doing your own thing too, Roxy. I really enjoy being driven by you.'

'You do?'

'Absolutely. Leaving aside the niceness of having a woman doing the work, you're an excellent driver. What's your star sign?'

'Excuse me?'

'Your star sign,' repeats Thea.

'Um, Capricorn.'

'I knew it!' She looks at me triumphantly. 'Capricorns are

good at pacing themselves and they're practical, realistic people. That's you. And that's why you're a good driver.'

Is she right? She might be. I've never really bothered with astrology. But if I had to describe myself, I guess practical and realistic is probably close enough. It would be nice to be gifted and artistic, though.

'What about you?' I ask.

'I'm Pisces,' she says. 'A dreamer. Great for acting but not so hot behind the wheel.'

I laugh.

'Anyhow.' She pulls the light cashmere shawl she's wearing more tightly around her shoulders. 'I'd better go in and put my game face on. Can't show the nerves.'

'You don't look nervous,' I tell her.

'That's because I'm a good actress.' She winks at me and then walks confidently into the building.

I bet she'd have reduced Julie Halpin to absolute ribbons.

The next couple of weeks are brilliant and scary at the same time.

I buy a new dress for Alison's Start-Up for Success course, which takes place over two days at the Convention Centre on the quays. I asked her advice on what I should wear and she told me my navy suit and blouse would be perfectly fine, but that I could certainly bling it up a bit if I wanted so that I stood out a little more. She suggested going into Arnotts, where they're in mid-sale and where, she told me, I could find some really nice alternatives to the Claire Danes/ Carrie Mathison look.

And I do. After trying on dozens of different things, I come home with a better than half-price polka-dot dress by someone called Joseph Ribkoff, which fits me perfectly. The black dots are scattered and clustered across the cream and faded-pink background, and it looks really good on me. Because it's sleeveless I had to buy a jacket too. In fact I bought a couple, one in black and the other in a dusty pink that goes brilliantly with it. The jackets were also better than half-price and great value because of course I'll be able to wear them with jeans and trousers as well. I also bought a pair of Nine West courts embellished with black bows, which look great – they were new-season stock but worth every penny. And as I put my PIN into the machine, I felt proud that it was all my own hard work that meant I could afford it.

I model my new outfit for Mum and the children when I get home, and they tell me I look awesome.

'Totally gorgeous,' Mica informs me. 'Not like my mum at all.'

'I hope that's a good thing,' I say.

'You need to Instagram it for your business,' she says, and immediately takes a photo which she shares with me. Maybe her new way of earning pocket money can be as my social media guru!

'You've got your mojo back,' says Mum. 'You look great.'

'I feel great,' I say, and upload the photo with the caption 'Driver Does Dressing Up', which Leona both likes and comments on with a 'Wow!!!!!'

On the morning of the course, I accessorise my new outfit with my favourite dangly earrings (though I leave out my extra piercings) and a silver chain bracelet. I also layer on a little more of my pearl-grey eyeshadow than usual. I look at myself in the mirror and think that I'm definitely a go-getting

240

entrepreneurial woman. But even though I'm confident leaving the house, I can't help feeling nervous as I walk for the first time into the futuristic glass building where I've dropped so many business people off in the past. It's hard to believe that I'm the one going to a meeting here now. I check the screens in the big foyer to see where I should be and then take an escalator to the designated room. It's flooded with light from the almost-full-length windows that look out onto the Liffey, and is set out like a boardroom. There's water on the tables and notebooks and pens placed in front of each person's place. It feels serious and important and so do I. My heart is hammering with anticipation.

There are two other women at the workshop. Harriet is developing low-tech gadgets for older people; Miriam's business is involved in some kind of leasing. Miriam is by far the most assertive of us and her all-red outfit seems to give her extra authority. I'm glad I took Alison's advice and bought myself some empowering clothes. It's important to look the part. The twenty or so men on the course, naturally enough, are in suits.

I don't know what to expect from the day, but after a brief introduction by the coordinator (a woman from Alison's company), we're broken up into groups and given different scenarios and projects to work on. At first I'm reluctant to say anything, but then I find my voice, and even though the leader of my group is a man named Brian who never shuts up, I eventually manage to make some points that everyone else agrees on. I feel quite proud of myself.

I get to talk to lots of people at lunch and am astounded by how many different business ideas people come up with. I guess I've always felt that there are only a few good ideas and most of them have already been thought of. But Harriet's gadgets are really clever, and lots of the others have good products too. I should tell Natalie about this course, I think. She might get more ideas on how to expand her candle-making empire. I realise that I'm thinking of all our businesses as empires now, and not ironically!

By the time the sessions are over, I feel totally confident in myself and my ability to bring Christy's Chauffeurs – or StyleDrive as it now is – in a whole new direction. Obviously driving people is what I do, that doesn't change, but I've got ideas about marketing (our coordinator loved my Instagram posts) and promotions and customer feedback – everything!

I exchange contact details with everyone on the course and some of them say that they will definitely use my cars in the future. I've already given them promo codes for special discounts on their first trips. I've also arranged to meet with both Harriet and Miriam for coffee, so that we can share our experiences together.

I go home on a cloud of anticipation and excitement.

Dave, when he gets back from Wexford, is tight-lipped about my plans.

'Don't throw good money after bad,' he says, and I'm not sure if he's talking about the discounts I plan to offer or the polka-dot dress, which I don't think he likes. I haven't told him that I had to pay for the course in the first place. 'Anything you need to know about running a business, you can ask me.'

'If it doesn't work out, I'll be the first to admit it,' I say. 'I promise you. Our family won't suffer because of it. And look.' I open my laptop and show him the profit-and-loss account. 'I'm making good money. Gross, though,' I add. 'I have to account for petrol and depreciation and—'

'I know how it works,' he interrupts me. 'I have a business too, Roxy.'

'Sorry,' I say. 'It's exciting for me.'

'It's driving a car, that's all.'

I look around for my phone so that I can sync the info on the app to the laptop and get an accurate figure for the week. I can't see it anywhere, so I ask Dave to ring it for me, which he does. But I can't hear it ringing either and I start to panic. The phone is an important part of what I do. It has to be around somewhere.

Mica and Tom help me search the house, but none of us can find it.

'Maybe it's in the car,' says Mica. I'm about to say that it can't be because one of my routines is taking it from the wireless charger as soon as I get out. But then I remember that a client needed to charge his phone and I told him to take mine out. He's either kept it – disaster! – or, hopefully, left it in the side pocket of the passenger seat. He was sitting beside me in the car because I had three passengers on that trip.

'I'll look,' says Dave, which makes me feel good because it's as though he's taking a bit of ownership of StyleDrive and being less negative about everything. I realise it's a big change for him too, and I want him to see it can be a positive thing for both of us.

He's outside for quite a while, and I'm getting anxious. Losing the phone is a nightmare on a whole heap of levels. Then he walks back into the living room and lobs the phone in my direction.

'Oh, thanks,' I say. 'That's a relief.'

'What's this?' he asks, and I see he's holding the box containing the perfume that Ivo Lehane gifted me.

I've meant to take it out a number of times, but as I usually store things in the space under the armrest or in my own door pocket and don't need to open the glove compartment very often, I keep forgetting about it. In the back of my mind I've not been sure about it anyway, because even though Ivo gave it to me it still doesn't feel right to keep it. Perhaps I've been expecting him to ring up wanting me to collect him and asking for the perfume back, though I haven't heard from him since his aborted visit to Kildare.

I explain this to Dave and his eyes narrow.

'This guy gave you – a woman he doesn't know – a bottle of expensive perfume?'

'I told you. He bought it for his girlfriend but the bottle was too big for carry-on liquids,' I say again.

'He could've checked it in.'

I tell him about Ivo's computer and why he didn't check in his bag, and Dave looks at me with a sceptical expression.

'He gave you perfume,' he repeats. 'That's . . . that's—'

'What else was he going to do with it?' I interrupt him. 'He wasn't coming back and . . . well . . . what should he have done?'

'Not give it to someone else's wife!'

'Oh for heaven's sake.' I throw him an exasperated look. 'It was just a matter of convenience. I'm never going to see the man again.'

'Good,' says Dave. 'Because I forbid you to.'

I laugh. I can't help it. 'You can't forbid me to do anything. This isn't the nineteenth century.'

'I always thought there was something dodgy about him,' Dave says. 'And now I'm certain.'

'You thought he was a drug smuggler,' I remind him. 'Which he isn't. And nor is he trying to get into my . . .' I'm about to say 'knickers' when I realise that Mica, who went upstairs after Dave found the phone, is standing in the doorway. 'He's not trying to do anything,' I amend. 'And, like I said, he's unlikely to need me to drive him again.'

Dave picks up the remote and changes channel.

He doesn't say a word.

Chapter 19

Dave is home for good the following weekend. I hoped we might be able to spend a weekend with him in Wexford when the job ended, but Jimmy's family decamped to the house near the sea and, with a sudden spurt of glorious weather, there wasn't another place to be had. So any holiday plans will have to wait until mid-term, because the children will be back to school as soon as the summer camps end.

We all go to the local Chinese to celebrate his homecoming, which is fun in the way that our nights out used to be. I needed that time on my own, but it will be easier to cope with all the different things we want to do now that Dave's back. We've been in a sort of holding pattern, but now we're about to get on with our lives.

I've carefully arranged my driving schedule so that I'll always be home before him, which means he'll hardly even notice that I'm working. I've also plans to be a proper domestic goddess in the kitchen whenever I have the time. I'll still use the Gina Hayes cookbook, but I'll be substituting chips for the quinoa that seems to be an integral part of so many of her meal choices, and I'll ease up on the chopped salads too. Given that Dave has called it the Punishment

Book, I think introducing some carbs will keep him happy. It seems to work, as in his first week home neither he nor the children kick up a fuss about the subtle shift from heavier meals to lighter ones, and the almost complete disappearance of pizza from the menu. (The other advantage of the Gina Hayes regime is that – while not having made it to the Slim to Win sessions for ages – I've lost three kilos! I haven't lost my coffee habit, but I've stopped having muffins and croissants with them. All in all, I think, I'm doing well.)

In fact, I tell myself as I stack the dishwasher, Dave and I are both doing well. Sure, there are little niggles to be sorted, but we've gone through our worst time and come out the other side.

My phone buzzes and I pick it up.

Hi, says the text message. *I'm hoping you can drive me again. A somewhat different trip this time and I understand if it's not possible for you to do it so there's absolutely no pressure if it doesn't suit. I'm visiting some pharma companies in Ireland and need a pickup from the airport to Arklow next Wednesday. Then to be collected from there the following day and driven to Tipperary, and after that on to Cork. I'd like you to overnight in Cork, then bring me to Shannon for a flight to the States the following day. Obviously I'll cover your overnight costs. If it's all too awkward for you, perhaps you could recommend someone else.*

Ivo Lehane then suggests a price for the trip that's way more than I would have charged.

I stare at the message. There are, of course, a million different reasons why I shouldn't take this job, the main one being that Dave, like some kind of feudal overlord, forbade me from ever seeing Ivo Lehane again. But that was just him being all macho and alpha male. Surely when he hears how much I'm going to make, he'll change his mind. All the same, I can understand why he might freak out at me taking a job where I have to stay away overnight. Not that he has anything to worry about, but it would certainly be a novel experience. As for Tom and Mica, I don't think I've ever been away from them for a night before. I'm not sure that I want to be.

And yet. And yet. The money is great, the trip sounds interesting and I want to drive Ivo again. Of all my clients he's my favourite, and not simply because he opened up about his father and his family and made me feel almost like a friend. He's not my friend, I know that. But driving him is as easy as driving a friend. While saying no would be like letting a friend down. I never let my friends down.

It's taken me thirty seconds to persuade myself that I'm going to do this job. But I won't text back straight away. I don't want to appear as though I'm not having to consider it very carefully.

I wait for almost ten minutes before I type: *Of course. Delighted to. Text me your flight details when you have them.*

I press send, and then I go out to work.

As it's a day when I'm not home until mid-afternoon, Mum is in the house when I return. There's no sign of Tom or Mica – they've headed to Andrew's and Emma's respectively. I feel guilty about having missed them, though I know that their friends spend a lot of time in my house too. I've already started to worry about how they'll feel about me staying away for a whole night. Ivo has sent me his flight info, which

I've saved. I couldn't help feeling a little thrill as I did so. But still, my family should really come first.

The coordinator at the business start-up workshop talked about work–life balance. She also said there were times when we'd have to choose and that sometimes that choice might be difficult. What she should have said was that the choice was easy, but that living with it afterwards might be hard.

I text Mica to let her know I'm home again, and then Andrew's mum so that she can tell Tom. Fortunately, both of their friends live around the corner on Beechgrove Green, so they're not far away. Mica replies to me almost immediately saying that she, Emma and Oladele are watching a movie and that she'll be home when it's finished. Andrew's mum says that she'll send Tom home in half an hour.

'You look tired,' says Mum when I've finished texting and have shaken my hair out of its ponytail.

'Two complete circuits of the M50 will do that to you,' I tell her as I put the kettle on. 'Would you like a cuppa?'

She nods, and resumes her crocheting. There are three octopussies on the table, but the rest have finally been brought to the hospital.

'I'm getting faster,' she says when I comment on them. 'And it's nice to think that I'm doing some good.'

'It's fabulous.' There was a piece about the women who crochet them on TV the other week, as well as an article in the weekend paper. June appeared in both of them, but there was no sign of Mum.

'I prefer to keep a low profile,' she said. 'I don't want publicity.'

I laughed and told her it might be good for her internet dating site, and she (rather sniffly) retorted that it wasn't a dating site. And then she laughed too and said that maybe the old men might select her ahead of the forty-five-year-olds, based on her new celebrity status.

I suddenly think of Leona Lynch and wonder if she'd do a vlog about the octopussies. I don't imagine many of her followers would crochet them, but their mums or grans might. I suggest this to Mum, who says she'll talk to the group about it, and agrees that it would be nice to think that someone as young and well-known as Leona might get involved.

'I really should take it up myself,' I remark as I pour us both a cup of tea but don't add any biscuits to the table. 'It would be a far better use of my time than playing games on my iPad when I'm waiting for people.'

'So how has the driving been going lately?' asks Mum, who is very interested in all the stuff I learned at the workshop, and as a result has been more gung-ho about the business.

'Better than I ever could have expected,' I reply. 'Dad had so many contacts, and all of them are really happy to give me work. Plus I've done stuff for one of the people I met at the Convention Centre. And I could get an exclusive contract for some kind of hi-tech manufacturing company in Leopardstown if I wanted, but that would mean only driving for them so I'd prefer not to.'

'Wouldn't that be better than what you're doing now?' she asks. 'Wouldn't it give you a degree of certainty and allow you to plan your time?'

'I can plan it now.' I give her a considered look as I think about next week and Ivo Lehane's trip. 'Is it imposing on you too much? Because we can make changes.'

'I adore spending time with my grandchildren,' says Mum. 'It's not a hardship, Roxy. All I care about is that you're happy with what you're doing.'

'I am.' I hug her and she hugs me in return.

'Anyhow, what about you?' I ask. 'Any news on the dating front despite you not being on TV?'

She allows the topic to be changed and makes a face at my question. 'I told you, I'm not looking to date someone, just a bit of companionship. It's too soon to even think of anything else.'

'Any news on the companionship front, then?' I amend.

'I did go out with someone,' she admits.

'Oh, who? One of the men I saw? Not the guy with the messy kitchen, I hope!'

'Are you off your head? No!' she exclaims. 'This was an older gentleman who was specifically looking for an older lady. I bet he was swamped,' she adds. 'He didn't respond to me for days after I messaged him.'

'What was he like? Where did you go? Did you enjoy yourself?'

'It was very posh,' says Mum. 'He brought me for afternoon tea in the Merrion.'

The Merrion is one of Dublin's most luxurious hotels. It's popular with American visitors, as well as with politicians from both Ireland and abroad. I've done quite a few pickups and drop-offs there.

'Of course it's ridiculously expensive for a few finger sandwiches and pastries,' continues Mum. 'But the setting is lovely and everything was very elegant.'

'What's the man's name? What does he do? Are you seeing him again?' I pepper her with more questions.

'Diarmuid. He's retired. Possibly.' She ticks the answers off on her fingers.

'How old is he?' I ask.

'Sixty-nine.'

'A young fellah, so.' I grin. 'Ooh, Mum, this is exciting.'

'Let's see if I hear from him again,' she says. 'He probably has so many offers that he doesn't need to drink at the same well twice. It's no laughing matter,' she adds when I chortle. 'It's a minefield out there.'

It would have been for me too, I think, if I hadn't gone back to Dave. There are no adults without baggage. And it's not that you don't want people not to have lived, but the idea of adding their problems to your own is simply too daunting to consider. At least it would be for me. If I had to think about it. Which, fortunately, I don't.

Chapter 20

As I suspected, Dave goes mental when I tell him about the Ivo Lehane job.

'I told you I didn't want you driving for that man any more!' he cries. 'Picking him up from the airport would be bad enough. But now you're talking about spending the effing night with him. Are you out of your mind? D'you think I'm out of mine to allow it? What if he's using you as a cover for one of his drug drops?'

'First of all, I'm not spending the effing night with him, as you put it,' I say. 'I have to overnight, yes. But it's hardly sleeping with the man. As for him being a drug dealer – get a grip, Dave.'

'It's you who needs to get a grip,' he retorts. 'How much of a fool d'you think I am? What's going on between you and him?'

'Absolutely nothing,' I say. 'Other than he's the best-paying client I've ever had.'

'What type of client?' Dave's tone is pure acid. 'Paying over the odds. Giving you bottles of perfume. Asking you to stay with him. I'm entitled to know what exactly it's all about.'

I guess Ivo's generosity could be misconstrued. But there's nothing between us. Nothing at all.

'I'll explain it to you in a way you'll understand, then, shall I?' I ask. 'You'll never be in the same position I was and come home to find me in bed shagging him. Because Ivo and I have a business relationship. And because I'd never break your damn heart the way you broke mine.'

'Every time I argue with you from now on you're going to bring that up, aren't you?' Dave's voice is quivering with anger. 'No matter what it is. No matter what you've done. Nothing will ever be as bad as my single mistake.'

'I don't always bring it up,' I say. 'Only when you're falsely accusing me of doing the same thing.'

'You are *not* going to take this job,' says Dave.

'Yes, I am.'

'You'll be sorry if you do.'

'I'll be sorrier if I don't. And so will you. It's easy money, Dave.'

'Selling the car like your dad wanted would be a damn sight easier,' he says. 'And our lives would be exactly the way they were before, only better.'

'I don't want them to be exactly the way they were before!' I retort. 'In fact, mine is already a good deal better.'

'Thanks for that,' says Dave. 'All the years, all the time I've put into doing my best for you and the kids, and you fling it back in my face.'

I'm chastened by the hurt in his voice. I can understand why he's upset. But why can't he understand me?

'I'm telling you not to do this,' Dave says. 'I won't tell you again.'

My chastened feelings have only lasted a minute.

'You can't tell me anything, Dave McMenamin. You can ask.'

'Oh for God's sake!'

And he goes to the pub even though it's Saturday afternoon and he's supposed to be bringing Tom to his soccer match.

I know I should call Ivo Lehane and say I can't drive him after all. But I don't. After bringing Tom to his match and cheering him along from the sidelines, and then collecting Mica from her ballet class (it's her second lesson, and although she wasn't interested at first, she's been unexpectedly seduced by the tutu!), I drop around to Mum's.

The children go upstairs to have their showers while I sit in the living room and watch her crochet. But she knows there's something wrong and she puts it to one side and asks. I take a deep breath and tell her about Ivo's request.

'Overnight!' Mum's eyes widen. 'He's paying for you to stay overnight!'

'Now you sound like Dave,' I say. 'He's paying for my accommodation. He's not asking me to sleep with him.'

'How do you know?' she demands.

'For heaven's sake, he's given me an itinerary.' I take the printout of the Arklow–Tipperary–Cork–Shannon trip out of my bag and hand it to her. 'There isn't time for illicit sex.'

'That means nothing,' she says as she glances at it and then gives it back to me. 'Honestly, Roxy, I can't help thinking you're being incredibly naïve.'

'He has a girlfriend!' I exclaim.

'So what?'

255

'Why are you so ready to believe this is some kind of dangerous liaison?' I ask. 'Why can't you simply accept that it's a brilliantly paid job?'

'Because men are men,' she says. 'Even the good ones.'

'Like Dave, you mean?' I ask. 'The good husband who slept with the neighbour? Or like Dad, who used your money to pay off a woman he might have got pregnant?'

Mum's lips tighten.

'That was uncalled for,' she says.

'I don't think so.' I pick up a little octopussy and play with its tentacles. 'Dave did what he did. Dad did what he did. And because of them, you're prepared to completely discount me and my judgement and say that I'm being duped by my own client. It's not very trusting, is it?'

Mum looks at me in silence. I continue to fidget with the crocheted toy.

'I'm sorry,' she says finally. 'You're right. I'm making it all about him and not about you. I know you. I do trust you.'

Tears flood my eyes and I don't manage to blink them all away in time. She hands me a tissue. I put the octopussy on the table, then wipe my eyes and blow my nose.

'He's a decent man and a good client,' I say. 'And I want to do this.'

'I see that.'

'Dave is annoyed because he thinks I'm not respecting all his hard work over the years,' I say after I give my nose another blow. 'But I've always respected him. He's the one who's not respecting me.'

'So do you want me to stay over while you're away?' she asks.

'Or maybe have Tom and Mica here?' I suggest. 'Whatever upsets Dave the least.'

I resent that I have to think about his feelings.

But I'm glad that my mum is onside.

Dave and I don't discuss the job at all over the rest of the weekend or even the following week. There's an edgy atmosphere in the house, which I try to deflect by being manically cheerful.

'Are you all right, Mum?' asks Mica the night before Ivo arrives.

'Of course, why shouldn't I be?'

'You keep laughing,' she says. 'About silly things.'

'Oh. Well I'm a very silly mother in that case, aren't I?' Even to my own ears I sound like a demented hyena.

Dave, who's engrossed in a game on his iPad, doesn't even look up.

Fortunately neither Mica nor Tom seems to have linked my job and their upcoming stay at their grandmother's (which they both elected over Mum coming here) with my hysterical silliness. But Dave does, I'm sure, and I'm afraid he thinks it's because I'm excited about seeing Ivo again. I'd like him to be OK with this, but I know it's impossible. And yet I can't do what he wants and back out.

On Wednesday morning, as he leaves for work, Dave doesn't kiss me goodbye. I decide not to get upset about it. Instead I go upstairs and get dressed in my navy suit and white shirt. I had my hair cut yesterday and it's still gleaming and silky. I pull it back into its ponytail, hold it in place with some clips, fasten my silver chain around my neck and finally spritz myself with Annabel's expensive perfume. I look in the mirror. Very *Homeland*. Very professional. And at the same time, very demure.

I track Ivo's flight on my phone and leave for the airport when it's close to landing. As I pull up outside the terminal, I see him already there and waiting for me. I get out of the car.

'Roxy,' he says. 'Good to see you again.'

'Flight OK?' I ask.

'Not bad,' he says. 'Glorious day.'

And, for the time of year, it is. The sky is a crisp blue with only a couple of bright white clouds, the sun is warm, and it feels more like late summer than the beginning of autumn. I open the boot of the car and he puts his wheelie bag inside. I'm not sure where he wants to sit, but I feel that I should be ultra-professional and so I move around to the rear passenger door. Ivo waits for me to open it.

'Music or silence?' I switch on the satnav, where I've already entered the address of the Arklow business he's going to.

'Silence,' he replies. 'I need to go through some paperwork.'

'Of course.'

I put the car into gear and we glide forward.

Dave doesn't need to worry about a thing. Ivo has returned to professional mode. And so have I.

The drive to Arklow, which takes a little over an hour, is beautiful. Although the N11 can be busy, it also runs through some of Ireland's most stunning countryside, and today, in its early autumn glory, it's magnificent. The leaves on the trees are copper and gold and the surrounding fields are a deep vibrant green. In the distance, shimmering in and out of view, is the steel blue of the Irish Sea. I wonder if being able to flit between Brussels and Amsterdam and Paris on a whim compensates Ivo Lehane for not being able to see views like this every day. I'm not sure it could.

Arklow itself is a pretty little town on the banks of the Avoca river, with brightly painted shops lining the streets. The business Ivo is visiting is on the outskirts, accessed from a winding country road where the trees on either side form a dappled canopy overhead. But the building itself is a modern glass and steel structure, a sudden surprise as we round the corner and see it standing there in the middle of all the greenery.

I pull up outside the main door and get out of the car.

'That was a beautiful drive, thank you.'

I didn't think Ivo was aware of it. Any time I glanced into the rear-view mirror, he was engrossed in his iPad.

'I presume you're staying here tonight?' I say. 'In the town? Do you need me to bring you to your hotel after your meeting?'

'I'll be here all day, so I'm hoping they'll organise transport and don't abandon me here in the middle of nowhere.' Ivo grins. 'It's a bit murder-mystery, don't you think? Out-of-towner ends up murdered in deserted factory surrounded by cows.'

I laugh as I glance towards the cattle in the nearby fields. It's the paradox of Ireland. Big business and old traditions side by side.

'Hopefully you haven't come all this way to be murdered. How would they do it?' I add. 'Hit you over the head with a hammer, or feed you one of their latest drugs?'

He pretends to consider the question. 'Dump me in a slurry pit,' he decides, with a nod towards the cows.

'Ugh.' But I laugh. We've been very professional until

now, but I'm sliding into the easiness I've always felt with him again. 'Take care, so.'

'I will.'

'Where will I pick you up tomorrow? And what time?'

'Early if possible.' He looks a little concerned. 'Perhaps I should've organised for you to stay over tonight too, but I was thinking you'd rather be with your kids.'

'Of course I would,' I say. 'No problem. Whatever time suits you.'

His meeting in Tipperary is at ten thirty. I've already checked out the journey from Arklow, which will take about two and a half hours. I suggest collecting him at seven thirty, and he nods. He's staying at one of the newer hotels in the town, he says, and then adds that he hadn't thought about how long it would take to get to places and asks if I'm sure I'm OK with this.

'Ivo – Mr Lehane – this is my job,' I remind him. 'If you want to drive to Donegal in the middle of the night, that's OK with me.'

He grins. 'Hopefully not.'

Then he extends the handle of his wheelie case and goes about his business.

The journey back to Dublin takes longer than the journey to Arklow, mainly because there's so much traffic heading towards the city. But I still enjoy it and sing along to Dolly and Shania as I stick to the speed limit and don't allow myself to be aggravated by other drivers doing stupid things.

I'm back just in time for Mica and Tom coming home from school, and make them a Gina Hayes pitta pocket for their lunch. Then I go upstairs and pack my travel bag for my overnight stay in Cork with Ivo Lehane. I'm beginning to understand why Dave is so annoyed with me, because I'm ridiculously excited at the idea of a night away from home. Obviously not a night away having sex with another man, as he thinks, but a night away being me. I wish he could understand it. I really do.

But he's still sullen when he gets in later in the evening, and although I've cooked a couple of chicken breasts in a lemon sauce accompanied by peas and roast potatoes for his meal, he does no more than grunt thanks to me when he's finished.

Later still, Debs phones and I get up from the sofa where I've been sitting (my legs curled under me instead of across Dave's lap as I sometimes do) and go into the kitchen for a chat.

'What does Dave think?' she asks when I tell her about my trip to Tipperary and Cork.

Everyone always wants to know what Dave thinks! But I very much doubt that his friends ask him what I think whenever he has to go away for work. It's a given that I'll go with the flow. Which I always do. So Dave's views on my work are irrelevant. It should be entirely up to me. But even as I say the words aloud to Debs, I know I'm being disingenuous. It matters a lot. And I'm living the consequences of it right now, with his thunderous face and stony silences. But I tell Debs he's fine with it and that Mum is looking after the children, so she turns the topic to a girls' night out with Michelle and Alison, and I say that it would be great fun and that I haven't seen Michelle in ages.

'We haven't been out in ages,' Debs says. 'We're getting old.'

'Speak for yourself,' I joke, and Debs says I'm right, we're not old, just busy, and I agree with that. I tell her that I'll leave it up to her to arrange the night out, but to count me in.

Dave doesn't look up when I return to the living room. He's changed the channel from the documentary we were both pretending to be engrossed in to darts on Sky Sports. We used to joke about darts hardly being a sport, what with the beer bellies on some of the competitors, and Dave would say it was the sort of sport he was prepared to take up when he was older, and I'd laugh and say that he was hopeless at throwing things, and he'd joke that he could throw me over his shoulder any time and . . . It's my fault that we don't have these conversations any more.

I've changed everything.

Yet I'm not the one who slept with the next-door neighbour, am I?

262

Chapter 21

When I wake up the following morning, I slide gingerly out of bed so that I don't disturb Dave, who's still asleep. But by the time I've had my shower, he's awake.

'Ridiculous hour of the morning to be going out,' he says.

At least he's talking to me. Last night he rolled away as soon as I climbed under the duvet.

'I know,' I reply. 'But needs must.'

I'm waiting for him to say that there's no need for me to be going out at all, but he doesn't. Instead he checks that Mica and Tom will be going to Mum's after school and staying the night with her.

'Yes,' I say. 'I've packed overnight bags for them. They're very excited.'

'Huh,' says Dave.

'And she loves the idea of having them,' I add.

'Huh,' he says again.

'I'm off now.' I did my make-up in the bathroom and dressed while talking to him.

'Drive safely,' he says, and then goes into the bathroom himself and closes the door behind him.

OK, he's been cool, but at least he's speaking to me, so

that's something. I tiptoe into the children's rooms and kiss Tom goodbye – he doesn't move – and then float a kiss in Mica's direction. I know they'll be happy at Mum's, but I have to clamp down on the feeling that I'm putting myself and what I want to do ahead of them. And then I tell myself that it's fine, they'll hardly notice I'm not there. But what if something happens? What if they need me? What if Mum can't cope? I know I'm being ridiculous. Mum raised Aidan and me. Mum dealt with the fallout from Dad's relationship with Estelle. Mum is like me. She can cope with anything.

And Dave is here. He can cope too.

It's dark outside. Obviously. It's a quarter past six in the morning and the sun doesn't rise for another hour. But I like the quiet of the early-morning roads under the yellow street lamps. I like driving past houses and seeing the square of light in the upstairs room that means someone is getting out of bed. I like wondering about their lives and what the day ahead holds for them. I like the bright green, orange and red of the traffic lights and the pearly white headlamps of an oncoming car. And I like my latest audio mix, Imelda May and Ciara Sidine singing about love and loss and everything in between.

Although dawn is on the horizon, the sun still hasn't risen by the time I arrive at Ivo's hotel. I made good time, but he's already in reception waiting for me. There's no stubble on his face today; he's as groomed as I've ever seen him. I think he may have had his navy suit pressed overnight, because it's sharp and wrinkle-free. His shirt is crisp and white. He looks steely and businesslike but he gives me a wide smile.

'Good to see you,' he says. 'I hope the drive down was OK?'

'Couldn't have been better.' I smile back. 'Are you ready to go?'

He nods and follows me out to the Merc. This time he doesn't wait for me to open the rear door but walks around to the passenger side and gets in himself. Are we back to a slightly less formal relationship? I hope so.

'Silence or music?' I put my usual question to him.

'I've done everything I need to do for this meeting,' he says. 'Music would be nice.'

I switch on the audio, forgetting that it's still Imelda and Ciara, but when I offer to change it, he tells me he likes it, and so we travel for the first half-hour or so listening companionably.

'Is that your sort of music?' he asks when the mix finally ends.

I wonder if saying yes will diminish me in his eyes. He's probably some kind of classical buff himself. But except for the popular classics I played for him before, I haven't a clue. So I admit to my country addiction and he laughs and tells me he's a big Shania Twain fan.

'Really?'

'Had a poster of her on my wall when I was younger,' he confesses.

I put on her greatest hits and when she starts belting out 'Man, I Feel Like A Woman', we sing along while the sun rises behind us and we close in on our first stop of the day.

Like in Arklow, the business premises where Ivo has his meeting is outside the town, but this time in an industrial estate. It's grey and generic, with no surrounding fields of cows and no canopies of trees in the distance.

'I'll be an hour or so,' says Ivo. 'I'll text you when I'm done.'

'Fine,' I say.

He nods and walks into the building while I turn the car around. The Rock of Cashel, with its gothic cathedral and tower, stands tall, looking over the town, and I head towards it. I find a small coffee shop that is busy with a mixture of townspeople and tourists, and before I go inside, I take a photograph of the Rock to upload to my Instagram account. Then I order a large cappuccino and a muffin (the deal of the day) and call Mum.

'Everything OK?' I ask.

'Why wouldn't it be?'

'I mean, you're still all right for looking after the children tonight?'

'Of course I am.'

'Dave hasn't been in touch?'

'Why would he?'

'No reason.'

'Are *you* OK?' She turns my words back on me.

'Yes.'

'It was an early start.'

'I like being up early.'

'Stay safe on the roads, Roxy,' she says. 'Your family needs you.'

Is she trying to lay a guilt trip on me?

'And have a great time,' she adds.

'I'm working.'

'I know. But have a good time anyway.' Her voice is warmer.

'I'll do my best.'

'Love you,' she says.

'Love you back.'

I open Instagram and edit the Rock of Cashel photo. I'm getting good at this, and when I'm finished, it looks gloomier and more lowering than in real life, but also much more dramatic. After I've uploaded it, I also take a photo of my cappuccino and muffin and upload that too, captioning it 'Driver's Elevenses'. As I sip the coffee and nibble at the muffin (the first I've had in ages, and much sweeter than I'm used to lately), I scroll through my photos. Most of them are ones I've taken when I've been out on jobs, and are now part of my Instagram story, but over the last few weeks I've taken plenty of Tom and Mica that I never share. I love having photos of my children with me. It keeps them close.

I have to scroll quite a way back to find the photograph of the boy with the football. It continues to nag at me that I might be looking at my half-brother, and I feel a sick sensation in the pit of my stomach when I zoom in on his face and think that he might have lived his entire life not knowing we exist. And then I remind myself that we don't know he exists either, and that I'm probably making links where there aren't any.

And yet I still feel a pull towards him. I really do. Or maybe what I feel is a pull back to a time when everything in my life was simple and I never had to worry about anyone except myself.

I close my photo stream and then send a message to Dave telling him I'm in Tipperary. *The heart of the bog*, I joke. Dave, like me, is a city person through and through. He doesn't reply, which isn't a big deal, because when he's on a job he's notorious for ignoring his phone.

I finish the coffee, use the loo, and then walk towards the Rock. It's seriously impressive and it's easy to imagine how it would have been a major fortress hundreds of years ago. I wonder if I've time for a quick tour, but even as I'm studying one of the information leaflets, my phone rings. It's Ivo Lehane saying that he's ready to leave, so I abandon the Rock and walk quickly to the car.

As I pull up outside the building, Ivo emerges alongside a tall woman with dark hair and impressively geeky glasses. I get out of the car and wait between the front and rear passenger doors while they exchange some last-minute pleasantries. He moves to the back of the car and I'm about to open the rear door for him when he shrugs and says, 'Front, if you don't mind.'

He gets in beside me.

'Good meeting?' I ask.

'Excellent,' he says. 'I'm really excited about the vaccine they're working on. It has great potential. My job is to make sure the finance is in place.'

Hah! Vaccines. There you go, Dave McMenamin! Not that I truly believed for a second in the drug-smuggling theory, but still.

'Was it your idea or theirs?' I glance at him.

'Huh?'

'Coming here for meetings. Your idea or your company's?'

'We talked about it earlier in the year and I wasn't that keen. But coming back and forward the last few weeks made me realise I was being stupid.'

'Have you been in touch with Lizzy at all?' I ask the question as ultra-casually as I can.

'It took a week,' he says. 'She rang me and apologised.'

'Does that make you feel better?'

'It makes me feel like a bit of a dick, to be honest,' he admits. 'I shouldn't have made you turn around. I was rude to her. And to you.'

'You weren't rude to me,' I say. 'You bought me coffee.'

'I made you stop for coffee,' he reminds me. 'When you would've preferred to get home.' He sighs. 'Sometimes I wonder why I'm so good at the business stuff and so bad with people.'

'You're not bad with people.' I join the motorway and speed up.

'It's generally accepted that I am,' Ivo says. 'I have a bit of a reputation for being cool and aloof at the company.'

'If you know that, then why are you cool and aloof?' I ask.

'I don't feel that I am,' he replies. 'But I don't . . . Well, I'm not that interested in what's going on with people I work with. As long as they do the job, that's all that matters.'

'It's lovely to be recognised for doing a good job,' I say. 'And I'm sure it's a lot better to work in a place where people are nice to each other.'

'You're right, of course,' he says. 'But then you're in a people business. You have to be nice.'

'I can be cool and aloof too,' I tell him.

'I doubt it.' There's amusement in his voice. 'You're too . . . too interested and too interesting to be cool.'

'I promise you I can be,' I tell him. 'I could do this entire journey in complete aloofness if that's what you wanted.'

'Actually, no,' says Ivo. 'I like chatting to you.'

'Or would you rather I put on some more music?' I ask.

'I also have Dolly Parton and Taylor Swift for your country delight.'

He laughs. 'Can we keep talking?'

'Sure.'

'Tell me about yourself.'

'I've done that already.'

'I know that you're married with two children,' he says. 'But tell me about your life and this job.'

So I do. Obviously I leave out the bit about Dave sleeping with Julie Halpin. I also leave out the fact that he's raging with me about driving Ivo. I do, however, tell him about Mum's obsession with crocheting and her efforts at online dating.

'She sounds great, your mum,' says Ivo.

'She is,' I say. 'She's all about picking yourself up and starting over again. And not letting things get you down.'

I think about sharing the story of Dad and Estelle with him, but that's Mum's private life, and no matter what, Ivo is still a client. So instead I say that she'd really like a paying job to go along with the octopussies and reading to patients at the hospice, but that she knows she's too old.

'And yet she's still looking after me and my children,' I say. 'It's definitely true that a mother's work is never done.'

'I guess you'll be the same for yours,' says Ivo.

'Probably.' I smile at him. 'No, definitely.'

'I might see if our company can offer some sponsorship for the octopussy knitting . . .' He suddenly starts laughing and doesn't stop, which makes me laugh too.

'Sorry,' he says. 'It's just that "octopussy knitting" is a phrase I never thought I'd say.'

'I'm sure they'd be delighted with some sponsorship,' I tell him when I stop laughing myself. 'Thank you.'

We continue in a companionable silence, and when I next glance at the satnav we're not far from Cork. I say this to Ivo, who suggests we go straight to the hotel and check in.

'I'll be most of the afternoon at the plant,' he says. 'And I'm sure you could do with a bit of chill time. So you can go back to the hotel after dropping me. I'll call you to pick me up – I'm having dinner with some of the management team there later this evening.'

The hotel where we're staying is the Castlemartyr Resort, which, from the website, seems pretty impressive. Like so many hotels now it has a golf course and a spa, and although I haven't said anything to either Dave or Ivo, I'm hoping to spend a bit of time lying around the indoor pool. I've packed my swimsuit specially.

Actually, it's not surprising Dave is pissed at me. He's never had a job that included staying in a five-star hotel.

The first issue that arises when we arrive is that a valet asks for the car keys so that he can park the Merc. I'm not sure if I'm supposed to stay with the car or follow Ivo into the stately home building. He's the one who takes charge, saying that we're checking in but have to go out almost immediately and so would it be possible to leave the car nearby. The valet tells us not to worry, that we can move it to one side while we check in, and Ivo nods at him in an authoritative way.

As I take Ivo's bag out of the boot, I sense the valet looking at me and trying to figure out the relationship between us. But I don't have much time for thinking, because Ivo has already taken his bag from me and is striding into the tiled foyer. I follow him, pulling my own somewhat tattier wheelie case behind me.

Dave and I have stayed in resort hotels before – they're great when you have kids – but never anywhere like this. There's an air of quiet luxury about it that's completely new to me, and as with the valet outside, I'm suddenly intimidated. Ivo isn't, though. He walks up to the reception desk and begins to check us in.

Which is when I have a sudden sinking feeling in the pit of my stomach. What the hell am I doing here? Why on earth would Ivo Lehane want me to drive him to a place like this and spend the night? Dave might not have been right about the drug smuggling, but perhaps he is about everything else. And perhaps Mum is too. Maybe this is part of some kind of crazy seduction scene and I'm a fool not to have realised it before now. After all, nobody needs to treat their driver to a room in a lavish hotel. A normal businessman wouldn't have bothered with a driver at all. He'd have taken trains or cabs or . . .

'Here's your key.' Ivo turns and hands me the electronic card. 'We're both on the second floor.'

What the hell is wrong with me? Ivo Lehane doesn't want to seduce me. And I don't want to be seduced. I'm not Dave, after all.

Ivo leads the way to the lift. I'm conscious that we're standing shoulder to shoulder in the confined space. I can smell his warm, spicy aftershave. I wonder if he recognises the perfume I'm wearing. Annabel's perfume.

The lift doors sigh open and we step out.

'I'm two doors down from you.' He stops outside my

room and glances at his watch. 'Is it OK to drop our bags and go? We're a bit tight for time now.'

I nod wordlessly, then unlock the door and step into the room.

Bloody hell.

It's amazing.

The carpet is so thick I'm literally sinking into it with every step. The room is decorated in shades of cream and gold and there's an enormous king-sized bed with a matching coverlet and ottoman at the foot. There are fresh flowers on a mahogany table beside the full-length window, and the door to the bathroom reveals something Dave would be proud of – marble walls and floors, a double sink and an impressive-looking shower.

This is how the other half live.

And just for today, I, Roxy McMenamin, am living it with them.

I'm Cinderella, although I have to remind myself that I'm actually the coach driver, not the princess.

There's a knock at my bedroom door and my heart does a backwards flip.

I hurry out and Ivo is standing there.

'Ready?' he asks.

'Just a sec.' I close the door in his face and use the bathroom. The soap is lovely and frothy, the towels soft and fluffy.

'Sorry about that,' I say as I step out into the corridor again.

The valet appears from nowhere when we reach the reception area and hands me the keys of the Merc. The car is parked a few metres from the entrance, and for a moment I almost forget to open the door for Ivo. Actually, it wouldn't have mattered. He is already on the way towards opening it himself before hanging back and waiting for me to do it.

'Is your room all right?' he asks as soon as we've moved away.

'It's amazing.' I glance at him. 'I'm not sure you should be paying for it.'

'Huh?' He turns to me. 'I'd hardly expect *you* to pay for it given I'm dragging you down here.'

'Not dragging,' I say. 'You're my client. So really, the cost of the hotel room should be part of my expenses. Like petrol.'

'Don't be daft,' he says.

'Or perhaps I should be somewhere a little less . . .'

'Less what?'

'It's very luxurious,' I say.

'It's a nice hotel,' he admits. 'But I have a rule about staying in hotels. They have to be at least as good as my apartment. Which, being honest with you, is pretty nice.'

'I like the bathrooms to be as good as the one I have at home,' I say. 'Which is a lot to live up to because Dave's a bathroom maestro.'

Ivo laughs. 'I hope this one is up to scratch.'

'More than,' I assure him. 'The whole place is lovely. And I have to admit that the room is absolutely amazing.'

'I'm glad you like it. The views are spectacular, don't you think?'

I didn't have time to check. I will, later.

I pull up at yet another anonymous building in another anonymous industrial estate and let him out of the car.

'Text me when you need me,' I say.

274

'Sure. Actually . . .' He turns back to me and shrugs. 'Don't worry about it. Like I said, I'm having dinner with Bob and his colleagues at the hotel this evening. I can get him to drive me.'

'But I'm sure you'll want to change and freshen up.'

'I'm not a woman.' He grins. 'I'll put on a clean shirt. That'll be me done. Honestly, Roxy, take some time out. Have a glass of wine or something. Get a massage in the spa. Relax. You've done a lot of driving today.'

'If you're sure.'

'Certain,' says Ivo.

'OK, then.'

'Oh, Roxy . . .' He calls me back.

'Yes?'

'Charge it to the room,' he says, and then turns away.

The valet takes the car from me and I forget about it and him as I walk back to my beautiful room. That last throw-away comment of Ivo's about charging things to the room has made me wonder all over again if he has an ulterior motive in having me stay here. And yet why would he? All the same, I'm totally paranoid and have no idea what I should be doing.

So I call Debs.

'It's amazing,' I tell her. 'The hotel, the room, everything. The total five-star experience.'

'Wow, Roxy.' Her voice is envious. 'You've so fallen on your feet with this client.'

'I know,' I say. 'But . . .'

'What?'

'What does he expect from me in return?' I ask.

'Decent driving?' she suggests. And then, when I don't say anything, she cuts to the chase and asks if I think he's after a bit on the side.

'I don't think he's the sort,' I say. 'Of course I didn't think Dave was the sort before he copped off with Julie Halpin.' I rub the back of my neck. 'I can't help feeling as though all this luxury needs a pay-off. Not,' I add, 'that I'd necessarily be his kind of pay-off. It's just that I'm being treated like I've never been treated before, but he's the one who's supposed to be the client. Though why would he want me as a pay-off, Debs? He has a gorgeous girlfriend.'

'Gorgeous girlfriends are no guarantee that men won't go offside,' says Debs. 'Is there some kind of big corporate thing happening there later? Where they ship in a load of women in short skirts for the men? Did he ask you to bring anything special to wear?'

'No. And I'm wearing my trousers and jacket,' I tell her. 'I'd hardly fit in in some kind of chicken-ranch scenario.'

She laughs, and so do I, which makes me feel a lot better.

'Does he make you uncomfortable?' Her tone is suddenly serious. 'Because if so, Roxy, you could do a flit. Leave a message, say you had some urgent family business to see to. I'm sure he'll manage to get back to wherever he's going.'

'He's never made me feel uncomfortable,' I say. 'In fact, he's one of the easiest people I've ever driven. He's fun when he wants to be. And he's quite charming, too.'

'And yet you're afraid he wants you to put out for him,' says Debs. 'Which isn't all that charming, is it? But if you wanted to . . . well, I wouldn't blame you, either. A bit of revenge sex with your hot client would put Dave in his place.'

'I don't want revenge sex,' I protest as I try to banish the image of Ivo Lehane naked in the room with me. 'It's not about that.'

'What's it about then?' asks Debs.

'I really don't know.'

'I'm not going to encourage you to cheat on Dave,' Debs says. 'But what happens on the road stays on the road.'

'I don't want anything to happen on the road,' I tell her. 'And I certainly don't want to cheat on Dave.'

She stays silent.

'I don't!' I repeat as forcefully as I can. 'Honest to God, Debs, it's bad enough that Dave thinks there's something going on without you encouraging me.'

'Does he? Really?'

I explain about the perfume.

'Jesus, Roxy, no wonder you think the luxury hotel is part of a great seduction.'

'But the perfume was totally accidental.'

'Yeah, right,' says Debs.

'I swear to God.'

'It's odd if nothing else,' she says. 'I understand why you're a bit worried. The whole set-up is peculiar.'

Everyone thinks there's something odd about my relationship with Ivo Lehane. Even me. We can't all be wrong.

And yet, I think, as I eventually hang up from Debs, Ivo has always behaved impeccably. My current uneasiness is more about what's going on in my own head than the man himself.

I think of Dave, sullen and angry. I think of Ivo, charming and kind.

I like the way Ivo looks out for me. I like the way he asks my opinion. I like the way he treats me as an equal.

I like him.

But I don't want to sleep with him.

Do I?

Chapter 22

Somewhat to my surprise, I fall asleep, and it's dark when I wake up again. It takes me a couple of minutes to realise where I am. I grab my phone, which shows the time as 5.30 p.m. There are no missed calls and no messages. I get up and close the heavy gold-coloured curtains. Then I call Mum.

'How are you?' she asks. 'Everything OK?'

I tell her that everything's fine and that the client is safely off at his meetings, and she asks about the hotel. She's never heard of it so she doesn't know I'm staying in the lap of luxury while she's looking after my children. I can hear them squabbling in the background and ask her to put them on to me.

'Tom is being really mean,' Mica tells me. 'He won't let me help with stirring the pot.'

'Are you cooking?' I ask.

'Gran's friend is making dinner,' Mica says. 'We're having dabbled beef.'

That sounds disgusting.

'Daube of beef,' Mum amends when I finally get talking to her again. 'It's stew really, but very posh.'

'Posh food by a friend? Is it *Diarmuid* who's doing the cooking?'

'Yes,' she says. 'He asked me to go out to dinner with him, and when I told him I couldn't, he said he'd bring dinner to me.'

I think I gasp out loud. Mum's voice was warm and affectionate when she spoke. And why wouldn't it be? He's cooking for her. Which is . . . lovely. Especially as he seems to be dealing with my children too.

'Ah, they're getting on great,' says Mum when I apologise for messing up her night. 'Diarmuid doesn't see his own grandchildren that often, so he's delighted to have some time with Mica and Tom.'

'And you,' I add.

She laughs. 'It's still just friendship, Roxy.'

Maybe, I think, after we've finished talking. But it feels like more than that to me.

Mum's talk of food has made me feel hungry. Ivo didn't say anything about the eating options to go along with the glass of wine I haven't yet had, but I'm hoping I can get some bar food and coffee. And maybe the wine too. But despite the swimming costume in my bag, I'll give the spa a miss. Now that I'm here, I really don't feel right about lying by the pool, and there's no way I'd charge a massage to the room.

I take my denim skirt and floral T-shirt from my overnight case, which also contains fresh underwear and another white blouse for tomorrow. I lay the change of clothes on the bed, then hop under the shower to freshen up. It's a blissful shower – maybe even as good as the one in Beechgrove Park.

The towels are excellent and so's the freebie body lotion, which is smooth and creamy. I get dressed, shake my hair out of its ponytail so that it falls around my face, slide my feet into the high heels I shoved into the case at the last minute, and finally spritz myself with Annabel's perfume. It's a heavier, muskier scent than my usual one, perfectly in keeping with my surroundings.

It's after six so I try Dave's mobile because he should be on the way home by now. It goes to his voicemail. Dave never listens to his voicemail; instead I send him a text to say I love him and miss him. Sending the message seems to centre me somehow, and I'm feeling a bit more like myself again as I go downstairs.

The receptionist directs me to the bar, which does indeed serve food; although after a glance at the menu, I see that it's mainly upmarket sandwiches. I select the chicken and also ask for a glass of white wine.

There are only two other people in the bar, both men and both alone. One is reading a paper and has a pint of Guinness in front of him. The other is engrossed in his iPad and seems to be drinking water. The bar itself is more like an elegant drawing room than a place where people get stuck into alcohol. It's furnished with armchairs, small tables and expensive-looking rugs. The ceilings are ornate and there are gilt-framed paintings and mirrors on the walls.

A waitress brings me my wine, followed by the sandwich, which is, of course, a cut above your average chicken sandwich. It's more of a mini meal, to be honest, beautifully presented and accompanied by a colourful salad. I'm sure Gina Hayes would approve. Although I am salivating at the sight of it, I take a photograph of both the sandwich and my wine, crop it, filter it and then post it to my Instagram page with the caption 'Compensations in a Driver's Life'. Leona Lynch likes it nearly at once and comments that every job must have its compensations. She adds the hashtag: *#bestdriverintheworld*, which is sweet of her.

It takes me no time at all to demolish the lovely sandwich, but I linger over the glass of wine and, when I finally finish it, order coffee. Then I decide to take a wander around the hotel on the off chance that sometime in my future I might be able to come and stay here myself. I suddenly hear Dave's voice in my ear telling me that if we sell Dad's car we could have a break here, and I feel bad that I'm denying my family the opportunity to have a nice time just because I want to be a driver.

He still hasn't replied to my earlier text. I send another one saying I had a chicken sandwich for my tea (although I don't include the photograph to show how fantastic a sandwich it actually was). There's still no reply. A sudden feeling of fear grips me. The last time I left him alone, he brought Julie Halpin into my bed. Could he do it again? He promised he wouldn't, but he's so angry at me that maybe he'd think of it as warranted. I told Debs I wouldn't have revenge sex. But what if Dave doesn't feel the same? What if he feels that my insistence on doing this job justifies him having some fun with another woman in our bed again? I laugh mirthlessly at the thought of both of us sleeping with other people out of anger. Surely this isn't what our lives have become.

I put the phone back into my bag and return to the room. Alone.

* * *

I watch TV for a while, but I'm too wound up to sit still. Besides, lovely though the room is, it's suddenly claustrophobic. I pick up my bag, slip on my jacket and go out, leaving the hotel and walking around the stately old building. My jacket isn't heavy enough to properly protect me from the chill of the night, and my heels keep sinking into the soft ground, but I don't care. After being cocooned inside, the biting cold of real life is welcome.

I don't know anything about the history of the hotel, but I suppose that, like so many of the big houses I've driven people to, it was originally owned by a single family. I try once again to imagine what it would be like to be properly rich, to never have to worry about money, but I can't. Having enough to pay the bills has always been the backdrop to my life, and it always will be. And maybe that's why I want to work so much. Because I want to know that no matter what happens, I can make a living. That I can be independent.

I never imagined that being independent was something I needed to think about when I married Dave. But it should have been. Because even if you're part of a great team, you still need to have a space for yourself.

Deep in my thoughts, I don't even realise that I've walked right around the building. I'm properly cold now, and the wind has whipped my hair into a frizz, so I'm happy to go inside again. I decide to have another coffee in the bar. I don't want to go up to my room yet. I've had enough of my own company.

As soon as I walk into the bar, though, I realise I've made a mistake. Ivo Lehane is sitting there on his own. I don't have time to walk out before he looks up and sees me.

'Roxy,' he says. 'Come and join me.'

I sit down beside him, feeling slightly frivolous in my skirt and high heels and thinking it might have been better not to have changed after all.

'Drink?' he asks. There's a half-full glass in front of him and I think it's gin.

'Coffee would be nice.'

'Sure you wouldn't like something else?' he asks.

I'd kill for another glass of wine. But we're leaving at seven thirty tomorrow morning, so I shake my head.

'Coffee it is, so,' he says, and orders it. Then he asks if I've been exploring.

I nod and run my fingers through my windswept hair before glancing down at my short skirt and shoes. 'I'm a bit of a mess, sorry.'

'Not at all,' he says. 'You look . . .'

I wait.

'. . . less intimidating,' he finishes.

'Intimidating!' I stare at him. 'I couldn't possibly look intimidating.'

'Oh, but you do.' He grins at me. 'You're so cool and professional that I'm always afraid of saying the wrong thing.'

I don't believe him.

'Seriously,' he says. 'You get behind the wheel and it's like you're the captain of a plane or something. You're in total control of everything around you.'

'I wish.' I can't help laughing.

'Anyway, you can chill out for a while now,' he says.

'How did your meetings go?' I switch the subject away from me. 'Did you have a nice dinner?'

'The dinner was great and so were the meetings,' he replies. 'George and Kristina are good people and I think they'll

284

handle our new projects well. I should've visited them before, really. Same with the others.'

'Are they all part of your company?'

'We own or part-own them,' he tells me. 'They don't work for me directly.'

'Do you have many people working for you?' I know I'm asking too many questions, but I'm interested.

'It's a big company,' says Ivo. 'But you know how it is, everything's in sections and departments and the number of people who actually report directly to anyone is quite small. Are you interested in management?' he asks.

'I'm a driver,' I remind him. 'So . . . no.'

He laughs. It's a genuine laugh and I relax a little more.

'I'm sorry,' he says. 'I've been caught up in it all today. Truthfully I'd love to be involved in the research and development stuff myself, but I'm not qualified. I wish I were.'

'How did you get into it?' I ask.

I listen as he talks about his career path and I think of how different it is from mine.

'Have you ever wanted to get married and have a family?' I don't know where that came from. We were having a proper business conversation and suddenly I've thrown a personal question at him. When I desperately don't want to get personal with him. What the hell is wrong with me?

'Never had time,' he replies. 'When I was younger, it wasn't something I was interested in. I was spectacularly bad at relationships, treated women terribly.'

'I don't believe that!'

'It's true.' He makes a face. 'I told you before, I'm not a people person. I guess I inherited that from my dad. I didn't want to make any woman as miserable as my mum, so I didn't really try to connect with them. I was the guy who says he'll call but doesn't.'

'Ah, that guy.' I make a face at him.

'And then I got busy so it hasn't been an issue. All the same,' he adds, 'it's something that in recent years I've come to regret a little.'

'Plenty of time,' I say.

'Yes and no.' His expression is serious. 'I'm forty, which seems young but isn't when you're talking about maybe starting a family and stuff. My dad was in his twenties. So was my mum. Though maybe it was because they were both so young that it went the way it did. Still, it's hard to make compromises when you get older, and I'm guessing marriage is all about compromise.'

I tell him about Mum and her dating site and the fact that all the men are looking for younger women, and he nods slowly before laughing.

'We're so vain, aren't we?' he says. 'Men, I mean. No matter how old and unfit we are, we still think that women see us as hunks.'

I laugh too. 'It's true. I'm not going to make you feel better by saying any different!' And then, not caring, I ask about Annabel.

'Oh, I'm punching way above my weight with her,' says Ivo. 'She's a properly qualified research chemist. Brains to burn. Beauty too.'

That's why she's so high-maintenance, I suppose.

'It's been a struggle, though, these last weeks, what with coming home to my father,' he says. 'We don't get much time during the week, so the weekends are really important.'

'You could have brought her,' I say.

286

'No!' He looks horrified. 'She wouldn't . . . I wouldn't . . .' He shakes his head. 'No.'

I wait a few moments before asking him if he's thinking of visiting his dad again, and he sighs.

'I know I've made it up with Lizzy,' he says. 'But seeing him is really hard. I want to forgive him, I honestly do. Yet even after all the therapy and stuff, I simply can't.' He shrugs. 'But as you said, I guess it doesn't matter whether I forgive him or not as long as I show up. I was thinking about a visit this weekend until the US trip came together. I'll call Lizzy when I'm back and sort something out.'

'You should call her while you're here,' I say. 'And tell her you'll see her when you're back.'

He raises an eyebrow and I realise that I've overstepped the mark. But then he says I'm probably right, he just hates dealing with family stuff.

'Is your dad's health any better?' I ask.

'He's not any worse,' says Ivo. 'I don't know if he'll improve much, to be honest.'

I feel like he wants to add that he doesn't care either, but he's afraid of my disapproval.

He signals the waitress and orders himself another drink (gin and tonic, as I thought) and asks if I'd like anything.

I shake my head.

'Another coffee, perhaps?'

'No thanks.'

'You're remarkably disciplined,' he says.

I think of my chaotic life and snort.

'You are,' he protests. 'You can make a decision and stick to it. Whereas I'm forever wondering if I've done the right thing.'

I'm thinking how wrong he is and then I suddenly realise that he's right. When I definitely decide on something, I do stick to it. Which is why I'm still driving, despite Dave's objections. And why I'm still with him, even though he broke my heart. But Ivo is wrong to think I don't wonder if I've done the right thing. I'm always wondering about that. Not about the driving. And not about Dave. Well . . . I take a moment to consider the Dave situation, which is, after all, inextricably linked with the driving situation. I want both to work out, but at the moment it seems I can only have one or the other. So does the fact that I've chosen driving mean that deep down I don't want to be with Dave? No matter what I say to myself?

'I don't mean to bore you with my problems.' Ivo's voice brings me back to the here and now.

'You're not,' I say. 'I was just processing what you said about me. You're right in some ways about me sticking to decisions, but I don't know how good that is in the long run. Or if it's because deep down I'm a stubborn cow.'

'Don't call yourself names.' He smiles at me.

'Dave calls me a stubborn cow sometimes,' I tell him. 'And he's probably right.'

'Stubbornness can be a strength,' says Ivo. 'A weakness too, I admit. But maybe women should be a bit more stubborn sometimes.' He looks doubtful for a moment. 'Or maybe not. Maybe that's why Lizzy and I lock horns so much.'

'She sounds like a really lovely person.'

'She is.' There's warmth in Ivo's voice. 'And she was right to make me come home, even though I didn't want to. I guess she got all the caring and sharing genes. Sadly, I inherited all of Dad's worst characteristics.'

'Even if you did, you don't have to turn out like him,' I say.

Ivo stares into his gin and tonic for a moment before looking at me. All of his successful-businessman veneer has been stripped away and there's a vulnerability in his eyes I've never seen before. 'I'm terrified I will one day,' he admits.

'You won't.' I resist the temptation to put my arm around him to reassure him. That would be stepping even further over the mark. 'You might be his son, but having the same DNA doesn't mean you're the same person.'

'Thanks.' He takes a sip of his G&T and then puts it back on the table. 'I shouldn't drink this. It makes me self-obsessed.'

'And I shouldn't drink coffee because it makes me meddle in things I've no business being involved in.' I stand up. 'I'd better go.'

'Stay for another couple of minutes,' says Ivo. 'I don't want to go up to my room yet, and I'd rather not be alone.'

It's a command. He's my boss.

And he realises it too.

'Christ, I'm such an arse,' he says. 'Ordering you around. I'm sorry, Roxy. We should both go. I've had enough to drink. I'm getting totally maudlin here.'

'It's fine,' I say.

'It's not fine at all,' says Ivo.

He stands up too.

We take the stairs side by side in silence. We don't say anything as we walk along the corridor to our rooms. I stop at mine and take my key card out of my bag. I'm aware that Ivo is close to me. I can smell his aftershave again.

'Goodnight,' I say. 'I'll see you in the morning.'

289

'Yes.' Ivo hesitates.

There's a ripple between us. I can feel it. Something drawing us together. And it's growing stronger. I tap the card against the door lock. The light goes green. Ivo is right behind me. I can sense the beating of his heart, the rhythm of his breath. I can feel my own heart beating faster too.

And then my phone beeps with a message alert. Ivo steps back. I release the breath I didn't know I was holding.

'That'll be Dave.' I step into the room and turn towards him. 'Goodnight, Mr Lehane.'

'Goodnight, Mrs McMenamin,' he says.

I go inside and close the door behind me.

Although I told Ivo the beep was from Dave, I actually had no idea who had messaged me. But as it turns out, it *is* my husband, asking how things have gone. I can't answer it yet. I feel as though my treachery will be transmitted through the keypad. As though Dave will be able to tell, regardless of what I type, that what was going through my head at the moment my door clicked open was the hope that Ivo Lehane would follow me inside. At that moment, I wanted him to. I wanted it more than anything. Despite everything I've said to Dave about never hurting him as he hurt me, I would have let Ivo in. I've completely lost the moral high ground. I'm burning with shame.

I'm lucky my husband has saved me from myself.

I slip out of my shoes, sit on the ottoman at the end of the bed and massage my aching feet before calling him.

'It's very posh here,' I say, and I'm shocked at how calm my voice is. 'I'm not sure how comfortable I feel with this level of poshness, to tell you the truth.'

'Make the most of it,' Dave says. 'Order room service.'

'It's a bit late for that.'

Besides, it was another sort of room service I was thinking about.

'What time are you heading off in the morning?' he asks.

'About seven.'

'You'll be knackered.'

'Ah, it's OK. I'm going to bed shortly.'

'I don't like you being away from home.'

'I know. I'm sorry.' That's a lie. I'm not sorry at all. Because even though I nearly made the biggest mistake of my life a few minutes ago, I'm enjoying being away. I'm enjoying staying in a gorgeous hotel. I'm enjoying somebody calling me a professional. Giving me credit for doing a good job.

Debs and I have talked about compartmentalisation before. How men can do it so easily. How they can put their personal feelings or problems to one side and get on with other stuff. How women find that more difficult. But I am a woman in a man's world. So I can compartmentalise too.

'You're my wife and I love you,' Dave says. 'I want you here, not holed up in some hotel in Cork.'

'I'll be home tomorrow.'

'We'll go out,' says Dave. 'It's steak and pie night down the road.'

Our local pub does a variety of meal nights. Mexican. Indian. Traditional fish and chips. Steak and pie is one of our favourites.

'Great,' I say, although going out means asking someone to babysit the children, and I can't do that when I've been away for two days. But I'm not saying that to Dave now.

291

'Sleep tight,' he says.

'You too.'

I get undressed, folding my skirt and T-shirt and cleaning the muddy heels of my shoes before placing them back in my overnight case. Then I put on the oversize robe I've taken from the bathroom. I feel a bit like Julia Roberts in *Pretty Woman*, in the scene where she's wandering around Richard Gere's hotel suite. Though this is just a room. And there's only me in it.

I wait for a knock at the door.

But it doesn't come.

I'm such a fool.

Chapter 23

I wake up having slept better than I've done in months. I expected to be tossing and turning all night, but instead I fell asleep within seconds of my head hitting the pillow. My sleep was so deep that even if Ivo Lehane had banged on the door to be let in for a night of rampant sex (revenge or otherwise), I don't think I would have heard him.

I'm unsure what has me feeling so chirpy this morning, but after my shower I head downstairs. It's not clear if breakfast is included in my reservation, but I'm not looking for much, just some coffee and toast, although when I see the extent of the buffet available, I reassess my priorities and have some of the fresh fruit as well. And a mini muffin. I can't help it. It looks so enticing. Also, it's some kind of organic, bran-based muffin, therefore it must be healthy! There's no sign of Ivo. Maybe he's having breakfast in his room, because even when I've finished mine, he doesn't appear. I gather my things and wait for him in reception.

He emerges from the lift at exactly the appointed time, suave and businesslike again in his tailored suit, pulling his case behind him.

'Sleep well?' he asks cheerfully.

'Yes, thank you.'

'Me too. It must be the country air.' He smiles at me, then goes to reception and checks us out.

The valet – a different man from yesterday – appears with the car keys and I see that he's left the Merc outside the door. He insists on putting Ivo's case in the boot and holds the passenger door open, clearly expecting me to get in and a bit surprised when it's Ivo who does. He apologises as he hands me the keys and I smile at him and say no problem. Because it isn't.

It's still dark as we set off; a more profound darkness than in Dublin, where the artificial light from offices, houses and street lights never allows it to be totally black.

'Music?' I ask, but Ivo says he's not good with sound in the early morning and would prefer silence.

So for the first thirty minutes that's what he gets. Then his phone rings and he starts talking in French again. Animated French rather than the more seductive tones he used before. I wonder if he and Annabel are having a row. Perhaps he's breaking up with her in the car. Dad once told me about a woman who asked her husband for a divorce while he was driving them to a wedding.

'What did he say?' I asked.

'Yes,' replied Dad. 'Then he told me to stop the car and got out. He told her she could go to the goddam wedding on her own, that he'd never wanted to go in the first place, and that he was glad to be rid of her.'

I wonder where she is now. How the divorce turned out for them.

Ivo's tone isn't angry, though. It's crisp and businesslike. Maybe it's not Annabel after all.

And then, suddenly, softer and gentler: '*Je t'aime.*'

Everyone knows *je t'aime*. Even those of us who can't speak French.

It's the language of love, after all.

The sky is lighter as I take the slip road that leads to Limerick. There's an open-backed pickup truck ahead of me, laden with tractor tyres and bales of hay that leave a steady stream of wisps in their wake. I like seeing bales of hay on trucks. It reminds me that, even though I love living in the city, there's another world not that far away.

I'm not sure at what point I realise something's going to happen. I think it's before it actually does. Because I've allowed the gap between me and the truck to widen slightly and that means I clearly see the moment the back panel drops down and the tyres begin to roll out onto the road ahead of me. They're big and black and coming straight for the Merc, but I've already checked for oncoming traffic, and even though there's a double white line in the centre of the road, I move across and push down hard on the accelerator. A tractor tyre passes within centimetres of the passenger side as I swerve back in front of the truck at the same time as a blue Ford Kuga approaches. He's flashing his headlights at me in annoyance, but then I register him braking hard to avoid the tractor tyre that's now in the middle of the road, before careering onto the verge and into the steel barrier.

'God Almighty!' Ivo is clutching the door handle. 'That was a close shave.'

I stop the car and get out. So does Ivo. I glance at the Merc but don't see any damage. The Kuga doesn't seem badly damaged either, but the airbags have deployed and people are already hurrying over to see if the occupants need assistance.

'Will I call the police?' Ivo is beside me.

'Somebody already has.' I can hear the sound of a siren in the distance and look around me. I don't yet see a Garda car, but there are at least half a dozen other cars stopped on the road, which is littered with tyres. One has rolled to the verge behind the Merc. I shudder to think how close it came to hitting us. And I don't want to think about what might have happened if it had.

Ivo is taking photos with his phone as he walks towards the truck. The driver is standing beside it, and they're joined by the driver of a grey Volvo. Meanwhile, the occupants of the Kuga, a man and a woman, have got out of the car and are being looked after by others. My legs begin to shake. I flop back into the Merc and lean my head against the steering wheel. A minute later, Ivo returns.

'Are you all right?' he asks.

I nod.

'Sure?'

I nod again.

'The police are on their way.' He's stating the obvious. The siren is even louder now. 'Obviously the truck driver is shocked, but he's also worried. He should have secured those tyres.'

'Why did the tailgate drop?' I ask.

Ivo shrugs. 'Dunno. I guess he's going to get a few questions about that.'

'Do you want to wait around for the police?' I'm not sure if we should leave. We're witnesses, I suppose, if there's anything that needs to be explained, but if we hang around here for too long, Ivo might miss his flight.

He doesn't have time to make a choice about that, because the Garda car arrives and suddenly they're setting up cones and asking questions anyway, and I'm giving a statement to a man who looks barely old enough to be out of school let alone in charge of a major incident. Ivo then speaks to him and tells him he's got photos, although they're pretty much the same as the scene is now, and he gives his details to the young garda and next thing I know we're being allowed to go. But we've spent nearly an hour at the side of the road and we're going to be pushing it to get to the airport in time.

'Are you certain you're OK to drive?' Ivo asks as he fastens his seat belt.

'Of course.' I'm not going to say otherwise, even though I'm still a bit shaken and the moment when the tyres came off the truck keeps replaying in my head.

I join the motorway and get us up to a few kilometres under the speed limit before engaging cruise control. I'm still trying to block out the image of the first tyre bouncing down from the truck and onto the road, heading straight for us. I tell myself that it might have hit the bonnet and simply leapt over the car, but I'm not convinced. I exhale slowly, trying to bring my heartbeat under control.

Ivo says nothing, but he turns on the audio system and pairs his phone with it. The soothing sounds of classical guitar music fill the car and I feel myself relax a little. Neither of us speaks until we reach the airport. Ivo's flight should be closing around now, but I know now that when they announce a flight as 'closing', they actually mean they've started boarding. So if he hurries, he should make it. I get out of the car as I always do, even though he doesn't wait for me to open the door but gets out himself.

'Thank you,' he says. 'Both for the driving, as always, and for your quick thinking earlier.'

'I don't know that I was thinking at all,' I confess.

'The very best way to think.' He smiles. 'I'm very glad you're my driver. Even though I seem to be the client from hell, bringing nothing but trouble.'

'I've had a lot worse.' I start to smile at him in return, but out of the blue my bottom lip starts to quiver and I have to blink away the tears that are filling my eyes.

He's around to my side of the car in an instant, and before I know it his arm is around me.

'Hey. Hey,' he says. 'You're in shock. Give yourself a moment.'

I lean my forehead on his shoulder while he squeezes me and tells me to take my time.

'I'm fine.' I lift my head again. 'It was just . . . just . . .'

'Shock,' he says again, and I nod.

He's studying me, concern on his face.

'I'm fine,' I repeat a little more steadily.

'All the same, I'm not sure you should drive.'

'I got us here in one piece, didn't I? I'm sure I can get home.'

'But I was with you then,' he says. 'You're on your own now and it's a long way. I'd rather you weren't by yourself.'

I feel the tears start up again, but this time I don't blink because I don't want them to fall. I'm a professional. I don't cry on my clients' shoulders. Usually.

'This is so silly,' I say. 'I'm really not . . .'

He keeps holding me and I can hear the beat of his heart beneath his jacket and the comfort of his arms around me. I feel safe. Secure. I don't want to break away. But I have to. Because he has to go.

'Text me when you get home,' he says. 'So that I know you're OK.'

'I'll be fine. And you'll be in the air, I hope.' This time I pull out of his hold and rub my eyes with the back of my hand.

'Are you sure? Really sure?'

'Absolutely. You'd better go,' I tell him. 'You don't want to miss your plane.'

'You're more important than the plane,' he says. He keeps his hands on my shoulders and he's looking at me with concern.

'I'm OK. Honestly.'

He smiles, then leans towards me. I move at exactly the same time so that the kiss that he clearly intended for my cheek ends up halfway between my lips and my chin.

'Sorry!' I gasp.

The two of us look at each other for a moment without moving. His deep blue eyes are locked on mine and I feel like we're actually held together by an invisible force. And while he's looking at me and I've no idea what's going through his mind, I'm imagining what a real kiss from him would have been like. Hard and demanding? Soft and gentle? Long and lingering? None of these? All of these? For as long as we're here, like this, I can keep imagining. So I can't pull away even though I know that I have to.

But Ivo can, and does.

'Take care of yourself, Roxy.'

'You too.' I can hardly speak.

He squeezes my shoulder gently, then successfully places the lightest of kisses exactly where he intended, on my cheek, before turning away and striding towards the terminal building.

I think about the near miss the whole way home. Not the near miss of the tractor tyres on the way to Shannon airport, but the near miss of Ivo's kiss that grazed my lips and left them burning. And I can feel the feather-light touch on my cheek, too. The casual goodbye kiss that ended up where it was supposed to. But that I still wasn't expecting. Because clients don't kiss their drivers goodbye. And clients don't hold onto their driver's shoulders and look deep into their eyes and make them feel as though nothing and nobody else in the world exists.

But Ivo is a different sort of client.

I've misread him in so many ways – thinking that he was callous about his father and offhand with his sister when the reality is a difficult childhood relationship that's been hard to overcome. Thinking that his high-maintenance girlfriend was a kind of trophy woman when she's a qualified chemist. Thinking that he had ulterior motives in wanting me to stay overnight at the hotel when it was simply necessary for his travel arrangements. Thinking that Dave's text last night saved me from something else. Yet everything I've thought about Ivo has been a product of my own fevered imagination. And a way of looking at things that probably comes from a diet of too many TV soaps and trashy celebrity magazines. Ivo Lehane is a good man. And right now, my heart is overwhelmed with longing for him. Because all the time our eyes were locked together, the only thing I was thinking was that I wanted him to kiss me properly. That I wanted to know what it would be like. That I wanted him to hold me tightly and protect me and love me.

I'm an hour into my journey home and I have to pull into the improbably named Barack Obama Plaza service station, because suddenly my hands are shaking uncontrollably and there are tears streaming down my cheeks. And I don't know if that's delayed shock from the tyres or if it's something to do with my inexplicable longing for Ivo Lehane.

I spent all day yesterday worrying that he might want to get me into bed. I'm spending today wishing he had. The woman who swore she'd never cheat on her cheating husband now regrets not being a cheating wife. I wonder what sort of song Dolly would write about it.

I fill the car with petrol and then buy a coffee from Bewley's, which I drink standing up, replacing the fresh mint of Ivo with the roasted taste of arabica beans. I look out at a day that has become bright and sunny, so that everyone coming into the plaza seems equally sunny in their outlook. But I'm here, hands around my coffee cup, and I've never been more confused in my life.

How can I now be wishing that Ivo Lehane was the sort of man who would've knocked at my door in the middle of the night and made mad passionate love to me without stopping? How can I possibly be thinking that if he had asked me to come with him into the airport and found a cupboard to make love to me in, I would have said yes.

While all he did was brush my lips with his – by mistake. What the hell am I like?

My phone beeps.

My heart does a triple jump.

Hope your trip was OK. See you later.

I stare at Dave's message and then send a thumbs-up in reply.

I realise that I didn't ring the children this morning. Not that there was a good time to ring them, but I could have broken my 'no personal phone calls while I'm driving rule' and Ivo wouldn't have minded. He likes hearing about Tom and Mica. He likes knowing that I have a happier family life than his.

A life I would have risked just for a quickie with him.

I'm worse than Dave.

I'm a different version of Julie Halpin.

I hate myself.

I turn on talk radio as a distraction from my thoughts, but I'm unable to concentrate on the discussion about the health service even though it's something that normally engages me. Instead I'm wondering if what happened to me is what happened with Dave and Julie, only with a different outcome. Was he taken over by an unstoppable desire to know what it would be like to be with another woman? Was it something he simply couldn't resist? Was it the same moment of madness I felt with Ivo Lehane?

When we first started going out together, Dave told me he'd slept with another girl before me. Only one. Which was one more than the number of boys I'd slept with before him. We were both teenagers, and back then, though there was a lot of kissing and fumbling, sleeping with someone was a very big deal. I know it seems ridiculous that Dave has been my one and only, but it's never bothered me before. In fact, it's been a source of pride.

Now I can't help feeling as though our lack of experience was a mistake. For both of us.

I pull up outside Mum's house. Her car isn't there, which means she's already gone to collect the children from school. I let myself in and wait for them to come home. When they arrive a few minutes later, Tom throws himself at me and tells me he's missed me. Mica follows behind, a little more circumspect.

'Did you have a good business trip?' Her voice is serious.

'Very good,' I tell her.

'Did you miss us?'

'Unbelievably.'

'Did you buy us presents?' asks Tom.

I hand them the bags of sweets I picked up along with my coffee at the Barack Obama Plaza, and they beam at me. I also give Mica the mini bottle of shampoo I took from the hotel bathroom, as well as the amenity kit of nail file and cotton buds. She kisses me with delight.

'Don't eat all those sweets at once,' I warn. But Tom's already tearing his bag open as they head to the living room. Mum follows them with sandwiches she made earlier and I cross my fingers that they'll eat more of them than the sweets.

'How was it?' she asks when she comes back.

'Tiring,' I say.

'You look terrible.'

Only a mother can say that to you without you taking complete offence. Even though it's bad enough her telling you.

'Early mornings.'

'Late nights?'

'It was only one night,' I remind her.

'I looked up that place you stayed. It's very flashy,' she says.

'Not so much flashy as luxurious,' I tell her.

She raises an eyebrow.

'His company was paying,' I say.

'That was generous of them.'

'It was convenient.'

'Did you like staying there?'

'It's probably the only time I'll ever stay somewhere that expensive. So yes, I liked it.'

'And you seem to like him too.'

'I like a lot of my clients. I like Leona Lynch. And Thea Ryan.'

'But you've never spent a night away with either of them.'

'I might if I ever need to.'

'And everything's OK?' asks Mum.

'Of course it is,' I lie. 'Why wouldn't it be?'

'Why indeed,' she says.

I round up the kids and drive home. The familiar scent of our house – Airwick, children and a kind of underlying whiff of the greasy lubricant that Dave uses on his jobs – wraps itself around me.

'What's for tea?' asks Tom.

'You had sandwiches at Granny's,' I remind him.

'But I'm starving,' he howls.

So I make them spaghetti hoops on toast, which they devour. As they get down from the table, I hug them both so hard that they complain.

'Well, I've missed you,' I say.

'You shouldn't have gone away,' says Mica. 'Then you wouldn't have missed us.'

Does she think this herself? Or is it Dave talking?

He arrives home at seven, and, as they did with me, the children rush to greet him.

'How's my man about the house?' he asks Tom. And then, ruffling Mica's hair, which normally she hates, 'How's my best woman?'

They tell him they've had a great time at Granny's and that I bought them sweets. He looks at me.

'I thought all sugary stuff was banned,' he says.

'Not all the time.'

'Only when I bring it home.'

'Dave. Please.'

He gives the children another hug and walks into the kitchen.

'Any food for me?' he asks.

'Fry-up?' I suggest.

'Sounds good.'

I cook a meal for him but nothing for myself. I sit down opposite him with a mug of coffee. He doesn't ask if I've eaten already but he does ask about the trip.

'Tiring.' I repeat what I said to Mum.

'I knew it would be.'

'I'm sorry,' I say. 'I should have thought it through more carefully.'

He looks at me in surprise.

'I didn't think it would be so full-on,' I explain. 'It was more than I expected.'

'And what about the hotel?'

'More than I expected too.' I keep my voice light. 'And then this morning . . .' I tell him about the incident with the tyres.

'Bloody hell, Roxy!' He's genuinely upset. 'You could've been killed.'

'I don't think so,' I say. 'But it was a scary moment all the same.'

'No wonder you look like a ghost.'

'I think I'll go to bed early.'

He nods. 'I'm glad you're home.'

'Me too,' I say.

We sit together in the living room once I've tidied up the kitchen and the children are in bed. Dave is watching an old war movie – he's a bit obsessed with them and the perfect English of the actors. I sit beside him on the sofa and take out my phone.

Home, I type. *All well. Hope is OK with you too.*

It's about an hour later when it pings in reply.

Greetings from New York. Glad you got back safely.

Glad you got there safely too. Take care.

Take care. I say it without thinking every time Dave or the children leave the house. But I mean the words. I want them to be safe. I don't want anything bad to happen to them.

I put the phone back in my bag and yawn suddenly.

'You have to stop.' Dave mutes the TV and turns to me.

'What?'

'The driving, of course,' he says. 'How would I have coped if you'd been killed today? How would the children have coped?'

Would you have mourned me or replaced me? I wonder, but I don't answer.

'You're too important to this family for anything to happen to you,' he continues.

I'm sure he doesn't mean to make me feel like a cog in the machine, but he does.

'Today was exceptional,' I say. 'Both the overnight and the accident.'

'It's too risky.'

I wish I hadn't told him about the tyres. But it seemed like the right thing to distract him from Ivo Lehane.

'The same thing could happen to you,' I remind him. 'You're out every day in the van. Sometimes you have to drive long distances. You can't wrap me in cotton wool, Dave.'

'It's my job to protect you,' he says. 'Look, I'm not saying you have to stop forever, but you should take a break.'

This is a new way of looking at it. But I know that if I take a break, I'll never go back. Besides, I have bookings. So I can't. That's what I say to him.

'Honour the ones you have,' he says. 'But then stop. You need a rest, Roxy. You've been burning the candle at both ends.'

Mum says that too. But I haven't. I've been doing something I love doing. I've managed everything else.

'Your family is more important than any business,' Dave reminds me.

He's right about that.

'So we're agreed,' he says when I stay silent. 'Good.'

He doesn't wait for me to say anything. He unmutes the TV and goes back to watching it.

I walk out of the living room and up the stairs. I take my time getting ready for bed even though I'm feeling exhausted. I cleanse, tone and moisturise my skin. I brush my hair. I get under the duvet. I lie in darkness and silence and tell myself that Dave has a point and that my driving is both unnecessary and troublesome. So perhaps it would be better for all of us if I gave in and sold the car. Perhaps that would fix everything.

I'm still awake when he comes into the room and gets undressed. He slides into the bed beside me, then puts his arm around me and pulls me towards him. I don't want this tonight, but I'm kind of relieved that despite our argument of earlier, he does.

He falls asleep afterwards.

I don't.

Chapter 24

I do my best to be Supermum over the weekend and then keep what could be described as a low profile for the following week. Fortunately the jobs I have booked are strictly during the children's school hours, so once again I'm home whenever Dave is home. I don't say a word about clients and I also adjust the cooking arrangements so none of the Punishment Book recipes appear.

But I feel like I'm walking on eggshells. I never used to feel like this in my own home. I never felt as though I was keeping part of myself from Dave either. And yet I am. I'm driving when he doesn't want me to, and although I've turned down some jobs that don't suit me, I know I'll agree to ones I like if they come. And that'll create an even bigger problem later.

Obviously I haven't heard from Ivo Lehane. He's off working in the States and he's forgotten all about me. I wonder, though, if he's planning to resume his visits to his dad. And if he does, will he want me to drive him? Leaving aside the fact that Dave thinks I'm about to take a break, I couldn't possibly have Ivo in the car again. I wouldn't trust myself. In my mind I've become an unfaithful wife.

And telling myself that my husband was actually unfaithful while I'm only daydreaming about it doesn't make it any easier.

Mum drops in to see me on Wednesday afternoon, shortly after the children come home from school. They're in the garden, jumping on the trampoline, even though autumn has become more tangible and it's chilly outside. I'm indoors, loading the washing machine. Mum waits for me to finish before following me into the kitchen. The kids rush in to say hello and she gives them a couple of chocolates each.

'Love you, Gran!' they cry before disappearing outside again.

'I'm trying to limit their eating between meals,' I tell her as we watch them leaping around. 'It's good for me too.'

'In fairness to you, the weight loss suits you. Just don't go too far with it,' she remarks.

'I won't. I still snack between jobs. But honestly, since I've started eating better, I have more energy. I shouldn't have been so dismissive of Gina Hayes before.'

'You weren't,' says Mum. 'You were envious of her.'

'Maybe of the fact that she's so successful and good-looking.'

'So are you,' says Mum, in the loyal way that all mothers have.

'You say the nicest things.'

'I speak the truth.' She grins. 'Anyhow, I'm here on a mission.'

'Oh?' I put the kettle on and she sits down at the table.

'I want everyone to come for a family lunch on Sunday,' she says.

'Everyone?'

'You and Dave and the children. Aidan, Kerry and theirs. It's your dad's birthday.'

Of course it is! How could I have forgotten?

'I didn't do a month's mind for him,' she continues. 'I'm not into that sort of thing. But I think it would be nice to celebrate his birthday.'

A month's mind is a memorial mass that's held about a month after a person has died. Dad wasn't remotely religious and Mum's relationship with the Catholic Church is pretty à la carte, so I never even thought of the possibility of a month's mind. But I like the idea of celebrating Dad's birthday, and say so.

'Good.' She smiles at me. 'I haven't had everyone around me since the funeral. It will be nice to have you together at a happier occasion.'

I'm not entirely sure how happy it'll be without Dad, but I swear to myself that I will be as positive and cheerful as Mum needs me to be. To be fair, she's looking positive and cheerful herself right now, and she's wearing her Charlotte Tilbury make-up as well as a nice blouse and trouser combo I haven't seen before.

'I needed new stuff,' she says when I compliment her on the blouse. 'It would be easy to flop around the place in tracksuits and T-shirts all the time, but I've got to make an effort, otherwise it's the beginning of the end.'

I glance involuntarily at my own tracksuit, which has a dusty streak across the arm. I'm conscious that I'm not wearing a scrap of make-up. There is something deeply disturbing about the fact that my sixty-two-year-old widowed mother looks more glamorous than me.

311

She laughs when I say this and tells me that no working mum can possibly look glamorous. When I say that some do, she shakes her head and then suddenly asks if I'll be driving 'that man' to Kildare again after my two-day jaunt with him.

I lean down and pick one of Mica's discarded chocolate wrappers from beneath the kitchen table. My face is flushed when I get up again.

'Dave and I are arguing about the driving,' I say.

'Oh, Roxy.' Her eyes are full of concern. 'Does he want you to stop?'

'He's never been a fan in the first place,' I say. 'He still wants us to sell the car and use the money for a holiday. And he's asked me to take a break although I know he really means stop for good.'

'There are worse things you could do,' says Mum.

'I know. But I really like driving.'

Mum is torn, I think, between wanting me to be happy and her overall feeling that Dave is probably right about my job.

'Besides,' I add, 'I did all the paperwork and everything to make it my business. I went on the course. I found new clients. I'm doing well.'

'I understand. I do, really. But when it becomes something that takes you away from home overnight . . .'

'That's a one-off,' I said. 'But . . . oh, Mum, there's something about being in the car that makes me feel good.'

'Hmm. Well you don't look it. You're as pale as anything and you've got dark circles under your eyes.'

I told her we'd already agreed that working mothers often looked wrecked and added that there was nothing wrong with me that a trip to the hairdresser followed by a nice relaxing massage wouldn't cure.

'Well, get your glam on before Sunday,' she says. 'Because I want you at your most fabulous then.'

Mum has only just left when Thea Ryan rings to ask if I can bring her to an interview at RTÉ the next day. I never say no to Thea and I can fit it in after collecting some businessmen from Heuston station and taking them to their hotel, which is beside the canal and not that far from Thea's house. It still leaves me time to be home and pick up the children from school. I'm pleased with my time-management skills as I slot Thea's job into my diary. I realise that I'm actually flouting Dave's express order not to take on any more work, and that there's going to be a real showdown about this sooner rather than later.

Right now, though, he doesn't need to know.

He's pleased when I tell him about Sunday lunch at Mum's. Despite her accepted lack of prowess in the kitchen, she's experienced at roast dinners, which I'm presuming will be what's on the menu. Dave says he'll get a nice bottle of wine to bring with us and I nod in agreement while making a mental note to get some flowers too. I wish we'd done this last year, before Dad became ill. We didn't celebrate any of his birthdays after the big do he had for his sixtieth, when we hired a private room at the local pub and surprised him. Lots of friends he hadn't seen for years came and it was a great night. Mum's own sixtieth was a smaller event because she reckoned it was too soon to have another big hooley. She was wrong. We should have gone mad then too. I make a note to celebrate every single one of her birthdays in the future. Because you never know, do you?

I'm not quite so pleased with my time-management skills when it actually comes to picking up the businessmen, because the rain has returned and the traffic is dreadful. After I eventually deposit them at their hotel, I do a bit of what I like to call bushcraft driving to get around some of the worst of the black spots, and I'm pleased to be only five minutes late pulling up outside Thea Ryan's house.

I grab her umbrella from the boot and hurry to her door, surprised that she hasn't opened it already, because despite her general air of scattiness, she's very punctual, and I reckoned she'd be peppering about my lateness, even if it is only five minutes.

There's a furious barking from inside, but although I've rung the bell, there's no sign of Thea, which makes me anxious. I take out my phone and dial her number, and I can actually hear it jingle in the hallway. I kneel down and peer through the letter box, but I can't see anyone. I know, because she told me, that Desmond was meeting a friend of his this morning, so he's not there. But she should be.

'Ms Ryan!' I call through the letter box. 'Are you OK? Can you hear me?'

There's more furious barking and I swear at the dog, who's jumping at the door.

'Be quiet!' I hiss. 'Where's your mum? Where's Thea?'

He barks again, runs a little bit down the hallway and then stops. A cold feeling of dread comes over me. Is the dog trying to tell me that Thea is lying unconscious on the floor, or worse? And then I hear her.

'Roxy!' Her voice is muffled. 'Are you outside?'

'Yes!' I shout back. 'Where are you? Are you all right?'

'Of course I am!' She sounds peeved but not in pain. 'I'm trapped, that's all.'

'Trapped where?'

'In the downstairs bathroom.'

I'm so relieved that she hasn't fallen and broken a hip, or had a stroke or anything so much worse, that I start to laugh.

'Are you still there?' she calls.

'Yes.'

'Come around the side of the house, for heaven's sake!'

Holding the umbrella over my head, I walk around the house and notice that there's a narrow frosted-glass pane in the wall with a small hinged window above it. I guess this is the downstairs bathroom.

'Ms Ryan?' I say tentatively.

The window, which pivots open horizontally, opens a little more and I see Thea's worried blue eyes behind it.

'I can't believe this has happened.' She's somewhere between anxious, raging and embarrassed. 'I came in to freshen up before you arrived, and the latch on the door has slipped or something. I can't get out.'

The window opening is too narrow for me to get in, and I say so.

'Well there's no point in you getting in anyhow,' declares Thea. 'We'd both be trapped in the bathroom then.'

I laugh again. I can't help it.

'It's not funny,' she says.

'No, it's not,' I agree. 'Do any of your neighbours have a spare key?'

'To the hall door, yes,' says Thea. 'The Mulcahys at number six do. But I don't know if Fiona is home, and even if she is, how will we get this door open?'

'If we can get into the house, I'm sure we'll come up with something.'

I head back down the pathway. Happily, my ring on the doorbell of number six is answered by a woman around my own age who insists on coming with me to Thea's.

'Poor dear,' she says as we open her hall door. 'I'm sure she's distraught.'

She's more like a spitting cat, I think, as Fiona Mulcahy and I unsuccessfully try the old-fashioned knob on the bathroom door.

'This is ridiculous,' cries Thea. 'I'll be trapped in here all day. I need to contact RTÉ and tell them I can't make it. If only I'd brought my phone in with me, I might be able to do the interview down the line. Not that talking to them from my bathroom would be my preferred option, but all the same, it would be something. Perhaps . . .' She pauses for a moment. 'Perhaps you could throw my phone through the bathroom window. I could call them then. That would be a solution, wouldn't it?'

'But not the one you want,' I say as I examine the door lock. 'Because after that you'd still be stuck in the bathroom. I'm going to have a go at getting you out. Could you stand well away from the door?'

'You're hardly going to try to break it down,' she cries. 'It's a heavy door, Roxy. You'd need a strong man to do it.'

'Yes, but the problem isn't the door, it's the lock. And I have a plan.'

316

'What kind of plan?' asks Fiona.

'My daughter got stuck in a room in my mum's house a few years ago,' I tell her. 'My dad got her out. There's a touch of brute force involved, so we might need the two of us, but it's as much about timing as anything else.'

'OK.' She looks at me doubtfully.

'Are you standing out of the way, Ms Ryan?' I ask.

'I'm cowering behind the toilet.' Thea's tone is acerbic, and I grin.

'OK,' I tell Fiona. 'When I say push, can you put your shoulder to the door with me?'

She nods.

I turn the doorknob all the way in the right direction and then pull it hard. As I do, I shout, 'Push!' and Fiona and I both bang hard against the door, which abruptly flies open. The two of us stumble inside, stopping ourselves from falling by grabbing the hand basin. Thea Ryan is standing between the loo and the far wall, looking at us with astonished delight.

'Oh my goodness, Roxy, you did it!' she exclaims. 'You clever, clever girl.'

'Probably wouldn't have managed it without Fiona,' I say. 'It needed a bit more than one shoulder.'

'That was impressive.' Fiona is smiling. 'I can't wait to tell my husband that I kicked in a door today.'

'It's all about getting the bolt back as far as you can, then sort of pulling it away from the hole and using the force of your body to bump the rest of it out,' I explain as I rub my shoulder. I'm going to have a bruise on it later. I banged into the door pretty hard, knowing that it needed a good jolt.

'Well, I'm very impressed.' Thea walks out of the bathroom and into the hallway. 'Fiona, my dear, thank you so much for your help.'

'You're welcome,' says Fiona. 'I'll keep your keys, shall I?'

'Of course.' Thea nods. 'You're a great neighbour. Thank you again.'

Fiona leaves the house and I wait while Thea puts on a royal-blue coat and a purple hat with a blue feather. Then I shelter her with the umbrella as we make our way to the car.

'Are you feeling OK?' I ask.

'Stupid,' she replies. 'I'm feeling stupid.'

'Could've happened to a bishop.' It was one of Dad's favourite rejoinders to mishaps, and Thea smiles.

We drive in silence the rest of the way to Donnybrook, and when we pull up outside the radio studio, I escort her up the steps to the reception area. I don't go in but leave her to her interview and wait in the car. My shoulder is throbbing now and I remind myself to put some arnica on it when I get home.

Thea's voice eventually comes over the airwaves. Her interview is about love – apparently she and Desmond have been married for fifty years and the presenter is asking for the secret of a happy marriage.

'Trust,' says Thea without pausing. 'Trust and respect. I respect my husband for the kind of man he is and for the work he does. I trust him both emotionally and practically. And I hope – I'm sure – he trusts me too.'

I feel myself go hot and cold at her words. Because trust and respect are in short supply between me and Dave, no

318

matter what we say or do. I know that I haven't truly been able to trust him since Rodeo Night, and I don't feel that he respects me and the need I have to keep driving. At the same time, I don't see how I can possibly have any views on a lack of trust in my husband given the fantasies I've been having about Ivo Lehane. OK, I might not have done anything, but I honestly think I would have. Which is just as bad.

What happened to us? I wonder. It was all so good and now it's slipping away like sand through my fingers. Were things going wrong before Dave slept with Julie? I didn't think so – but then I thought that I was content with my life before, and now I want it to be different. We used to share everything, yet there's an invisible barrier between us where I don't tell him things and I'm pretty sure there's stuff he's not telling me. So where does that leave us? Will we find ourselves again? Will we last for fifty years like Thea and Desmond? Or . . . not?

But if not, when will it change? When will one of us decide enough is enough? And why would we decide anything like that now, when Dave has sworn never to speak to Julie again and I've decided . . . Well, I haven't decided anything yet really.

Thea finishes her interview and I bring the car back to the front of the studio to collect her. I tell her that she spoke really well, and she smiles.

'I was lucky with Desmond,' she says. 'Given the crowd we moved in, he could've had plenty of other women over the years. I could have had other men. But whatever temptations lay in our paths, we both knew that we had something good, something we couldn't risk destroying. It's not only how we are as husband and wife,' she adds. 'It's how we are as people together.'

That's how I thought Dave and I were. That trust is what I thought we had.

'Have you somewhere you need to be now?' asks Thea when I pull up outside her house. 'Because if not, it would be nice if you could have a coffee with me. It's the only way I can say thank you for rescuing me earlier.'

'Oh, you don't have to . . .'

'Not if you're busy, obviously,' says Thea. 'I don't want to put you under pressure.'

I don't socialise with clients. I stepped over a line when I had coffee with Ivo Lehane, and see what that led to! But coffee with Thea Ryan is entirely different. And I don't need to go home yet. So I tell her that coffee would be lovely, and a couple of minutes later I'm sitting in her warm and cosy kitchen while she's switching on a very impressive-looking machine.

'Desmond bought it last Christmas,' she says. 'He drinks far too much coffee.'

'So do I.'

'In his case it's a diversionary tactic,' observes Thea. 'He does it to put off the moment when he has to get working. I guess it's the opposite for you.'

I nod.

'Either way, this is a nice blend,' Thea says. 'Though I'll have a camomile tea myself.'

I feel as though I should be helping her, but she bats away my offer by saying I'd be more of a hindrance than a help. I'm hoping she means it in a kind of generic way.

She serves the coffee in a wide blue china cup with a

matching saucer, and then shakes some bite-sized biscuits onto a bright green plate, which she puts between us. Her camomile tea is in a floral-patterned cup with gold edging. It's all very Miss Marple.

'How's your mum doing?' she asks when she's sitting opposite me.

'Not bad.' I tell her about the octopussies and she's charmed by the idea, saying that it's something she should do herself.

'I used to crochet a lot,' she tells me. 'When I was on the stage I used to sit in the wings with my hook and wool. I have more crocheted caps than I know what to do with. They were all the rage back in the seventies! I found it relaxing to do, and at the same time it helped me keep my focus.'

'I can send you the link to the website if you like,' I offer. 'Or you can google "knitted octopus".'

'I'll google it,' she says. 'And I'll definitely do it. It's such a lovely idea.'

'Mum's house is overrun with them.' I smile.

'I can imagine it occupies her,' says Thea. 'Has she got out much since the funeral?'

'Actually . . .' I take a sip of coffee, then put my cup back on the saucer. 'She's sort of dating.'

'Really!' Thea looks both astonished and impressed. 'Good for her.'

I explain about the website and about the men who only want women twenty years younger than themselves, and Mum's surprise when Diarmuid got in touch.

'I haven't met him,' I finish. 'But he sounds nice. Mum says it's only friendship, which makes me feel better about it

321

because it's still quite soon after Dad, but as she says herself, she's not at a time in her life when she can sit around and wait . . .' I falter, because once again I'm thinking of Dave and me, and I can't help wondering what's going to happen to us in the years ahead.

'Are you all right?' Thea is looking at me quizzically. 'You seem a little distracted all of a sudden.'

And then, for no reason I can think of other than that she's the sort of person who makes you tell her things, I'm blurting out the story of Rodeo Night.

'Oh, my dear.' Thea's blue eyes are full of sympathy. 'I can imagine how that must have hurt.'

It's funny, but I haven't really thought much about how hurt I felt. I've focused on my anger and humiliation and devastation and betrayal, but every single one of those emotions is wrapped up in hurt. And perhaps it's the hurt that's so difficult to put to one side, no matter how I try.

'We place our trust in someone, and when they break it, it's not easy to repair,' observes Thea. 'It's like the matching cup to the one you're drinking out of.'

I look at her in confusion.

'They were a pair,' she says. 'I dropped one of them and the handle broke off. My daughter Juno, who's the super-practical one of our family, glued it on for me. She did a wonderful job and it looks perfect. But I know what happened, and I'm afraid that if I use that cup, the handle will fall off and I'll be scalded by the tea.'

I replace my cup on the saucer.

'That one's fine.' Thea smiles. 'I have total faith in it.'

But she has a point. That's exactly how I feel about Dave now. I truly don't think he'll even look in Julie Halpin's direction ever again. But there's a nugget of doubt that something – or someone – might break his resolve. It doesn't have to be Julie.

Thea gets up suddenly and takes the second blue cup from the cupboard. She tips the tea she's been drinking from her floral cup into it.

'But sometimes you need to go for it,' she says as she takes a sip and then winks at me. 'How's your chauffeur business?'

I tell her that it's doing well but that it's another bone of contention between me and Dave.

'It's not up to me to give you advice,' she says. 'My children always tell me I dispense far too much of it and that most of it is worthless. But . . .' she shrugs, 'what's the point of having lived to my age and not being able to share stuff?'

'No point at all,' I say.

'A woman must have money and a room of her own,' Thea says.

Once again, I look at her in confusion.

'Virginia Woolf,' she explains. 'She was talking about writing fiction, but it's true in every respect. A woman needs her own space and her own money to be her own person.'

The car is my room. The money, even though it all ends up in our joint account, is mine too. Virginia Woolf, whoever she is, is right. And maybe that's why Dave doesn't like me driving. It's not that he's a controlling sort of man, but he likes to be the one in charge. He likes to be the one to say what we can afford to do and what we can't. He likes being the head of the house.

Are all men like that? Do they need to feel important all the time? Does it matter to them that much?

Thea is looking at me as she continues to drink her tea from the mended cup. I have to be more honest with her.

'It's not just Dave,' I say.

'Oh?'

'I wanted to sleep with someone. He sort of kissed me by mistake and I wish it had been for real, and now I can't stop thinking about it and about him.'

It sounds ridiculous when I put it like that. Thea refills her cup and asks me if I'd like another coffee. I nod.

'What happened?' she asks when she puts the fresh coffee in front of me.

I explain and she looks thoughtful. 'Which are you more upset about? Your husband and the other woman or how you're suddenly feeling about this man?'

'I had right on my side, but now I don't,' I say. 'So I guess I'm most upset about that.'

'It was a fantasy, Roxy,' says Thea. 'Everyone has fantasies. I often had them with my co-stars, but they didn't mean anything. It's hardly a massive betrayal.'

'It's how it makes me feel,' I tell her. 'Ivo's kiss was . . . well, it was supposed to be friendly, you know? But every time I think about it, I can't help feeling what it would've been like to kiss him back properly. And wishing that I had. And wishing that he'd come to my bedroom the night before, which is awful of me, isn't it?'

'It's still fantasy,' Thea says. 'When I kissed my co-stars, I believed in it. I wanted them too. Sometimes it was hard to separate Thea the person from the character they were kissing or holding or pretending to make love to.'

324

I tell her that what's happened to me is very different.

'Not entirely,' she says. 'When you're being Roxy the chauffeur, you're playing a role. This man is part of a scene that isn't your real life. You felt something. Maybe, for a time, you wanted something. You didn't actually do anything. Unlike your husband. Whom you've very generously forgiven.'

'I know. On a practical level, I know. It's . . . well, it's a long time since I've had feelings like that. And I should know better. I'm the grown-up, after all.'

'Your husband isn't?'

'He's Dave,' I say. 'I look after him. I make sure he's OK.'

'Roxy!' she exclaims. 'He's an adult and he can look after himself.'

I cover my face with my hands. I don't know why I said that. I know Dave is an adult. I know he can look after himself. But I suppose when it comes to our family unit – despite everything I think about Dave being the one to make the decisions – I'm actually the person who keeps it all together. And so Dave's behaviour is OK because I can fix it by forgiving him. How *I* feel is entirely different, because I can't forgive myself.

'Why are you punishing yourself so much?' asks Thea. 'If all you're doing is imagining how it would be with a man who's not your husband, but you've no intention of taking it any further, then why are you so upset?'

Because I wanted to take it further, even if it was only a one-off. I wanted to see what it would be like with someone else. Which is maybe what Dave thought when he slept with Julie. I believe him now when he says it didn't mean anything. It wouldn't have meant anything with Ivo either, but it would have been great.

'You're a good person, Roxy,' Thea says. 'Whatever you want to do, you're doing from the position of being a good person. Truly.'

'I know it's daft,' I say. 'I really do. But I can't possibly drive him ever again. And that's hard.'

Thea nods slowly.

'Maybe Dave's right about me driving anyhow,' I say. 'Money and a room of your own are all very well, but there has to be give and take.'

'Is Dave the teeniest bit jealous of you, do you think?' Thea puts the question to me very casually, and I look at her in surprise.

'Jealous? Of me? Of course not. Why would he be?'

'Because you're smart and resourceful and you've taken this business by the scruff of the neck and are making a success of it. You're good at what you do and I'm sure all your clients like you. *I* like you. I told you before, you're an excellent driver.'

'But not very professional.' I sigh. 'I'm lusting after one client and I'm sitting here having coffee and biscuits and sharing my problems with another. Which is really not in the job description.'

'Breaking down the door to my loo isn't in the job description either, but you did it,' says Thea. 'Don't be so hard on yourself.'

'I'm not.'

'You are. Nobody's perfect. Nobody can be. You can only do your best, and that's what you've been doing. So cut yourself some slack, forget about one little kiss at a time when you were in shock, for heaven's sake, and allow yourself to chill.'

'Is this the kind of advice you give your daughters?' My smile is a little wobbly.

'Absolutely,' she grins. 'But as they're my daughters, they hardly ever listen. That's why I'm hoping it's different with you.'

Chapter 25

I'm looking forward to Sunday lunch at Mum's and am hoping that having all the family around will bring back a sense of normality to my life. I also hope that the lunch gives us some kind of closure on Dad. I know a funeral is supposed to be closure, but it wasn't, not really. Maybe Dave is right after all and the reason I want to drive the Merc so much is because I still miss my father. Maybe he knows me better than I know myself.

Dad and Dave got on well. There were occasional times when they fell out over something relatively trivial, but their arguments were usually short-lived. Dad liked Dave's work ethic. He told me that my husband would always be able to take care of me, and he was right. Despite the fact that we needed my wages in the early years, and that we've never been entirely financially secure, I've never felt pressured by it because I've always trusted Dave to look after us. He's a hard worker, and unlike some husbands, he never criticises how I spend the household income. He might be a traditionalist in many ways, but he's a good traditionalist.

Dave insists we take a taxi to Mum's so that we can both

have a glass of wine with dinner. When we get into the cab, Tom and Mica start squabbling, and when I tell them to be quiet, they ask me if I ever say that to passengers in my taxi. I say that it's a bit different for me and they want to know why, and Dave lobs in the fact that most taxi drivers don't have to spend a night away from home. I don't know the guy who's driving us now, but I'm sure he thinks we're all mental. I tell my children to sit quietly and they both get into a huff, and I sigh and hope the rest of the day ahead will be calmer.

Tom is first out of the cab and races up the path to ring the doorbell, but Mica chases after him and they fight about who gets to buzz, which is utterly ridiculous, as ringing a doorbell is hardly a novelty for them. So I press it instead. Mum opens the door looking positively radiant in a chic purple dress and matching court shoes. She's also wearing gold earrings and the pretty gold chain that Dad bought her for Christmas a few years ago.

She smiles at the children and suddenly they're on their best behaviour, hugging her and telling her that it's lovely to see her. I exhale with relief.

'Something smells good, and it's not just you, Selina,' says Dave as we step inside. He's right: the savoury aroma of cooking permeates the house, and I feel hungry right away. Mum waves us to the living room, where Aidan and Kerry are already sitting, a beer in his hand and a glass of wine in hers.

There's a flurry of hellos and Mica scoops Sheryl, Aidan and Kerry's three-year-old daughter, into her arms. Deacon and Tom, who are close in age, immediately start punching each other and Kerry tells them to stop play-acting.

Aidan offers to get Dave a beer, and when he returns with a bottle of Bud, the two of them start talking sport.

Kerry tells me that I'm looking well, though beside her – a slender woman with chestnut curls, chocolate-brown eyes and cheekbones to die for – I usually feel pale and uninteresting. However, today I'm wearing the polka-dot dress I bought for the start-up workshop, and I'm empowered. Even Dave, who was lukewarm about the dress before, commented on how sassy I looked when I came downstairs earlier.

'Food will be on the table in five minutes.' Mum comes into the living room, her face slightly flushed, and I offer to help her serve it all up.

'No, no,' she protests. 'I'm doing everything today.'

When we troop into the dining room, I gasp. The table is beautifully set with the linen tablecloth that was only ever used at Christmas when I was small. There are also linen napkins at each place, as well as a menu card with a picture of Dad on the front.

'Granny, it's fabulous!' cries Mica. 'It's so pretty. Like a party.'

'Thank you.' Mum looks pleased

'You've excelled yourself.' I pick up one of the menu cards. 'This is a lovely idea!'

The menu has a shrimp terrine starter, garlic and rosemary pork for the main course, and lemon cookie fruit tarts as a dessert. I'm pretty certain she didn't get any of it out of a Gina Hayes book, but it sounds like a meal the nutritionist might put together.

'I had some help,' admits Mum. 'But for the moment you can pretend it's all my own work.'

'What help?' asks Aidan, but she shakes her head at him and refuses to answer.

Shrimp has never been on the menu in Mum's house before, and I know Dave isn't a fan, but he eats it anyway and compliments Mum on the taste. Even the children are happy to dig in.

'I'll help you clear away,' I tell her when we've finished. For a moment it looks as though she's going to refuse, but then she nods. I carry some of the little ramekin dishes to the kitchen – they're new, I've never seen them before in my life.

'What's all this?' I murmur as she takes the carving knife out of the drawer. 'Have you been going to classes without me? You've turned into Nigella Lawson.'

'Ah, it's just a bit of home cooking,' she says. 'I've been impressed with what you've been doing over the past few weeks and I thought I'd give it a go myself.'

'How many times have you practised this?' I take the plates out of the oven where she's been keeping them warm.

'It's my first go,' she admits. 'But I was able to do the shrimp things yesterday, and a roast is a roast – the garlic and rosemary is just fancying it up a bit.'

I stick a metal skewer into the accompanying potatoes. Mum's relationship with roast potatoes (even McCain's frozen ones) has always been a bit hit and miss, but these are perfectly done.

'I got the timings right,' she says with a hint of pride.

I'm stunned. I inherited my 'can't cook won't cook' attitude from her, and now it seems that both of us could give Nigella and Jamie a run for their money!

We bring the pork to the table. Dave makes more appreciative sounds, which Aidan echoes.

'Don't ever remember this sort of stuff when we were kids,' he remarks, and I think Kerry kicks him under the table, because he nearly chokes on a carrot.

'How's business?' Dave asks him when he recovers.

'Not bad.' Like me, Aidan has driving in his bones. In his case, though, he was never interested in driving people. He prefers inanimate objects. My brother has a furniture removal business, although it's not only furniture he moves – he'll transport anything for anybody.

'Economy picking up again,' observes Dave. 'Should keep you busy.'

Aidan nods. Dave makes some comment about the amount of new-builds going on and the number of people renovating bathrooms. The two men get stuck into their conversation about their respective businesses and what the government should be doing to make things easier for them and how the tax is still a killer. It's the sort of stuff Dad would have been talking about too if he was still with us, and I feel a stab of pain that he's not here to tell them – as he so often did – that they have it easy these days and it was all different when he was a boy. I wish, oh how I wish, he'd lived to enjoy his retirement. If he'd actually ever retired. Because he was always on the go.

I imagine him as a young man, like Aidan and Dave, and then, perhaps inevitably, I think about Estelle. I should have another conversation with my brother about the possibility that she had a child by Dad. If it's true, knowing about Estelle's son would be like a glimpse into another world. Of how it might have been if she and Dad had stayed together and raised a family. Well, obviously Aidan and I wouldn't have existed, but with Estelle by his side, would Dad have lived the same sort of life he had with Mum? Or would it have been very different?

What has life been like for her son? Did Estelle ever return to Ireland with him? Do I really have a half-brother I've never met?

It's impossible to believe. And yet part of me does.

The conversation gets more and more animated and the topics more and more diverse. Mum brings out the lemon cookie fruit tarts, which are both sweet and sharp and are absolutely delicious. She's been hiding this latent talent as a cook all of her life. It's a tragedy. I say so.

'Ah, it's easier now with the YouTube videos telling you what to do,' she says. 'And of course you can get all sorts in the shops.'

'That's true,' observes Kerry. 'It was a delicious meal, Selina, thank you.'

'You've gone from zero to hero in a flash,' I say, and Mum beams with pride.

'You did a great job, and Dad would be proud of you.' Aidan nods his agreement.

At the mention of Dad, we all go silent. Then Mum stands up with her glass in her hand.

'We're here to celebrate the birthday of a man who can't celebrate with us,' she says. 'But we'll never forget him. I'll never forget him. He'll always be the love of my life. Happy birthday, Christy.'

We're all a little emotional as we raise our glasses. The children run around the table clinking their plastic beakers, thus making sure that nobody actually cries. But, I think as

I wipe my eyes, it's OK to cry. And it's OK to miss my dad. I look across the table at Aidan, who gives me a small smile. I always thought I had a special relationship with Dad, but he and Aidan were close too. Dad was the one who gave him the money to buy his first van. He was a good man, no matter what.

We return to the living room. Mum puts on music from one of the playlists on Dad's old phone. It's music from the seventies and eighties, heavy on Donna Summer and Crystal Gayle. It takes me back to my childhood, when he used to play the same music on an enormous portable stereo system while he tinkered with the car in the driveway. I say this and then wish I hadn't, because the talk turns to Dad's time as a taxi driver and a chauffeur, and then, annoyingly, to me and what my plans might be.

'I thought you were only doing it for Dad,' says Aidan. 'I can't believe you're still at it.'

'Not for much longer,' says Dave. 'She's taking a break. But ultimately we'll be winding down the business and selling the car.'

I knew all this talk of a break was stonewalling.

Mum looks at me in surprise. 'Have you finally decided enough is enough?'

'No. I have,' says Dave.

'Dave's a bit fed up with me,' I tell my brother. 'I've been inundated with jobs lately and I had to overnight for one of them.'

'In a very flashy hotel.' Dave's voice is sour. 'She's got a taste for the high life now, has our Roxy.'

'Don't you have enough to do?' asks Kerry. 'I'd love to

get back to work, but I'm run off my feet with the kids and I don't have the time or the energy.'

'I like it,' I say. 'And of course my two are a little older than Deacon and Sheryl.'

'But it has to change.' Dave opens another tin of beer.

I'm pissed off with him at raising what's basically our personal business in front of everyone and turning it into a topic of conversation. I don't need other people's advice. Especially as they might side with Dave.

'Are you making money?' asks Aidan.

'Yes,' I say. 'Quite a decent wedge, actually.'

'I should really have had a look at the books before she started so we can assess it properly,' Dave says. 'She got so-called business advice from some friend of a friend, but you're better off with family.'

'He's a colleague of Alison King's,' I say. 'A professional. And I'm perfectly capable of seeing that I'm making money.'

'Dave's right, though. Family will always be better at looking out for your best interests,' says Aidan, and I want to hit him over the head.

'Roxy likes driving.' Mum speaks when it's obvious nobody else is going to say anything.

'I know she does,' says my husband. 'But it was always going to be temporary. The key thing will be to get out at the right time and sell the car before it depreciates too much. Christy was very generous in leaving it to her, but I'm pretty sure he never expected her to keep the business going. He wanted us to sell it so that we could treat ourselves. We could go to the Caribbean for Christmas.'

'Dave!' I shoot him a horrified look. 'We'll be here for Christmas. With Mum.'

There's an awkward little silence broken only by the Bellamy Brothers wondering if they said I had a beautiful body would I hold it against them.

'Anyway, Roxy can find something else to do,' says Dave. 'She was happy enough before.'

I nearly say 'Before what?' but I don't. When was I happier? Before I got married? Before I had children? Before Dad became ill? Before he died? Or was I simply happy before my husband cheated on me with the woman next door? And what does 'happy enough' really mean? Isn't that a watered-down version of happiness, where you're making the best of a bad job? Yes, I was happy enough. But is happy enough really enough? Shouldn't I just be happy? Also – and I can feel myself getting angry at both Dave and my brother – why are they talking about me as if I'm not here? Or as if I don't know what I'm doing?

Mum looks between us and then takes charge of the conversation.

'We're here to celebrate Christy,' she says. 'Not to talk about Roxy.'

'Of course we are,' says Aidan. He takes out his phone and shows us some photos of himself and Dad that he's scanned. We all smile at the pictures and reminisce about Dad as Aidan continues to flick through them. He pauses at one of him standing in the garden, a football trapped beneath his foot. Dad must have taken it. It's almost identical to the photo in the seat pocket of the car, the photo I've saved to my phone. I look at Aidan, but he's already swiped to the next picture.

Neither he nor Mum wants to believe that Dad might have fathered another child. When it comes down to it, no matter how fascinated I am by the idea, I'd rather it wasn't true either. Thinking about it is a waste of my time and energy. I should delete the photo from my phone and throw the actual picture away.

The day I stop driving, I will.

Nobody is in a rush to leave Mum's house. Dave, replete with food and beer, has nodded off in an armchair. Mica, Tom and Deacon are playing in the conservatory. Aidan is replacing some light bulbs in the utility room. Mum, Kerry and I are chatting about TV programmes. Kerry asks if we've seen the series starring Thea Ryan, and Mum nods enthusiastically. She adds that I'm Ms Ryan's driver, which makes Kerry's eyes widen.

'I'm not employed by her,' I clarify. 'She calls me when she needs to be driven somewhere.'

'And she's driven that celebrity nutritionist woman with her own show. Gina Hayes.' Mum sounds proud of me and I can't help feeling a little proud myself. Especially when she adds that I've also had the vibrant Leona Lynch as a client. 'It's good to know that the younger crowd like her too,' Mum adds, which makes me chuckle.

'Dave is right about you living the high life,' says Kerry. 'I can't believe you're an actual celebrity chauffeur.'

'There's not that much celebrity in it,' I say. 'But it's nice to have some famous people in the car from time to time.'

'You should have a website,' Kerry says. 'And list them.'

'I'm not sure they'd want to appear on a site like that,' I say. 'But I've set up an Instagram account and Leona Lynch

is one of my followers. I'm up to nearly five hundred now,'
I add as I take out my phone and show her. 'Gina's PR
company follows me too, and they've used me for a few of
their authors. They've booked me to pick up Kieran Kelly
next month.' Kieran Kelly is the hot Irish actor currently
making a name for himself in Hollywood. There's talk of
a Golden Globe nomination and possibly even an Oscar. I
was very excited when Melisse called me.

'Oooh!' Kerry is equally excited. 'Now I see why you want
to keep driving. Who wouldn't want a sexy man like Kieran
Kelly in the back seat!'

I laugh. 'Men like him are the exception rather than the
rule,' I say. 'It's usually boring business people. But still . . .
it *is* kind of cool, isn't it?'

'But Dave says you're taking a break.' She lowers her
voice even though my husband is snoring gently in the
corner. 'And he's made it plain that he wants you to sell
the car.'

'Ah, you know.' I shrug. 'I think I can talk him around.
It's all about managing our time, really. Making sure the kids
aren't neglected.'

'With men, a lot of it is making sure *they* don't feel
neglected,' says Kerry.

She's echoing my mum and she's right. Dave wants to
believe he's the most important person in my life and that
everything revolves around him. And in a lot of ways it does.
Before Dad got sick and before I started driving, I always
took account of my husband before I agreed to doing
anything. The weekends were crafted around him. He made
an assumption that I had plenty of time for my own stuff
during the week. Which was partly true, of course. But my

time then was every bit as taken up by other things as it is by driving now. The common theme, though, was making sure Dave was happy. Not just happy enough.

These are uncomfortable thoughts and I don't like the way they're worming through my head. It's not wrong to put your family ahead of yourself. The same as it's not wrong to want to do something for yourself. But if that's the case, how come I feel guilty about doing both?

Kerry is talking about another celebrity now, a beauty blogger I've never heard of.

'If you ever drive her, Roxy, be sure to ask her for samples,' she says. 'I bet she has loads of stuff she never has time to use.'

My phone beeps suddenly and wakes Dave up. He's trying to pretend he wasn't asleep at all as I fish it out of my bag and look at the message. It's from Leona Lynch's agent asking if I can drive her next weekend to a tech event in Trinity College where she's a guest speaker.

Dave has announced to everyone that I'm taking a break and winding things down. And despite telling Kerry that I can talk him around, I'm not sure I can. But neither am I saying no to Leona Lynch. So I agree to the job without anyone even knowing that I was offered it in the first place.

Sometimes technology is great.

'We should probably get going.' Kerry looks at her watch. 'I'll see how Aidan is getting on.' She walks out of the room.

Dave stands up too and stretches his arms above his head.

'Great meal, Selina,' he says. 'Very impressive. I'll call a cab.'

Everyone is bustling around now and Mum and I are momentarily alone in the living room.

'It was a fantastic lunch,' I tell her. 'You said you had some help. It wasn't Diarmuid by any chance, was it?'

Mum flushes and then gives a little shrug of resignation.

'He gave me some tips,' she admits.

'So he hasn't dumped you for a younger model yet?' I tease. 'You're managing to keep him interested?'

'Shh, for heaven's sake,' she hisses at me. 'I'm telling you because . . . well, I don't know why, really.'

'Are you properly dating him?' I'm happy for her, but it's a bit weird to think that my mum's male friend helped her make a celebration dinner for my late father's birthday.

'Not dating,' she says. 'I told you before. It's companionship.'

'How many times?'

'He brought me to dinner in town. A really good restaurant with proper tablecloths and leather-bound menus. And then he advised me on this. He's a good cook, Roxy. He enjoys being in the kitchen.'

That's a turn-up for the books for certain.

'Nobody will ever replace your dad,' says Mum. 'I swear to you.'

'Mum, you're a grown-up. We're all grown-ups. Your life is yours to lead.' I think I'm being very mature even though I suddenly feel quite wobbly inside.

She puts her arms around me. 'I don't care how grown up you are, darling. You'll always be my little girl,' she says, and kisses me on the cheek. 'And listen to me,' she adds. 'I know I mightn't always have seemed supportive about it, but if you want to keep driving, you keep driving, no matter what Dave says. I'm always here to back you up and keep an eye on Mica and Tom.'

My husband walks in carrying my jacket and holds it out

so that I can slip my arms into the sleeves. I emerge from my mother's hug and slide it on.

Dave checks his phone and puts his arm around me.

'Taxi's here,' he says, and there's authority in his voice. 'Time to go.'

So we do.

Chapter 26

I want to pick the right moment to tell Dave about driving Leona, because I know it's going to annoy him, particularly as it's at the weekend. I also have to pretend that it's a job that's been in the pipeline for a while, otherwise we'll definitely have a row about my so-called break. When he comes home on Tuesday night in great form because the company has landed a very profitable contract, I think that this is the time. He can't complain about me getting good business when he's getting it too.

Obviously I don't say anything while the children are around, but when they've gone to bed and we're sitting on the sofa together, I'm ready to give the speech I've been rehearsing for the past couple of days. But before I can start, he pulls me towards him and brings his mouth down on mine, and I think that this is what it's supposed to be like, that we're husband and wife and we only want what's best for each other. And I truly do want what's best for Dave. What's best for both of us. Everything else is a distraction.

'I hope the kids don't—'

'Shut up,' he says, and kisses me again.

I shut up.

'We should do it like this more often,' he says afterwards.

'You're usually watching football.'

'I'd pick you over Arsenal any day.' He grins. 'Certainly the way they're playing now.'

'That's good to know.' I make a face at him and he kisses me again.

'I've been thinking,' he says after a while.

I look expectantly at him.

'I know it's been a tough time, and maybe I haven't been understanding enough of what you've gone through.'

I'm not sure if he means about Dad dying or him and Julie.

'Things have been out of whack,' he says. 'It's hard to get it back sometimes.'

Clearly he really *has* been thinking. And this is a good thing. Because it means our marriage matters to him as much as it matters to me. Hopefully we'll be able to talk about it like adults, and he'll understand my desire to have my own business.

'What we really need . . .' His tone is serious and I look at him intently. 'What we really need,' he continues, 'is to make the family complete.'

I'm not sure exactly what he's talking about. Our family *is* complete. Unless he wants to get the dog that Tom badgers us about every so often. So far we've always stood firm. But does Dave seriously think adding a dog to the mix will help?

'We only have two,' he says. 'I know your family is small, Roxy, but I come from a larger crowd. And I'd like more.'

I say nothing as I process his words.

'We were strapped for money before,' Dave continues. 'During the recession and everything. But now we're in a better place. I have lots of work. You've made a nice little pot with the driving, and as soon as we sell the car, we'll have even more. So it's a good time.'

I know what he's saying but I want to hear it all the same. To be sure I'm not mistaken.

'You're a great mother,' says Dave, 'and you deserve another baby.'

I love Mica and Tom more than anything. I've loved them since before they were born. I loved carrying them, giving birth to them, bringing them home and watching them grow. I think of what that would be like again. And there are bits of it that are appealing. But I'm done with the whole baby thing. I really am.

'I don't want another baby, Dave.' I feel the tension in my body. 'We're fine the way we are.'

'You wanted one when Tom started school,' he reminds me.

And it's true. I did. For about a day. Because when I went home to an empty house, I felt bereft. But then I started childminding. I'm done with that too.

'It would be lovely to have a baby in the house again,' says Dave. 'And great for Tom.'

I don't want another argument with him. There have been so many and they're always about him wanting something and me saying no. Instead I say we'd have to consider it carefully.

He squeezes my shoulders and kisses my hair and tells me he loves me again.

This is clearly not the ideal moment to mention the Leona Lynch job, but I decide to tell him anyway. Leona's agent has sent me more information about the event itself and has said that I can have some free tickets. I use these as bait, saying that Mica is crazy about Leona and that tech is really important and it would be good for her to go, so it's not so much me doing a job as doing something for our daughter.

'But you've to collect this Lynch wan from Drogheda first? And bring her home?'

'It's no big deal, Dave. And she's an important client.'

'Your important client is going to have to start looking elsewhere,' he says. 'Besides, you've only been driving her a few months. She can't be that important.'

'Leona is great,' I say. 'She taught me how to edit photos to make them look good on social media. StyleDrive has a lot of followers now.'

I wriggle away from him and take out my mobile phone to show him the Instagram account. He's never looked at it before. Dave only bothers with Facebook.

'What's the point of sharing all these photos?' he asks. 'How does that get you any business?'

I say that it's all about exposure, and he snorts. But then I suggest that his plumbing company could put up photos of the work they've done. People would see his wonderful bathrooms and be inspired. He looks at my photos again and scrolls through some of the accounts I follow.

'Click on Leona's,' I say.

He does, and grimaces. 'She's far too in love with herself for me.'

'She's not posing for you,' I point out. 'Dave, she earns a six-figure sum from all of her blogging and stuff. She talks about beauty products and people buy them. OK, a lot of her followers are too young to be hiring cars and buying bathrooms, but other people see the pictures too.'

He's scrolling through my pictures again, more slowly this time.

'You should think about it.'

'Maybe,' he says. 'But it doesn't alter the fact that you've taken on a job *at the weekend* when I don't want you to drive at all.'

'We'll work it out,' I say, even though I'm not sure how we will.

'Where's this?' he asks, stopping at a photo I took of Castlemartyr. It doesn't do it justice because the light was poor and even the filters didn't really help. I tell him that it was where I overnighted in Cork, and he's saying that it doesn't look like much when he moves on to the room. Which by any stretch of the imagination was fabulous. But very fortunately his attention is caught by the bathroom and he's looking at the tiles and the shower and suddenly I can see he's interested in the whole idea and has been distracted from our conversation.

'So I would post pictures of the bathrooms we do,' he says.

'Yes.' I nod. 'I think they'd look great. You could do them as you're working on them. Or before-and-after pictures.' I'm actually getting quite excited on Dave's behalf.

'I'll download the app,' he says.

'Brilliant.'

'What's this?'

It's the chicken sandwich I had in the bar. The photo makes it look even better than it was in real life.

'My dinner,' I tell him. 'A chicken sandwich.'

'"Compensations in a Driver's Life"?' He reads the caption.

'It was a very nice sandwich,' I say.

'Best driver in the world?' This time he's reading Leona's hashtag.

I shrug.

Dave takes out his phone and downloads Instagram.

We don't talk about Leona Lynch again.

Mica has obviously been telling Emma all about the tech event, because her mum rings me for more information. After I give her the lowdown, Audrey offers to bring the two girls to the venue while I collect Leona, which is really helpful.

'No bother,' says Audrey. 'Emma is very excited. She's a big Leona Lynch fan too.'

Until I met Leona, I hadn't realised how popular she was. But now that I recognise her name, I've seen it pop up all over the place. So Audrey and I make an arrangement for her to collect the children on Saturday morning. They're going to get the Dart into town, which will leave them near the venue. Meantime I text Leona to check on the time I'll be picking her up.

Dave has agreed that he might bring Tom and his friend Andrew in later, but as they have a football match in the morning, he's promised them burgers afterwards. They're looking forward to it, he says, and he's not going to let them down.

'Absolutely fine,' I say with a determined cheeriness. I'm not going to rock the boat.

The event is good fun and Leona is an absolute star. After her talk, everyone mills around trying to get selfies. I ask Mica if she wants to push forward, but my daughter is suddenly shy and shakes her head. However, after Leona eventually manages to escape, she sends me a text and asks if I'd like to bring Mica to the security guard's room for a selfie of her own. Mica and Emma are over the moon with excitement.

'Hi!' Leona beams at them when we walk in. 'It's great to see you. Which of you is Mica?'

And then she's chatting to them and letting them take as many selfies as they want and generally making their day.

'Thank you,' I say when they eventually have enough and Audrey tells them it's time to go home. 'That was so generous of you.'

'No problem at all.' Leona smiles. 'I like your daughter. She's feisty.'

'She can be a handful sometimes, but she's got a good heart,' I say.

'She reminds me of me,' says Leona. 'Knows her own mind.'

'Which can be good and bad.' I grin. 'Are you ready to go home yourself now?'

Leona nods and drains her bottle of water.

'I have to get the car first,' I tell her.

'I'll walk with you,' she says.

'Sure?'

'Of course.'

We walk through the college. It's where she was studying for her degree and she knows her way around.

'I told all those kids how important education is, but I dropped out myself,' she says, her tone rueful. 'I will definitely finish my degree at some point.'

'That'll keep your mum happy.'

She laughs. 'The most important thing, obviously.'

We don't talk on the way back to Drogheda. Unlike the

last time I drove her, she's spending a lot of time tapping on her phone. After half an hour or so she takes a call.

'Liam-o,' she says. 'How are you?'

I try to tune out as I always do when clients are having conversations, but I can't help hearing that her tone is getting more and more irritated.

'I told you. I have a car bringing me home. I'm on the way now,' she says. She adds that she has to update her vlog later tonight and that she's getting stuff together for a meeting on Monday. Liam clearly isn't impressed.

'It's my job!' she cries eventually. 'For crying out loud, Liam, don't you see that?'

No, it seems he doesn't. I try even harder not to listen, but she's getting more and more annoyed and eventually she says that she's not carrying on with this conversation and cuts him off.

Do all men resent the women in their lives working? Surely not Leona's generation. They've been brought up with equality. So were we, sort of, because we all thought we could have a go at whatever we wanted, but I guess I never thought that anything I could do would be equal to anything Dave did. I do now, though.

I say nothing, and after a while she leans forward.

'Why is it that men think whatever it is they want to do is way more important than anything a woman wants?' She puts words to my own thoughts. 'It's the whole bloody alpha-male thing. They're like babies really. Which isn't very alpha at all.'

I still don't say anything.

'Liam wanted me to go to his place after I finished up today. I already told him I was too busy. But he won't listen.'

349

'Is he your boyfriend?' I ask.

'My ex-boyfriend,' she says.

'Ah, Leona, don't do anything rash.'

'It's not rash to dump someone when they don't respect what you do,' she says. 'And he doesn't.'

The issue of respect seems to be looming large in my life at the moment.

'I bet you wouldn't take any of that crap from your husband,' she adds.

Hmm.

'I admire you,' she says. 'You're strong and determined and your daughter is an absolute peach.'

I'm admired by a Generation X-er. Or Z-er. Or whatever they are. But someone young and relevant. It would be a great feeling if I thought for a second that I deserved it.

Chapter 27

Debs rings me on Sunday morning and asks if I'd like to go to IKEA with her. She wants some new lamps for her living room, and because Mick won't even set foot in the superstore, he's perfectly happy to let her do the grunt work.

Dave says he's going to watch the soccer at home and that he's happy to keep an eye on Mica and Tom while I go shopping. He says this in a jokey, blokey kind of way and I'm relieved there's an easier atmosphere between us, even though I know he was irritated by the Leona Lynch job and that he's still waiting for me to give the green light on another baby.

The more I think about it, the more I see how having another baby kills two birds with the one stone for him – it makes selling the Merc almost inevitable, as there's no way I could keep driving with a small baby at home, and it means I would revert to the Roxy I was before. I can understand why he wants her back. She knew what she wanted. She knew what other people wanted. And she made sure that both of those things were the same. But today's Roxy isn't like that at all. She really doesn't know what she wants. Yet she knows what she doesn't. And she's not quite so prepared to let other people dictate her life.

Debs and I follow the prescribed route around IKEA, which, as always on a Sunday, is like a bear garden. But she manages to find two lamps she likes and we make our way to the market hall, where (as always) I load up with scented candles and paper napkins. I know I should probably support my neighbour, Natalie, in the candle purchases, but in all honesty, how can anyone walk out of IKEA without buying something, if only to justify the effort in getting around it in the first place.

When I arrive home, Dave is in the front garden with a man I don't recognise. The driver's door of the Merc is open and Dave is leaning against it. He's talking to the man, waving his arm expansively as he often does when he's explaining something. I park the Toyota on the street and get out.

'Hi,' I say as I walk into the garden.

'Hello,' says the stranger.

'The kids are acting up,' Dave tells me. 'It's doing my head in. See if you can sort it out, sweetheart, will you?'

I give him a surprised glance but I leave him and the man together. Dave has an eclectic mix of mates who drop around from time to time – other plumbers or electricians or carpenters – and I'm thinking that this guy is probably here to talk about a job. Which is good. Dave likes being busy.

I break up the row that's going on between Mica and Tom over the PlayStation controller. Mica flounces off to her bedroom and Tom settles down in front of the TV. It's unusual for him to argue with his sister over technology – normally he gives in and reads instead. But I can see that his face is set and this was an argument he definitely wanted to win.

I go upstairs. Mica is lying on her bed, looking at the ceiling. 'You OK?' I ask.

'I hate boys,' she says. 'They always want what you have.'

'You sometimes want what Tom has,' I remind her.

'Yes, but when he wants it, he makes such a fuss he always gets it,' she says.

Does he? Tom is my gentle child. But perhaps Mica has a point. When his mind is set on something, Tom is unyielding. The thing is, it's a rarity for him to dig his heels in.

'I didn't care about the stupid game,' Mica continues. 'I minded because I was playing first and he said it was his turn but it wasn't.'

'Oh well.' I sit on the bed behind her. 'Boys can be very silly sometimes.'

'I know.' She heaves an enormous sigh. 'I don't think I'll ever get married.'

'Why is that?'

'Because you have to be nice to them then,' she says. 'You're stuck with them.'

I can't help laughing.

'It's true.' Mica's voice is deadly serious. 'Granny says so.'

What on earth has my mother been telling my daughter?

'When you find a man you love, you'll want to be nice to him,' I say.

'But will it be worth it?' Mica doesn't wait for my reply but gets up and takes a book from her shelf.

Role reversal, I think, as I hear Tom blasting away on the PlayStation. I hope it's temporary.

I'm unwrapping my candles in the kitchen when Dave comes in.

'Who was your friend?' I ask.

'He's not a friend.' Dave opens the cupboard and takes out a jar of coffee. Then he begins to fill the kettle. 'He's buying the car.'

I think I've misheard him over the sound of the running water. 'What?'

'He's buying the car.' Dave spoons coffee into a mug.

'What car?'

'The Merc, of course. I uploaded the details onto a few sites yesterday and this guy is interested.'

'You did what?' I look at him in disbelief. And then, when he doesn't answer, I add, 'You can't sell the car. It's mine.'

'We're married,' says Dave. 'What's mine is yours and what's yours is mine. That's always been the way, Roxy. As long as it's there, you're going to keep finding excuses to drive whenever someone wants. You won't do like you promised and take a break.'

I never promised to take a break. That was Dave's idea.

'This guy, Garrett, will arrange a bank transfer,' he continues. 'He's paying exactly what I wanted – a grand under the price I listed it for. You should be glad, Roxy. You'll have your life back and we can have another baby and—'

'You can't sell the Merc,' I repeat. 'It's registered to me.'

He says nothing.

'Besides . . .' I feel the anger bubble up inside me. 'Besides, I don't want another baby. I like my life as a driver. It's interesting.'

'Well thanks a lot for that,' says Dave. 'I've done everything to give you and the kids the best I can afford, and now you're telling me that your life is boring.'

'Oh, for God's sake!'

'Don't throw your eyes to heaven like that,' he says. 'These last months you've disrespected me in every possible way. You've ignored my feelings about the car. You've done what you want whenever you want. You don't consult me about anything. It's like I'm not good enough for you any more. It's like you prefer strangers in your car than your own husband. Although they're not all strangers, are they? Giving you perfume? Putting you up in expensive hotels? I saw that bedroom, remember?'

'How dare you!' I don't know if Dave's accusation, with its kernel of . . . well, not truth exactly, but something, has made me even angrier than I should be. I wonder fleetingly if that's why he can get so angry when I accuse him of anything. Because he knows that there's a nugget in there that might not be totally wrong. 'Can I remind you, Dave McMenamin, that you were the one who shagged the neighbour?'

'You're going to bring that up as a trump card every time, aren't you?' He looks at me in disgust. 'I thought we were over it. You said you forgave me. I promised it wouldn't happen again, and it won't. We have to get back to normal and I'm doing my best. But you're carrying a grudge and using the car against me. It's time for me to take a stand.'

'Your stand still doesn't seem to take account of the fact that you've no right to sell it.'

'That car is a symbol of everything that's wrong in our lives,' says Dave. 'And it's got to go.'

'But—'

'No buts. It's over, Roxy.'

'It's not!' I cry. 'I'm building up a good business and I

want to keep doing it. You're right – I don't want to take a break. And I don't see why you're being so bloody pig-headed about it.'

'*I'm* being pig-headed!' He snorts. 'It's all about what *you* want, not what I want or what the kids want.'

'That's so not true.'

'You've become self-centred,' he continues. 'You don't care about us at all.'

'That's not true either.' I'm getting angrier by the minute. 'Before I take a job, I always make sure that there's someone around to look after the children.'

'Yeah. Instead of them having their mum at home, they're being shunted around the neighbourhood.'

Is he right about that? I've had the same thought myself when I'm arranging childcare. And yet is it selfish to want to have a life of my own outside of Beechgrove Park? Why do I feel so damn guilty when he clearly doesn't?

'You don't care what happens to this family as long as you get what you want,' he says.

We're facing each other across the table and neither of us is backing down. I can see Dave's jaw clenching and unclenching.

'It's either that fucking car or me,' he says eventually. 'Your choice, Roxy. Your choice.'

And then he walks out of the room.

A few months ago, if Dave had stormed out of a room after an argument, I would have given it a few minutes and then gone after him. I would've tried to fix things, to find a compromise. But today I don't. Because there is no compromise. He's trying to tell me what I can and can't do, and it's not right. It shouldn't be a case of the car or him. It shouldn't be a case of the car or the children. It shouldn't be a case of me having to be the one to stop doing what I want so that other people can do what they want instead. I will always sacrifice stuff for my kids because they are my life. But I've already done my very best to make sure that driving fits in with their timetables. I could be out on the road from morning till night. And there are times when I'd quite like to be. But I'm not. So I'm going to ignore the guilt, at least as far as Tom and Mica are concerned. I don't feel one bit guilty about Dave. He's always done what he wants. And I've always supported him. So why can't he, for once in his life, get behind me?

And how dare he try to sell Dad's car – *my* car – behind my back?

I'm working myself up into an even greater temper and I decide that I need to get out of the house. So I grab my bag, shout upstairs to Tom and Mica that I'll be back soon, and go outside, slamming the front door behind me. I get into the Merc and drive to Malahide Castle. I park the car and then stomp around the grounds while my anger bubbles and seethes.

I think of the last time I was here, with Mum, when I'd left Dave and we accidentally bumped into him and the children. I think of how impressed I was with his parenting skills (even though I didn't really acknowledge it at the time), and I think about how I allowed the pendulum of forgive and forget to swing in his favour. I wanted to go back to him then. I thought we could make a go of it. Yet we're not.

Is that my fault or his? If it's his, it's because of Julie

Halpin and because of the macho crap he's coming out with. If it's mine, it's because I'm putting myself first. It's definitely not because I had a silly lustful crush on Ivo Lehane. One that made me think of what it would be like to be with a different sort of man. A man who doesn't see life in black and white, even if he confesses to having no people skills. Besides, Ivo has issues. I don't need a man with issues! But the fact that I could fancy someone other than Dave was a shock. I don't know if I'm impossibly naïve. Or just stupid.

I'm craving a coffee, so I go into the Avoca café and order a large cappuccino with extra cinnamon on top. I add a slice of chocolate cake to my tray. I haven't had cappuccino and chocolate cake since I started sticking more closely to Gina Hayes and her healthy-living lifestyle. But when you're feeling angry and upset, a quinoa bar won't cut it.

I'm taking my tray with its comfort food to a table when I hear my name called. I turn around.

'Mum!' I smile, and then my eyes widen in surprise as I look at the man opposite her. He seems vaguely familiar.

'This is Diarmuid,' she says.

The man from the site that's not Tinder. The man who was happy to go out with women closer to his own age. The man who helped her cook Sunday lunch. I eye him warily.

'Nice to meet you.' I feel I should shake his hand or something, but I'm laden down with the tray and my bag.

'Are Dave and the children with you?' asks Mum. 'Do you want to join us?'

'It's just me,' I reply.

'Oh. Well sit down.' She pulls out the empty seat at the table and I put down my tray.

'Do the children have a football match?' she asks.

'No, they're at home.'

'You have your husband well trained.' Diarmuid grins at me.

If only, I think.

'Is everything OK?' asks Mum when I don't say anything.

'Of course. I had a bit of a headache, so I needed to get out.' I rummage in my bag and take out an unnecessary Panadol, which I wash down with a gulp of cappuccino. I can see Mum giving me a quizzical look, but Diarmuid – who actually looks better in real life than in his photograph, which must be a first for anyone – is saying that Mum has told him a lot about me.

'All good, I hope.' I keep my voice as cheerful as I know how.

'She says you're a powerhouse,' Diarmuid assures me. 'That you have your own business and drive celebrities all around the country, as well as raising two of the cutest children in the world.' He grins again. 'Obviously I think my grand-children would equal them in cuteness, but well done you, anyway.'

'Thank you.'

'Times have changed so much since I was a young fella,' continues Diarmuid. 'There's my own daughter working in the bank and her husband at home.'

'Seriously?' I know the house-husband thing happens, but not among any of my friends.

'Oh yes,' says Diarmuid. 'She's quite important, but don't ask me what she actually does. Ronan is a musician. He gives lessons from home, though obviously they have to fit in around their own children.'

'How old are they?' I cut off a piece of my chocolate cake.

The rich cocoa taste explodes in my mouth and I'm instantly calmer. It's been such a long time!

'Tuirean is ten and Luagh is six,' he says.

'Similar ages to my own.'

'Yes, so Selina told me. I admire women who can do it all.'

'I don't think any of us are doing it all,' I say. 'I think all we're doing is our best.'

'I admire you anyway,' says Diarmuid. 'I was a desperately unreconstructed male until Cara had Tuirean. When she told me that Ronan was planning to stay home with the baby, I nearly had a fit. But her job was way better paid than his, and she's a real business dynamo. So it made sense. Took me a while to see it, though. I kept thinking of her being under huge pressure and him being a bit of a wimp. Not the case. Not at all.'

'Roxy's situation is a little different,' says Mum. 'She only started driving to help out her dad.'

'But I love it,' I say firmly. 'And the business is going from strength to strength.' I take out my phone and show him my Instagram account.

'They're great,' he says as he scrolls through the photos. 'You have a talent.'

I explain about the filters and he says he has no real idea of what I'm talking about, but then asks if I'll take a photo of him and Mum together.

'If you like.' I look at Mum enquiringly and she nods, so I get up and wait for them to move so that they're sitting next to each other. I spend a little bit longer than usual making sure that I have them properly framed, then I switch to portrait mode and take the photo.

They look good in it. Comfortable together. I feel a lump in my throat for Dad.

'Can you do something with it like you've done with yours?' asks Diarmuid. 'You know, make it look more moody or professional?'

I experiment with a few filters, then show him the final result.

'Amazing what technology can do,' he says. 'I remember the days of leaving film with the chemist and being surprised when you got your photos back because you'd forgotten what was on the roll.'

I can't imagine that. I really can't.

'Send it to me and I'll share it with him,' says Mum, who's totally up to speed.

I do, and she does, and Diarmuid exclaims again at how good it is.

We finish our coffees and leave the café together.

'Everything OK?' asks Mum again, as Diarmuid walks slightly ahead of us.

'Of course. Why wouldn't it be?'

'Because you're here on your own on a Sunday afternoon.'

I sigh. There's no point in lying to her. She always knows.

'Dave and I had a bit of a row. About the car,' I add, although I'm pretty sure Mum is aware that the car is the main thing Dave and I row about.

'Oh, sweetheart.'

'He's trying to sell it behind my back, not that he actually can. And I'm not going to let him. I'm not going to be forced into giving up my job.'

'Is it worth it?' Mum's voice is matter-of-fact.

'It is to me.'

361

'You've got to make the right decision for you,' she says. 'I told you before and I'll tell you again – I'm here for you, no matter what. Just be certain of what it is you really want.'

'Thank you.'

'And although your dad would hate to think that the car has come between you and Dave, he'd also be behind you.'

I take a tissue from my bag and blow my nose.

Diarmuid is still ahead of us, allowing us to talk privately.

'He's a nice man,' I say.

'I know.'

'Still only companionship?'

Mum says nothing.

'Mum?'

'So far,' she admits eventually. 'But . . . well, we'll see.'

'Whatever makes you happy,' I say.

I mean it. Though it's a bit bleak that my mother's new relationship seems to be running a lot more smoothly than the one I've been in for over twenty years.

Chapter 28

It's almost dark by the time I get home.

Dave and the children are eating pizza in front of the TV. I say nothing about the fact that it's been a rarity in the house for weeks.

'Mum!' Mica scrambles to her feet. 'You're back. Where did you go?'

'I had things to do.'

'What things?'

'I had to see your granny,' I tell her.

'Do you want some pizza?' Tom picks a triangle from his own plate and offers it to me.

'It's OK,' I tell him. 'I had cake with Granny. I'll go upstairs and change.'

I hurry up to the bedroom, but Mica follows me.

'Why didn't you bring us with you to see Granny?' she asks.

'You were all busy.'

'I would've stopped doing what I was doing,' says Mica. 'I like going to Granny's.' She frowns. 'Are you . . . are you upset about something? Is it my fault?'

'Not at all,' I assure her. 'But maybe I'm not having my best day today and that's why I needed to see Granny.'

'Poor Mum.' She wraps her arms around me. 'Everything will be fine.'

'Of course it will,' I say cheerfully. 'Everyone has down days sometimes.'

'Like when I had the row with Emma and Oladele.'

'Exactly.'

'We had a row because they were mean. Was someone mean to you? 'Cos I wasn't.'

'I know you weren't,' I say.

'Was it Dad?' She looks anxious.

'Why would you think it was Dad?'

'Because he was annoyed when you went out. And he said that you wanted to be Superwoman but that only Superwoman is Superwoman.'

'He has a point.'

'He says that you have to stop driving and be our proper mum.'

I might actually punch Dave.

'I'll always be your proper mum,' I say.

'I know.' She cuddles up to me. 'I don't mind you doing other things. Except if I want to go to football or swimming or stuff.'

'Good.'

'And I like that you're friends with Leona Lynch. Which is very cool for an old person.'

'Thanks.'

'I love you,' says Mica.

'I love you too,' I tell her in return.

But later that night, there's no love between Dave and me. None at all. We don't speak until the children are in bed, and when we do, I tell him, with all the finality I can muster, that he's not selling my car. And that I'll wind down the business when I want to and not before.

'You know, I don't think it's about the driving at all,' says Dave. 'I think there's something else. I think you use it to get out of the house with no questions asked. Because don't think for one second I haven't wondered about it, Roxy. Friday nights. Sunday afternoons. Overnight stays. A guy who gives you perfume.'

'Not this again!' I'm totally exasperated now.

'What am I supposed to think?'

'Maybe that I'm doing my job.'

'Or that you're using it as an excuse.'

'I thought I was driving because I'm incapable of forgetting my dad.'

'That too,' says Dave. 'Look, I've been talking to people about you. And they all agree—'

'What people?' I demand.

'Friends,' Dave says. 'Family.'

'Who?'

'Aidan, for one,' replies Dave. 'He said you were upset because Selina told you that Christy might have had a baby before he married her. He says that your mum thinks it's unhinged you a bit. I can imagine it would. And I can't believe you didn't tell me about it. Which shows how much you've changed, Roxy. Last year, I would've been the first to know.'

Aidan wouldn't talk about Dad's possible baby to me, but he did to Dave? I'm filled with rage towards my disloyal brother. As for Mum – well, she might have said that to Aidan a few weeks ago. But she's in my corner now. If I need her to be.

'I've made allowances for you,' says Dave. 'I've been patient and fair. But my patience is at breaking point and you haven't been fair to me.'

I have. At least, I think I have. Although there's still the issue of Ivo Lehane. But he was my fantasy man. Thea Ryan said it was OK to have a fantasy. And I trust her.

'Look.' Dave sighs deeply. 'Let's agree that we've had a tough few months and that both of us have done things we regret. But we're over the hump now and we'll move forward.'

I want to say yes. I want to believe that things can be better. But I'm very afraid that we may have passed the point of no return.

'That car is a symbol of everything that's gone wrong between us,' says Dave. 'The offer for it is a good one. I can buy you a really nice replacement for the Toyota and still have money left for a decent holiday afterwards. We deserve it, Roxy.'

Is it possible he's right? About the car? About everything?

'I need to think about it,' I say.

'And the baby,' he adds. 'Think about the baby too.'

No matter what he says, I'm definitely not thinking about a Band-Aid baby.

I don't have any jobs the next morning, but I'm up before Dave and make toast for his breakfast before he heads out for the day. He doesn't say anything as he eats the toast and drinks a large mug of coffee, which only takes him five minutes. He's gone before seven. I stand under my state-of-the-art shower and worry about the future.

The children are up soon afterwards. In contrast to the silence in the kitchen while Dave had breakfast, the two of them squabble and rile each other up over their porridge. Because it's drizzling, I drive them to school. By the time we get there, they're best friends again and are holding hands as they walk through the gates. If only it were that easy for adults to resolve their differences.

I go home and make my second coffee of the day. I'm about to sit down with it when my phone pings with a message.

Just to let you know my father died last night, says Ivo Lehane. *I know it's short notice, but is it possible for you to pick me up at the airport later. 3 p.m.?*

I stare at the message for a long time. I made a decision never to have him in the car again, but this is different. I reply that of course I'll meet him and that I'm sorry for his loss. Though I can't help wondering how sorry he is himself.

I ring Mum, explain the situation and ask if she can look after Tom and Mica for the afternoon.

'Oh, the poor man,' she says, and I don't know if she means Ivo or his dad. 'Of course I'll look after them. I'll come to yours so you don't have to collect them later.'

'Thank you.'

'It's not a bother. I hope everything's all right.'

This time, I don't know if she means with Ivo or with Dave. But I don't spend time chatting about it.

I finish my now lukewarm coffee and clear away the breakfast things. Then I go upstairs and change into my navy suit and white blouse. I have a job this morning, meeting a client from Connolly station and bringing him across town. Fortunately that still leaves me time to get to Ivo later.

My client is a taciturn man who doesn't speak during our journey from the train station to the office park on the west side of the city. He does, however, take the two bottles of water from the car, so I stop and buy more in case Ivo needs any. He never has, but there's always a first time. I get to the airport early but don't bother with coffee; I simply stand at the barrier and wait for his flight to arrive.

It takes a while, but finally I see him walk through the doors and scan the faces of the crowd of people waiting for incoming travellers. He smiles when he sees me and then turns slightly to the person who's a step behind him, putting his hand beneath her elbow and steering her in my direction.

She's nearly as tall as him, though her high-heeled boots clearly help. Her hair is silver blonde, and she's wearing it in a chopped pixie cut that enhances her angular face. She has the same confident air as Gina Hayes, her white coat making a statement in the same way Gina's signature raincoat does. She's pulling a small cabin bag behind her. Its bright red colour matches the red of her lipstick. She looks amazing.

'Thank you for coming at such short notice,' says Ivo as they reach me.

'I'm sorry it's under these circumstances,' I say.

His smile is tight and then he introduces me to the woman who's with him. Not that he has to.

'Annabel Mauret,' he says. 'My driver, Mrs McMenamin.'

Has he emphasised the Mrs a little too much?

'Pleased to meet you,' says Annabel.

The mental image I'd built up of the high-maintenance Annabel shatters into a thousand pieces. I know Ivo said she was a qualified chemist and I accepted that she had her own career, but wow – this woman isn't simply a girlfriend. She's a force of her own. She wouldn't have been upset about Ivo not coming to her birthday party, only that her arrangements were messed up. I admit to myself, as I lead them to the car, that she could have been disappointed on a personal level too, but she seems too poised and self-assured to allow herself to become upset over things that are out of her control. I wonder, suddenly, if she recognises the perfume I'm wearing. Her perfume.

I realise that I feel like the other woman.

I open the rear door of the Mercedes and she slides along the seat so that Ivo can get in beside her.

'Thank you,' he says as I close it.

I get into the front and switch on the engine. Annabel begins to talk to Ivo. I recognise two words. *Mon cher.*

I can't speak French . . .

They talk on and off for the entire journey to Kildare, and it's not until I'm about to take the exit that Ivo speaks to me.

'Sorry,' he says. 'I should have said. We're going to a different address.'

I have to admit that I was wondering how the glamorous Annabel would feel about Banville Terrace. But Ivo has booked them into a guest house outside the town. I'm a little surprised he hasn't chosen somewhere a bit more upmarket – after all, he's used to the five-star treatment, and clearly Annabel is too; those hundred-euro main courses are way beyond anything Kildare has to offer – but when I pull up outside the guest house, I can see why he picked it. The elegant period house is undoubtedly appropriate for their stay, although as it's a good twenty-minute walk from here to Banville Terrace, I hope Annabel has flatter shoes with her!

'Thank you,' says Ivo when I open the door to let them out.

'I really am sorry,' I tell him.

'I can't truthfully say that myself.' His expression is a mixture of guilt and resignation. 'But I'm glad I did my bit. And thank you for making me see that it was something I had to do. The funeral is tomorrow at eleven,' he adds. 'Lizzy has made the arrangements, so our transport is already organised for that. But Annabel will need to be driven back to the airport the following day, though I'm staying a little longer. If you can drive for both of us, I'd really appreciate it.'

'No problem. Just let me know when you want me.'

'Thank you,' says Annabel in her perfect English. 'Ivo was right. You are an excellent driver.'

I smile briefly at her and get back into the car.

I'm glad Ivo thinks I'm a good driver.

I'm glad he told her I was too.

Although I'm caught up in commuter traffic, I still make it home before Dave. Mum is watching an episode of *Endeavour* on the TV. She hits pause when I come into the room.

'How's your client?' she asks.

'Oh, all right,' I reply. 'I guess it wasn't entirely unexpected.'

'This means you won't have to drive to Kildare any more.'

'I know. That'll cheer Dave up. And you,' I add. 'You were never keen either.'

'It was just that you seemed . . . oh, I don't know, very eager to work for this man. That two-day trip . . .'

'He was paying me more than double my other clients. Of course I was keen.'

'He gave Mum perfume.'

370

I jump. Mica's head has popped up from behind the armchair in the corner.

'What on earth were you doing there?' I demand.

'Reading.' She holds up a book. I'm delighted she's reading, but behind the chair! 'It's a quiet place,' she tells me when I ask her why.

'What perfume?' asks Mum.

I explain about the bottle of perfume, and she frowns.

'It's nothing,' I say. 'I didn't want to take it, but he insisted because at the time he wasn't planning to come back. But he did. So that's that.'

'Right.' Mum looks doubtful.

'Oh, stop it!' I drop my bag on the sofa. 'I'm going upstairs to change. D'you want to stay for something to eat, or would you prefer to go home?'

Mum glances at her watch. 'Actually, I'm going out.'

I look at her.

'Diarmuid is bringing me to dinner in Howth,' she says.

'Right. You'd better head off if you want to make yourself look beautiful.'

'Granny always looks beautiful,' says Mica.

'I know.' I plop down on the sofa beside Mum and give her a hug. 'Sorry. I'm a bit tired. And ratty.'

'Like I said, burning the candle at both ends.'

'Truly not,' I tell her.

I fall off the healthy-meal-choice wagon and order a Chinese takeaway for dinner. I don't have the energy to cook and it turns out to be a good decision, because Dave arrives at the same time as the takeaway.

'Great,' he says as he tucks in to kung po chicken. 'It was a busy day and I'm starving.'

After dinner, he waits in the kitchen while I stack the dishwasher. Tom and Mica take themselves off to watch TV.

'Look, I'll accept not selling the car,' he says abruptly. 'It's yours and you like driving it. Plus I'll also accept that you want to keep driving for a bit longer. But *you* have to accept that the family comes first.'

'My family always comes first.' I'm pleased and relieved that he has finally seen my point of view. It truly is like a weight rolling off my shoulders.

'Yeah, well.' He shrugs. 'We're nothing without family, Roxy. Mine is very important to me. And I know I kind of blindsided you with it before, but I've thought about it a lot and I really want us to have another baby.'

So on the one hand he's given me the green light to drive. But he also wants me to have a baby, which would make it impossible.

'I can't have a baby and keep working,' I say.

'Think about it, sweetheart.' He stands behind me and, to my surprise, puts his arms around me. 'All I want is for things to be the way they were before.'

He keeps talking about how things were before. But we can't go back.

And I don't want to.

Chapter 29

I decide to go to Mr Lehane's funeral the following morning as it seems like the respectful thing to do. Ivo has been a good client and I'm aware that his father's illness has been a difficult time for both him and his sister. Until my own dad died I wouldn't have considered going to the funeral of someone I didn't know personally, but many of Dad's regular customers turned up at the church, and seeing so many people there was a great comfort to all of us. I want to be part of the comfort that's offered to Ivo and Lizzy. By the time I organise Mica and Tom for school, I'll be late getting there, but I reckon the church will be full and nobody will notice me slipping in after the mass starts. I arrange with Eric Fallon to take my jobs for the day and, in case I get delayed, I ask Natalie if she could look out for the children after school. I know this is two days in a row that they're being cared for by someone else, but it's exceptional.

I stick close to the speed limit on the motorway and make it to the church shortly after the service has started. I expected to see it overflowing, but there aren't many mourners inside. The first pew is taken up by family. I recognise Ivo, of course, flanked by Annabel, now wearing a chic black jacket with elegant beading, and an auburn-haired woman who I guess must be his sister, Lizzy. There's also an older woman and two men in the pew.

Scattered around the church are a number of elderly parishioners who probably come to every funeral. But the total number can't be more than twenty. I'm glad I came, if only to add one more person.

I take a seat at the back, and as I listen to the priest, who clearly never knew Mr Lehane, I remember how Father Kaminski spoke warmly about Dad – a family man, kind and generous, loved by all who knew him. To be fair, Father Kaminski didn't know Dad that well himself; he was new to the parish and Dad wouldn't have been a regular at the local church, but he visited him a number of times at the hospice and, according to Dad, he was 'broad-minded enough for a cleric'. Those words about Dad were true, though. His family – Mum, Aidan and me, along with our own families – was the most important thing in his life. Everything he did was for us. Everything.

But I suddenly think of Estelle and the money he gave her, and I have to accept that maybe not every single thing he did was for us. That not every single thing could be. I also think of the photograph in the car that I've ignored for these last weeks and wonder what more Dad might have done without telling Mum. Why did he give Estelle the money if he didn't believe, on some level, that she might be telling the truth? Why did he keep her photograph if he didn't care, at least a little? Is it possible he might even have met her on one of the days he left the house early and didn't return until late at night? Could he have met her child, too?

I shiver in the chill air of the church as I tell myself that even if it's true, it hardly matters any more. Neither Estelle nor her son has ever tried to contact us. The past is behind us and it's probably better that way. But it has marred the memories I have of my dad and of the sort of person I thought he was, and that's still hard to accept.

I'm lost so deep in my thoughts that I hardly even realise Ivo is walking to the lectern to give the eulogy. I'm surprised he's doing it, but he keeps it very short. He says that his father lived the kind of life he wanted to live and that he will be missed by many people (though clearly not that many, I think, given the numbers in the church). Then he thanks everyone for coming. He says that his father is being buried in the local cemetery and that there will be refreshments for all the mourners in Kielty's pub on the Monasterevin Road afterwards.

I stand along with the sparse congregation, partly shielded by the woman in front of me, as the coffin is wheeled out of the church. I feel like an intruder. I came out of a sense of obligation, yet it's hard to be part of another family's grief. The chill wind whistles through the open doors and I wrap my green scarf more tightly around my neck.

I'd like to make a quick escape, but the tradition after the funeral mass is for those who attended to express their condolences to the family, and I hang back as the strangers in the church approach Ivo and Lizzy. Annabel is a little apart, out of place both because she isn't part of the family and because she's a splash of Continental glamour on a grey Irish day. Beneath the clearly expensive jacket, she's wearing an elegant black and white houndstooth dress that comes to just above the knee; and I recognise her black shoes with the gold stiletto heels – they're Kurt Geiger and I saw them in Arnotts when I was buying my polka-dot dress. They're new this season.

The man who's been monopolising Ivo and Lizzy walks away. This is my opportunity to go over and tell Ivo once again how sorry I am.

He thanks me and introduces me to his sister. She's very pretty, with wide hazel eyes and a warm, open manner quite at odds with the irate woman I overhead on the phone to him before.

'You're very good to come.' She gives me a hug. 'Thank you.'

'Indeed,' says Ivo. 'You didn't have to be here. I appreciate it.'

I don't really know what to say to them. To him.

'Will you be joining us in Kielty's afterwards?' asks Lizzy.

'Oh, I don't think—'

'Please do, if you can,' she says. 'There aren't going to be many people there and I'd like . . . well, I hate to think that he wouldn't have anyone . . .'

We hired a private room in Dad's local for after his funeral. It was packed with people. Aidan had put together a montage of photos of him, which were projected onto a giant screen, and we used a soundtrack of his favourite music to accompany them. Later in the evening, Dessie, one of Dad's closest friends, played guitar and we sang lots of the songs he'd loved.

I can't bear to think of a sparse gathering for Mr Lehane.

'Well, of course,' I say.

'You don't have to come to the cemetery,' Ivo tells me. 'Head straight for the pub. That's what the others are doing.' He nods in the general direction of the small knot of people I saw in the church.

'I'll see you a little later, so,' I tell him.

I walk away and get into the car. I don't know the pub he's talking about, but by now I'm very familiar with the Monasterevin Road. As I start the engine, a woman in a blue coat knocks at the driver's window and I roll it down.

'Are you going to Kielty's?' she asks. 'Could you give us a lift?'

What can I do but agree? The woman, along with two others and an elderly man, gets into the car.

'Very nice.' She pats the leather upholstery approvingly. 'Do you know the family?'

'I know Ivo,' I say.

'Very glamorous woman he's got with him,' says the elderly man. 'Dressed for a wedding, not a funeral.'

Which is a little harsh on Annabel. Like me, I'm sure she dressed well as a mark of respect.

'The pub is about a mile down the road,' he says as I pass the Tesco where I used to pick Ivo up. 'On your right. There's parking.'

I follow his instructions and a minute later pull up in front of Kielty's. My passengers pile out, heading straight inside. I'm not in a rush to follow them, so I sit in the car and check my messages. Melisse Grady is looking to book me for another author visit next week. A company I do a lot of work for also wants me for a number of pickups and drop-offs. Baz Cadogan, one of the people I met at the workshop in the Convention Centre, wants me to drive him to an event. And I've got an enquiry from a retired judge in Howth, who's asking about transport to his regular hospital appointments on the other side of the city. *I can't drive any more,* he's written. *But I want to travel in comfort.*

I respond positively to all of them and add them to my schedule.

The skies above me have turned a deeper shade of grey and the wind has whipped the trees into a sudden frenzy so that their remaining leaves scatter and whirl around the car park. Even as I think it might rain, hailstones begin to fall, clanging onto the roof of the Mercedes and smashing against the windscreen.

The sun shone on the day of Dad's funeral. I was too hot in my black dress and jacket, and I'd developed a blister from my feet sweating into my tight black shoes. I recall Julie Halpin saying to me, as I did to Ivo Lehane, that she was sorry for my loss. And then I remember her blue sundress, a bright pool on the floor of my bedroom, and her sparkly flip-flops twinkling merrily in the early-morning light.

If I hadn't gone home that morning, I wouldn't be here now, sitting in the almost-empty car park of a country pub, a hailstorm raging around me. I'd be at home, or maybe at Mum's. My life unchanged and unchanging. All the drama of the last few months would never have happened. Everything would have been so much simpler. I would have remained the Roxy I was before. The Roxy Dave still wants me to be.

And then I tell myself that's not necessarily the case. I'd still have had to make decisions about driving or selling the Mercedes. And that decision would have changed our lives anyway. But it would have been made without the constant backdrop of Dave's betrayal. Maybe without that I would've chosen differently. Or maybe I would have made the same choice and still be here in the pub car park, in a hailstorm.

Life is random. And short. And sometimes it throws you curveballs you never expected.

As abruptly as it started, the hailstorm ends, and almost unbelievably the clouds part to reveal a bright blue sky. I loosen my scarf, get out of the car and walk into the pub. The other mourners are already on refills of tea and munching on the sandwiches.

In the forty minutes or so before the Lehanes arrive, my head is almost melted by the incessant gossip about the late Mr Lehane (a troubled soul, according to most of the women), Lizzy (a saint) and Ivo (a bit above himself). I'm relieved to see him finally walk into the pub with Annabel, followed by Lizzy, the older woman and the two men. There are some general introductions, and I learn that the older woman and one of the men are distant relatives, while the other man is a neighbour.

Ivo is immediately cornered by one of my passengers, the woman in the blue coat. Annabel holds back and talks to the relatives. Lizzy herself comes over to me, a cup of tea in her hand.

'Did you get anything to eat?' she asks.

I nod. Although I wasn't particularly hungry, I had an egg sandwich along with coffee.

'Ivo told me all about you,' she says, and I wonder what that actually means. 'He says you've been great about driving him here – and collecting him,' she adds with a grin. 'Idiot that he is.'

'Oh well.' I shrug. 'Clients have their preferences.'

'He also said that you were responsible for making him keep in touch.'

'I'm not sure that—'

'After that weekend when there was a crash on the motorway and we rowed because it wrecked my evening.'

She sips her tea. 'He said that he brought you for restorative coffee afterwards and you told him to cop on to himself.'

'I didn't quite put it like that!' I exclaim. 'And I haven't driven him to Kildare since, so . . .'

She smiles. 'I was paraphrasing. And I know he hasn't been over, but he called me every day. So you've been good for him. Thank you.'

'I'm not sure that's down to me,' I say.

'Maybe not. But at least he was able to talk to me about Dad's care without making it obvious that he hated him.'

I'm dying to know, but don't want to ask. However, Lizzy seems eager to chat. She's clearly decided that, as Ivo's driver, I'm not a complete stranger.

'Ivo always blamed his mum's death on Dad, which I accept is a tough thing,' she says.

'His mother? Not yours too?' I look at her in surprise.

She shakes her head. 'My mother was Dad's second wife. Ivo was very young when they married.' She scrunches up her eyes. 'The first Mrs Lehane was killed in a hit-and-run when he was small.'

'Oh, how awful!' I exclaim. 'But why would he blame your dad? He . . . he wasn't driving the car, was he?' It would be unsurprising that Ivo would have issues with him if that was the case.

But Lizzy shakes her head. 'No, no. She was walking along one of the unlit back roads near the house when she was hit. The driver didn't stop.'

'The poor woman. And poor Ivo, too.'

'He was devastated. He blamed Dad because she'd gone out after an argument.'

'What a horrible thing to have happened.' I'm picturing

Ivo as a boy, younger maybe than Tom, knowing that his mother would never come home again. It's no wonder he had issues as an adult if his tragedy wasn't dealt with properly when he was younger. My heart constricts with sympathy and I glance over at him. He's still in conversation with the woman in the blue coat, although Annabel has now joined them. She's listening, but there's a glazed look to her eyes, which isn't surprising given that Blue Coat was the most gossipy of all the mourners and peppered her conversation with allusions to people nobody from outside the town could possibly know.

'From what I can gather, Dad's first marriage wasn't great,' continues Lizzy. 'Ivo told me about it when we were older, but of course he always painted Dad in the worst possible light. Every single row between them was his fault, not hers. From my point of view, though, he was talking about a completely different person. Dad was always lovely to me and Mum, although the truth is that they were seeing each other while he was married to Ivo's mum, and I completely understand that that's hurtful to Ivo too. But it doesn't make Dad a bad person,' she adds. 'Lots of marriages break down.'

'I got the impression that Ivo's feelings towards your dad are very deep-seated.' I can't quite believe Lizzy is being so open about their family. Ivo is like a locked safe by comparison.

'They certainly didn't get on,' agrees Lizzy. 'Like I said, Ivo blamed Dad for all the problems with his mum. They had to get married, that was part of it. She was pregnant with Ivo, and back then it would have been a massive source of shame for her to have the baby as a single mother. So maybe it's not surprising that Dad's relationship with Ivo, not to mention his mum, was a bit patchy.'

'It's harsh to take it out on your own son, though,' I say. And then I recall Estelle and my dad, and how she was also pressurised into getting married and couldn't stand it and ran away. Women were treated badly by society in the past. Blamed and shamed for things that were the fault of men too. It's good that it has improved, although probably not as much as we'd like.

Lizzy makes a face. 'Apparently during one of their rows he told Ivo that his mum had been with loads of other men before him and that she was "loose". That he took her on as a favour. That his dad could be anybody. As far as Ivo was concerned, he could never love him after that. I know,' she says as I open my mouth to speak. 'I know it was cruel and hurtful and I'm not defending him, but people can say some awful things when they're angry. All I know is that while he was married to my mum he was a good man. Easy to rile up,' she continues. 'But certainly not the monster that Ivo likes to paint him.'

'I guess we all see things from our own perspective,' I say, though honestly I'm completely on Ivo's side. His dad sounds awful no matter what Lizzy might say in his defence. 'Was he telling the truth? About Ivo not being his?'

I glance over at her brother. Though he's actually only her half-brother, unless the late Mr Lehane was right when he made his hurtful remark that Ivo's dad could be 'anybody'. Yet he and Lizzy both have the same way of tilting their head to one side when they're thinking. And when Lizzy smiles, her eyes crinkle up just like his. Anyhow, her story explains a lot about Ivo. His reluctance to come home. His insistence that he's bad with people. His desire not to be like his father. Most of all, in fact, his desire not to be like his father. He catches me looking at him and grimaces slightly as he nods at the woman in the blue coat.

Meanwhile Lizzy shakes her head as she answers my question. 'Not as far as I know. It's possible, I suppose, but I don't think his folk would have agreed to the marriage at all if she'd had a reputation.'

And now my sympathies shift entirely to Ivo's mum. The idea that women have a 'reputation' while men can put it about and be thought of as studs has always enraged me.

'Anyhow, when Ivo went to college, we pretty much lost touch,' says Lizzy. 'We hardly spoke again until a few years ago, when my own mum passed away.'

'I'm sorry,' I say. 'She must have been very young too.'

Lizzy nods. 'Cancer.'

Despite everything, I feel sorry for Ivo's dad, who buried two wives and was left alone in his old age.

'Dad never got over Mum's death,' says Lizzy. 'He started drinking heavily, and gambling too. I didn't know because I'd moved out by then and was living in Dublin. Even when Dad sold the farm and moved to Banville Terrace, I didn't twig there was anything wrong. It wasn't a big farm, but I assumed that as he was getting older, he'd had enough of it and had been made a good offer. But actually he sold it to pay his debts. Online gambling. It's a bloody curse.' Her hand shakes and a splash of tea washes over the side of her cup into the saucer. 'Sorry,' she says. 'I get so angry on his behalf.'

'Did Ivo know about the gambling?' I ask.

'Not until Dad tracked him down and asked him for a loan,' replies Lizzy. 'Ivo said no.'

'Oh dear.'

'In retrospect, he was right,' admits Lizzy. 'But when I heard, I was furious. Ivo has done well for himself. He could've paid off Dad's debts. When we argued about it, he said that Dad would've started gambling again anyway. I know he was right, but still – to refuse straight out. He didn't even talk it through with Dad. He put the phone down on him mid-conversation. It was a lot of stress and pressure and eventually Dad had the stroke . . .'

'Do you blame Ivo for that?' I ask.

She sighs. 'It probably would've happened anyhow, but there was a time when I felt it was partly his fault and so I was really angry with him. I told him he had to come home and face up to what he'd done.'

No wonder Ivo's feelings about coming to Kildare were so mixed. The picture Lizzy is painting of him as hard and uncaring is very different to the man I've driven. I look across at him again. He's smiling at the woman in blue now, his head bent towards her as she continues to talk. I wonder who the real Ivo is. The man who needed therapy to get over a difficult childhood. Or the man who's hard enough not to want to help his own father.

'I'm sorry, I'm babbling away and I'm sure you have better things to do than listen to other people's family histories,' says Lizzy. 'It's just . . . since Dad fell ill, I haven't had the chance to talk to people. So it all kind of came spilling out of me. Ivo would be furious if he knew. He likes to keep things to himself.' She suddenly looks anguished. 'You won't tell him I've said any of this, will you? He already thinks I'm a terrible chatterer. He'd go mental.'

'That's OK,' I say. 'Sometimes it's good to share with a

stranger. Anyway, I won't be seeing him any more, will I? He'll hardly be coming back.'

'Who'll hardly be coming back?' Ivo has finally escaped from the woman in blue and joins us.

'You,' says Lizzy. 'Now that Dad has died, I won't see much of you.'

'I'm sure I'll be back from time to time,' he tells her. 'It would be nice for us to meet up. Maybe you'll visit me in Brussels, too.'

'I'd like that,' she says.

'Roxy – Mrs McMenamin – I was wondering if you could lend me your services for a short while,' says Ivo.

'Of course.'

'Mrs Preston gave my dad a holy relic when he had his stroke,' he says. 'She was wondering if I could return it to her. It's in the house and it would be more convenient to collect it and give it to her now than have her call around for it at some other time.'

'Too right,' says Lizzy with a glance at the woman in blue. 'If she gets in the door I'll never get her out, nosy old bat that she is.'

'Oh well, it was good of her to give it to him in the first place,' says Ivo. 'Maybe he got some comfort from it.'

'Not that I believe for one second in all that mumbo-jumbo,' he says to me a few minutes later when he's in the passenger seat and we're heading to Banville Terrace. 'And I particularly doubt very much that a piece of some long-dead saint's tunic has any powers other than infectious.'

'You have a point. But,' I add, 'even though I don't believe in relics and stuff, I have to admit that I sometimes feel my dad's presence in the car. And that's kind of comforting too.'

Ivo looks around as though he expects to see Dad in the back seat.

'Not like a ghost,' I say. 'Just . . . well, looking out for me.'

'That must be a nice feeling,' he says. 'Maybe he can do the honours for me too whenever I'm in your car.'

'He already did,' I say as I pull up outside the house on Banville Terrace. 'When we escaped the tractor tyres.'

Ivo laughs. 'In that case, thanks very much, Mr . . . oh, not McMenamin, obviously.'

'Carpenter.'

'Thanks, Mr Carpenter, for keeping an eye out for us and passing down your great driving skills to your daughter. She saved my life.' He smiles at me and opens the door. 'You can wait here,' he says. 'I know where the relic should be.'

I do as he says, but it's a good five minutes before he emerges again, a folded card in his hand. When he gets into the car, he opens it to reveal a small scrap of fabric stuck inside. There's a prayer opposite, asking the saint to intercede with God for the intentions of the supplicant.

'Can you imagine?' he asks as he fastens his seat belt. 'All these saints clamouring to speak to God like lobbyists in Parliament so that he'll intervene on behalf of a farmer in Kildare or a nurse in the Philippines or a business owner in Latin America. It's utterly bonkers. But,' he adds, and there's humour as well as a touch of sincerity in his voice, 'maybe sometimes we do need the comfort of believing in something. And I have to remember that your Dad is in the back seat.'

I smile at him and we lapse into silence as I drive back to the pub. By the time I'm pulling into the car park, I can see him pinching the bridge of his nose between his thumb and forefinger, something I do myself when I'm trying not to cry. That's the thing about funerals. No matter how you feel about the deceased, they're a reminder that our time here is finite, and that when people are gone, they're gone forever.

'There are tissues in the glove compartment if you need them.' I keep my voice matter-of-fact.

Ivo says nothing. He clears his throat, opens the glove compartment and finds the tissues. He takes one and then hesitates. I'm trying not to pay him any attention, to allow him his moment of grief in some privacy, but I'm suddenly aware that the glove compartment is still open and that he's holding something else in his hand.

'You have it.' He turns to me and I see that it's the photograph he's holding. The photograph of the boy and the football. 'You have it,' he repeats.

'It's yours?' I'm astonished. '*You* left it behind?'

'I didn't realise . . .' He's looking at it again. 'I thought it was caught up in one of my files. It never occurred to me that I could have dropped it in the car.'

'It's yours,' I repeat as a million different thoughts swirl around in my head and I try to put them in some kind of order.

The most important thing, the realisation that floods me with overwhelming relief, is that if the photo belongs to Ivo, then he dropped it the first time I picked him up and it has nothing at all to do with my dad. He wasn't the one to leave it in the car. Estelle didn't send it to him. He didn't keep it hidden from Mum for all of their married life. He told her the truth about everything. He's as good a man as I always believed he was.

'It's me.' Ivo, unaware of the turmoil of my mind, gives me a rueful look.

I wasn't expecting that. Although perhaps I should have been, because of course he's the right age for the boy in the photo. But there's zero resemblance between young Ivo and Ivo now. Nobody would have recognised him.

'I've had it for ages,' I tell him. 'I thought someone might have dropped it but I didn't think to ask you because . . . well, I sort of assumed it must belong to a woman. And even if a man did leave it behind, there have been so many in the car that it was an impossible task to check with everyone. Besides,' I add, a little defensively, 'it looks nothing like you.'

'Possibly a good thing.' He looks at the picture again, then continues. 'Lizzy gave it to me the first day I went home. She said that Dad had kept it in a book. She said it proved he loved me.'

'Oh, Ivo.'

'I wasn't all that convinced, to be honest.' He clears his throat again. 'I reckoned she found it shoved in a drawer somewhere and spun that story to make me keep coming back. It didn't bother me when I lost it. It's not a great photo.'

It is to me. Because of what it represents. Estelle's child wasn't Dad's child. He told the truth all along. I can't wait to let Mum know.

'I remember it being taken, though,' Ivo continues. 'It was the day Ireland played Switzerland in the European Cup qualifiers. Dad bought the tracksuit for me and made me watch the game with him. I didn't want to because he used to get so angry when we lost and he was awful to be around then. But we won that match and he was delighted.'

I smile.

'Then we lost away in Moscow and were hammered by the Danes at home,' he adds. 'Which wasn't so great.'

'You know a lot about football,' I say.

'It was the only thing I could talk to Dad about.' He grimaces and looks at the photo again. 'That day . . . that day he bought ice creams to celebrate.'

I'm glad Ivo has a good memory of his father. I'm glad he found the photograph today.

'Anyhow.' He gives himself an almost imperceptible shake. 'Best be getting back in and hand over the relic to Mrs Preston.' He smiles at me. 'Could be that it worked its miracle after all. It's supposed to be from St Anthony, and he's the one who finds lost things, isn't he?'

We share a laugh. That's the thing about being raised an Irish Catholic. You might not believe a word of any of it and only go to mass for births, marriages and funerals, but you'll still give credit to St Anthony when you find something you've lost, and you still have a vague hope that your departed relatives are looking out for you.

'I should head off,' I say. 'There's no need for me to go back inside.'

'Say goodbye to Lizzy first,' says Ivo. 'She was really pleased you came. Me too. Thank you.'

I follow him back inside, where he gives the relic to Mrs Preston, who blesses herself before putting it in her handbag. Meantime I go over to Lizzy, who's now chatting to Annabel.

'Sorry to disturb you,' I say. 'But I'm heading home now.

389

It was lovely to meet you, Lizzy. I hope everything goes well for you in the future.'

'Thanks,' she says. 'And thanks again for everything you did for Ivo.'

'I didn't do anything.'

'You helped both of us,' she says.

Annabel is looking at me from her sky-blue eyes.

'You are more than a driver,' she says. 'You are a complete friend of the family.'

'Not really.' I don't want her to get the wrong impression.

'But I think so,' she says. 'You are friends with everybody.'

'It's my job,' I say. 'It was lovely to meet you too, Annabel. I'll see you tomorrow when I pick you up.'

'Yes,' she says, and moves away from us.

'Perhaps we'll meet again sometime,' Lizzy says.

'Perhaps.' Although that's highly unlikely.

I walk towards the stairs and suddenly Ivo is behind me.

'I'll see you to the car,' he says.

We step out into the bright sunshine. It's positively warm now after the hailstones earlier.

'I'll text you details of Annabel's flight later,' he says as I unlock the Mercedes.

'That's fine,' I say. 'And let me know when you're going back yourself when you can.'

'Annabel's right. You've been way more than a driver to me,' says Ivo. 'You made me . . . Well, I can't thank you enough.' He gathers himself and gives me a half-smile. 'If it hadn't been for what you said when I made you have coffee with me, I would have broken off contact with Lizzy again. And that would've been wrong. Also,' he adds, with slightly more of a smile this time, 'you saved my life when we were attacked by mutant tractor tyres. So thank you for that too.'

'All part of the service,' I say.

He's about to say something else when Lizzy hurries into the car park, my green scarf in her hand.

'This is yours, isn't it?' she asks.

'Oh, thank you! I'm hopeless with scarves.' I drape it around my neck and smile at her. 'I'm forever leaving them behind.'

I open the car door. Ivo has stepped back a little, but Lizzy embraces me in another hug.

'If you're driving him back later in the week, you won't say anything, will you?' she murmurs. 'About Dad and Stella? His mum? He doesn't like talking about her and . . . well, he'd probably be a bit annoyed at me if he thought . . .'

I tell her no, of course not, before I've even registered what she's said.

I switch on the engine and drive slowly out of the car park. I glance in my rear-view mirror. They've turned away and are walking back into the pub arm in arm. Brother and sister. Half-brother and half-sister. Same dad, different mother. Different mother, same dad.

Ivo's dad and Stella. My dad and Estelle.

I've only gone about fifty yards, but I pull into a cutting at the side of the road.

Stella. Ivo's mum. A woman forced to marry a man she didn't love because she was pregnant. A man who didn't believe the child was his. Who treated her badly. Who didn't love his son.

Estelle. Dad's first love. A woman forced to marry because she was pregnant. A woman who didn't believe the child was her husband's. Who ran away because he was violent. Who was afraid for her son.

They can't be the same woman, can they? Stella walked out of the house and was killed in a hit-and-run accident. Estelle came to Dublin and was given money to escape by my dad. But what if one of those stories is wrong? What if Estelle didn't go to London after getting money from Dad, but returned to Kildare? What if she had another row with her husband over her son? What if she left the house and was hit by the truck? And what if that row was about the fact that Ivo wasn't his son, but my own dad's?

What if Ivo is my half-brother, not Lizzy's?

My stomach is churning.

'Get a grip, Roxy.' I say the words out loud as I lean my head on the steering wheel. Ivo's mum and Dad's first love might have similar names, but they're not the same woman. It would be a coincidence too far. Wouldn't it?

Yet I can't help remembering how I felt a connection to the boy in that photograph, and how I felt a connection to Ivo Lehane too. I thought the boy in the photo might be related to me. I thought Ivo and I . . . Well . . .

As I fight the nausea that's overtaking me, I remind myself that Ivo and Lizzy look alike. Because they have the same father. The man who was buried today. Not my dad. Definitely not.

I take a deep breath, restart the car and drive home.

Chapter 30

Mum knows there's something wrong as soon as I walk in the door. She ushers me into the kitchen and puts the kettle on before asking me what's happened. For once in my life I truly don't know what to say to her.

'Roxy, sweetheart, was it a very sad funeral?' she asks when I've been sitting at the table for what seems like hours without speaking.

'It's not that at all,' I eventually say. 'It's that I found out who owns the photo. The one of the boy in the car that I thought might be Dad's son.'

'You did? That's good.' She sounds pleased, but not as excited as I would have expected.

'Don't you care?' I ask.

'Well, I'm glad you found the owner,' she replies. 'But I already know it's nothing to do with your dad.'

I look at her in astonishment. How could she possibly know anything when I only found out a couple of hours ago myself?

'I did some investigating too,' she tells me. 'I have to be honest with you, Roxy. When you first told me about it, I was more upset than I let on. Your dad spun his story, and I believed him all those years because I wanted to believe him. But I also knew that I couldn't rest until I knew the truth.'

'You said you wanted to leave it,' I remind her.

'It's impossible, though, isn't it?' asks Mum. 'Once there's a doubt in your mind, you have to find out. So I did some research of my own.'

'How? When?' I can't imagine that while she was manically crocheting octopussies she was also looking for the owner of the photograph. She's been tracking down Ivo when all the time I've been driving him!

She smiles. 'Before he retired, Diarmuid was a senior official in the Department of Social Welfare,' she says. 'I didn't know that when I first met him, of course. But when we were talking, sharing our stories, I told him about Estelle and your dad. And the baby. He knows a lot of people. He offered to help.'

I'm gobsmacked. Both at the fact that she shared intimate details of her life with a man she'd only just met, and also because he happened to be the one man who was able to help her find out what she wanted to know.

'He discovered enough to make me sure he was talking about the right person.'

I swallow hard. She knows Ivo's name. It's not a common one. So she must surely have put two and two together and realised that he was the man I was driving.

'He found Estelle's son?' I ask.

'No,' says Mum. 'Estelle herself.'

Once again a million thoughts are colliding in my head. If Diarmuid has found Estelle, she can't be Stella. Because Stella is dead. Unless Estelle is too. Unless he's found her grave.

'She's living in Donegal.' Mum seems totally unaware of my inner turmoil. 'She's married to a businessman. From what Diarmuid managed to learn, they moved there from London ten years ago.'

Estelle is alive. Estelle isn't Stella. Ivo isn't Dad's son. My head is properly spinning now. I truly can't keep it all together. I can't cope with the information overload.

And I don't.

I faint.

When I open my eyes again, I'm lying on the kitchen floor and my legs are propped up against a chair.

'Don't move,' says Mum, who's bending over me. 'Take your time.'

'I'm OK.' I struggle into a sitting position and then pull myself onto the chair. 'I'm fine, honestly. It was a shock, that's all.'

'It's not the shock,' says Mum. 'Like I said before, you're burning the candle at both ends. I thought you'd grown out of your habit of fainting when you're upset but clearly you're not able for anything out of the ordinary right now.'

It was a childhood thing and of course I've grown out of it. Otherwise I would have keeled over when I saw Dave and Julie together, wouldn't I? But my body had finally rebelled after everything that had happened in the last few weeks.

'It's been a tricky day.' I take the mug of sweetened tea that she's handing me and grimace. I'd much rather have coffee. But she's standing over me with a determined expression on her face.

'Even so.'

'Tell me everything,' I say.

395

'I'm not saying another word until you drink your tea and have a biscuit.' She thrusts a Penguin in front of me. They used to be a staple in my cupboard until I cut out sugary snacks in the house. But I need the sugar now. I wolf down the Penguin, and begin to feel better.

'There's not much more to tell,' says Mum. 'Diarmuid's contact found out that she spent a lot of her life in the UK, where she married an Irishman called David O'Shea. He's involved in the textile industry and she's a designer of sorts. They moved to Letterkenny about ten years ago and opened a factory. They've lived there ever since.'

'And her son?' I ask.

'Peter,' says Mum. 'Works in the Department of Foreign Affairs. He's a cultural attaché in Brazil.'

She picks up her iPad and opens a website. It shows a photo of the current foreign affairs minister along with the ambassador and his team at an Irish promotional event in São Paulo. Peter O'Shea is standing at one end of the group. He's a heavy-set man, his dark hair liberally sprinkled with grey. He's wearing horn-rimmed glasses and a blue suit. He doesn't look a bit like Dad. Or Aidan. Or me.

'I can't believe you found this out and didn't tell me,' I say.

'Diarmuid only got the details last night,' Mum tells me. 'And you were in a hurry this morning so I planned to tell you when you got home. Which now I have. Though it's funny that we should both have found out different things about the same situation at the same time.'

Funny peculiar, I think. Not funny ha-ha. All the same, I feel a weight lift from my shoulders again.

'So who *is* the boy in the photo?' asks Mum.

'The man whose father's funeral I went to.'

'Ivo from Kildare?'

I nod.

'For heaven's sake, didn't you recognise him?' she demands. 'Honestly, Roxy, after all that fuss! I know the photo was of a little boy, but surely you could have seen a resemblance.'

This time I shake my head. 'Ivo's nothing like the boy in the photo,' I say. 'He's sharp and confident. That boy was geeky and worried.'

'I could see he had a bit of a worried look about him,' agrees Mum. 'But he's OK now, obviously. A successful businessman with my daughter on tap to drive him wherever he needs to go.'

'Not for much longer,' I remind her.

She doesn't comment but I can tell she's pleased.

'Are you feeling better now?' she asks as I finish my tea. 'Maybe you're taking this Gina Hayes stuff a bit far. Eating too many of her damned chopped salads. You have to look after yourself.'

'It's nothing to do with that at all.' I decide to give her a tiny piece of the information that rattled me so much. 'When Ivo told me that the photo was his, I was very relieved. But then his sister made a comment that made me think there was a connection to Dad after all. I was leaping to some mad conclusions, but it was a shock all the same. When you told me the truth, I guess I was overcome.'

'I didn't realise you were quite such a fragile flower.' But Mum's eyes are still anxious as she looks at me.

I give her a reassuring smile. 'I guess the last few months have finally caught up with me,' I say. 'So listen – now that you know about Estelle, are you going to try to find out more? Like . . . if her son, Peter, really is Dad's too? Even though he doesn't look a bit like any of us.'

'I don't know,' says Mum. 'There's a part of me that would like to know for certain, but your dad was adamant and why shouldn't I believe him? Besides, I've no idea what Estelle has told that boy over the years. He's done really well for himself, hasn't he? So who am I to interfere in their lives? Christy is gone. There's nothing to be gained in trying to find out about something that doesn't matter any more. Let's leave the past in the past and plan to do our best for the future.'

She's right. She's always right.

'Which you have to do too, Roxy. Let go of your dad as some kind of ideal man that nobody can live up to. He was my ideal man but he wasn't perfect. He made his mistakes and you can't measure everyone against him. Accept that he had his faults. Accept that Dave has his. Do what's right for you.'

'I *do* accept those things,' I say. 'And I know that I have to make choices.'

'Choose to be happy.' Mum puts her arms around me. 'That's all I want for my children. That they're happy.'

'I am,' I say.

I'm happy that the mystery of the photo has been solved.

I'm happy that Ivo Lehane is not related to me in any way whatsoever.

I'm happy that he and Lizzy are close to each other again.

I'm happy that Mum has made her peace over Estelle.

I'm happy that Estelle's son has done well for himself.

I'm happy about lots of things.

But there's still a sense of unfinished business in my life. And I won't be truly happy until that's finally sorted.

* * *

The next day I collect Annabel from Kildare. She's ready and waiting when I arrive at the guest house exactly on time. Today she's back in her white coat and high-heeled boots. She really is a stunning woman. There's something about her that says she was born to be high-maintenance, and I can see why Ivo takes her to expensive restaurants and buys her extravagant gifts. But, I remind myself as I place her red suitcase into the car, she's also a qualified chemist with a career of her own. She doesn't need a man to make her high-maintenance. She can do that all by herself.

Ivo waits while I open the passenger door for her. Then he puts his arms around her and hugs her. She hugs him back and they kiss, briefly, on the lips. He says something to her in French and she replies in the same language. Then she gets into the car and I close the door.

'I'll send you a message when I'm ready to leave myself,' he says. 'If that's OK.'

'Whenever suits you,' I say. 'No problem.'

'Drive safely,' he says.

'Of course.'

As if there's any other way I'd drive with his glamorous girlfriend on board.

She's quiet for most of the trip, but when we join the M50, she begins to ask me about my job and the people I drive.

'What happens in the car stays in the car,' I tell her.

She looks at me in confusion and I explain that I don't talk about my clients.

'Ah, *bon*,' she says. 'You are like the priest in the confessional.'

I laugh at her using the same analogy as Dad so often did.

'But you can tell me about Ivo,' she says, and I feel a

399

shiver running down my spine. 'He was OK when you drove him?'

'OK?' I ask. 'In what way?'

'Because it has been difficult for him,' she says. 'Coming back here. To that place where his father lived.' I hear the shudder in her words. And I'm surprised that Ivo brought her to Banville Terrace.

'Yes, it was difficult,' I agree. 'But he's happy to be friends with his sister again. So that's all good.'

'And you,' she says. 'He is friends with you.'

Is there a warning in her words? A threat? A question? Or simply a statement?

'When you spend a lot of time in a car with someone, you get to know them a little,' I say to her. 'But that doesn't make us friends.'

'I see.'

I'm relieved when we arrive at the airport and I pull up outside the terminal building.

'ID? Mobile? Credit cards?' I ask.

'Yes, thank you,' she says.

'Have a good flight.'

'Thank you, Mrs Roxy McMenamin,' she says. 'It was good to get to know you.'

And then she walks off, pulling her red bag behind her.

Ivo's message arrives on Sunday evening asking if I can collect him in the morning. I say yes.

Obviously Dave is up to speed with Mr Lehane's passing and the funeral-related jobs I'm doing for Ivo. When I first told him, he looked at me from granite eyes and said he was glad that the old man had finally popped his clogs and that at least it meant I wouldn't be driving his son any more. And I said that I knew I wouldn't and that it would be a pity to lose such a lucrative client, but if it meant Dave was happier, then so was I. And Dave said he still wasn't happy and that neither was Garrett, the guy who was going to buy the car. But that we'd sort something out sooner rather than later.

It's a relief to get into the Merc after a weekend that, leaving aside all Dave's concerns, has been prickly and awkward. The weather has turned completely wintry, with such heavy rain that the children's football and GAA matches were cancelled. That meant they were around the house the whole time with excess energy that I didn't know how best to contain. Inevitably it led to arguments between them, and even the bread-making I suggested ended up in a row over who was in charge of putting the dough into the loaf tin. (I'd had to go to the supermarket to buy the tin, as well as the mix for the bread. Naturally, I didn't already have anything like that in the cupboard.) Tom was scornful of using a mix. Mica didn't think the finished product looked professional enough. And Dave, when he poked his head around the kitchen door before heading off to watch Arsenal versus Chelsea, remarked that it seemed like an awful lot of effort to go to when you could just buy bread in the shops.

I will never be a domestic goddess. No matter how much effort I put in.

But I am a good driver. I arrive at Banville Terrace exactly on time.

There's a To Let sign on the house already.

The door opens and Ivo comes out with his small travel bag. Lizzy follows him with a bigger one. It turns out that she's going to be in the car too, although she wants to be brought to her apartment, which is close to the business park where she works and is also near one of the motorway exits.

'So it's not taking you out of your way,' she explains as she settles into the back seat.

'Nothing will take me out of my way,' I tell her. 'I'm your driver. I'll go wherever you want.'

Ivo gets in beside her. At first they sit in silence, but then they start chatting about the last few weeks, the funeral, and finalising their father's estate.

'Not that there's much to it,' says Lizzy. 'He sold the farm and gambled away his money. You were right not to lend him anything. He wouldn't have paid his debts; he'd have gambled even more.'

'I know,' says Ivo.

'I shouldn't have been so horrible to you about it.'

'You had a point.'

'Especially as you were paying his rent. I never knew.'

I sense rather than see Ivo shrug.

'You're a good man, Ivo.'

'Ah, I'm not that great.'

She laughs. So does he.

'We're OK, aren't we?' she asks.

'Yes,' says Ivo. 'We are.'

I'm glad for them. I really am. I know Aidan and I aren't the closest, but I also know that he'd be there for me if I needed him. It's good to know Lizzy has Ivo. And that he has her. And that despite everything, he looked after his dad.

'Annabel is an impressive woman.' Lizzy changes the subject.

'She is rather,' says her brother.

'Super-intelligent.'

'Yes.'

'And super-gorgeous.'

'That too.'

'You lucky thing.'

Ivo laughs. 'Stop fishing.'

'I'm not,' says Lizzy. 'I'm saying that you're going out with a hell of a woman.'

'And?'

'She's a bit distant, though.'

'Oh?'

'Maybe even . . . oh, I dunno, judgemental?'

'I can't talk,' says Ivo. 'I was judgemental about Dad. And about you too, I guess.'

'You didn't look down on us, though.'

'Nor does Annabel.' Ivo sounds offended.

'Sorry,' says Lizzy. 'That came out wrong. All I meant was . . . well, she's from a different world, isn't she? Have I got it right that her grandfather is actually a German prince? And that she grew up in a castle?'

'A count,' says Ivo. 'And no, she didn't grow up in a castle, although the family does have a big house in Bavaria. Annabel's mother was a bit of a free spirit and moved to a commune in France when she was seventeen. She didn't go home again until she'd had Annabel. She never married Annabel's father, but they're still together. They live in Nice and have an apartment in Paris.'

'Gosh, it all sounds very *Hello!*.'

It does rather. And it's not altogether surprising that Annabel might have looked down on Banville Terrace and Kielty's pub.

'They're very nice people,' says Ivo. 'And although they're quite rich, they're not extravagant.'

Extravagance is relative, I think, as I recall the fish at a hundred euro a pop.

'Just think, my future sister-in-law is an aristocrat.' There's a wickedness about Lizzy's voice that makes me smile.

'You're not going to get a rise out of me,' says Ivo.

'Spoilsport. Are you going to marry her?' Lizzy's obviously bored with teasing him and wants a direct answer to a direct question.

So do I.

'We haven't discussed it,' says Ivo.

'I like her,' says Lizzy. 'But I'm not sure she's the right woman for you.'

'Why's that?'

'Maybe she's a little bit self-centred? Or is it self-confident? Or self-contained, like you. You need someone warm, Ivo. Someone open. Someone to hold you tight at night.'

I glance in the rear-view mirror. Ivo's face is expressionless. Then he glances up and his eyes catch mine. I look away at once.

'What about you? What about the man in your life?' he says.

For a moment I think Ivo is talking to me. But then I realise he's speaking to Lizzy.

'As you well know, there isn't one right now,' she says. 'And I'm happy to keep it that way.'

'Don't *you* need someone to hold you tight at night?' he asks drily.

'Yes. But I'm waiting for the right someone. I'll let you know when he comes along.'

And then she switches the conversation back to her father's estate and the things they need to do, and they keep it up until we reach her apartment, which is in one of the many modern blocks that have been built in the slipstream of the motorway.

'I'll go up with you,' says Ivo. 'You'll wait here, Roxy?'

'Of course.'

I hope he'll maintain his relationship with his sister now that their father has died. Ivo needs family. After his horrible childhood, he needs to know that people care.

I care about him.

I cared about him when he was a complete stranger. I cared about him when I had my imaginary flirtation with him. I'll always care.

Out of the corner of my eye I see him emerge from the apartment building and walk towards the car. I get out to open the rear door for him, but he diverts to the passenger seat. I get back in again.

'I hope our conversation didn't irritate you,' he says as I pull out of the apartment complex.

'What conversation?'

'Me and Lizzy,' he says. 'She seems to think her mission in life is to meddle in mine.'

'I don't hear people's conversations,' I lie. 'It's a special driver skill.'

'Of course it is.'

We continue in silence. I feel as though he wants to say something to me, but he doesn't. I also feel as though I want to say something to him, but I've no idea what it is.

We're only a few minutes away from the airport when his

phone rings. When he begins to speak in French, I know that it's Annabel.

'*Oui. Oui. D'accord.*' His tone is soft and gentle. I'm listening out for the one phrase I definitely know – *je t'aime* – but I don't hear it. I'm so distracted that I almost run the red light at the airport roundabout.

'Shit,' says Ivo as I slam on the brake.

'Sorry,' I mutter.

I pull up outside the terminal building a couple of minutes later and get out of the car.

'Thank you for all your help over the last few months,' says Ivo. 'And over the last few days too.' He takes out his credit card.

'Please don't,' I say. 'You've already paid me a lot of money this year. This drive and Annabel's to the airport are free.'

'I can't possibly—'

'I didn't get flowers for your father's funeral,' I say. 'I'd like you to accept my driving services instead.'

'That's—'

'Please.'

'Well . . . OK,' says Ivo. 'You've been great, Roxy. Really great.'

'Thank you.'

'I'll miss you.'

'I'm sure you'll be far too busy with your corporate stuff to miss me,' I say. 'And in any event, it's Lizzy you'll miss if you don't keep your promise to stay in touch.'

'I thought you didn't listen to conversations in the car.'

'You already told me you'd be staying in touch with her. And you should. She's fabulous.'

'She's a great person, isn't she?'

'So are you.' I can't help myself. 'Who we are isn't down to DNA, you know. It's what we're like inside. And you're a good person, Ivo. You may not have wanted to, but you did the right thing every time. You're not your father and you won't turn into him either.'

He smiles at me. 'It's good to have you on my side.'

'I'm always on my clients' side,' I say.

It's only now that I realise it's raining and we're both getting wet.

'You'd better go,' I say. 'ID, mobile, credit cards?'

'And carry-on bag,' he says.

'Have a safe flight.'

'Thank you.'

We look at each other for a moment, and then he puts his arms around me and hugs me. I've had a lot of hugs from his family, one way or the other. I feel his stubble graze my cheek.

This time I'm the one to pull away.

'Goodbye, Mr Lehane,' I say.

'Goodbye, Mrs McMenamin.'

And then he walks out of my life.

Chapter 31

Back in my own world again, I cook fish fingers and beans for the children's dinner. Mica is full of chat about school; Tom wants to keep reading his newest book at the table, something that is strictly forbidden.

'But it's very exciting, Mum,' he complains. 'I want to know what happens.'

I wish my life was a book. I could skip a few chapters and see how it all turns out in advance. But what if I didn't like the ending? What then?

Dave arrives home early, and I slide the chicken enchiladas we're having for dinner into the oven when I hear his key in the door. I bought them from the local supermarket on the way back from the airport. They're spicy and full of flavour and probably as good as anything Gina Hayes has to offer. I've been seduced by her and her feel-good lifestyle over the past few months. I've thought that if I eat like her, I can be like her. I've been seduced too by Leona Lynch and Thea Ryan and Melisse Grady and all those women who seem to glide towards success without any of the messiness of life. Maybe even by Alison King, too. I've put my own life and happiness at risk, and for what? A job that involves getting far richer, more successful people than me to the places they want to be. Nothing more.

Dave puts his arm around me and gives me a kiss. He wolfs down the enchiladas and then says he's going to the pub with the lads to watch the footie. I ring Debs and ask her if she'd like to come over.

'Sure,' she says. 'I'll get Mick to drop me up. Crack open the wine.'

Intravenous wine would be good, I think, as we sit down at the kitchen table. I could do with a certain amount of oblivion to wipe away the last few days. Tom and Mica are watching a cartoon on TV and their laughter floats in to us.

'So what's new?' asks Debs.

'I've lost the lucrative client, I've stopped Dave selling the car and I'm not sure if I'm doing the right thing any more,' I say. And then, out of the blue, I burst into tears.

Debs grabs some tissues from the box on the table and thrusts them at me. I mop my eyes, blow my nose and take a slug of wine.

'What's all that about?' she asks.

I tell her about Estelle and Dad, and the photo in the car that I thought might have been Dad's son and that turned out to be Ivo. Which might have meant me fancying my own half-brother. Which still makes me feel sick inside.

'Well, yes,' she says in her sensible way. 'I can see that would definitely have been freaky. But he isn't your half-brother, so you didn't. Although,' she adds, 'you told me when you were in Cork that you didn't want revenge sex with him. Did you, in the end?'

'No!' I exclaim.

'Whew! But why are you so upset if that's the case?'

'I don't know!'

And I don't. It's just . . . there was so much going on outside the house that it took me away from the things I needed to think about. Like me and Dave and how I really feel about the Julie Halpin situation that's supposed to be in the past but that I can't leave in the past like Mum wants me to do and like I know I should do. It's easy for me to tell Ivo Lehane to put his past behind him. It's a pity I'm not able to do it for myself.

'Where are you with Dave and the driving now?' Debs asks.

'God knows,' I reply. 'He's tolerated me running back and forwards to Kildare this last while because he knows it means the end of Ivo. And maybe he thinks that without someone like him as a great client, the business won't be so profitable. He doesn't want it to be profitable. What he wants is another baby.' I down an enormous gulp of wine. 'I'm done with babies, Debs.'

'Are you done with Dave?'

Her question has cut to the chase. Am I? But if so, why? Because of Julie? Because of his attitude about my driving? Because he wants a baby? Because of Ivo?

Because of me?

'It's taking you a long time to answer,' she says.

'I'm done with things the way they were,' I say. 'But Dave isn't. He says he wants everything to be how it was before.'

'And you don't.' She sloshes some more wine into my glass.

I shrug helplessly. I used to be so good at stuff. At making decisions. At knowing what to do. But I've lost it.

'Nancy Barrett said you were great driving her to Kinnity Castle,' Debs remarks.

'Nancy's a friend. And besides, she hasn't been driven by a chauffeur since her wedding day. Of course she'd enjoy it.'

'Perhaps. But she told me that you were a really calm person to be in the car with. That you made it all part of the experience. You're good at it, Roxy. You really are. Dave should accept that and support you.'

'And if he doesn't? If he keeps on at me to stay home and have another baby?'

'Don't get trapped,' says Debs.

But it's too late. I'm trapped already.

I call in to Mum after I've done another airport pick-up on Tuesday. She's sitting in the kitchen surrounded by her octopussies, but she gets up and puts the kettle on for a cup of tea.

'Some of them are Diarmuid's,' she tells me as I sift through the tiny purple creatures. 'In all honesty he's not great at the crochet, but he's doing his best.'

'I'm impressed he's even trying,' I say. 'And it's nice that he's still around, and that he helped you over the whole Estelle thing.'

'I'm a bit surprised he's still around myself.'

'Why?' I ask. 'You're a great woman. He's lucky you're . . . seeing him.'

She grins. 'Seeing him. That's diplomatic of you.'

'Well, dating sounds a bit weird. But are you dating now, Mum? Is he a fixture in your life?' I honestly don't want to know if she's sleeping with him. That's way too much information.

411

'I guess we're sort of exclusive,' she says, and blushes.

'Oh, Mum.' I give her a kiss.

'Steady on. It's not . . . I'm not going to marry him or anything. I couldn't.'

'Not now,' I agree. 'But maybe in the future.'

'Your dad wanted me to get married again,' says Mum. 'He didn't want me to be on my own. I suppose he thought I couldn't manage. But after those first few weeks, I've been managing perfectly fine. I miss him. I'll always miss him. But I'm OK on my own too. I said before that women mourn, men replace. I should've added that women get on with their lives. We pick up the pieces and start living. It might take some longer than others, but we do.'

Is she trying to tell me more than I'm asking here? Is she talking as much about me and Dave as her and Dad? Can my mum fix my life for me when I can't fix it for myself?

'I'm trying to pick up the pieces after Dave and Julie Halpin, but every time I think I'm OK, he says something that makes me feel . . . oh, I don't know! I want us to be good again, Mum. But I want it to be different too.'

'He's deflecting all the wrong he did by sleeping with that woman onto you and the car,' she says. 'The more he can make you feel guilty about driving, the less guilt he has to carry about cheating on you.'

I look at her in utter amazement. She's clarified everything for me with one single sentence. She's right. Again.

'It's no easy task living with someone your whole life,' she tells me. 'There'll always be ups and downs. But you have to want the same thing in the end. Do you and Dave?'

We did once, but do we now?

I've changed. I've changed because of him. Because after Rodeo Night I knew I had to be more than just a supportive wife. And yet I was great as a supportive wife. I loved it.

'It's not like he beats me up or is having multiple affairs or is hateful to the children,' I say. 'He's a good man.'

'But being a good man may not be good enough any more,' says Mum.

'We made vows. For better or worse.'

'I know.'

'I feel like I'm letting myself down.'

'Oh, grow a pair, Roxy,' says Mum. 'Whatever you do, you're not letting anyone down.'

Grow a pair! Mum has changed in the last few months too. She'd never have said anything like that before.

'Do you think I should leave him?' I ask.

'Only if that's what you want,' she says. 'I told you I'd support you no matter what, and I will. Always.'

'What d'you think Dad would've said to all this?' I ask. 'He liked Dave.'

'You know, when you get on in life a bit, you take it all far more philosophically,' says Mum. 'You've seen things, learned things, put up with things. Your dad would have cared about *your* happiness, not Dave's.'

Well, yes, he would.

'And he would have said the same as me. That he'd support you no matter what. He also would have said that you only have one life and you have to make the most of it,' she adds. 'He'd be proud of you, Roxy, and the business you've built up. He always was proud of you. And so am I.'

'I didn't realise quite how wise you were, Mum.'

'Not wise. Just experienced.' She leans over and takes my

hand. 'Experienced enough to know that life comes in chapters. And sometimes you finish one and you move on.'

Her phone pings. She reads the message and smiles.

'Diarmuid is dropping around,' she says. 'He wants to take me to lunch.'

'My mother, the merry widow.'

'Not always,' she says. 'But working on it. You have to work at happiness, Roxy. It doesn't simply land in your lap.'

I get up and put my cup into the dishwasher.

'It's always therapeutic talking to you, Mum.'

'Ah, go away with yourself.' She gives me a hug. 'You'll be fine, you always are. And I'll be fine too.'

'Tell Diarmuid I said hello.' I pick up the car keys.

'Do what's right for yourself,' she says as she walks me to the door.

I love her.

She's amazing.

Chapter 32

On Thursday, I go to my Zumba class for the first time in weeks. I'm a step behind everyone else and out of breath by the end. Afterwards Debs, Alison and I head to the pub for a drink, though we keep it non-alcoholic in order to stay virtuous.

'So how's everyone been?' asks Alison. 'You especially, Roxy. How's the business going?'

'Roxy has been feeling a bit swamped,' Debs tells her when I don't answer straight away. 'And Dave hasn't entirely been on her side.'

'Dave needs to cop himself on,' Alison says. 'He's lucky to have you and he's a fool if he doesn't see it.'

Normally I'd be annoyed at one of my friends for dissing my husband. But tonight I don't care.

'The business has been going great,' I say. 'Though I've lost my best client.'

'Which may not necessarily be a bad thing,' says Debs.

Alison looks at me quizzically and I fill her in on all the details about Ivo, including the perfume and the trip to Cork. She raises an eyebrow at me.

'So it's not entirely surprising that Dave freaked,' I finish.

'Why should he?' demands Debs. 'Roxy, you haven't done anything!'

'Would you have liked to?' asks Alison.

'Oh, I don't know,' I say. 'Maybe I was a bit tempted. But I didn't fall off the wagon, unlike my husband who clambered onto her! And now Ivo's back in Brussels or Paris or wherever, with no real need to come back to Ireland. He has a girlfriend there.'

'You should look at it all in a businesslike way,' Alison says. 'Your marriage, the chauffeuring, your relationship with Ivo—'

'There's no relationship with Ivo,' I point out.

'Your fantasy one,' she amends. 'Anyhow, put it all under the microscope and be businesslike about it.'

'How can I possibly do that?' I demand. 'It's life. It's too messy to be businesslike.'

She says I should write down the pros and cons of everything and list my priorities in relation to their importance, then look at what's feasible and how I can achieve it.

Or, I say, when she's finished giving me advice that she would normally get paid for, I could ask myself: what would Dolly do?

They both look at me as though I'm bonkers, and I tell them that Dolly has been a kind of mentor to me, and they laugh and tell me that I am seriously cracked. We all laugh hysterically then. Just like we used to do when we were young and foolish and I was Dave's girl and I thought I was the luckiest person in the world.

Two weeks later, I finally find out if I can make it all work.

I'm driving Gina Hayes again. I've collected her from the

airport and we're going to the TV studios for her appearance on an afternoon lifestyle programme when my phone rings. I have to take it. It's from Mica's headmistress.

'She was feeling unwell and she's thrown up,' says Mrs McCrae. 'She should be at home.'

I'm less than ten minutes from the studio, but even if I was to abandon Gina Hayes on the side of the motorway and turn around now, it would still take me at least half an hour to get to the school.

Using my best business voice so that Gina doesn't know there's anything wrong, I tell Mrs McCrae that someone will collect Mica soon. Then I call Mum. But there's no answer from her phone. I try Dave, but there's no answer from him either. Nor is there a reply from Natalie. By the time I end all the attempted calls, I'm at the studio. I leap out of the car and tell Gina that she'll be picked up when she's finished. Fortunately she's not on for about an hour, so I'll have time to organise something for her. I can see a puzzled look on her face and I know I've been abrupt to the point of rudeness with her. Before she's even gone through the studio door, I'm driving out of the car park and towards the motorway again.

I try all the phones again with no luck. Where the hell is everyone? Where's my working mother's support network? I undertake a car that's plodding along in the middle lane and think I see the telltale flash of a speed camera. I swear loudly and then use my voice control to ring Eric Mallon. He can't collect Gina Hayes but he knows someone who probably can.

'Let me know if there's a problem, will you?' I ask. 'I don't want to abandon the poor woman.'

Eric tells me not to worry, that he'll sort it, and I allow myself to relax very slightly.

The phone rings again. It's Mrs McCrae. She wants to know when someone is going to collect Mica.

'I'm on the way,' I tell her. 'I'm caught in traffic.'

Mrs McCrae is a working mother herself. She should know what it's like. But I can feel her judgement and disapproval across the ether.

I'm nearly at the school when Mum calls me back. I tell her what's happened and she says she'll be there in a couple of minutes.

'I'm nearly there now,' I tell her.

'I'll go too, in case you're delayed,' she says.

But I'm not. We arrive at the same time and I head straight for Mrs McCrae's office.

'One of you sooner would have been better,' says the headmistress when Mum and I both walk into the room.

Mica is lying in the small armchair in the corner, covered with a blanket. Her face is shockingly pale and I'm immediately very worried about her.

'Sweetheart, what happened?' I ask.

She says nothing, but puts her arms around me and buries her head in my chest as I pick her up.

'I'll wait here for Tom,' says Mum. 'School finishes in ten minutes.'

I nod at her and bring Mica to the car.

She perks up slightly when I carry her into her room and help her get undressed.

'Do you still feel sick?' I ask.

'Only a bit.'

'Was it anything you ate?'

Mica normally has the stomach of an ox. There's nothing she can't chow down.

She shakes her head and says she felt icky and then couldn't help getting sick.

'Any of your friends sick?' I ask.

'Emma.' She looks at me accusingly. 'I told you she was.'

She did tell me. Yesterday. I meant to phone Audrey. Which I do now.

'Oh God, Roxy, I'm so sorry. I sent you a WhatsApp this morning.'

I haven't looked at my WhatsApp groups. There are so many of them and I didn't think there'd be anything important. Instead I focused on the Gina Hayes job and other messages from my driver's app.

'Mrs McCrae didn't tell me Emma was ill when I called in,' I said. 'It would've been good to know. Is she OK now?'

'I brought her to Dr Massoud this morning,' says Audrey. 'He reckons it's a gastrointestinal bug. I'm keeping her hydrated and she's perked up in the last half-hour or so.'

'Right,' I say. 'Thanks, Audrey.'

I ring Eric, who confirms that another driver will collect Gina, then I call Melisse and tell her what's happened.

'But you've sorted out Gina?' she asks.

'Of course.'

'In that case, no problem.'

Mica has been lying on her bed all this time. She looks at me from wide eyes.

'Have I messed up your job, Mum?'

'No. Don't worry. I always have backup.'

She gives me a weak smile.

'And you're always my number one priority,' I add, as I

Sheila O'Flanagan

hear Mum and Tom arrive home. Although I let her down today. I should've phoned Audrey earlier and I should've checked my WhatsApp messages.

I share Mica's diagnosis with Mum and we use the sanitising gel in the kitchen on our hands. I open a small bottle of 7 Up so that it can go flat. I don't know if this is a medically sound method of hydrating a vomiting child, but Mum used it for all of us any time we were ill, and I swear by it.

'Can I go up and see Mica?' asks Tom.

'No,' says Mum. 'You can stay down here and not pick up her germs.'

'But I want her germs,' he complains.

Mum goes up to sit with Mica while I give Tom something to eat and then spend the next hour rearranging my schedule for the next few days.

'Thanks for being here,' I say to Mum as she leaves.

'I told you I'd be here for you anytime,' she tells me. 'And I am.'

When Dave comes home, he's in a bad temper, not made any better by hearing that Mica is ill. And then, an hour after he's eaten, he's sick too. Dave isn't ill often, but when he is, he might as well have five kinds of terminal disease, because he groans and sighs and whimpers as though he's at death's door. (Unlike his daughter, who's now asleep in her room, having taken a little of the flat 7 Up.)

I feel for Dave, I really do, because being sick is awful, but every time I go downstairs to do something, he calls me up again, saying he's going to throw up. I've left a bucket beside the bed, but that's not enough; he wants me there to mop his fevered brow.

I'm not good at watching people being sick. It was the

420

one thing I couldn't bear whenever Dad had treatment sessions that made him nauseous. I want to ring Mum and ask her to look after my ailing family, but of course I don't. They're my problem, not hers. (And they're not a problem. They're my family.) Meanwhile, I hope against hope that Tom and I don't succumb to the bug too. I'm less concerned about me. I never get bugs. The only time I ever feel ill is if I've been out on a night with the girls and have over-indulged in alcohol. And it's a long time since I've done that.

It's a grim night. Dave is in and out of the bathroom as often as he chucks up into the bucket. Mica, probably disturbed by the constant flushing of the loo, wakes up and is sick again too, although there's not much for her to be sick with by now. But she's frail and forlorn and my heart breaks to see her like this.

Things don't settle until after four, when both she and Dave fall asleep and stay asleep. I've left Dave on his own in the bedroom and have lain down beside Mica, where I doze on and off until six thirty, which is when I should be driving Thea Ryan to the airport. She's heading off to visit a friend, not for an acting role, and I feel bad that she's going to have to get an ordinary taxi.

'Don't be silly, Roxy, it's fine,' she said the previous night. 'You have to look after your family. Of course I prefer to be driven by you, but I'm perfectly capable of calling a cab.'

Still, she's an old lady and I treat her with a certain level of respect that I'm not sure she'll get from someone who doesn't know her.

I tiptoe into the main bedroom to see how Dave is. He's sleeping (and snoring), and I'm relieved to see that the bucket is empty. Tom is asleep too. I go downstairs, rub my hands with the sanitising gel, make myself tea and toast and hope again that the two of us will escape the dreaded bug.

When they eventually wake up, Dave and Mica are much better. I've already rung the school to say that Mica won't be in and that I'm keeping Tom home too. He, of course, is delighted at having a day off. Dave isn't quite so delighted, as he's on a bit of a tight schedule for the job he's doing.

I leave Tom in charge while I go to the supermarket to buy chicken soup for the invalids, and then we bunker down for the day. I'm trying to keep Tom away from Dave and Mica, even though I know the bug probably isn't airborne. It just makes me feel better. So we stay in the kitchen while the two of them watch TV upstairs in our room.

By the evening we're over the hump and I allow myself to breathe again. I check all of my messages: WhatsApp, Facebook Messenger and the car app. I can't believe I get so many of them. Honestly, there are far too many ways for people to get in touch.

My phone pings while I'm looking at it. It's Dave asking me to make him a cup of tea and some toast.

When I bring it in to him, Mica takes some of the toast but she's sticking to the flat 7 Up. I suggest she might like to go back to bed and promise her she doesn't have to go to school the next day.

'Me neither?' asks Tom, who's followed me.

'You're staying home too,' I assure him.

He jumps up and down with glee.

I hope he doesn't get sick. It would ruin it for him.

Fortunately he doesn't, and Mica is practically back to herself, so both of them can enjoy their unexpected day off school.

Dave, on the other hand, stays in bed. He spends the day alternating between sleeping, playing games on his tablet and asking for tea and toast.

'And this is why,' he says, as he hands me his empty cup, 'you have to give up that job. How would we manage if you were working?'

'I *am* working,' I remind him. 'I cancelled all my clients.'

'Which is no way to run a business,' he says with a note of triumph in his voice. 'They don't make allowances for things like sick children.'

'No,' I agree. 'But I made sure that everyone was looked after. I've called them all today to make sure everything was OK.'

And it was. In fact Melisse Grady was very complimentary about how I'd handled things, which is good, because along with having to find another driver for Gina Hayes, I got Eric Fallon to drive one of her other clients this morning. She was pleased at how seamless the switch was – Gina had called her from the TV studio to tell her that a different driver had collected her but everything was fine. I feel grateful to Alison for insisting I go on that small business training course. It helped me to realise the importance of having professional as well as personal backup in place.

I say all this to Dave, but he gives me a knowing look and tells me that Melisse will probably deal with Eric instead of me in the future because he'll be more dependable. I can't believe how bloody sexist my husband has become. It's as though he's regressed to some 1950s notion of women at home in their aprons, not having a clue about the outside world. As if those housewives didn't know what was going on. I bet they were all as sharp as tacks. They were just constrained by the times. But I'm not. I'm being constrained by my husband.

I take the tray away from him and stomp down the stairs. I'm not going to drive for the rest of the week, to be sure that Mica is fully recovered and Tom doesn't come down with the bug, but I'm damn well going to fill my diary for next week. And Dave can feck off if he doesn't like it.

Fifteen minutes later, he sends me another message asking for a cup of tea. Then the phone pings again. He's added that maybe he could manage another slice of toast. With butter this time. I wonder savagely what his last slave died of! Nevertheless, I'm not going to fight with him while he's unwell. That would be horrible.

'I'm going back to work next week,' I say when I bring him the tea and toast. 'I've got bookings.'

'Roxy—'

'And I don't want to hear any more guff from you about having to be at home, or babies, or selling cars or anything.'

'Give it a rest.' He groans. 'I'm sick. I can't cope with this right now.'

'I'm telling you now,' I say. 'So that you're prepared.'

'You're still hell-bent on punishing me, aren't you?' he asks. 'I wish I'd never set eyes on Julie bloody Halpin.'

Julie bloody Halpin. The catalyst. But I can't blame her forever.

What happened happened, and yes, I can think that Dave is the one most at fault (because he bloody is), and maybe I threw myself into work to prove to him that I could live without him. I know now that I can. It's not all his fault. I have to shoulder some blame too.

But we both need to fix it. Not just me. And not just him.

With a sudden jolt, I realise that I don't care about fixing it.

I look at him without speaking.

I've loved him for most of my life.

I don't love him any more.

I don't say anything right away. I don't say anything until he's well again. And then I sit down with him and say I want a divorce.

He looks at me in utter bewilderment.

'Why?' he asks.

I've thought about it. It's not because of Julie Halpin and I say so. It's because I've changed.

'Because you're being selfish,' he says. 'We took vows, Roxy.'

'And you broke them.'

He doesn't have a comeback to that.

'You can't want a divorce,' he says. 'You're being . . . It's still your dad, isn't it? Upsetting you. You need time. It's coming up to Christmas. You can't break us up before Christmas. The children will hate you.'

Yes, they will.

'You love me, Roxy. You've always loved me. It's been you and me from the start.'

'I loved you,' I say. 'I'll always care about you. But I don't want to live with you any more.'

'This is crap.' He's getting angry now. 'I suppose you want me to move out. You want to take everything for yourself. You want the house and the kids and the job, and I'll tell you why. It's because you've got yourself into the mindset of those rich people you drive around. You think you can have a life like them. But you can't. You're my wife. That's what you're good at. Everything else is play-acting.'

Does he really think that? Did he always?

'You're not some superwoman. Or some ball-breaking feminist icon. You're a mother and you've been doing a part-time job. You need to look in the mirror and see yourself properly.'

I remember Thea Ryan asking me if Dave was the teeniest bit jealous of me. Now I wonder if she's right.

I put the question to him.

'Why would I be jealous of you?' he asks. 'You're nothing without me.'

And that's the nail in the coffin. He doesn't respect me. Maybe he never did.

'I want a divorce,' I say. 'And I won't be changing my mind.'

We look at each other in silence. I thought that I'd cry. But I don't.

The next day, Dave moves out.

He moves next door.

Chapter 33

Mica's birthday falls on the third of January, which has always been a bit of an issue as it's the tail end of the Christmas celebrations. This year, I organise a party for her. Owing to the fact that it's been the coldest winter in living memory – it snowed on Christmas Day – I don't have to bother with the whole bouncy-castle scenario, which is almost obligatory in the summer. I have a much better plan anyway. Leona Lynch has agreed to come and talk to Mica and her friends about clothes and make-up and other girlie things, as well as some tech stuff. But, she says, in an empowering way that doesn't make them feel they have to conform. When I tell Mica this, she puts her arms around me for the first time in ages and tells me she loves me.

'And Dad too,' she adds.

'Of course Dad too.'

Dave is coming to the party. I've no problem with that, but I've told him that I don't want Julie in the house.

'At some point you'll have to accept we're in a relationship,' he tells me.

I do accept it. I wonder if he lied to me when he said that he'd never noticed her before Rodeo Night. I wonder if he lied when he told me he'd never even speak to her afterwards. If she lied when she told me she was seeing someone else. I wonder how it was he was able to move in with her so quickly. What was said between them. I wonder about it but I don't care about it. It's almost frightening how easily I've accepted that Dave and I aren't together any more. How he's completely lost the ability to hurt me. The day after he moved out, I looked at our wedding photos and I felt the same sort of nostalgia that I felt when Mum and I looked through Dad's old photos. But I didn't feel ripped apart. My heart wasn't broken. I hadn't fixed it, but it didn't matter to me any more.

Though I wish he wasn't next door. At the same time, it makes it easy for him to see the children, and as they're my biggest priority in all of this, my feelings about where he lives and who he's with (and what gossip fodder it is for the neighbours) don't come into it.

They were upset when we sat down and had the conversation with them. I tried to be as even-handed as I could, but Dave – possibly unsurprisingly – said that he would rather we weren't splitting up but that there was nothing he could do about it because I didn't love him any more. They cried at that. Obviously I had to spend a lot of time telling them how much I loved *them*, and that of course I loved their dad too but we'd decided we couldn't live together.

I don't stop Mica and Tom going into number twenty. But I'm not sure how much Julie actually wants them to be there when they do.

Anyway, we've settled into a life that's liveable if not perfect. And it's proved to me that even if you can't fix things, you can live with them in an altered state.

Thea Ryan was very pleased when I said that to her. She told me it proved that I was in touch with my inner self. Maybe I am. Maybe before, when I wanted to make everything right all the time, I was being the person I thought I should be. Not the woman I am.

Although it's a children's party, Mum and Diarmuid are coming. They (like Julie and Dave) are now very definitely in a relationship. I try not to think too much about Diarmuid spending the night in what was Dad's home, because even though I really like him and Mum is happy, the idea still makes me a bit wobbly inside. I think that I was worried Mum was erasing Dad's memory, but she hasn't and she wouldn't. Their wedding photo is still on the living-room wall. The picture they had taken on holiday shortly before he got sick is still in the kitchen. She's moved to another chapter in her life, but the part of it with Dad in will never be forgotten. And the part of mine with Dave will never be forgotten either. It's just not a part of my future and who I am now.

Emma, Andrew and Oladele arrive first. Even though it's Mica's party, Tom has been allowed to ask some friends too. Mica has also invited Jamie Shore and Killian O'Carroll, two boys she practises her soccer with, so it's a good mix of girls and boys.

The excited chatter level has risen to fever pitch by the time Mum and Diarmuid arrive with the birthday cake, which Diarmuid has made. It's shaped like a football and Mica loves it. Dave arrives a few minutes later. His present to her, chosen after discussion with me, is a pair of football boots. Mica insists on wearing them straight away. I watch her put them on and lace them up. I don't say anything about the studs marking my wooden floors.

These last few months have changed my daughter. Leaving aside the fact that she's shot up an extra couple of inches, there's a seriousness about her that wasn't there before. After Dave moved out, we had a long discussion about being married, and she reiterated her view that she wasn't going to bother with it herself. I told her that she might feel differently if she found the person she loved, and she pointed out that I'd found the person I loved but that I'd changed my mind. And so we talked a lot about how your feelings can change and how you can still care about a person and not love them. She doesn't know about Rodeo Night. I will never be the one to tell her about that.

Tom was quiet and withdrawn at first, but when he realised that he would still see his dad every day, he seemed to cope better. Two of his friends have divorced parents so it's not a new thing in his experience. But I'm sad that it happened to him. I can't help feeling I let both of them down.

About an hour after the last guest has arrived, Leona Lynch turns up. Eric drove her here today and will drive her home. Eric and I have pooled a lot of our clients and cover for each other all the time. I used to be afraid of him poaching them from me (Dave was actually right about that), but he pointed out that it would be a futile thing to do and that we would be better off working as an unofficial team. It's good to have Eric to fall back on, and I know he feels the same way about me.

Leona is brilliant with the girls – and the boys, too. She can talk make-up in one breath and tech in another. Clearly, though, while the girls are interested in both, the boys only want to talk about the app she's developed. I'm not sure exactly what it does, but it's all to do with friends and groups and (she tells them) it's very inclusive. Whatever. They're happy as anything talking to her.

Dave and I don't speak very much to each other. Although we are as hands-on and practical as possible when it comes to parenting our kids, he hasn't forgiven me for asking for the divorce, and I don't think he ever will. We haven't sorted out the practicalities of the house yet and I know there are going to be some hard words between us, but I'm hopeful it will work out in the end. I'm not trying to fix it by myself, though. Alison put me in touch with a good divorce lawyer, a fiercely competent woman who takes no guff from anybody. So I'm leaving it all up to her.

The noise level in the dining room has become almost intolerable. I leave the children to Leona and go upstairs. I sit on my bed and for the first time since that fateful day, I don't think of Dave and Julie in it. I open my driver's app and look at the schedule for the week ahead. I'd thought it would be quiet with people coming back to work after the Christmas break, but I'm busier than ever. Nevertheless, I'm coping. Between Mum, Natalie and Dave (some evenings), I've got it covered. And even if there's another incident like Mica being sick, I know that Eric has got my back.

Everyone, in fact, has got my back.

Even Dave.

I know I did the right thing. I still feel guilty about it, but surprisingly, it was Melisse Grady who told me that I had nothing to feel guilty about. We'd met for a coffee one day when she wanted to book me for a series of jobs. I'm not sure how the conversation turned to our personal lives, but I ended up telling her about me and Dave and how it had all gone wrong. I said it was my fault we ended up separating, because I wanted to drive. She looked at me in utter disbelief and told me that it wasn't. He was the one who'd slept with someone else, she said. He was the one who broke our trust. And if the result of that was me finding a different part of myself, well, tough luck on him. She was quite animated about it and I left her feeling a lot better about myself and my choices. All the same, it's hard not to feel a failure if your marriage breaks down. Regardless of whose fault it is.

Debs, of course, has been a brick. So have Michelle and Rachel and Alison. There's something about female friendship that's strong and empowering. Dave used to tease me about us getting together and bitching, but actually we don't. Except, very occasionally, about Julie. And even then without venom.

I click from the schedule to the accounts, but I know, even before looking, that December was a spectacularly successful month. I've brought people to lunches and dinners and parties, all of them dressed up and excited for the holiday season. All of them leaving big tips too, even though the majority pre-paid on the app and so could have spilled out of the car without a thought.

The biggest tip was from the father of a girl from Castleknock. He'd paid for the car for her and her friends to be brought to a party and home afterwards. A clever way, I thought, of making sure they were safe. She left a pair of shoes behind. They were crystal-encrusted Manolos, with four-inch heels. It was the first time I'd ever held a pair of Manolos. They were a thing of beauty.

I brought them to her house the next day and her dad, who answered the door, was disparaging about girls who wore shoes they couldn't walk in and left behind in taxis.

'You're only young once,' I told him, and he shook his head in disgust. But then he laughed and said he supposed I was right and that she was a good girl really, and then he handed me the generous tip. I told him it wasn't necessary and he told me how much the Manolos cost and I pocketed the money without another word.

I glance at my watch. There's still at least an hour's worth of party left. I know I should go downstairs but I'm enjoying my moment of solitude in my room. I repainted it when Dave left and the walls are now a midnight blue, startling in their intensity. But I like it. I like my midnight-blue duvet cover too. I always slept in light-coloured rooms before, but I seem to sleep better in darkness, although I still wake up ten minutes before the alarm.

I take a picture of the duvet cover and post it to Instagram. It's not my usual kind of post, but I caption it 'Driver's Day Off' and the likes start to come in straight away.

I have no other messages, though.

The school, the Zumba, the mothers' WhatsApp groups are all silent. I've muted Slim to Win for a year. I haven't put on the weight I lost and I can manage on my own now.

I'm about to go downstairs again when the phone pings.

Hi, says the message from Ivo Lehane. *Hope you had a lovely Christmas. I'm visiting Lizzy next week. And after that I'm going to have another schedule of driving – for those restructuring projects I told you about. I know this might be completely unworkable for you, especially as it would mean a*

433

couple of nights away from home again, but would you be able to drive me?

I haven't thought of Ivo over the last few weeks. I certainly haven't followed the advice Debs gave me the night I confessed that I missed sex with Dave more than Dave himself, and she told me it would be OK to fantasise about Ivo again. To be honest, I've been mostly too tired for fantasies. But even if I could, he's not someone I want to fantasise about. He's too real for that.

I didn't expect to hear from him about business any more. Good business, though, I think, as I look at his message.

If you'd rather not, that's fine, he adds. *But you know me, poor people skills. I do better with drivers I know. Don't want to mess up anything for you, though. Your husband and children come first.*

I continue to look at the message and then I take a deep breath.

No problem, I reply. *Always delighted to drive my best client. The husband part isn't an issue any more. The children are for life, though.*

There's a long silence before he replies.

Are you OK? he asks.

Getting there.

Sure?

Absolutely.

Christmas must have been difficult.

We got through it. We went to my mum's. Always a joy.

He sends a smiley Santa emoji. And then another message.

Lizzy came to me for Christmas. That was a joy too.

I'm glad. I'm about to send the reply and then I add, *How's Annabel?*

The response comes back quickly.

Annabel's got a job in Canada. She leaves next week.

I'm sure you'll miss her, I send.

It was too good an opportunity for her to turn down. She's heading up her own department. It's always been her dream.

I can feel my heart beating a little faster as I read his words. Is Annabel's dream different to Ivo's dream? Is it over between them? Do I care? Does he? I exhale slowly. The most important thing about my relationship with Ivo right now is that he's my best client and he's coming back on a business trip. That's what I have to focus on.

But I can't help smiling as I remind him to send his flight details.

He sends a thumbs-up and adds, *Look forward to seeing you.*

I wait for a moment before replying that I'm looking forward to seeing him too.

I walk downstairs. The children are still being entertained by Leona. Dave is sitting in a corner talking to Diarmuid. It's the first time they've met. They seem to be getting along well. But that's the thing about Dave, he gets along with everyone. He always will.

Mum walks over to me.

'You OK?' she asks. 'This isn't too much for you?' She glances across at Dave.

'I'm fine,' I say. 'I can cope. It's all under control.' Then I grimace as Oladele jumps up and knocks over her glass of orange juice and a bowl of popcorn. I grab some paper towel and clear up the mess before anyone has time to get upset.

As I throw the paper in the bin, Mum grins and so do I.

If I've learned anything over the last few months, it's that control is an illusion. Anyone, any time, can do something to upset the balance of our lives. Sometimes it's good, sometimes it isn't. Sometimes we cope, sometimes we don't. Sometimes we have to let other people do the coping for us for a while.

We're all hanging on by our fingertips.

But now I know that I can get up again if I fall.

Acknowledgements

Every time I type 'The End' on the last page of my manuscript, I'm relieved that I've finally managed to get the story from my head and on to the page. And when I see the finished book on the shelves, it's a very proud moment. Much as I'd like to take all the credit for myself, there are a lot of people who have a part to play in turning my initial idea into a published book and they all deserve a lot of thanks.

My publisher and editor, Marion Donaldson, is as generous with her advice as she is gentle with her criticisms, as she helps me to develop the novel from those first nebulous thoughts into something someone might like to read. It's a great pleasure to work with her and I want to thank her yet again for helping me to bring Roxy's story to life.

More wise words come to me from my agent, Isobel Dixon, who looks after the business side of things so I don't have to. Thank you, Isobel, and thanks also to Hattie, James, Daisy and everyone at Blake Friedmann who know how to mix work and pleasure in just the right quantities.

As always, I have to give a great vote of thanks to the Hachette group for being such fun to work with, and for all those champagne moments! A very special thank you to the fabulous Breda Purdue in Ireland who has shared the journey with me for twenty years, and who has never stopped being a great champion of books and authors.

There's an old saying that no man is hero to his valet. An updated version might be that no writer is a heroine to her copyeditor! For noticing that characters put down phones they've never picked up and leave rooms they never entered, and for allowing me the chance to fix it, thank you again, Jane Selley.

To Jean Denihan, who knits octopussies for premie babies and gave me the idea for Selina's new interest, thank you for both the knitting and your enduring friendship.

My extended family continues to be supportive and enthusiastic even after so many books – thanks again, although I can never thank you enough!

As always, massive thanks to Colm, for reminding me that there are more things in life than my laptop, and for making sure that I enjoy them.

Every writer is, first and foremost, a reader too. There's nothing more exciting than starting a new book and getting lost in the story. To all my readers – those who've been with me for many books and those who are new – thank you for choosing *Her Husband's Mistake*. I really hope you enjoyed it. I'm always happy to hear from you through my website and social media, where I try my best to answer all your messages.

Author's Note

Back in February 2018 I attended a fundraising event for the wonderful Shabra Charity (www.shabracharity.com). At that event Mr Paul Doran made a substantial donation to the charity so that his children could have their names used in a book. *Her Husband's Mistake* is that book, and I hope Emma and Andrew are happy to have their names in print as Mica and Tom's best friends. The fact that Emma's mum is Audrey both in real life and the book is entirely co-incidental!

Read on for an extract of
Sheila O'Flanagan's new novel

The Women Who Ran Away

Chapter 1

Grand Canal, Dublin, Ireland: 53.3309°N 6.2588°W

Even after she'd put her luggage in the tiny boot of the convertible, Deira still wasn't sure if she was going to go through with it. Which was crazy, she told herself, because this was the easy bit. The harder part had been the previous night, when she'd walked into the dimly lit underground car park and waited for the Audi to unlock automatically. Even as she'd told herself that nobody would take any notice of her, she'd expected one of the residents to suddenly appear and ask her what the hell she was doing. But the one person already there, a young man in head-to-toe Lycra, was more concerned with unchaining his bike than with Deira's actions.

Nevertheless, the familiar click as she slid her hand along the driver's door was comforting. So was lowering herself into the driver's seat and finding that it still moved automatically to her favoured position when she pressed the memory button. She'd been afraid it would have changed. But there was no lingering scent of an unknown perfume or a different shampoo. No sense that someone else had taken her place. Nothing at all was different. Her heartbeat slowed down. Everything felt normal. Easy. Right.

Driving slowly out of the apartment complex, she'd told herself that her criminal career was off to a good start.

Of course she had a key, which surely meant that taking the Audi wasn't actually a criminal act, no matter how anyone else might see it; but she wasn't supposed to be here, doing this. Deira didn't care. She was past caring. And being back in the car was comforting in a way she hadn't expected. So it was worth it.

Now, as she slammed the boot closed and walked back into the granite mews overlooking the canal, she felt a sudden rush of tears fill her eyes and clamped down hard on her jaw to try to stop them falling. It didn't matter that she was tired of crying; the slightest thing still set her off, blubbing uncontrollably and embarrassing both her and anyone around her. She rubbed her eyes with the back of her hand. If for no other reason than the sake of her skin, she needed to get over it. Her complexion was ruined from the salt of her ever-present tears.

She glanced at the clock on the kitchen wall and released a slow breath. Unless she was going to chicken out at the last minute, she'd have to leave soon. After all the trouble she'd gone to, missing the ferry would be a complete disaster.

But instead of picking up her keys and bag and heading back outside, she put a pod in the coffee machine and made herself an Americano. She sipped it slowly as she studied the tickets in front of her, making doubly sure that she had the right date. It would be idiotic of her to go on the wrong day, but over the last couple of months she'd done so many idiotic things that she didn't trust herself any more. She recalled the phone calls, the emails and – worst of all – the scene in the office, and she shuddered. She'd been made a fool of, but she knew she'd been a fool too. And that was hard to take.

She put the tickets back in her bag. She had the right date. She wasn't a complete idiot, no matter what other people might think.

Although the trip had been booked nine months previously, she'd totally forgotten about it until the direct debit for the balance had resulted in her account being overdrawn. She hadn't even realised she'd gone into the red until her bank card had been declined at her hairdresser's. It had been one more humiliation added to all the others. Naturally she'd burst into tears again.

It had been Gavin who'd first suggested taking the car to France, confessing a need to drive a stylish convertible along some decent motorways before people judged him a sad old fart and passed comments about his virility and the size of his penis.

Deira had laughed when he said that, and wrapped her arms around him.

'Nobody would think that of you, ever,' she'd told him. 'They wouldn't dare.'

Because Gavin Boyer looked at least a decade younger than his fifty-seven years. True, his hair, once even darker than Deira's, was now almost entirely silver-grey, but that only made him appear even more distinguished than when he was younger. He was still tall and broad, and even if his waist was thicker than it had been in his twenties and thirties, he'd managed to maintain his athletic build. Rather unfairly, in Deira's view, he achieved this without any great effort other than golf twice a week and an occasional visit to the swimming pool of the nearby gym. Metabolism, he'd say airily, when she complained that, at seventeen years younger, she put on weight simply by looking at a packet of biscuits. He made no comment at all about her monthly trip to the hairdresser to have her own increasing number of greys covered with an approximation of her natural chestnut brown.

Definitely not fair, she thought now. But life wasn't fair, was it? Because if it was, she wouldn't be standing here with a rapidly cooling cup of coffee in her hand wondering if he would set the police on her when he got home.

She took a sip of the coffee. There was no need to worry. He wouldn't set the police on her because he wouldn't know that the car was gone until the end of the following week, and even then he wouldn't know she was the one who'd taken it. Besides, even if he did suspect her, she'd be miles away and there'd be nothing he could do about it. Interpol would hardly worry about a missing car, after all.

She shook her head. Car thief. Interpol. None of that was part of her life. France was supposed to have been a holiday. For both of them.

Their original plan had been to explore Brittany for a few days before heading to Paris. Deira had told Gavin that if he was going to indulge in his dream of open-top cruising down the motorway, she wanted to be able to say she'd driven around the French capital in a sports car with the warm wind in her hair. When he'd looked at her in bewilderment, she'd explained that one of her late mother's favourite songs had been the haunting 'Ballad of Lucy Jordan', in which a thirty-seven-year-old woman feels so trapped in her life that she knows she'll never get to do just that. When Deira was old enough to understand the lyrics, she'd sympathised with Lucy Jordan and wondered if her mother had ever felt the same way. Now approaching her own fortieth birthday, she'd visited Paris on a number of occasions but had never driven an open-top car around the city's streets – and had never particularly wanted to until the day they'd collected the convertible.

Until recently, she would have felt enraged at the notion that any woman would feel washed up by the age of thirty-seven. But she'd come to realise that there was more to it than how you felt, and she knew there were things she'd previously considered unimportant that she'd never have the chance to do. And that, more than anything else, was why she'd cried every single day for the past two months.

She glanced at the clock again. She knew she was cutting it fine. It was a three-hour drive to Ringaskiddy, and she was supposed to be at the ferry terminal forty minutes before the ship sailed. Unless she was going to abandon her plan, she had to leave now. Yet something was holding her back. She wasn't sure exactly what. A reluctance to commit herself to all the driving? The knowledge that she was poking a hornets' nest? Fear of what people would say?

'If he rings, it's a sign and I won't go,' she said out loud, even as she knew he wouldn't ring, and that if he did, she'd be in a panic to get the car back before he realised it was gone. Even thinking about him ringing was a sign of her weakness, not her strength. Anyhow, she didn't believe in signs or omens, good or bad.

Life was life, she often said to her friend Tillie, who had a more open view on random signals as pointers for making important decisions. Seeing a white feather floating on the air or a sudden shaft of sunlight on a dismal day didn't mean anything more than the fact that a bird had flown by or there was a momentary break in the clouds. Tillie would shake her head and tell her that she needed to be in touch with her inner self a bit more. But Deira was afraid of her inner self. She wasn't sure it was a part of her that needed being in touch with at all.

Maybe the very fact that her account had been debited without her actually noticing it was a cosmic sign. Perhaps the fact that she'd had no problem taking the car was a sign too. Or the sign could simply be that the sun was shining in a clear blue sky and the drive would be lovely.

On the other hand, it was always possible there would be something on the way to Cork that would make her come to her senses and turn around again.

'Plenty of signs on the road to Cork,' she muttered as she picked up the car keys. 'Mostly telling you about motorway exits.'

She slung her bag over her shoulder, set the alarm and walked outside.

The morning air had warmed up and the bright sunlight dazzled off the canal water as she sat in the driver's seat and lowered the roof of the car. Truth was, she rarely drove it with the roof down. She lived in Ireland, after all. There was always a good chance that a torrential downpour would arrive out of the blue. And even on the sunniest of days, the wind-chill factor meant that it wasn't always ideal for open-top driving.

But today was perfect.

So maybe that was the sign.

Deira wondered if she should call Gillian and tell her what she was doing. But if she did, her older sister would want to know when she'd decided to make this trip and who she was

going with and why she hadn't said anything before and . . .
No, talking to Gill would definitely be a sign, Deira thought.
A sign that I've lost my mind completely.

She started the car and pulled away from the kerb. Her
phone rang almost at once, and her heart began to beat wildly.

'Are you on your way?' asked Tillie.

'I've just set off.'

'You'll be late.'

'No I won't.'

'No phone calls?'

'No,' said Deira.

'Everything will be fine,' said Tillie. 'Have fun.'

She waited for Tillie to remind her not to do anything
crazy, but when she didn't, Deira simply replied that she'd
do her best to have a good time.

'You deserve to,' said Tillie. 'I'll send you positive vibes
and keep in touch.'

'Thanks.' Deira ended the call and continued to follow the
canal before turning onto the industrialised Naas Road. The
traffic on a Saturday morning wasn't too heavy, and she
nudged her speed up a little. Her hair whipped across her
face and she tucked it behind her ears. My life hasn't been
wasted, she told herself, as she thought again of Lucy Jordan.
It really hasn't.

And yet as she drove on, she was regretting once again
the choices she'd made and the decisions she'd taken that
now meant that, in ways she'd pretended to herself didn't
matter, the last thirteen years of her life *had* been entirely
wasted. There was no point in thinking otherwise. Nothing
could change it. That was the thing. Not taking the car, not
driving to Paris, not telling herself that forty was the new

thirty. What had happened had happened and the worst part of it all was that she'd been complicit in it. Which really did make her an absolute, utter, complete fool.

'Of course you're not a fool.'

Tillie's words, spoken when Deira had first broken the news to her, came back to her.

'Yes I am,' Deira had told her. 'I'm the same kind of fool that all women are. Thinking they're doing what they're doing because that's what they want when really it's just because they're in love with the wrong man.'

Tillie had hugged her then.

And Deira had felt the rage and the hurt ball up inside her so tightly that she literally doubled over with the pain of it.

She felt it again now. A horrible feeling in the centre of her stomach. And the pain higher up too, the one that had made her think she might be having a heart attack. But she knew she wasn't. She knew it was simply her anger at being played. At allowing herself to be played.

She was angrier with herself than with him.

She blamed herself more than him.

But she blamed him too, and that was why she was going away and taking the damn car with her.

To find out what happens next, pre-order

The Women Who Ran Away –
publishing in summer 2020.

The Women Who Ran Away

Deira isn't the kind of woman to steal a car. Or drive to France alone with no plan. But then, Deira didn't expect to be single. Or to suddenly realise that that only way she can get the one thing she wants most is to start breaking every rule she lives by.

Grace has been sent on a journey by her late husband, Ken. She doesn't really want to be on it but she's following his instructions, as always. She can only hope that on the way she'll find a way to forgive him. And then – finally – she'll be able to let him go.

Brought together by unexpected circumstances, Grace and Deira find that it's easier to share secrets with a stranger, especially in the shimmering sunny countryside of Spain and France. But they soon find that there's no escaping the truth, whether you're running away from it or racing towards it . . .

Available to pre-order

REVIEW

When a shocking news report shatters Juno Ryan's world, she suddenly finds herself without the man she loves – and with no way of getting the answers she needs.

Juno flees to the enchanting Villa Naranja in Spain. The blue skies and orange groves – along with Pep, the local winemaker's handsome son – begin to soothe her broken heart. But just when she begins to feel whole again, another bombshell drops.

Juno might have run away from her secrets, but the past isn't finished with her . . .

REVIEW

Then

When Lola Fitzpatrick catches the eye of Philip Warren, she's new to Dublin and loving it. He's used to getting what he wants . . . and she can't resist him. Until one night he forces her to make an impossible choice.

If she'd known then what she knows now, everything might have been different.

Now

Lola's daughter Bey has inherited her mother's impulsive streak and it takes her down dangerous paths.

Then one night she too finds herself in front of a man she loves, with impossible choices of her own to make.

For both women, what happened that night changes everything.

For better. For worse. For ever.

REVIEW

When Imogen Naughton vanishes, everyone who knows her is shocked. She has a perfect marriage. Her handsome husband treats her like a princess. She's always said how lucky she is. So why has she left? And how will she survive without Vince?

What goes on behind closed doors is often a surprise, and Imogen surprises herself by taking the leap she knows she must. But as she begins her journey to find the woman she once was, Imogen's past is right behind her . . .

Will it catch up with her?
And will she be ready to face it if it does?

REVIEW

Sheila O'Flanagan

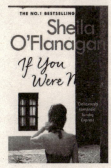

REVIEW